Kathleen Rowntree grew up in Grimsby, Lincolnshire, and was educated at Cleethorpes Girls' Grammar School and Hull University where she studied music. Her other novels are *Brief Shining, The Directrix, Between Friends, Tell Mrs Poole I'm Sorry, Outside, Looking In*, and *Laurie and Claire*, and she has contributed to a series of monologues for BBC2 TV called *Obsessions*. She and her husband have two sons and they live on the Oxfordshire/Northamptonshire borders.

D0599883

Also by Kathleen Rowntree

BRIEF SHINING
BETWEEN FRIENDS
TELL MRS POOLE I'M SORRY
OUTSIDE, LOOKING IN
LAURIE AND CLAIRE

and published by Black Swan

THE QUIET WAR OF REBECCA SHELDON

Kathleen Rowntree

BLACK SWAN

THE QUIET WAR OF REBECCA SHELDON
A BLACK SWAN BOOK : 0 552 99325 5

Originally published in Great Britain by
Victor Gollancz Ltd.

PRINTING HISTORY
Victor Gollancz edition published 1987
Corgi edition published 1990
Corgi edition reprinted 1990
Black Swan edition published 1994
Black Swan edition reprinted 1994
Black Swan edition reprinted 1995
Black Swan edition reprinted 1997

Set in Linotype Melior

Black Swan Books are published by Transworld Publishers Ltd,
61–63 Uxbridge Road, London W5 5SA,
in Australia by Transworld Publishers (Australia) Pty Ltd,
15–25 Helles Avenue, Moorebank, NSW 2170
and in New Zealand by Transworld Publishers (NZ) Ltd,
3 William Pickering Drive, Albany, Auckland.

Printed and bound in Great Britain by
Cox & Wyman Ltd, Reading, Berkshire.

To my mother
Doris Paine

Contents

The Family Interest

(1892–1898)

I

On and on prattled Louisa. 'How tiresome she is,'
thought Rebecca, watching her friend through half-
closed eyes. She had been glad enough to find Louisa's
note of invitation when she returned home from her
boarding school, glad indeed, for it was eleven weeks
and two days since she last set eyes on George; but it
was tedious listening to breathless confidences in this
stuffy little room – the sewing room, Louisa's refuge
from her alarming sisters – when she could be outside
in the sun.

'Of course, the big excitement was Augusta going to
nurse in South Africa. She sailed a fortnight ago. Oh
Rebecca, such a *thrill* to see her setting off in her
uniform . . .'

The thought of Augusta in her uniform did not
thrill Rebecca. They were an ungainly lot, the Ludbury
girls; insufferable too, except for Louisa who, though
a bit of a duffer, was reassuringly predictable and
good-hearted.

'I've made you a bookmark. Now where did I put
it? I know I put it somewhere safe . . . Here it is!
I embroidered "To R from L" on it. Do you think that's
silly of me?' Louisa's eyes bulged anxiously.

'Of course not.' Rebecca, her dark, glossy head
lolling back against the shabby leather of the chair,
stretched out a leisurely hand. 'Thank you, Louisa.'

'I hope you like it.' Louisa could hardly breathe.

But there was no time to inspect her handiwork. Outside, a cow lowed; not in the yard; further off. Rebecca's ears had been alert for this sound for the past half-hour. She rose and strolled to the window, remarking: 'How hot it is in here. Quite stifling.'

The cows were swinging down the meadow to their afternoon milking. Soon they would enter the yard.

'Shall we go down to the dairy? It will be deliciously cool in there. I'm sure you'll have something to show me, Louisa.'

'Why, yes,' Louisa cried eagerly. 'The new cheeses. And then we'll go to the hen-house and look at my Rhode Island Reds.'

'Perhaps,' murmured Rebecca, who did not care for poultry.

'And you should see the plums in the orchard! We're in for a bumper crop; I've never seen branches so laden.'

Rebecca was already on the stairs.

In the yard the commotion was under way: thronging cattle, bumping and defecating; men shouting; chains and pails ringing; cats rushing by with high, expectant tails; hidden dogs, hysterical for release; dust and steam swimming in the heat. George saw her at once and became immobile in the midst of chaos. Rebecca, too, was turned to stone. Many miles away she could hear Louisa in the dairy chattering on about cheese muslin – and was that another voice calling her name? No matter. Across the seething yard George and Rebecca stared at one another along a shaft of stillness.

'There you are,' Louisa cried, running back to the yard from the dairy. And then, with a start: 'Why, Charlotte!'

Rebecca turned.

Charlotte Ludbury was standing in the shadows, just inside the kitchen doorway. Her eyes were hard and fixed upon Rebecca. 'Your friend appears to have lost the use of her tongue, Louisa. I wished her a good afternoon fully sixty seconds ago.'

'I'm sorry, I didn't hear,' Rebecca said.

'You were occupied with other matters, perhaps.' Charlotte came out into the yard and looked across to where George was now closing a cowshed door. 'But I came at Mama's bidding, Louisa. She says you are to bring Miss Sheldon to the drawing room.'

'Well!' Louisa exclaimed when Charlotte had gone. 'How kind of mama, Rebecca.' But her eyes were troubled. Was this a good omen, or was their friendship about to be scrutinized with regard to the family interest?

'We had better go, then,' Rebecca said calmly. But she, too, was apprehensive: until now Mrs Ludbury had considered her beneath notice; what had she done to merit this sudden attention?

Mrs Ludbury was dark, tiny and round. Her resemblance to the dear Queen was no accident for she worked hard at it: dress, demeanour, conduct, all dedicated to the Victorian mode. She had borne children with similar patriotic regularity: Augusta Rose, Charlotte Victoria, George Albert, Louisa May, Edward Charles, Caroline Anne, Frederick Arthur, Sophie Alice and Gertrude Henrietta – though sadly, these two last did not survive their baptisms – and she had wasted considerable energy in grooming her husband for the Albertian role.

The relationship between Monarch and subject was not entirely one-sided. Mrs Ludbury's popular 'Daisy Polka', a gallant composition for pianoforte, was reputed to have pleased the royal ear, and the dedication of much stirring verse – for Mrs Ludbury was a poet, too – had been graciously accepted. It may not have escaped the royal notice that Mrs Ludbury was an advocate for the British Israelites, an ingenious sect, keen on the notion that the lost tribe of Israel was none other than the British race; keen as well to see Victoria assume the mantle of Moses. In thrilling tones Mrs Ludbury penned many an exhortation to her Monarch: imperial expansion would gain the promised land.

This had been rather too much for her husband. Harold was a simple farmer, a plain, uncomplicated man. He had farmed at The Grange, Headley Green, six miles south of Birmingham, since the death of his father.

Harold's distinctive features were common to all his children. The Ludbury nose was a narrow, high-bridged promontory between close-set eyes of palest blue; the hair was frail, wispy, inclined to reddishness; and the Ludbury frame was large. Once Harold had been a cheerful fellow, confident in his calling: as consort to Mrs Ludbury, however, it gradually dawned on him that farming did not do. He could not say why this was so, but there was no doubt about it. Farming, if it was to go on, must not be spoken of indoors; special pleading for its requirements was anathema. Surely, Harold had argued – mildly and not for long – the farm was necessary to the family's sustenance? Doubt was cast on this view by the success of Mrs Ludbury's school for the daughters of British Israelites. Harold had come to exist in a state of confusion and shame. Try as he might he could not grasp the rationale behind life's edicts and proscriptions. That his wife was infallible he did not doubt: was not her work sealed by royal approval? 'Never forget,' he urged his son, whenever George's enthusiasm for the agricultural side of life threatened to get out of hand, 'your Mama is a wonderful woman.'

Mrs Ludbury was unimpressed by her husband's uncomprehending loyalty. There was nothing within Harold's power to do that could please her. (Perhaps there was one thing, but to give Mrs Ludbury, prematurely in widow's weeds, her due, that thing had not occurred to her. She wore black because the

12

dear Queen was obliged to wear black: if the Monarch mourned then so must she.) She pushed Harold to the back of her mind and got on with a life dedicated to Higher Things.

She was listening attentively to a pupil at the pianoforte when the door flew open.

'Here we are; here is Rebecca,' Louisa called – too loudly, Rebecca thought.

Mrs Ludbury frowned. For a moment she could not think why Louisa's friend – the rather dubious Sheldon girl – should enter her drawing room. Then it came back to her, and she jabbed a forefinger in the direction of a sofa.

They sat, one at each end.

Mrs Ludbury stared speculatively at the visitor. It was not Rebecca who interested her, but her stepmother, formerly Miss Annie Blincoe from a well-respected local family. Annie had outraged Headley Green by marrying the widower, Sheldon, a Birmingham manufacturer and thus beyond the pale; decent country folk had been personally affronted. Some comfort was derived from evidence that the sharp-tongued Annie was giving Sheldon a hard time of it – already the elder girl had left home in a huff and the son was seldom seen; the schoolgirl, Rebecca, had only the holidays to endure, but Sheldon was stuck with her daily and looked a beaten man. The rector's wife, a not infallible informant, had upset this pleasing theory by reporting Annie to be in an interesting condition. Mrs Ludbury, like her neighbours, was anxious to know how things stood.

Rebecca, unsettled by this scrutiny, cast her eyes about the room. It was enormous, and stuffed full of furniture like a waiting room – deep armchairs, wide sofas, high-backed settees, Pembroke tables, revolving bookcases, magazine and music racks, pouffes and footstools – and it was in two distinct halves: this end where they sat was warm and bright, fed by sunlight from the deep front windows; the far end was dim, streaked by dust-laden rays from a side window, a ghostly marble fireplace just visible in the gloom. A boy of ten or eleven sat in an armchair on her right, hunched like an ape, gnawing his fingernails, eyebrows raised in mournful abstraction: Freddy Ludbury, youngest of the tribe, Ludbury in every feature. Would those uncompromising looks suit him as he got older, as they complimented George's strong personality, or would they hang on him apologetically as they did on Edward, the middle son? The girls, poor things, had the same stark features and looming presence; their mother's compactness would have been a kinder inheritance. Thinking of this, Rebecca returned her attention to Mrs Ludbury.

To her discomfiture she discovered she was still the object of unsmiling scrutiny. 'How rude she is. No wonder Charlotte and Pip are so frightful,' she thought, gazing stolidly back. Mrs Ludbury was not embarrassed by detection. She stared on, her eyes two pinpricks of light in her dingy face. Grime lurked in the lines around nose and mouth. Abashed at this discovery, Rebecca looked away.

'How is your mother, Miss Sheldon?' Mrs Ludbury suddenly yelled above the piano's din.

Rebecca's heart lurched.

'Mama!' Louisa cried.

'That will do, Flora,' Mrs Ludbury shouted towards the piano. 'Omit the next reprise. It requires a coda, about sixteen bars.'

The pianist gathered up her manuscript and made for the door.

'Your own composition, Mama?' breathed Louisa, all set to rave.

'Certainly not. That was Miss Gaunt's latest effort.'

'Mama,' interrupted Freddy nervously, 'might I go now?'

14

'And would *you* confuse Miss Gaunt's composition with your Mama's, Freddy?'

'No fear. Hers are not nearly so jolly as yours.'

Mrs Ludbury smiled; Freddy was a discerning child. And Freddy decided it was safe to go. 'We'll continue our reading later on,' she called after him. She did not delude herself: boys, like men and dogs were, generally speaking, hopeless; susceptible to filth, smells and rudery; disinclined towards the Higher Things. She had failed with George, and he had been such a clever child, every bit as clever as Augusta, cleverer than Charlotte, though not as brilliant as Pip. Yet George had proved quite obstinate in his opposition to the Higher Things. Edward, of course, did not count; being thoroughly stupid he was suited to agriculture. But she still had hopes for Freddy. There were times when he smelled too strongly of stable for her peace of mind, and how she wished that George would refrain from praising Freddy's horsemanship. Still, she must persevere . . . Now, what was she about? She collected herself and returned her piercing gaze to Rebecca. 'I refer, of course, to your *step*mother, Miss Sheldon. How is she, pray? I have heard a whisper – nothing more – that a happy event may be in the offing.'

Louisa, who had no idea to what her mother alluded, gasped encouragingly: 'How wonderful!'

'Be quiet, Louisa. Go and find Charlotte. I can't think what has happened to the girl.'

Whereupon the door flew open and there stood Charlotte, flushed and disarrayed. 'Mama!' she cried, 'it really is too bad . . .' She paused to remove hair from her eyes.

'Well, get on with it. What is too bad?'

'Pip is, Mama. She has led me a terrible dance. She lured me into the boxroom and locked me in. I should be there still were it not for George. He heard my cry at the window and sent the man to get me out. Really, I'm so vexed, I've a good mind to box her ears.'

'Do no such thing. Pip is highly strung. Now sit down and compose yourself. One would imagine you'd been dragged backwards through a hedge.'

This was not reassuring news to Charlotte who had already caught Rebecca Sheldon frowning at her in distaste and patting her own sleek, raven head in a self-congratulatory manner. 'Preening, the little minx,' concluded Charlotte.

'You have interrupted Miss Sheldon, Charlotte. She was about to give us news of her stepmother. Pray continue, Miss Sheldon.'

And Rebecca racked her brains for something to say about the second Mrs Sheldon.

'I'm sorry Mama was out of sorts.'

Louisa and Rebecca were picking peas in the kitchen garden.

Rebecca thought 'out of sorts' an inadequate phrase to describe Mrs Ludbury's alarming and erratic behaviour. The insistence upon her stepmother had been trying, for Rebecca had so little to do with the woman, but she had done her best. In desperation she had hit on the subject of Mrs Sheldon's pug – her stepmother was inordinately fond of her dog – and had managed several minutes on the pug begging for sugar lumps, dying for the Queen, and howling to piano accompaniment: all to no avail; her effort was received in silence. Mrs Ludbury perked up when Rebecca recalled her stepmother's collaboration with the rector's wife over preparations for a forthcoming bazaar, only to scowl as she enlarged upon the benefits that would accrue to the heathen from their efforts. In fact, there had been no pleasing her, and Rebecca had given up, confining herself to monosyllabic replies until she and Louisa were dismissed like tedious children.

(At that very moment Mrs Ludbury and Charlotte were discovering new and soothing unity in their opinion of Rebecca. Sly and deceitful, they agreed. Vain, Charlotte added as an afterthought.)

'It had nothing to do with you, very probably,' Louisa was saying. 'Time and again I've thought to myself: "Mama is vexed because I spent the egg money on embroidery silks," or "she is cross because I spent so long with old Mrs Harris," and then I discover she knows nothing about it. And she was only a bit put out this afternoon. Why, you should see her sometimes! I shouldn't really say, but you're my closest friend!' – 'Good heavens!' Rebecca thought. 'Am I really?' – 'and I know I can trust you to be discreet . . . Mama is sometimes very, very cross; mad as a bull! There! I've said it! It is *nice* being able to confide in you. I don't care what the others say, I put up with their teasing. And dear George always sticks up for me . . .'

'So she is persecuted on my behalf,' thought Rebecca, feeling guilty. 'You're a dear, Louisa,' she said breaking into the other's flow.

Louisa was silenced for a moment: 'You'll come again soon?'

'Today week.'

'Oh, look at the time! If we hadn't picked the peas I could have walked with you to the road; as it is, I must go and hurry the girl; Mama's digestion will be upset if tea's late.'

'Goodbye,' Rebecca called, turning away with a run, a bit of a skip, then settling to a brisk walk. How glad she was to be alone in the sunlight, how glad to be gone.

Five o'clock and still a scorching sun; no hint of evening in the air. Rebecca slowed a little as she went beneath the trees, savouring their shade before the long, exposed walk to the road. A small missile hurtled down, stinging her arm, and rattled into silence at her feet. How strange – a stone from a tree? She peered upwards.

17

A low chuckle, a rustle of greenery, and a hailstorm smote her. Laughter screamed from the shaking branch like the whooping of a huge, demented bird. She willed her legs to move, to move faster, to run.

'Booby! Just you wait, Rebecca Sheldon! You'll catch it next time,' a voice promised, shrill with spite.

'She's mad,' Rebecca told herself as she hurdled the gate. 'Pip Ludbury is mad.'

Hovering in a heat haze above the meadow a horseman came galloping. 'Oh George, George!'

'Whatever is it?' he cried, drawing up.

'She terrified me.'

'Lou?'

'Pip.'

'Oh, Pip.' He laughed indulgently as he jumped down beside her. 'She upset Charlie earlier on. What did she do to you?'

'Pelted me. Back there in the trees.'

'I'll give her a shaking, the little wretch! But the trick with Pip is never to let her see you're rattled. She is a terror, though. Mama says it's because her brain's too active. She's quite brilliant, by all accounts.'

Brilliant. So that was it.

'You look a bit peaky, Becky. Get up on Gypsy; we'll take you to the road.'

'I couldn't. No, George, don't. Oh, I'll fall.'

'No you won't. She's steady as a rock. Hold on here; she won't mind. Put your leg over. Go on. Who's to see?'

Astride, clutching Gypsy's mane, squealing a little, and the sun beating, beating, the smell of him made a memory more urgently real than this dreaming walk: their first meeting, four years ago, she eleven years old, he two years older. Her mother had died that morning, and she had run from the house, from the terror of that grey immobility. She ran through lanes, then fields, until it was certain she was lost, then flung herself to the ground, drowning in tears and mucus in the sodden grass.

'You're in a fair old paddy,' a voice, creaky with adolescence, remarked.

Shocking intrusion. 'Go away,' she managed in a rush.

'This is our land, if it's all the same to you. I'm George Ludbury. You're the little Sheldon girl, aren't you?'

Raising her head, she saw that he presented no threat; he was a gangling youth whose growth had outstripped his trouser-length. 'Rebecca,' she told him; then, with a violent exhalation: 'My mother's dead.'

He considered this. 'I should cry it out, then. Go on, have a good bawl, you'll feel much better afterwards.' And he waited in silence as she followed his advice. 'Here,' – he reached into his pocket when her crying faltered, and produced a handkerchief – 'have a good blow.'

She blew and wiped and gave the handkerchief back.

He got down on all fours. 'Climb on. I'll give you a piggy-back home. They'll be worried to death about you, I shouldn't wonder.'

He smelt of cow, hay and milk.

At the Sheldon gate he set her down, opened it, and pushed her gently through. 'Go on. I'll watch you to the door.'

With dread, she walked along the path. His voice called after her: 'Chin up, young Becky. It'll be all right – you see.' The unfamiliar diminution of her name startled, then comforted her: it was an appropriation, sweet in this hour of maternal abandonment. When she got to the door she looked back. He was still watching.

'I say, Becky,' he said now.

'Mum?' She was nearly asleep.

'It's jolly nice of you, coming to see Lou.'

'I like her.'

'She's a good sort, even if she is a bit of a chump. Mama says she's simple, but I don't know . . .'

Simple. Funny people these Ludburys. Lethal, lunatic Pip was brilliant. Capable, industrious Louisa was simple. Ah well . . . too hot to be bothered. Lovely, dozy silence. Could go on like this for ever, George, Gypsy and me, lolloping, dreaming . . .

> Dear Rebecca,
>
> You had better not come on T" ,rsday, after all. There is a terrible to-do here. Augusta writes to say that she has married a man on the boat. Can you imagine? Mama is mad as a bull. I will let you know when it is safe to come.
>
> Your affectionate friend,
>
> Louisa
>
> P.S. Pip put a frog in Miss Gaunt's bed. Miss Gaunt has gone home.

2

'I'm finished with Augusta,' Mrs Ludbury bellowed looking very black. 'Finished!'

The breakfast table fell still. Those seated at it looked grave and rather bemused, for Mrs Ludbury had finished with Augusta some days ago on receipt of a gushing letter mailed from South Africa. Now, it appeared, a letter from London made it necessary to finish with Augusta all over again.

'These vile people seem to imagine we are now related.' She jabbed today's correspondence with a rigid forefinger. 'What's more, they treat the whole thing as some kind of joke. It is the most disgraceful communication I have ever had the misfortune to read. How dare Augusta get us into this, this *loathsome* familiarity? Has she no consideration at all for the family interest?'

'But Mama,' ventured Charlotte, 'I'm surprised these people are so bad. After all, he is a doctor' – she referred, rather daringly, to the bridegroom – 'and Augusta says his people are well-to-do in Wimpole Street.'

'Silence! I think I'm about to be ill.' Mrs Ludbury clutched at her throat.

Groans rose up, great cries of dread; and cries of joy from Pip who scented a scene.

'My heart!' Mrs Ludbury yelled above the din. 'I shall never stand it. Never mention her name again!'

George, looking on, decided that Augusta was well out of it. At seventeen he was eager to get on with life. Unfortunately his ambition – to lick the farm into shape, to make it a finer inheritance – did not coincide with his mother's. She had a plan for him and agriculture formed no part of it – just as marriage had formed no part of her plan for Augusta. She had arranged for George to be employed in the office of Mr Henshaw, land agent, surveyor, and devotee of the British Israelite cause. From first inkling George had demurred, but not – at his father's behest – violently. Now Augusta's independent line fired him. All morning he thought about it as he worked in the hayfield. Later, at the dinner table, he observed that the world had not yet ended and that his mother, in spite of a morning's indisposition, was at this very moment making brave headway through a plateful of cold mutton and caper sauce.

'Mama,' he said, turning white, 'I've been thinking things over. I'm obliged to Mr Henshaw, I'm sure, but I shan't go to work for him.'

Mrs Ludbury was caught with a forkful of mutton between plate and open mouth. After a moment's indecision the mouth was favoured. 'What?' she cried indistinctly.

'There's plenty of work to be done here on the farm. If we don't look sharp it will soon be in a bad way. I'm thinking of ploughing the long meadow; we could do with another cash crop, and when you think of the price Harry Hawkins got for his beet . . .'

'How dare you? That you should mention these things at table – and Charlotte about to give us her "Thoughts On A Departed Child", I dare say! Of course you will work for Mr Henshaw.' And Mrs Ludbury reattended with confidence to her plate.

'That I shan't, Mama. My mind's made up. I shall stick to farming; here if I'm let, elsewhere if I'm not.'

Mrs Ludbury rose up with a savage cry. 'See how your children serve me!' she instructed her mate. 'First Augusta's treachery, now this from George. It will be the death of me. Girls! Assist me to my room. You,' she snarled at Harold, 'need not come. Stay and instruct your son. Teach him his duty to the family interest.'

Charlotte and Louisa hauled their mother out of the room and through the hall to the stairs while Pip danced and squealed around them.

George watched them go, then turned to face the accusing eyes of father and brothers. 'I'm done,' he declared, throwing down his napkin. He rose and strode to the door.

From the lych gate he saw her and stood for some moments watching: Rebecca, busy with hand fork and trowel, kneeling by a grave in the sun. As always he was struck by her extraneousness, for she was far removed from the Ludbury norm; his attachment to her felt faintly dangerous. He unlatched the gate and stepped on to the loose gravel path. She looked up and was temporarily blind against the sun.

'Thought I might find you here.'

'George!' Pleased, she sank back on her heels and indicated her handiwork. 'Do you like it?'

He glanced at the grave. She had made a tiny garden of it. 'Very nice,' he said politely. 'Bit unusual, though, for a grave.'

'Yes. Mama would be pleased with it.'

He got to the point. 'Look here, Becky, I've something to tell you, but I shan't tell another soul, so keep it under your hat.'

She scrambled to her feet. 'Whatever is it?'

'I'm done for at home. They're quite content to let the farm go to wrack and ruin and they expect me to stand idly by. They've a notion to put me in an office. Where's the sense in it, I ask you? Well, I've had enough; I'm clearing out; first light tomorrow.'

'Oh, George, Where?'

'London. They won't find me there.'

'Oh, George.' She was desolate now.

He took her hand. 'The thing is, Becky, I'll be back. You can count on it. It'll be a few years, mind, I've got to make something of myself. I can do that, you know.'

'Of course you can.'

'Well, what I want to say is: I'll be back. For you, Becky. See?'

She was silent.

'I'll miss you like anything,' he told her.

'I'll miss you, too.'

'But at least we've got things straight, got it settled between us.'

'Well, yes.' But she was not altogether clear.

He stepped closer and put his lips briefly against her cheek. 'Goodbye, Becky,' he said hoarsely, then squeezed her arms and turned away.

Now it was her turn to watch: George Ludbury – dear, dependable George; George smelling of cow, hay and milk – striding from the churchyard, from Headley Green, from her girlhood years.

George's absence from the breakfast table next morning was ignored. The grumbles at milking, the rumpus when Harry Hawkins turned up and helped himself to the pigs, were not allowed to invade the house. An empty chair at the dinner table, however, could not go unremarked.

'Pip, go and find him,' Mrs Ludbury said. 'Tell him his father is waiting to carve.' (Carving, it was understood, could not take place without the rapt attention of all partakers.)

Beneath a water jug on the wash-stand the sharp-eyed Pip spotted the note intended for her brothers. Probably one, or both, of the boys had seen it, connected it with George's absence, and concluded that ignorance would be the safest position to adopt. Pip was less squeamish. She snatched up the note and read avidly:

Tell them I've gone to London to make something of myself.
Tell them not to worry. Let Harry Hawkins take the black sow and piglets. (I sold them to him last night). Edward can have my calves. Freddy can have Gypsy. *Edward is not to be let near Gypsy.* Papa can have everything else of mine.
Your affectionate brother, George.

Pip, who had been baptized Caroline but nicknamed by George after her propensity to give all and sundry the pip, moaned and hugged herself. There would be an almighty one this time. She flew down the stairs, across the hall and into the dining room. 'He's gone,' she cried, 'gone for good. Here, read this.' She thrust the note into her mother's hand, stood back, and waited for the heavens to fall.

Dear Rebecca,
The most dreadful thing has happened – I can hardly bear to write it. George has gone. He has left us without a word. It is the worst thing in the world

because he was so good at putting things right and smoothing us down. Whatever shall we do without him? I know you will be distressed to learn of this, Rebecca, and, of course, it would not do for you to come here for some time. Mama is distraught; she has suffered numerous heart attacks.

Oh dear, when *shall* we meet? I am doing the Lady Chapel flowers on Saturday afternoon. Will you go to the grave? We may spend a few moments together, then.

Your affectionate friend, Louisa.

P.S. I came across Papa weeping in the orchard. (I would not tell this to anyone but you.) The shock has unsettled him. He said George had gone because he, Papa, had failed him. Isn't that strange? I am worried about Papa.

3

'I must say, I'm pleased to see you taking this so well,' Miss Hyslop said. Miss Hyslop lied: wretched herself, she would have preferred a degree of agitation, some show of sorrow; but Rebecca's eyes, though grave, were untroubled. This steady calm in the face of sorrow had impressed Miss Hyslop over the years, for the silver-lining theory of life was Miss Hyslop's pet philosophy. Many of the maidens at her Stratford-upon-Avon school were orphans or at some similar disadvantage, and it had been her life's work to persuade them that God was working His purpose out despite appearances to the contrary. Rebecca had been her most striking success. She had joined the school at the age of eleven having just lost her mother; two years later her father had remarried and her sister, Edith – to whom Rebecca was devoted – had taken a position as lady's companion in Gloucestershire rather than remain under the same roof as her stepmother; then there was anxiety about her brother, Thomas, who had gone missing; and lately the death of her father. Yet through it all Rebecca remained calm, deeply affected, but, Miss Hyslop saw, staunchly trusting in God's Plan.

(If Miss Hyslop had only known, Rebecca paid scant attention to God's Plan. It was her ability to reflect on her experience that had stood her in good stead all these years. Good and bad, she had found, tended to walk hand in hand.)

Rebecca was seventeen; it was high time, her stepmother had decided, to embark on more fruitful occupation. Accordingly, she had secured for her stepdaughter an apprenticeship with the Birmingham firm of Jevons and Mellor, art needlework specialists of repute. And Rebecca was grateful; she had not been enamoured of the prospect painted by Miss Hyslop – pupil teacher now, assistant mistress in the fullness of time – there was more to life, she had felt, than this little school. She understood that her stepmother wished to be rid of her, but was touched that she sought to accomplish her ambition with sympathetic imagination, for Rebecca was a talented needleworker and pleased by the chance of attachment to such a prestigious house.

'It's kind of my stepmother to have gone to such trouble,' she told Miss Hyslop.

'But it's a *shop*!' Miss Hyslop cried, forgetting in the heat of the moment due respect for God's Plan.

'Yes, there's a shop – Edith and I have bought silks there on several occasions – but primarily it's a place of instruction and artistry. The most beautiful things are done. William Morris was associated . . .'

'Well, as I said before,' – Miss Hyslop was in no mood for enthusiasm – 'I'm relieved you can contemplate leaving us with such tranquillity.'

'I'm not happy to be leaving, I know I shall be very sad when the time comes, but I'm trying to think sensibly about the future.'

'But I had such plans!' Miss Hyslop almost shouted, full of wrath against Jevons and Mellor, Mrs Sheldon and Divine Interference. Not only had she planned plans, Miss Hyslop had dreamed dreams. Dreams of a future in which Rebecca played a leading role were her favourite sleeping draught: the two of them toasting muffins in the study on a winter's afternoon; walking beneath streaming willows, throwing bread to swans; together at the theatre, heads inclined, sharing wonderment; Rebecca supportive at her side on the school platform; then, years later – a moving scene, this – Rebecca assuming the mantle of Headship – 'With you at my side, dear Miss Hyslop, I shall steer our beloved school into the future.' . . . Suddenly, with ice in her heart, Miss Hyslop foresaw an eternity of comfortless nights. 'I had such plans,' she wailed.

'I know,' Rebecca said gently, laying a light hand on Miss Hyslop's arm. 'I shall come and stay here often, if I may.'

At once a new scenario flew into Miss Hyslop's mind: Rebecca as weekend guest, dainty at breakfast, fellow stroller along the river bank, intimate beside the evening fire. All was not lost. Bedtime horrors receded. 'Why, yes,' she cried joyfully. 'You are quite right to have faith in Providence. I see it plainly now: you will have your employment, as I have mine, but this dear school will be your refuge, your place of recreation – I daresay you won't want to go home for your holidays very often now.'

'No. I dare say not, Miss Hyslop.'

4

Rebecca walked carefully over the bare wooden boards to the bare, narrow, twisting stairs; carefully, because every sound in this sparsely furnished farmhouse reverberated and it was important not to wake the children. At the bottom of the stairs, at the entrance to the room, she closed the slatted door behind her, letting down the iron latch without a sound. The extremities of the long, low-ceilinged room were in darkness, but the looming blackness of a dresser, the pale glint of crockery, the unhurried, metallic beat of a longcase clock set boundaries to the shadows beyond the table where an oil lamp gleamed. The best light came from the fire, glowing and darting in the inglenook. Here Edith sat in an ancient Windsor chair.

'Brr.' Rebecca hurried to join her sister. 'Where's Sam?' – Sam, who had been gay during the midday meal, teasing Rebecca, provoking his children to laughter, catching Edith's hand to cover in kisses; who had been despondent at tea time and in the depths of despair by sundown.

'Gone into Lipscombe – The Ram, I expect.'

'Oh.' Good. They could relax. She held out a slim parcel. 'For you, with my best love.'

Edith took it and peeled back the paper. For a moment she looked at it, the white cloth in its snowy wrappings on her knee, then she picked it up and shook it out to study at arm's length. It was beautiful, worked all over in broderie anglaise. She rose, went to the table and smoothed it over the scrubbed deal surface.

Rebecca leapt to her feet and saw at once that the cloth was out of place; it was too small, too fine, and, she remembered too late, there was no suitable table in the house. 'It's my best work to date. I thought you'd like it as an example,' she hurried to explain, and rushed on to cover her embarrassment:

'There's such a variety of work done – bed linen, stool and chair covers, firescreens. Have you seen the new Jacobean embroidery? Oh, I wish you could visit us, Edith; you'd laugh – a lot of rather grand ladies come for instruction, they get into some awful pickles . . .' She came to a halt, then said: 'Whatever made me bring that? I wish I'd thought of something useful.'

'I shall treasure it.' Edith folded the cloth and replaced it in the tissue. 'I'll put it with my special things – Mama's things – in my chest. You know that I took quite a few of Mama's things when I left?'

'Well, our stepmother did remark . . .'

'I'll bet she did. But they're for you as well, Rebecca. We'll go over them tomorrow. No trace of Thomas in Birmingham, I suppose?'

'No. I called at the factory, but Mr Dimmont hasn't seen him for months. *She's* often there, of course.'

'Evil woman! I hate her.'

Rebecca looked down at the floor. 'Father's equally to blame – you must see that, Edith. After all, he left everything to her; he had no thought for his children. I don't really mind for myself, but it's a tragedy for Thomas.'

'I hate her,' Edith insisted. 'She drove our brother to drink, then poisoned our father against him. And *you* may take a lofty view, but with children to feed and clothe *I* feel very bitter.'

'Oh, Edith. She's not all bad. I'm sure if you wrote to her . . .'

'Never! We won't talk about it. Come on, put another log on and get closer.'

Chairs squeaked on stone flags. The fire shuddered then sprang into new life.

'Your letters are very cheerful. You said something about a promotion.'

'Yes.' Rebecca smiled into the flames.

'You intend to make a career of it, then?'

29

'I don't know about that. I'm not sure I should stay there for ever.' (Miss Crowthorn had stayed there for ever – a brilliant designer, a dazzling needleworker, everyone agreed about that. Now, though, her eyesight was failing, she made mistakes, people were sometimes impatient. And wasn't there a subtle repository of disrespect in the title 'Miss' after a certain age? Rebecca recalled young, personable Mr Patterson's off-hand tone when he addressed the fifty-year-old spinster, and contrasted it with the complimentary manner of his approach to her – 'Miss Sheldon, what a charming colour scheme, if I may say so!' At what age did Miss Crowthorn cease to be paid homage and earn distant contempt? And to what quality in Miss Sheldon was homage paid? To her colour sense? To her prospects with the firm? Or to her good looks, her youth, her buoyant matrimonial chances?) 'I suppose,' she said reflectively, 'there are other considerations in life.'

'Yes.'

The sisters sat in silence for a while, thinking of other considerations. A burning log sank lower in the fire; ash shifted with the sound of sudden rain.

'Any nice young men?' inquired Edith.

'Yes . . .'

'Well, then?'

'There's a curate. I met him at a church social evening. He's quite . . . attentive.'

'Mmm. A curate.' Edith's tone was doubtful.

'And there's Mr Patterson, I suppose. He's very . . . attentive. And he's Mr Mellor's nephew.'

'There you are, then.' It was settled, evidently.

Rebecca shuffled her feet. In spite of the nearness of the fire a damp chill had attacked them. Then it came to her that she would make Edith a rug, warm and bright – just the thing. Now, where to get rug wool and large-holed canvas? Mr Patterson would know, he did most of the buying. She would ask him first thing on

Monday. 'The trouble is,' she said thoughtfully, 'I'm not sure that I like him particularly. He's very pleasant, but I hate the way his hair clings to his scalp. And he's very pale.'

'Who?'

'Mr Patterson. The curate's pale, too, and he's got buckteeth.'

The sisters gazed sadly into the fire.

'Of course,' said Edith after a while, 'looks aren't everything. Don't underestimate position. I think Mr Patterson sounds promising in that quarter.'

The fire was making Rebecca drowsy. She yawned and stretched. 'And all he smells of is hair oil,' she reflected.

'Who?'

'Mr Patterson.'

'What would you have him smell of, for goodness' sake? Sheep? Pigs? Beer?'

Rebecca thought her sister's tone a trifle sharp. 'I was just thinking about what I like in a man,' she explained. 'You know: earthiness, ruggedness, plenty of go . . .'

'Ever hear from George Ludbury?' Edith asked slyly.

'Yes.' Then, realizing she had been caught out: 'Oh, you!'

'You always were a dark horse, Rebecca.'

'Nothing to get excited about. Just a few letters about himself. He sounds fine. Perhaps he boasts a bit, but he gives the impression of being in charge of a whole string of butcher's shops in London.' She stretched luxuriously. 'There's something awfully nice about George.'

'Be careful, darling. Those Ludburys always struck me as odd.'

'Me too.'

'Don't be too set against other . . . prospects.'

From a dark corner of the room the clock spoke up: ten rickety chimes.

'Ten! Good Lord! And that clock's always slow. Look, go up now, will you, dear? Sam will be home soon and his moods are so unpredictable these days.'

The sisters got to their feet.

'Are you coming up? You look very tired, Edith.'

'Soon.'

There was something about the way she moved, heels dragging, hand in the small of her back . . . 'Oh, Edith. You're not, are you? Not again . . . so soon?'

'Goodnight, Rebecca.'

5

'Get on with it, man!' snarled Mrs Ludbury. 'Carve!'

Husband and wife contemplated one another along the length of the dinner table. Their children Charlotte, Louisa and Pip on one side, Edward and Freddy on the other kept their heads down, though Pip shot the odd glance at her mother and Louisa muttered something to Great Grandmama Ludbury who was hanging on the wall opposite in a gilded frame.

'I am very worried about Papa,' was Louisa's muttered observation. She said that all the time. It had become involuntary. Walking through the hall she would become transfixed by the bentwood hat-stand and feel obliged to confide in it. 'I am very worried about Papa,' she told the blue and white dragon plates on the kitchen dresser, the broody hen, the butter churn and the monkey puzzle tree. The cook and the gardener overheard and nodded their agreement. But to members of the family it was nothing to remark. Louisa's utterances were part of the ambience – the back stairs creaked, the landing window rattled, the drawing room mantle clock hiccuped during the quarter chimes, and Louisa, for reasons best known to herself, muttered.

Harold sat in his chair and thought. His wife required him to carve, and she had sharpened the knife personally not quarter of an hour ago. 'So no excuses,' she had said. He hauled himself to his feet and took up the carvers. If only she would stop boring into his skull with those black, baleful eyes. Looking down, he saw that his hands were shaking.

'I will go to him,' Louisa told Great Grandmama Ludbury. 'I am not afraid of Mama. I will get up and go to him. He is ill. He is quite beyond it. Yes, I will go to him,' she promised, frozen for ever in her chair.

Whatever was the matter with the man? wondered Mrs Ludbury. Why did he stand there slavering like an idiot? She considered telling him to mop his chin before the dribble dropped on to the meat, but restrained herself; they'd be there all day without a morsel to eat if she suggested a diversion. The man didn't seem to know what he was about. Why did he not pull himself together? No backbone. No willpower. Weak as a jelly. Thinking of jelly . . . her eyes darted longingly to a sauceboat of the redcurrant variety, a great dollop of which she intended to spoon on to her plate of roast lamb, if only the man would carve her a slice. She swallowed and gripped the arms of her chair. For two pins she'd rush over there and carve it herself. 'Carve, man, carve,' she groaned through clenched teeth.

'They are waiting,' Harold observed to himself. 'All of them waiting. All except George and that other one, that girl. Dear old George . . . too late now. Sorry, old fellow . . .' His stomach, boiling with bile for a week, now gave way. An iron fist thrust upwards into his chest and ruptured his throat. 'I am suffocating,' thought Harold as the hammer in his ears went wild. A curtain of fire blinded him. At the last moment he thought: 'Done it again. Failed her. Couldn't even die decently – nice and orderly in bed. Forgive me, my dear . . .'

'My God he's died on us, and all over the joint!' thought Mrs Ludbury. She found her voice: 'Move it! Move the joint!'

'Oh, Papa,' Louisa cried. 'I was about to come to you, indeed I was.'

Charlotte took charge. 'On to the sofa, quick. Edward! Freddy! Loosen the necktie. Undo the stud.'

'Papa, Papa,' moaned Louisa, chaffing lifeless hands.

'Send for the doctor, Mama,' Charlotte commanded.

'Let me see.' Mrs Ludbury elbowed her way through. She gave her husband a poke, then put an ear to his breast. 'Dead,' she proclaimed. 'Dead as a doornail. Edward, go and get one of the men. He can't stay here. He must be put in the boxroom. You'd better go for Mrs Knight, Freddy. Quick, take the trap. Call on the doctor, too, but don't let him bring that Pickles woman – I won't have her in the house. Go on, hurry!'

Fists struck the table with considerable force. Abandoned cutlery jangled like nerve ends. 'I want to *know*,' screamed Pip, still in her place at the table. 'I want to know,' she repeated, more quietly, but on a warning note.

'Know what?'

'Why dead? What reason?'

'God . . .' began Charlotte.

'Not God reasons, *body* reasons. What happened *inside*?'

'Doctor Forbes will tell us,' Mrs Ludbury said soothingly.

'How will he know? He can't know without looking inside. Will he cut Papa open?'

'Pip!' shrieked Louisa.

'Stop her, Mama,' Charlotte begged.

'Papa is dead because his heart stopped,' Mrs Ludbury said, recalling the delicate state of her own organ.

'Why did it stop? That's the question. Silly answers make me cross. I think he should be cut open.'

'Mama, this has gone too far,' Charlotte protested, and Louisa clapped hands over her ears and began to weep.

'Silence!' the widow roared, and then peace being restored 'I'm about to be ill.'

Footsteps in the hall. Charlotte pulled the door wide open. 'Edward's brought the man,' she reported, surveying the arrivals – an apologetic farmhand, limbs a-twitch with the vain effort to remove evidence of his toil, and Edward, grinning fatuously.

Mrs Ludbury joined Charlotte in the doorway. 'You might have brought a cleaner one. Never mind. He'd better get on with it. In here, my man. Get hold of him; and you, Edward. Upstairs. Boxroom.'

'I'll help,' Pip cried.

'I don't think she should, Mama . . .'

'Nonsense,' Mrs Ludbury snapped, suddenly ravenous. 'Pip can run ahead and open the door. Off you go. Now, Louisa, take the joint into the kitchen and tell Harriet to give it a good wipe. I'll have a little on a tray in my room. Mind you slice it thin. I don't know that I shall manage it, but I must try. I shall have to keep up m'strength now I've the burden to bear alone.'

'You've got me, Mama,' Charlotte pointed out.

'I know, dear,' Mrs Ludbury sighed. 'Help me to my room.' Hanging heavily on to Charlotte's arm, she staggered into the hall and went towards the stairs. The door to the kitchen was ajar. 'Louisa, make haste with that meat. And don't forget the redcurrant jelly.'

Harold, a disappointment to his wife in life, gave complete satisfaction in death.

Mrs Ludbury stood at the foot of the coffin in the freshly spring-cleaned drawing room and was moved by his nobility. As a corpse, she reflected, Albert himself could not have been more impressive. She thought of the greatest widow of them all, in deference to whom she had worn black for so long, and resolved to cut no corners in following the royal example. No degree of mourning could be too rigorous for Harold. The dressmaker installed in the sewing room must double her effort; every member of the household must be clothed in black from head to toe; purple and grey periods would follow in due course. And Louisa and the girl had better buck up; everything in the house must be draped in black or, at the very least, garnished with black ribbon.

Mrs Ludbury felt called to widowhood. Tears of gratitude coursed over her leathery cheeks as she knelt in homage to the man who had elevated her to that state. 'Harold, Harold,' she murmured, one hand on her heart, the other touching his coffin. Her art, she knew, would be enriched by the poignancy of her position. Already a panegyric stanza was taking shape:

> No earthly care disturbs thy noble brow,
> Husband! Nature's prince! Grave knight at
>   peace,
> A Higher Love than mine has claimed thee
>   now . . .

'Mama! Come away, do. You'll upset yourself. Come with me.'

'Damnation!' thought Mrs Ludbury, allowing Charlotte, nevertheless, to lead her from the room.

'There is a matter we must discuss,' Charlotte said, arranging her mother comfortably on the chaise-longue in the dining room. 'Bearing in mind that the funeral will be a public occasion . . .'

'George,' Mrs Ludbury put in.

'Augusta,' Charlotte corrected her. 'George, I feel, presents no problem. He is a dear boy; his letters are full of affection. I think we may find that he has got it out of his system, that he is ready to play his part, here at The Grange. After all, he is now head of the house. As long as we handle it carefully . . .'

' "Head of the house", eh?'

'Augusta is the problem,' Charlotte said.

Mrs Ludbury pressed her lips into a firm line. 'There need be no thought of Augusta. *Her* offence was irretrievable. We have discarded her like a diseased branch for the health of the tree. But what you say about George fills me with hope, for *he* is a mainline stem, the family's future depends upon him. That is why I have encouraged your correspondence. In the family interest he must be recovered.'

'You are right, of course, Mama. But, with regard to Augusta, it would be unpleasant to be in the wrong. You see, she may turn up for the funeral.'

'With that awful man in tow?'

'Possibly. But I think I can write to her in such a way as to make her hesitate before adding to your anxiety on such a painful occasion. Do you agree that I should write, Mama? I'm sure I can handle it.'

And Mrs Ludbury, not entirely to her satisfaction, saw that she could. Charlotte, who could make fine copies of her mother's work, perform her mother's pieces for pianoforte with a degree of *bravura*, and remember the steps of every dance, but who had small talent for original composition and was as ungainly as an ox (even that idiot, Louisa, could dance), evidently had hidden talent, and the suspicion grew in Mrs Ludbury that this talent was powerful: it was imperative that it remained at her mother's disposal. 'Of all my children,' Mrs Ludbury began slowly, 'you, Charlotte, are the one whose discretion and judgement I trust. It is a great comfort to have a daughter on whom I can absolutely rely.'

'At last!' thought Charlotte, purple with pleasure, 'Mama values me, acknowledges my worth, loves me. . . .'

Fearing an embrace, Mrs Ludbury reached briskly for a book. 'Make haste, then,' she said curtly. 'The funeral's on Friday. Go and get it written.'

'Yes indeed, Mama,' said Charlotte.

As the door closed Mrs Ludbury threw down her book and closed her eyes. Interesting, that about George. Head of the house. She began to paint a picture in her mind to see if it would do.

'George!' Charlotte cried in the tones of a parched desert wanderer espying an oasis. 'Dear boy! I knew you'd come.'

'Steady on, old girl.'

'George, oh it's George!' Louisa rushed into the hall from the kitchen.

Thunder on the stairs. 'What? Did you say "George"?' Pip tore into her sisters, scattering them, and leapt upon her brother, legs around his hips, arms around his neck, whooping joy into his left ear.

'Pip! Get down! Remember Papa!' Charlotte remonstrated, tugging at her sister's skirt.

Pip slid to the floor, and George fell back against the hall table.

'Yes, come and see Papa.' Pip seized his hand.

'Sh. Go quietly,' Charlotte called after them. 'I'd better go and prepare Mama.'

Alone in the hall, Louisa wrung her hands. 'George is back. Isn't it wonderful?' she asked the hatstand doubtfully.

In the drawing room George swallowed hard and cleared his throat.

'They've put something on his face,' Pip told him, darting forward. 'It feels waxy. But if you poke your finger under his collar . . .'

'Stop that! Clear off! Give a fellow a bit of peace, can't you?'

Grinning, she left him.

Later, returning to the hall, he almost collided with Louisa. 'Hallo, Lou.' He sounded surprised, noticing her for the first time. 'What are you doing hanging around here in the gloom?' He squeezed her arms and kissed her cheeks.

'Mama will see you now,' Charlotte called, putting her head round the corner.

'Oh, it is wonderful,' Louisa decided, giving the hatstand a playful shove and setting walking sticks jostling with croquet mallets.

In the dining room the curtains were closed and there was so much black stuff about that George found it difficult to make out his mother. But there she was on the chaise-longue, her eyes bright as stars in the night sky.

'Mama?'

'Come closer.'

'How do, Mama?'

'Nearer.'

A hand, swift as a snake's tongue, encircled his wrist and pulled tenaciously. He was obliged to kneel beside her.

'You may kiss me, George.'

The strong, stale smell of mother engulfed him: camphor, vaseline, moth-ball and unwashed lace. Suddenly he was full of dread. 'I'm sorry I wasn't here . . .'

'You're here now, George.'

A stuffy silence, during which George heard the rustle of a skirt behind the half-closed door.

Mrs Ludbury heard it too. 'Go and close it,' she said, pointing. Charlotte was taking too much upon herself; advice was one thing, listening at keyholes to ascertain the degree of adherence to said advice was quite another. 'Now, open the curtain a crack. Let's have a look at you.' She studied him, frowning. 'Taller than ever, but you've filled out nicely. You look prosperous, George. Are you?'

He grinned.

'Well, are you? Speak up! Don't beat about the bush. Have you made your fortune or haven't you?'

'I've not done badly, Mama; tidy sum in the bank, learnt a few tricks of the trade . . .'

'Trade?' Mrs Ludbury interjected sharply.

'Business, then. I reckon I've a good head for business.'

'We won't talk about that now. Come close again.' She lowered her voice dramatically and went on: 'I am left a widow, alone in the world with two children still to rear.'

'I bet old Charlie can help you there; she'll keep 'em in order. And good old Lou runs the house like clockwork . . .'

'A man!' Mrs Ludbury cried. 'This house requires a man!'

'There's Edward . . .'

With a shriek of despair Mrs Ludbury felt back upon her cushions. Alarmed, George leaned over her, and at once the snake hand struck, imprisoning his wrist in a stranglehold. 'You, George,' she hissed. 'We need you. Oh, my strength is failing, I am plagued by fatigue . . . George, I look to you for support in my hour of need, you who are Head of the House.'

George, much moved, bowed his head, and his mother's free hand caressed it like a blessing.

'Don't worry, Mama,' he choked. 'You've got the right man here.'

'Thank you, my son,' Their work accomplished, the snake hand and the benedictory hand fell in lifeless collapse across her stomach.

George got off his knees. 'I shan't mind getting out of London, giving up the shops.' (His mother winced.) 'I always meant to get back to farming once I'd put a bit by. Mind you, I might combine the two – farming and butchery – not a bad combination. But I expect this place'll take some licking into shape first. I'll invest in some decent machinery . . .'

'Not now! I am in mourning!'

'Sorry, Mama. Stupid of me. Wrong time altogether. Anything I can do for you?'

'Send Charlotte to me. And tell Louisa to see about tea – perhaps a slice of Madeira cake; something easy to digest. I hardly ate a scrap at dinner, and I must keep up m'strength.'

6

'A gentleman to see you, Miss,' the maid said doubtfully.

'Gentleman?'

'Ludbury, I think he said his name was. I put him in the sitting room.'

The sitting room; where Lady Anne waited upon Lady Marjorie, where Mrs Beaumont-Gibbs took tea while Rebecca unpicked her knots. 'I'll be down at once,' Rebecca said, abandoning her work, pausing only briefly in front of the looking-glass.

Halfway down the stairs she saw him through the open sitting-room door. He was gazing down into the street through the long window, his hands deep in his trouser pockets, jingling small change; a rather sharp-looking fellow. She had decided to flee, had gathered up her skirts in readiness, when he turned as if suddenly sensing his imminent loss. He saw her and smiled, and was at once restored to an approximation of George Ludbury; dear, very dear George.

They moved swiftly towards one another, but at the foot of the stairs he hesitated. 'My goodness, Becky! You're so . . . I mean, you've become so . . .'

But she caught both his hands in hers and shook them, laughing.

'It's very grand here,' he remarked politely. 'Charlotte said it was a shop.'

'The shop's through there,' Rebecca said, nodding in its direction.

Somewhere a bell rang and footsteps hurried. They loosed hands.

'Shall we go for a walk? It won't matter if I'm out for a while. The park's lovely at the moment.'

He was relieved. 'Right-oh.'

In the park the wind was blowing blossom from the trees. Pink and white petals fell like confetti.

'My father's dead,' George said, staring at a bed of scarlet tulips.

'I know. Mrs Smythe told me when she came in to match some silks. I'm very sorry, George.'

'So I'm back.'

'For the funeral?'

'For good. Now Papa's gone I'm head of the house.'

'I see.' But she did not. Had he not broken free to go about his own business? In her favourite daydream he returned to whisk her off to London.

'I'm sick of city life, Becky. I'm not really cut out for it. Though I must say I've done very well in London. But now it's time to get back to the land where I belong.'

She quite saw that; a city pallor diminished him, she decided, recalling with a pang his former weather-beaten looks. 'I expect there are plenty of farms about the country for sale or rent,' she suggested timidly.

'None with land to better The Grange: I've always said that, and now's my chance to prove it. Oh, Becky, won't it be grand? I've dreamt of it all these years, you and me at The Grange. I used to watch you coming up the drive to call on Louisa; one day, I'd promise myself, she'll be coming here for good.'

To The Grange? With the Ludburys? In the midst of her panic she recognized that this, at last, was his proposal of marriage. But to live at The Grange? Had that really always been his intention? She had never guessed it, not for one moment. The pain of her confusion overwhelmed her and his words mingled incoherently with her horrified reaction.

42

'. . . plenty of room, there, Becky . . . and you were always such friends with Louisa . . . Mama and Charlotte may be sticky at first, but they'll come round . . .'

Mama and Charlotte. There was no doubt about it. He proposed that she live with his mother and Charlotte.

'. . . times when I've had my doubts, I can tell you. But Charlotte seems to have found the knack of handling Mama; she's sure that once this mourning business is out of the way I'll be able to get on with it – buy some new stock and machinery, repair the barns and the cow sheds . . . Not a bad old stick, Charlie. You'll soon be getting on like a house on fire . . .'

Never! Never, never, never . . .

'. . . Just think of it, Becky: you and me – Mr and Mrs George Ludbury of the Grange, Headley Green.'

'George, I must go.'

'Must you?' He pulled a watch from his waistcoat pocket. 'In that case I'll catch the twelve ten. How about Sunday? Here, of course. Too soon for The Grange. Have to prepare the ground a bit before you show your face.'

She swallowed, feeling sick. 'I'm going to Stratford to stay with Miss Hyslop for the weekend.'

'Sunday after, then.'

'I'm sorry, George; we're giving a tea for the children from the orphanage. Can't let people down.'

'Have to be Sunday fortnight, then.'

'Well, I may be going to Lipscombe to stay with my sister that weekend. She married a farmer there, you know.'

'Old Edith? Fancy her marrying a farmer! Lipscombe, eh? That's in Gloucestershire, in the Cotswolds, ain't it? I wouldn't mind taking a look at the farms around there. Tell you what: if you do decide to go I'll meet you there. I'll put up at an inn; take a look at the future brother-in-law.'

'George, I don't know. Things are a bit difficult for Edith at the moment.'

'Write to me and let me know. That'd be best.'

'Yes. Yes, I'll write.' A letter. Much easier to explain in a letter . . . 'Dear George, I cannot countenance close quarters with your family; the very idea makes me shudder . . .'

'You're cold, Becky. Shivering. We can't have that.' He put an arm around her shoulder and tipped up her chin with his hand to stare fondly into her eyes. 'Got to take care of you, little lady. Come on. Let's get you out of this wind.'

How hurt he will be. Oh, George . . .

Dear Becky,
Sorry to hear poor old Edith's unwell. I hope you'll find her better at the weekend. Perhaps we can visit her together at Whitsun.

Things are not going too well here. Truth to tell, Becky, I'm beginning to wonder whether our plans will work out at The Grange. It turns out that Mama is as set against progress as ever, as far as the farm is concerned. And this carry-on with mourning worries me; there seems to be no end to it. I shall have it out with her. I am not one for wasting time.

I hope to see you Sunday week. My regards to Edith and her husband,
Your ever loving George.

'What do you think?' Rebecca asked Edith, as her sister continued to study George's letter.

'Oh, darling, I don't know. It *sounds* as if he's lost patience with them, but they still might give in to him. And then where'd you be, if you'd agreed to marry him and found you were expected to live with them at The Grange after all?'

'It's so *difficult*,' Rebecca groaned.

A boy of two or three came unsteadily across the grass towards the sisters sitting in the shelter of the porch. They watched his progress without enthusiasm. Suddenly, he tripped and fell.

'Up you get,' Edith sang out with false brightness.

Getting to his feet, the boy eyed his mother with sullen speculation. Surely he was owed a rush of maternal concern? His pouting mouth trembled.

Rebecca clapped her hands. 'Well!' she cried. 'Did you see that? The most *enormous* butterfly.' She was careful to address the question to her sister.

'Where?' demanded the child.

'Over there. Quick! Oh, it's gone behind the rosemary bush.'

The child hurried off in pursuit.

'Well done,' Edith acknowledged, handing George's letter back to Rebecca. She sighed. 'I must say, I've always had my doubts about you and George. I was sure the Ludburys would never allow it, even if you were mad enough to contemplate an alliance.'

'But by the time it dawned on me that George and I might be leading to . . . well, marriage . . . he'd left The Grange – cut himself off from them. I never dreamt he'd think of returning.'

Edith sat up straight and drew in breath. She was about – her stern expression indicated – to speak plainly. 'The Ludburys are the most appalling people I have ever come across . . .'

'Yes, but not George. George isn't a bit . . .'

'. . . Snooty, rude, insular, suspicious,' Edith insisted, her voice rising. 'Do you remember the to-do there was when Maudie Dimmont invited Gussie Ludbury to stay at Willen Lodge? You'd have thought the Dimmonts were white slavers. And the sort of people who visit The Grange are most peculiar. And you know about Mrs Ludbury cutting Mama in Chapmans? Did she ever tell you about that? So unspeakably rude . . . They'd

45

hardly so much as nod to us after church, even.'

'That was because of the factory . . .'

'But it wasn't just us they were rude to. They were suspicious of everyone. I always wondered how you managed to get on terms with Louisa.'

'George put the idea into Louisa's head – she's very suggestible – so that we'd have an excuse to see each other. But you're right about the Ludburys being suspicious. Charlotte was forever spying on Louisa and me – Lord knows what she imagined we got up to – perhaps she guessed about George. And as for that terrible Pip . . .'

'So it would never do, darling. You must see that.'

Rebecca looked down at the letter in her lap. 'George,' she began, and was then obliged to clear her throat. 'George is the kindest, dearest person in the world. Not a bit like them. He wouldn't hurt anyone's feelings. He's a very . . . tender person.'

Edith reached for Rebecca's hand. 'I know. I remember how pleasant it was to meet him in the village. . . . Even so, dear, the Ludburys are his people. He grew up with their ideas, their outlook on the world. Remember that.'

Rebecca turned. Her eyes engaged those of her sister with wide, shining purpose. 'If there's a chance, Edith, I shall take it. As long as I don't have to live amongst *them*, it'll be all right. I know it will.'

'You'd be related to them. They'd probably visit you.'

'But I'd receive them as mistress of my own house.'

'George would probably expect you to visit The Grange. Just imagine – they'd be sour as anything to you – you'd be the despised sister-in-law.'

'I could put up with it – I can deal with Charlotte, you know; I found I could get her quite rattled by adopting a sort of queenly air – I can put up with it, so long as our life – George's and mine – is quite

46

separate from theirs. And it would be best for George, too. Don't forget he had to break away from them years ago because of his mother's obstinacy. He's not the sort of person to stand being dictated to. No. I can see how it was. He came back for his father's funeral. He thought his mother had mellowed. But' – she waved the letter fiercely – 'he soon found he was mistaken.'

Edith shook her head.

'I want him – more than anything. But not them. On no account them.'

'Then tell him. Be frank with him, Rebecca.'

'Oh, Edith!' She flung out a hopeless hand. 'How can I? How can I tell him that I detest his people? The trouble is, he's fond of them. He's a very . . . fond sort of person. I couldn't be so unkind.'

'Even so; I think you ought . . .'

The child came charging round the corner. 'Couldn't catch it. Me *stung*.' He held out a nettle-pocked hand.

'Spit on it and rub it in,' Edith advised vaguely.

The child spat and rubbed.

'So what will you do?' Edith asked.

'Write. Agree to meet as he suggests. Find out what he intends to do.'

'Me still stung!' the child roared accusingly.

'Oh dear!' Edith stood up. 'We'd better look for a dock leaf.'

Rebecca stuffed George's letter into her skirt pocket and hurried after them. She linked arms with her sister. 'Oh, Edith, I know it's right, George and me. I know it.'

'Darling, I do hope so.'

Dear George,
Edith is better and sends her regards. I am sorry to hear that things are not as you had hoped at The Grange. However, do bear in mind that there are other farms to be had. My brother-in-law knows of

one or two around Lipscombe, for example. Things often turn out for the best.

I will see you on Sunday afternoon at three o'clock.

With love, Rebecca.

The brave little darling, marvelled George, placing Rebecca's letter in his writing box and turning the key. 'There are other farms to be had,' she had written, as if quite unmoved by fading hopes of becoming mistress of The Grange. And yet, he told himself, putting the key in his waistcoat pocket, the loss of such a prospect would dash the spirits of any girl; it was only natural. But *she* kept her chin up; there was no special pleading from *her* to wait and see, to play his mother along, to ignore the imminent collapse of the cowsheds.

'Georgy! Georgy Porgy!'

That blighter Pip. Not going to be caught by her this morning; things to do. 'Out of my way!' he cried, brushing past her on the stairs. 'I'm in a hurry.'

His feet carried him round the turn of the stairs out of Pip's sight; but his voice, loud and urgent, rose up the stairwell. 'Louisa! Come quick! The farm accounts. Where do you keep them?'

An indistinct reply.

'To the dairy, then. Yes, now! Leave all that. I want you to go over them with me. You're the only one around here who knows what's what . . .' They passed out of earshot.

Pip went into action. Within seconds she had sped along the landing, returned with a manicure kit in her pocket, turned the handle to George's door and stepped down into his room. All without a sound. But a heavy tread on the stair made her hesitate. She listened. Not George – it was Charlotte.

Pip closed the door noiselessly and considered. It was not improbable that Charlotte was on her way to this room on a mission identical to her own: she, too, had seen the letter with the Birmingham postmark lying on the brass plate in the hall. In fact, thought Pip, recalling the look of righteous anger in her sister's eyes, for two pins Charlotte would have snatched it and made off with it, if George had not come striding into the hall. Yes, she'd stake her life on it, Charlotte was now on her way to this room.

She raised the counterpane and shot under the high iron-framed bed. The chamber pot rang out like a cracked bell. 'Shush,' hissed Pip, dampening the sound with a quick finger. Just in time; for the door opened and, after a breathy hesitation, a weighty foot stepped down into the room. Putting her face to the floor she observed, between carpet and counterpane, a pair of tiptoeing feet passing by. There was a shuffling and a shaking, and the sound of wood drawn across wood. She's at the writing box, Pip decided, removing a piece of under-bed fluff from her mouth. But a grunt of disappointment came from the region of the chest-of-drawers, followed by cross sounds of drawer rifling. Surely, Pip thought, she has not given up on the writing box? Surely she has discovered a means to unlock it? Evidently not. In which case Charlotte must be unaware of the contents of *last* week's letter, the one giving old George the brush off: ('Edith is unwell and cannot do with visitors, please postpone your visit to Lip-something-or-other.') How glorious to be one up on Charlotte!

'Blow it!' Charlotte said under her breath. She tidied the drawers, closed them, and hurried to the door where she bungled her exit by tripping over the step.

Hopeless, thought Pip, crawling from under the bed. Charlotte had no finesse. She listened at the door for a moment or two. Quiet as the grave. Good. To business. Taking out her manicure kit, she advanced upon the writing box.

*

The sun, hidden by thick cloud all morning, suddenly broke free and poured its radiance on Mrs Ludbury at her writing table. Diverted, Mrs Ludbury raised her face to the bright intrusion and, since there was no one there to see, raised her arms as well and had a good stretch. It was as if the sun, shooting in like that, had sought her out particularly to caress with warm fingers. This thought made her smile and close her eyes; for she had once been a lively beauty and Harold an impressionable young man.

Dear, dear Harold. How indebted she was to him. Her mind had obliterated the irritation of recent times and dwelt only on his tender years and his final magnanimity in relinquishing life at a moment when her muse was unobliging and she was in sore need of inspiration. And there was no doubt that his passing had inspired her. Already The Hyacinth Press was in receipt of a slim 'In Memoriam' volume, and those vouchsafed a glance at the manuscript declared themselves moved to tears. A rich vein had been struck, pure gold brought forth.

High on the wall Harold gazed into the distance with tired eyes. His widow rose from her chair and went to stand beneath the photograph, craning her neck to peer up at him. Suddenly she threw back her head and stretched up her arms. Warm fingers pressed cold glass. She held the pose for some time, enjoying the eloquence of her straining body. The sun went in. Mrs Ludbury forgave it and returned briskly to her desk where her eyes contemplated her present opus in which the poet, now alone, fearlessly embraces the new unsullied century. Refreshed, she took up her pen.

A tap, and Charlotte put her head round the door. 'Mama, you'd better come down at once. George wants to talk to us.'

Really! There was no peace. It was a miracle she ever completed a stanza. The wretched girl had come into the room wearing that calculating look of hers – most objectionable – and having resumed speech she was using a confidential, self-important tone.

'. . . convinced it requires careful handling, Mama, else, I must warn you, the consequences may be most unpleasant.'

'I haven't the slightest idea what you're talking about, Charlotte, and if you don't mind . . .'

'Do attend, Mama. George is determined to have it out with you, and I beg you to be a little more conciliatory. If his wishes are completely thwarted I fear we may lose him altogether. The cowsheds really are in a bad way . . .'

'Cowsheds? You dare to come in here, interrupting my work, talking of cowsheds?'

'Please, Mama. Do come down and talk to him. He's pacing and stamping like a stallion. I wouldn't put it past him to come charging up here; then where'd you be? Much better meet him on neutral ground.'

Exasperated, Mrs Ludbury got up and pushed past her daughter.

'Only, *do* be a mite conciliatory, Mama.' – Mrs Ludbury bounced down the stairs with Charlotte lumbering after her – 'We don't want to lose him again when we've spent so much energy getting him back. Think of the waste . . .'

Such excitement in the dining room: George at the paper-strewn table, thumping it, Louisa at his side, wringing her hands, Pip at the opposite end, elated, and Edward shaking by the door. Only Freddy was missing: he had seen how the land lay that morning and had gone for a long gallop.

Mrs Ludbury and Charlotte swept into the room.

'What, pray, is the meaning of this?'

'Sit down, Mama, and take a look.' George had the air of a man doing his best to keep calm. 'Louisa has been showing me the farm accounts . . .'

He got no further. Mrs Ludbury was quick as a cat when it came to pouncing on unorthodoxy. 'Louisa? What have the farm accounts to do with Louisa? Well? Speak up, girl!'

'Oh dear!' wailed Louisa as all eyes turned upon her. 'I thought it was for the best, truly I did. I knew you would not wish to be troubled, Mama, and someone had to see to them when Papa died. I used to help him when he felt tired, so it seemed quite natural . . .'

'Natural? For a young lady? Surely Edward . . .'

'Edward required assistance; now didn't you, Edward?'

'Er . . . don' know 'bout that,' Edward said cagily, resolving to make a bolt for it at the earliest opportunity.

'It seems a sensible arrangement to me,' Charlotte pronounced.

'Indeed?' Mrs Ludbury scented schism. 'And were you consulted?'

George brought his fists down heavily upon the table; 'Can we get to the point?' Papers leapt into the air, Pip squealed, and Edward took off muttering something about seeing to the bull. 'The point being that these accounts show the farm's broke. It's so run down it no longer covers your living expenses. Why, Louisa had to sell a couple of dairy cows last month – in full milk!' (At this revelation Louisa fainted with fright across the table.) 'I've noticed, Mama, that you like to do yourself well; always a couple of joints on the go, a ham for breakfast, a Stilton for supper, all those new clothes for mourning . . . Don't you know it all costs money?'

'How . . . dare . . . you?' spluttered Mrs Ludbury, beginning to feel ill.

'George, tell them what you propose,' Charlotte interposed urgently. (The significance of the word 'them' was not lost upon Mrs Ludbury.)

'I propose that Mama signs the farm over to me – with provisos, of course – then she need never be bothered with it again and I can guarantee us all a decent living.'

'What a splendid idea!' Charlotte cried artlessly.

Mrs Ludbury saw it all. They had planned it. They were all in it together – perhaps not Pip and Freddy, but the other four, certainly. They were bent on ousting her, crushing her; their greedy eyes were willing her annihilation. 'Rubbish!' she shrieked. 'I won't have it! I'll thank you to give me those papers immediately; every one. I shall send them to Mr Henshaw; he will advise me . . .'

'Henshaw knows nothing about farming.' George got to his feet and wagged a forefinger at his mother. 'I warn you, Mama, I've run out of patience. This is my last offer. If you don't take it I shall clear off and the farm can go to rot . . .'

'Take it? I wouldn't touch it with a barge pole . . .'

'Mama, don't! George, give her time to think . . .'

'Right! I'm done! I shall set up on my own. There are plenty of good farms to be had.'

'Now see what you've done, Mama!'

'Let him get on with it,' Mrs Ludbury cried. 'Let him see how he likes being stuck on some farm with no one to see to his comforts.' (But here a nasty thought occurred to her.) 'Louisa won't go with you,' she added hastily. 'She's needed here. I hope you haven't encouraged him, Louisa . . .'

'I wish you'd stop, Mama,' cried Charlotte, fearing this new direction. And at once her fears were confirmed.

'I've no need of Louisa; I'll have a wife!' George announced.

'There! Now you've done it!'

'Rebecca Sheldon,' said Pip.

'That *shop* girl?' Mrs Ludbury felt the world had gone mad.

'I knew it.' Charlotte's voice was low, it trembled with venom. 'I always knew that girl meant to have George.'

'That *shop* girl,' Pip reminded them.

Mrs Ludbury clutched her throat. A massive heart attack was imminent; it would probably kill her. 'If you knew,' she hissed, 'why did you not say? You thought you could handle it yourself, I daresay. It is just possible, Charlotte, that I might have prevented it. I have lived in this world a little longer than you. I hope this will be a lesson . . .'

George was going, he was striding from the room.

'Wait,' Charlotte implored, lunging at him.

Evading her, leaving her sprawled over the raised end of the chaise-longue, he charged to the doorway.

At the last moment Mrs Ludbury gathered her wits in time to spring into his path. 'You propose . . . that creature,' she marvelled in a voice low and ominous as distant thunder, 'for a daughter to your mother, a sister to your sisters, a mother of future Ludburys?'

He had taken hold of his mother's arms to thrust her aside, but she clung to him tenaciously. 'Think of the family interest!'

Roused beyond considerations of filial delicacy, he hurled her to the wall and made for the stairs. Pip darted after him and watched him mount them two at a time.

'Shop girl!' her shrill voice called, and continued lest he should ever forget: 'Shop girl, shop girl, shop . . .'

And later, on the train to Birmingham, her cry persisted in the rhythm of the rails: *shop* girl, *shop* girl. 'Damn and blast them!' he cried to the empty compartment. But beneath his hot anger a tiny grub of fear stirred, sickening him.

'Darling! Darling Becky!'

'George, dearest!'

'It's been dreadful. I don't know how I've stood it.'

'Poor darling. But it's over now. Don't think about it. Look to the future.'

'You're right, Becky. But I'm afraid the future won't be quite as grand, now. Not at first.'

'As if that matters to me, George. The thing is, we'll be together.'

'Dearest love! I'll make it up to you, losing The Grange. You'll see. I'm going to get on, really make something of myself. Tell you what: let's go and pay Edith a visit; take a look at the Cotswolds. I feel like getting right away from here. Shall we?'

'Oh yes! Do let's, George.'

The New Alliance

(1899–1909)

I

To come upon Lipscombe from the south, east or
west is to be startled by its unexpectedness, for it
lurks secretly at the foot of tall hills. Only from the
north is it approached with foresight; a long curving
line of weathered grey stone buildings visible ahead
in the valley of the Lip. The road running from north
to south becomes High Street through the town. The
transition begins with a farmhouse or two by the
roadside, then houses separated by gardens. In High
Street, houses of substance stand cheek by jowl with
cottages and shops – poky shops, double-fronted shops
and emporiums. And there are inns, tiny inns catering
for lesser mortals, and one large sprawling coaching
inn, The King's Head, attending to the comforts of
travellers and townsfolk of consequence.

George Ludbury, taking his first exploratory stroll
in the town, paused at The King's Head for a glass of
sherry wine. He emerged much encouraged by a genial
ambience and a pleasant passing of the time of day,
and proceeded past the town hall (Victorian mock-
Tudor) and a ramshackle drill hall, and on into the
square. This, a brief broadening of the street sufficiently spacious for markets and fairs, housed the gentle
class – doctor, lawyer, parson – behind a row of horse
chestnut trees. Becoming narrow again, the street
hugged the side of a churchyard. George approved
of the church; it was great in size, castellated and

gargoyled, a monument to the prosperity of fifteenth-century wool-trading. Beyond the church was a school and a cluster of cottages. Then the street lost heart and became a road again, nerving itself to scale the cliffs and ridges separating Lipscombe from Cheltenham.

George the trader looked thoughtfully at the hills. It occurred to him that they formed a formidable barrier to competition, and among them, he had been reliably informed in The King's Head, nestled several great houses positively broody with wealth. Turning westwards, George the farmer contemplated Astly Hill, a gentle promontory where Samuel Biggins, future brother-in-law, farmed. Last night Sam had let slip that there was land for sale adjacent to his own.

Sam had not intended to tell George about the land, for he himself coveted it – though there was scant hope that he would ever meet its price. The news dropped from a tongued loosened by the sudden lifting of daily, dragging depression and the wild delight of becoming the centre of attention. It all began when he introduced George Ludbury to the regulars in The Ram. George caused quite a stir there, with his winks and his side-of-nose tappings and his nicely judged condescension. (George, a natural King's Head man, knew he was rather too good for The Ram.) The fellows were flattered by the company of this countryman who had conquered London. Reflected glory fell on Sam. He grew bold, his depression lifted, his mind became nimble. One of the fellows made an ambiguous remark. Sam was on to it at once, repeating it with a wry twist, making a rude addition, bringing off a ripe, red-blooded joke. A cracker! The fellows loved it! To a man they threw back their heads and roared. 'This is it!' thought Sam, the moment when convulsions shook him until there was nothing in the world but a rollicking wave of exhilaration. Oh, the joy, of it! The camaraderie! How he searched for it among feeble sallies, wondering if he would ever possess it again. Well, now it was his. He was riding the wave. Now! Now! He turned to display his triumphant jaw-splitting smile to the far corners of the room. Those who had been out of earshot smiled, like automata, in response. The room was aflood with bonhomie, and he, Sam Biggins, was the cause of it.

Nothing lasts. The mood faded, and though Sam refined and embellished the joke, the last chuckle died. Terrified of his returning gloom, Sam grew reckless. He interrupted a man who was telling George about vacant shop premises. 'Old Duncan's ready to sell that land next to mine, I happen to know.'

'G'arn.' 'Bet you'm arter it yourself, Sam.' 'Old Duncan's a stubborn beggar, he'll never sell.'

Damn and blast his loose tongue! George would have that land – Sam could see it in his greedy eyes. George would rob him of his dream, his faint hope.

The one drawback to the land, from George's point of view, was the lack of a farmhouse. 'We'll have to rent a house,' he told Rebecca.

'Nonsense. We'll live over the shop,' Rebecca cried. 'We must put all our resources into the business.'

The businessman in George was much taken with this attitude; but the child in him, long silenced and suppressed, rose up in apprehension, for the shop they had taken was a poky little place (the only premises currently available in town). 'We'd be living side by side with some pretty rum folk: small shopkeepers, cottagers and the like.'

'I'm sure they'll be perfectly pleasant,' Rebecca said airily.

The businessman won, and George proposed to take his bride to 48 High Street, where Rebecca would smile at her neighbours and George, who was easily embarrassed, would rely on curt nods.

Charlotte Ludbury came to the wedding.

A tentative communication from George had arrived at The Grange informing his mother of time – ten o'clock, Saturday week – and place – The Parish Church, Lipscombe – and saying how jolly it would be to see members of his family there, and particularly a brother or two to stand up for him at the chancel steps. Afterwards, he suggested, they might all take refreshment at The King's Head. By the same post a letter had come for Louisa. This was from Rebecca who wished it to be known how fervently she hoped her girlhood friend would be at the wedding. Louisa was made to read this communication aloud, an experience so horrible that any gratification she may have felt on receipt of the letter was thoroughly extinguished.

'Golly! *I* wouldn't go if they paid me. Watch old George make a fool of himself with that shop girl? No thanks!' cried Pip after this painful reading.

Mrs Ludbury and Charlotte remained seated at the breakfast table long after the others had departed. 'Shut the door,' Mrs Ludbury snapped when Louisa and the maid had folded and put away the giant tablecloth and were preparing to depart with crumb trays and brushes. Their first decision was taken unanimously and at once: Louisa could not possibly be spared from The Grange on the day in question. The hopelessness of Edward as candidate for best man was acknowledged soon afterwards, and Pip, they reminded each other, did not care to go. Then they hummed and hawed and traced the grain of the wood on the surface of the dining table with their fingers. Eventually, Charlotte's political flair enabled her to persuade her mother of a right course: Mrs Ludbury would preserve her dignity and stay at home; Freddy, who had such nice manners and would be a credit to them, would be the groom's best man, and since Freddy was yet a minor, Charlotte would accompany him. Thus would the right note of distant magnanimity be struck, and a link between the family and its senior son be maintained should that prove valuable in the future.

George was delighted when this decision was communicated to him. 'Charlie's a good old stick. This' – he referred to his family's decent decision – 'is her doing, I'll wager. She always tried to get Mama round to my point of view. She really did her damnedest for me over those cowsheds.'

Rebecca, who had heard more than she desired to know about the cowshed difficulty, changed the subject.

Rebecca and George were married – Rebecca given away by Sam Biggins and attended by sister Edith, and George supported by Freddy – before a small congregation of farming folk pleased to welcome the newcomers into their midst, and Charlotte, her eyes hard as beads, her face mottled and swollen with the misery of the occasion. The sight of the sister-in-law in possession triggered a pain of such violence in Charlotte's heart that she was obliged to resume her seat during the Wedding March; and later, when George wondered aloud whether his sister and brother would care to inspect the shop and living quarters comprising 48 High Street, Charlotte gathered to her a protesting and wine-invigorated Freddy and fled to the station. Watching them go, Rebecca felt cheered, concluding that she was most unlikely to be called upon to play hostess to Charlotte in the foreseeable future.

Friendships with local farming people were consolidated by George's membership of the hunt (a courtesy extended to all farmers owning land in the hunt's terrain). Friendships were made also – though more cautiously – with certain of the commercial community. This was tricky ground. It was Rebecca's nature to be on pleasant terms with all her neighbours, but her husband's nervousness over any ambiguity concerning their social status made her circumspect with her 'Good morning, Mr Tovey' and 'Beautiful day, Mrs Green', substituting a mute smile when caught with George. But there were traders, those high up in the pecking order of the Lipscombe Chamber of Commerce, whom George was pleased to know – Mr and Mrs Harry Webb of the drapery and soft furnishing emporium, the Misses and Mr Slatter, purveyors of high-class provisions (a triple-fronted establishment) and the discreet widower Dowse, ladies' and gentlemen's outfitter (patronized by The Hall) – and a pleasant social round got under way.

It was the elder Miss Slatter who recommended Nurse Ballinger to Rebecca. Not, of course, that Miss Slatter spoke from personal experience, but she did know that Nurse was an indispensable accompaniment to all the best confinements. Nurse Ballinger, however, did not think 48 High Street quite what she was used to. As she explained, when George called at her little almshouse dwelling in Castle Lane, she spent a month every year at The Hall for the sewing and held herself in constant readiness for a summons to the Square where many ladies relied upon her. Mr Ludbury must understand, she went on in tones of hushed gentility, she was used to living in, and he could hardly expect. . . Feeling hot, George mumbled and left. But a few days later Rebecca herself paid a call, and Nurse Ballinger went the way of Miss Hyslop of Stratford-upon-Avon. (Mrs Ludbury was such a sweet lady; hardly more than a girl; motherless, too, the poor thing. Nurse Ballinger could not recall prettier manners, nor when she had looked into a lovelier pair of eyes – green as pools they were, fringed with black lashes. . .) George, having declared that he would not have the old witch in the house, turned the two attic rooms into nursery and bed-sitting room.

Nurse Ballinger proclaimed herself satisfied.

Nurse Ballinger came to the side of the bed with the precious bundle and lowered it into Rebecca's arms.

Rebecca, weak from her labour, light-headed with relief that it was over, loosened the tight shawl around the baby's face and gazed down. Wizened, miraculously shrunken, Charlotte Ludbury gazed back. 'No! Take it! Quick, Nurse!'

'Mrs Ludbury, dear! Have you a pain?'

'Just take it.' She thrust the bundle into the nurse's arms. 'What's the matter with her? She can't be right.'

'Not right?' Nurse Ballinger was scandalized. 'She's a beautiful baby; all present and correct.'

A tap at the door. The maid had been sent to fetch George.

'We'll see what her father thinks of her,' Nurse Ballinger said, bustling reprovingly towards the door.

George recognized his daughter at once. 'Well, well, well. What a little beauty! A real Ludbury, ain't she? Just look at the way she's staring at me, Nurse. I reckon she knows whose little girl she is. What are we going to call her, Becky?'

But Rebecca was slumped against the pillows, mouth and eyes tight shut.

'Mrs Ludbury's very tired,' whispered Nurse, mollified by this display of proper parental pride. 'It's only to be expected. She'll feel more like it later on.'

He was still there, Rebecca sensed with irritation. She flexed her feet and hands and took a deep breath. Then, opening her eyes, she saw that the light from the window was fading and the lamp had been lit. She had slept for some time.

'You're awake,' he cried gladly. 'Feeling better, old thing?'

She smiled to indicate that she was.

'I've been having another look at her. Do you know, she reminds me of Charlotte? Fancy that! What do you think we should call her? It occurred to me. . .'

'Margaret.' Sensing danger, she uttered the first name to arrive in her head.

He was surprise. 'Nice enough name, I suppose. But I was thinking of . . .'

'I've set my heart on "Margaret", George.'

'Right you are. Very nice, too. I say, though: how about Margaret Charlotte? How does that strike you?'

She had not the energy to say.

When she awoke again the curtains were drawn together. George was there, over by the cradle.

'I can't get over her,' he was marvelling. 'Spittin' image. You know, it might be an idea, seeing as she's to be christened Margaret Charlotte, if we were to ask old Charlie to be godmother. What do you think? I bet Charlie'd be tickled pink.'

Why not? The child was a Ludbury, that was plain. Dear Lord! She hadn't bargained for this. The idea had been to escape the Ludburys, not bring Ludburys of her own making into her own world. 'Whatever you like, George,' she muttered, turning her head into the pillow. 'Oh!' She looked up with a sudden thought. 'But we must ask Edith, too. I won't have her hurt.'

'Couldn't be neater. Her two aunties, eh! What do you think of that, little 'un? She smiled! She did! Did you see it, Nurse? Oh, this little Meg's a clever 'un, and no mistake.'

'Little who?' asked Rebecca from the bed.

'Meg. Margaret's a bit of a mouthful. Ain't it, Megs?'

If Charlotte was tickled pink to be the child's godmother it was not evident from her demeanour. Her terror on being obliged to step over the threshold of 48 High Street was pitiable to see – furtive looks up the street, muttered prayers that she should not be observed, shudders and distracted cries. Later, the arrival of the Misses Slatter bearing christening gifts sent her scurrying for the safety of the attic room – recently vacated by Nurse Ballinger – in which she was to pass the night. 'I can smell meat,' she announced, coming down when the coast was clear. 'It's all over the house.'

George winked at his wife, and Charlotte, turning her head, caught the grin with which it was received.

'I dare say you've become accustomed to it,' she fumed. 'Unfortunately, I have a particularly sensitive nose. I just hope my stomach doesn't turn.'

'Perhaps you would be more comfortable at The King's Head,' Rebecca suggested.

'No, no. I shall put up with it. But I do wonder at you, Rebecca, not noticing the odour.'

'There is no odour, Charlotte. You imagine it,' Rebecca said. Heaven help them. How *were* they to get through the rest of the afternoon and evening? What a good thing it was that Charlotte was going home straight after the christening tomorrow. Rebecca yawned behind her hand and went to the scullery door. 'Daisy!' she called to the maid. 'Be a dear and listen out for the babe. I'm going to have my afternoon nap.'

'Good girl,' George said approvingly. (Before leaving, Nurse Ballinger had impressed upon him the importance of afternoon naps.) 'I'll bring you up a cup of tea in an hour or so.'

With studied weariness, Rebecca raised the latch of the door to the stairs and closed the door carefully behind her.

In her bedroom she was all animation. She kicked off her shoes, bounced on to the bed, punched pillows upright against the bedstead and pulled the eiderdown snugly around her. Then she took a book from the bedside table drawer and settled down for a good read.

2

A storm had been hanging over the hills all day. 'If only it would break,' people called to one another in the street, and muttered to themselves in hot airless rooms. In 48 High Street Rebecca hauled down the scullery window as far as it would go and peered up at the glowering sky.

'Mama,' a voice wailed, '*have* you seen Malakie? I've searched everywhere. He can't just vanish.'

Rebecca turned wearily. Her second child was due very soon; and in any case, she had been asked this question too many times today. 'Look here, I've already told you,' she began crossly. Then stopped. The child was desolate. Her heart softened, for she loved Meg dearly.

Not always so. As a baby Meg had seemed a bore and a chore. Rebecca had left her largely to the maid, Daisy Major, a capable girl, and appeased her conscience with the production of nourishing delicacies and the enforcement of afternoon airings. But Meg had grown fast and become attractive and interesting. Charlotte Ludbury had been exorcized by an abundance of curls, fat dimpled cheeks, and dancing lights in green eyes. Now Rebecca saw only Meg, though George still liked to remark on her resemblance to his sister.

'Darling, it's a mystery,' she said now, catching Meg to her. 'Where can he be? Have you asked Daisy?'

'I'll ask her again,' Meg said, breaking free. She was not a cuddlesome child.

At supper that evening George was irritating. He chuckled to himself and shook his head at a private joke.

'Perhaps we should share it,' his wife suggested.

'Blind as bats! Both of you!' he chortled. 'Haven't you missed someone today, Megs?'

'Malakie,' Meg said promptly. Her eyes narrowed.

'D'you know he's watching you playing with that meat? He can't abide the way you're picking at it. It's made him quite ill, by the look of him.'

'Where?' demanded Meg, abandoning knife and fork.

Rebecca's eyes flew up and raked the room. Meg's passion, the doll Malakie, was astride a biscuit barret in a corner of a high shelf of the dresser. She groaned, for Malakie was transformed. The jaunty little chap in jester's costume, who had been steady of eye and clear of face, was now grotesquely cross-eyed and moustached. Not at all himself.

Meg's eyes followed her mother's. Her face turned white and she clenched her fists until her knuckles, too, were bloodless.

'Darling,' Rebecca said, reaching towards her; but her voice was drowned by fatherly uproariousness.

'What do you think of him now? Still going to take him to bed with you? Oh, I shouldn't if I were you, not a rum-looking rascal like that. Reckon he's had a drop too much to drink.'

'No,' said Meg.

'No? No, what?'

'Not going to take him to bed.'

'Oh-ho! Kicking him out, are you? You hear that, Malakie? She's done with you. Poor ol' fellow!'

An uneasy silence developed, during which Rebecca sent meaningful looks of reproach down the table.

'Come on, old girl. Just Daddy's little joke.' (George preferred to be 'Daddy'. It was friendly, relaxed, very twentieth century.)

Meg ignored him and picked up her knife and fork.

'Come here.' He seized her arm and reached up for Malakie and dragged them both into the scullery. 'Look, the eyes and the 'tache'll come off in no time. Just you watch.' He worked on the doll's face with a wet cloth. 'What did I tell you? Good as new.'

Meg raised her eyes and regarded him coolly. She set her lips in a thin determined line.

'Here, take it!' George commanded, getting annoyed.

Meg took it, climbed on to a chair and hurled it through the open window.

George was dumbfounded. But his daughter, well satisfied, returned to the supper table.

'My God! She's tossed it into Tovey's yard,' cried George.

Rebecca rushed to see. 'You naughty girl! How could you? Daddy was only playing a joke.'

'She'll have to go and ask for it back.'

'I shan't,' said Meg, getting on with her meal.

'That you will, my girl. Right away.'

'No.'

'I'll go and ask Mr Tovey for it,' Rebecca volunteered.

'What? Wife of mine beg favour at a cottage door! You'll do no such thing.' He advanced threateningly on the supper table. 'Now look here, my girl; do as you're told. This minute! Do you hear?'

Meg continued to eat stolidly.

Rebecca ran to her with a mother's urgent appeal. 'You see, darling, there wouldn't be the same difficulty for you knocking on Mr Tovey's door. But it would be very awkward for Daddy. And, after all, it was you who threw the doll into Mr Tovey's yard.'

Meg put down her knife and fork. She wriggled out of her chair and went to the staircase door. Standing on tiptoe, she raised the iron latch, and when the door swung open, mounted the first stair and turned to face them. 'I shan't go, so say no more about it,' she advised, and pulled the door shut behind her.

Later that evening a shame-faced George was obliged to pay a call on his neighbour. Later still it was decided that Meg (who, according to her reluctantly approving father, was a downright little madam and determined not to be beat) should go to The Grange until after the baby's birth. When they had agreed on this, Rebecca suffered a momentary qualm, for although Meg had visited The Grange many times with her father and was reputed to be a great favourite with her aunts, she had not so far spent a night away from home. Furthermore, Rebecca was not entirely sure that a large measure of her Aunt Charlotte's company was quite what she had in mind for her daughter's formative years. Then, recalling Meg's defiance of her father that evening, she reassured herself with the thought that a less impressionable child would be hard to find. It was a good decision, they would stick to it; for she was so very weary, Nurse Ballinger would be moving in soon, and 48 High Street was rather a cramped little house.

'There's a good-sized plot for sale in West Street opposite the Post Office,' George said ruminantly. (West Street was Lipscombe's advance into modernity possessing, as well as the big new Post Office, the cottage hospital, and further away from the town, the station yard. It ran between High Street and Astly Hill, and was the route taken daily by George on his way to the farm.) 'Perhaps it's time we made a move. That site, with the farm just up the road, and still very close to High Street might be just the job. We could build to suit ourselves. What I've got in mind is a three-storey house over a double-fronted shop. There's a good long garden with an orchard at the back; and against the back lane we could build stables and outhouses. What do you say, Becky? Shall we take a look? I should think the business can stand it now.'

And Rebecca, who kept the accounts and could reckon at the speed of light, agreed that it could.

3

Rebecca at her dressing table paused on the twentieth brush stroke of her long, heavy hair. Fifty strokes was her rule, but she had been distracted by the jangle of a hand-bell in the street below. She put down the silver-backed hairbrush and waited expectantly.

'O-yez, o-yez, o-yez,' rasped the crier with bad-tempered emphasis on the final 'yez'; and all the householders and shopkeepers in West Street paused in their doings to catch the Saturday evening bulletin. Notice of a hunt ball, a meeting, a bazaar, a catalogue of items lost and found, and then the announcement for which Rebecca waited. 'Mr George Ludbury, premier butcher of Lipscombe and district, announces his remove to new and imposing premises: Mallory House in West Street. No expense has been spared in the installation of the latest equipment to ensure the wholesomeness of his provisions; to wit, ladies and gentlemen, an icewell, the first of its kind in the town. Mr Ludbury presents his compliments and assures one and all of a hearty welcome at his new establishment. Orders collected and expedited daily. Try Ludbury's new Lipscombe sausages. . .'

The bedroom door flew open and Meg, curly-topped, sturdy-legged, five years old, burst in. 'Did you hear him, Mama? Did you hear him say "new and imposing premises"?'

'Yes.' Rebecca smiled at her daughter in the dressing-table mirror.

'It made us sound grand.'

'Of course. We are grand now.' Rebecca swung round and adopted a superior pose.

Meg, an earnest child, was not amused. 'But are we really?'

'I'm sure Mr Tovey thinks so, and the rest of our former neighbours. Anyway, I feel grand. Mallory House is grand.'

'I suppose Aunt Edith thinks so. She said we'd be *too* grand when we moved here.'

A sore point. Trust Meg not to miss it. Rebecca turned back to her dressing table and shuffled hairpins on a china tray. 'Relatives are excluded. We cannot be grand where they are concerned.'

Meg frowned. 'Well that's a pity. I s'pose Aunt Charlotte will still turn her nose up, then.'

'Just a minute.' Rebecca's voice became serious. 'We do not conduct our lives for the satisfaction of Aunt Charlotte. Is that clear? Moving here is an achievement. It shows what a successful businessman Daddy is.'

'But I know that,' Meg said, thinking of the hours she spent 'minding the horse' at the service doors to great houses while her father flattered and flirted inside, making mutually advantageous deals with cooks. He would emerge smiling broadly, leap on to the cart, gee-up the horse, and give her a blow-by-blow account of his businessman's prowess. 'I know all about that.'

'Of course you do, darling,' Rebecca caught her and kissed her, and thought what a pair they were, George and his own little Megs.

Meg caught sight of a grey chiffon gown hanging over the back of a chair. 'Oh, you chose that one?'

'Well,' hedged Rebecca, a gleam in her eyes, 'I kept the green satin, too. But I sent the mauve silk back; it clashed with my cloak.'

'Mama! You couldn't have kept three? What would Daddy have said?'

'Three would have been wicked,' agreed Rebecca. 'You can fasten the buttons for me later. There are little pearl ones all down the back.'

'And you'll save me the dance programme and the little pencil? And you'll say "goodnight" to me in your red cloak?'

'Of course. But go down now and help Nurse with Baby.'

'I'm busy reading, Mama.'

'Don't let your father catch you. He thinks reading ruins the eyes.'

'Silly man!' snorted Meg as she left.

It was a terrible child, Rebecca sighed, returning her attention to her hair. 'Twenty-one, twenty-two, twenty-three. . .'

Outside a newspaper lad called: 'Echo. Evenin' Echo.' Footsteps hurried, and end-of-week noises – sweeping, sluicing, shuttering – proclaimed the approach of leisured hours; time to spread in armchairs, dawdle over supper, repair to The Ram, to The Fox, to The King's Head, or get ready, like George and Rebecca, for the ball.

But not yet. The room was mellow with lamplight and firelight. Rebecca, satin-wrapped from her bath, stretched luxuriously and considered the bed. Plenty of time for a read. She raised the bedclothes and slipped between the sheets, then reached over to the bedside table to pull the lamp a little closer, and took up her book.

Some time later there was a tap on the door and Meg flew in again, coming to a frowning halt at the sight of her mother in the bed. 'What's the matter?'

'Nothing. I'm just having a rest. It's going to be a long and exhausting evening.'

'Well, I'm surprised you haven't heard him, banging about in the kitchen, shouting and cussing. . .'

'Why? His supper's on the dining-room table.'

'Nurse Ballinger's in the dining room, darning socks.'

'Oh, no! Look, shift her, darling. I don't want to come down. You can do it. Tell her Baby's crying, or the fire in her room needs attention. . .'

'All right.' She was off, unruffled, confident of her powers.

Then, on the floor below (for George and Rebecca had a bedroom on the second floor over the first-floor sitting room), an infant howled, surprised and disappointed, woken, no doubt, from sleep. Damn, thought Rebecca. Why must she be so thorough? She could see Meg now in her mind's eye, scurrying down the final flight of stairs, crying: 'Quick, Nurse. Baby Jim's crying. Can't you hear? Shouldn't wonder if he's fallen out of his cot.' And then, observing the flurried departure with satisfaction, 'You can come in here now, Daddy. She's gone. I got rid of her for you, so you can stop making a fuss. Shall I cut you some bread?' And George, instantly restored to good humour, would wag his head at her in admiration. 'Saw her off, did you? What d'you do? Give Jim a poke? Pull his nose? You're a rascal and no mistake. Come and give your Daddy a kiss.' Yes, a horrible child, thought Rebecca fondly, finding her place in her book.

A hand on her shoulder. She sat up. 'Heavens! I fell asleep. What time is it?'

'It's all right. I've just come up to get washed. Meg's pestering about doing up your frock. You promised, she says.' George sat on the side of the bed and gathered a handful of her hair. He sank his face into its black voluptuousness.

She caught his wrist and they gazed at one another speculatively. But practical man heaved a sigh and placed a chaste kiss on her cheek. 'Big night tonight.'

She yawned and stretched. 'Oh, how I've slept. Exhausted by all that cooking, no doubt. I hope there's enough for tomorrow.' (George and Rebecca were 'at home' to friends the next day; at least a dozen families were expected to come and marvel at Mallory House.)

'Then I'm very glad you've had a good sleep. You must shine tonight. By the way, isn't it time the Galloping Major moved in with us?' (He referred to the maid, Daisy Major, nicknamed after a popular song.) 'We've plenty of room here, and I'm sick of having that old biddy to stay with us every time we go out.'

'Daisy's busy with her own plans now.' (Daisy had engaged herself to Tom, George's erstwhile apprentice and now trusted foreman.) 'But I'll write to the Shipston orphanage on Monday; Mrs Webb swears by it. I'd rather have a raw recruit and get her into my ways. Daisy has been such a success. She can help me train the new girl.'

George rose.

She put a hand on his arm and wheedled: 'Be nice to Nurse, darling. She means well.'

'She mollycoddles that boy.'

'He appears to need it.'

'In nature,' George said darkly, 'things take their course. The weak are let go. Keeps the stock strong and healthy.'

'Heavens! The child's not as bad as that! And don't talk to Nurse about nature. Go on, you horrible man, go and wash.'

He paused in the doorway, ruminating. 'Pity Meg's not the boy.'

'Possibly.' Rebecca sprang from the bed and went to the dressing table to put up her hair.

When she was almost ready she put her cloak over an arm, took up gloves, bag and fan, and went across the corridor to Meg's room.

Meg sat bold upright in the bed.

Rebecca sat beside her and leaned backwards.

'Golly! There are a lot,' Meg said, doing up the buttons on her mother's dress. And when she had finished: 'Twenty-three.'

Rebecca stood up and swung the cloak around her shoulders. 'There. Will I do?'

Meg grunted, her mind too busy to find words, her eyes darting over the swirling magnificence. The colour! *What* a colour – violent as a field of poppies. It was a cloak for an empress: Mama was an empress now. She was coming towards the bed, gliding close, rustling and glinting in the lamplight.

'No kiss?'

Hastily Meg offered her mouth, impatient for the cloak to be totally visible again.

'Lamp out now,' said Rebecca, turning it out. 'Goodnight, darling.'

'Goodnight,' Meg mumbled, listening to the luscious progress of silken folds towards the door.

In the black void that was her room, Meg waited for the darkness to soften, for shadows to come. Her breathing slowed and her thoughts, still whirling, fell away, sucked into a long hollow tunnel. Down, down. . . . She watched them recede with regret, for now she would never know. A central truth had escaped her in that dreamy falling away. Then she tensed and set a stern face. She *would* know. Come back! What was it? What *was* it? Oh . . . *that*! Yes, it was true. She sighed and settled down to sleep, accepting with perfect equanimity the knowledge that she, Margaret Charlotte Ludbury, would never, never in a thousand years, wear such an extravagant garment as that beautiful scarlet cloak.

Below, Nurse Ballinger was cooing. 'My dear! A vision! Is she not, Mr Ludbury? I can't think of another lady who could wear such a colour. Certainly not in Lipscombe. It sets you apart, indeed it does, my dear. A poppy! A silken poppy! Do you see? The scarlet ruffle framing your black hair?'

'A poppy, for heaven's sake!' George chuckled, drawing her close as they hurried down West Street to the Town Hall on the corner.

Rebecca snuggled closer.

'It'll be our night tonight. There'll be a fair number of toasts to the Ludburys before the night's out, you mark my words.'

'Are you glad we came here, George?'

'To Lipscombe? I certainly am, my love.'

'So,' thought Rebecca, 'it has all turned out for the best.' How thankful she was that she had trusted her instinctive optimism. How right she had been not to make an issue of her dislike for his family. For here they were, a world away from The Grange, and her husband bursting with happiness and pride for the life they had created together. And it was only just beginning.

4

George turned his copper-coloured mare through the Castle gateway, on to the soft greensward and squeezed gently into canter. Ahead, a half-mile distant, lay the Castle, its stark refurbished quarters united in fragility to its Gothic ruins by a haze of silver mist and unripe sunlight. He had come this way before. On meet mornings, elegant in hunter's attire, he rode straight on to the Castle forecourt. On delivery days, aproned and straw-boatered, he turned his butcher's cart right at the fork halfway along the drive and took the circular route to the rear. Today, at the fork, he did differently. He turned left and rode into unknown territory behind the tree-sheltered chapel, for this was the way to the Castle stables.

A hundred eyes were on George as he braced into trot, then eased to a cautious walk. Rooks screamed in cedar and elm. The mare shuddered and pricked her ears. 'It's all right. It's all right, old girl,' he said, leaning forward to pat her neck with counterfeit confidence. Yes, a hundred eyes – he could feel them: eyes eager for mishap, eyes that would feast on a hanging, given the chance; not for the first time he shivered under their intent, unblinking, meanly speculative gaze. The sterner the test, the more aware he became of their presence. And there is no sterner test of a man's judgement than the obligation to put down his money: there it is, in pounds, shillings and pence, a precise public measure of his wisdom and nerve. Oh, yes; George knew all about it. Weekly in the cattle market – daily when he was London-based – he was obliged to prove himself under this relentless scrutiny. And he had earned a grudging respect. The name of Ludbury had become synonymous with sound judgement. Today, however, was different. The flesh, today, was horse. The supreme test. And they knew, those meanly cunning eyes, they knew full well and gloated: if ever George Ludbury was to come a cropper it would happen today.

The horse for sale was not simply a horse; it was Samson, a black giant of a stallion, the most magnificent hunter George had ever clapped eyes on. George was not given to covetousness, but his lust for the Honourable Peter Elton's mount made him weak at the knees. The point was, had it made him weak in the nose? Pondering this, he pulled a handkerchief from his pocket and applied it to the problematic member – the anatomical centre of his business acumen. The devil of it was, he reflected, blowing hard and wiping thoroughly, the opinion of hunt members had been well aired in The King's Head: George Ludbury would sell his soul to possess Samson. 'They're watching you like hawks,' his friend, John Poulter, had warned. 'They reckon her ladyship's set you on, good and proper. What with her husband playing the fool in Italy with his fancy woman, and the bookies after young Peter's blood, she's strapped for cash.'

As purveyor of fresh meat and savoury delicacies to the Castle, George was well aware of its financial embarrassment. Rebecca had been loud with complaint: it was not right to press ordinary mortals for payment if the big houses were to be allowed unlimited credit, especially, she had added, provoked by George's decision to delay the purchase of a piano, when that credit resulted in the postponement of Ludbury gratification. (There was another thing, George thought, reaching again to pat his mare who seemed rather jumpy this morning, the arrival of Samson in the stable would inevitably be followed by the arrival of a piano in the drawing room. George was not fond of the instrument.) But Rebecca had been very encouraging about Samson. 'You have him, darling,' she had urged after observing the Boxing Day meet. 'You'd do him justice, where as *he* merely looks peevish on him.'(An astute observation, for the Honourable Peter was scared to death of his mount, his mother had good as admitted it.) The Lady Amelia. . . What a horsewoman! A silly smiled spread over his face.

'I must say, you do like to go, Mr Ludbury!' Lady Amelia had yelled, standing astride him in a ditch. 'But your mare ain't up to it. Here. Haul on me arm. Many bones broke? I wonder you don't bid for Peter's stallion. Wasted on him. He don't care for leaping.' And later, confidingly over a stirrup cup: 'Must say, Mr Ludbury, you'd go frightfully well on Samson. Come up to the stables and have a talk with Peter. I'll put in a word f'ye.'

Well, here he was. Lamb to the slaughter? Bones for the picking? No, no. Not likely. They'd find it a hard job to bamboozle George Ludbury. Rubbing his nose for luck, he reflected that his reputation for astute dealing was more precious than a dozen Samsons.

The mare put up her ears and whinnied. 'What is it, old girl?' he asked, wondering whether his turmoil had somehow been communicated. But then he heard a sound that explained the mare's distress: a bellow, faint because distant, but emitted with force from a considerable chest. It came again, a fearful noise, full of rage and terror. 'Gee up,' he cried.

The stable yard was in a lather. Great gobs of froth flew from a loosebox to swirl and fragment in the air and fall in showers of spittle to the ground. George took in the scene then retreated to tether his mare considera ly out of sight. Returning on foot, he called: 'What the devil's going on?' A red-faced groom staggered back from the loosebox, and an ashen-faced lad took the opportunity to scurry out of sight, but the Honourable Peter Elton continued to shout and wave his crop. As George went forward the groom seized his arm. 'Keep back, sir. He's crazed.'

'My God! It's the butcher!' the Honourable Peter screamed. 'Don't think much of your timing, Ludbury. The brute's gone and done for himself. Broke his leg, the devil! And that incompetent fellow' – he indicated the groom – 'had a hand in it, I'll be bound. D'you see, Simmonds? Here's the good butcher, right on time, with a pocket full of money. All set to buy the beggar, ain't you, Ludbury? Hey! watch out, man,' he yelled as George placed steady hands on top of the stable door. 'The brute's beside himself.'

'I should keep back, Mr Ludbury,' the groom agreed. 'Samson's always had the strength of two stallions, but worked up like this. . . MacGregor's been sent for. He'll know if there's a chance for him. But I doubt it, from the look of that shank. Do be careful, sir.'

But George remained steadfast at the stable door, his eyes never leaving the thrashing horse.

A new grievance had occurred to Elton. 'By God! Damn surgeon's bill as well! That beggar's cost me a mint of money – eats his head off, damages the box – and what for? For as nasty a ride as I never care to endure again. I tell you, the brute's done for. Any fool can see that. Not much use to you now is he, Ludbury? Meat for your dogs, eh? By God and by Christ, I could murder the beggar! Dashed if I won't stick a bullet in him meself and be done with it. . .'

'No, sir. You'd not make a job of it, sir. You're too hot. Best wait for MacGregor.'

'MacGregor be blowed! The fellow's forever in my stables. Shouldn't wonder if he cuts you in, Simmonds. Just look at the brute!' Emboldened by George's unmoving presence at the stable door, he thrust himself against it and let off a volley of violent curses into the steaming interior. The stallion swung his head and sent his master flying.

Bruised, covered with dust, half-blind with horse spittle, Elton picked himself up and charged forward. 'Devil! Take that! And that! And . . .'

George leapt for the whip, wrenched it from the man's hand and held it fast.

'Hand it back, Ludbury.'

George took his time. Then: 'If I have to take it from you again, Elton, I shall set about you,' and he tossed the whip away towards the centre of the yard.

'Get off my land. Clear off before I set the dogs on you.'

'I'm going in,' said George. 'Bolt the door after me, Simmonds.'

He entered the box so swiftly that there was no time for protest. Minutes ago he had determined on the best spot, and now he crouched there, in a corner beneath the high manger, his back to the wall. And he talked incessantly, a steady, soft flow of inconsequential matter: 'There, there, old boy. Poor ol' fellow, poor ol' lad. Worked yourself up into a fine old lather. But it's all right, Samson, it's all right. You trust George, let him see. . .' Slowly George straightened, slowly he put out a hand, and all the time his voice ran on – a flat river of sound, a tuneless hypnotic murmur conveying 'this is not the end of the world.'

Samson appeared to hear the message, for he slowed, hesitated, gave a half-hearted thrust or two, then fell still, intent upon the hand that had arrived on his back, that grew bold over his rump, that slid slowly down his injured leg. A thrill of shivering shot through him. 'Steady, boy. Good ol' boy.'

'Well?' asked the Honourable Peter, unable to sustain a cool indifference.

'What d'you want for him?' George asked softly, backing smoothly away from the horse, unbolting the door, moving backwards out of the box.

The Honourable Peter could hardly believe his ears. 'You think he'll do?'

'I'm not an expert. MacGregor's the one to ask. But you're a gambling man by all accounts. Tell you what I'll do. I'll do a deal before the quack gets here. If the verdict's bad, I lose. If it's good, I get a bargain, but you save the expense of his keep while he comes good – if he ever does. One thing's certain; it'll be a dickens of a long time before he's sound. What d'you say, man?'

Hope dawned anew in the Honourable Peter's eyes. 'You're on, Ludbury. Make me an offer.'

George was all nose now. He thought of the sum he had come prepared to pay for a sound Samson, divided it by this and by that, added ten guineas for luck and took five of them back again. He came to a decision; the sum appeared illuminated in his mind's eye. He named it.

'Done. Shake on it, Ludbury.'

'My word'll have to do yer,' George said with a disdainful sneer. 'I'll be along to settle later.'

The Honourable Peter did not care for his tone. He recalled his position, and felt it incumbent upon him to put this butcher in his place. 'My man'll see to you. At the back door. I'll bid you "good day", Ludbury.'

'I shall be up here regular, mind; till I can move him,' George called after the retreating figure.

Without turning, the Honourable Peter waved a bored, dismissive hand.

'Darling! What a bargain!'

'It's an injured horse we're talking about, and there's never any certainty with an injured horse. MacGregor thinks he'll come good, but we can neither of us know for sure.'

Rebecca brushed this aside. 'But how clever of you to be able to tell from a quick feel!'

'I couldn't.'

'But you did.'

'No. It was what I saw that told me. While I was watching him he put his weight on that leg. Twice. Oh no, I only went in to be sure I could get him to trust me. He was in such a paddy I'd begun to have me doubts. Of course, he'd been severely provoked, poor fellow, but I had to be sure of him. As soon as I put my hand on him I knew we'd get on. Whether he ever does again as a hunter is another matter. I could still end up a laughing stock.'

'Darling!'

'Oh, yes! The story'll go round tonight. "Heard about George Ludbury paying good money for a three-legged horse? He let that young fool, Elton, get the better of him!" There are one or two around here who'll be delighted if I come a cropper – your brother-in-law for one. It could affect the business.'

'What nonsense! And you won't come a cropper. I'd back your judgement any day!'

He smiled politely, discounting, as always, admiration from the ill-informed.

'And now, darling, about the piano. You said we'd think about it when the Samson business was out of the way. So do let's. I miss not being able to play, and it's time Meg was taught. All young ladies must learn to play the piano, you know.'

'I suppose they must,' George agreed glumly, recalling the musical education of his sisters. 'Not that she'll take to it,' he added, brightening. 'She's too much of a tomboy.'

'All the more reason,' his wife said firmly.

A piano duly arrived in the Mallory House drawing room, and George's grin, as he watched his wife settle herself to play upon it, betrayed a secret satisfaction.

Rebecca was not unaware of her husband's pride in the way she had embellished the house and made it a favourite calling place. He teased her endlessly about her tea parties, but checked on their progress and encouraged their regularity with keen promotional interest. All this was evidence, if she needed it, that their life together more than made up for any disappointment still lurking in his heart over loss of The Grange. Not that there was any reference these days to what might have been. George was entirely caught up in his expanding businesses and prominent civic position. These were the result of joint effort, for as well as running the household, Rebecca managed all their accounts so that George could devote himself to shop, yard, farm and market, deal with cronies in The King's Head and ride regularly to hounds. Her success as a hostess, the tea parties and the after-Evensong Sunday supper parties, put a high gloss on their success.

There was just one snag in all this, Rebecca acknowledged to herself – not for the first time – as she set off along West Street towards Astly Hill: Edith. Edith did not care for tea parties with the Lipscombe ladies. Edith's husband was not a respected man of the town or tiller of the soil. It was most unfortunate, Rebecca reflected sadly, but there it was. She had done her best to include her sister, to demonstrate that whatever Sam's shortcomings, she, Rebecca, considered Edith's presence a bonus at any gathering; but Edith would not have it. Edith sometimes called at Mallory House for a chat or a calm moment in the garden, but she excused herself hastily if other callers were announced. Only on Astly Hill was their companionship entirely easy, when there was purpose and momentum in being together – mushrooms or berries to gather, cattle to be driven to milking sheds, brooks in need of a clearing or children in need of an airing. With light and shade scudding over them as wind drove clouds in the low sky, the petty difficulties of the town seemed stale and unimportant. And there was always a moment when they would link arms and gaze across to neighbouring hills; nearby, the verdant slopes of Neith, Honnington and Bowery, and in the southerly distance the highest peak of all, the dark, brooding shade of Knoller Knap.

Today, as she made her way up the track to the Biggins farmhouse, she hoped as she always did when the weather was fine that the visit would be spent out of doors. But today was unlucky; the afternoon destined to be spent indoors. Edith sat at the kitchen table with a mountain of mending, and bristled with pent-up feeling. Overhead, the intermittent wail of a sick child goaded her further towards the inexorable outburst.

Knowing this, Rebecca sighed. She sat alone on the window seat. Meg was not with her today, she was at home with Daisy Major, safe from the Biggins infection. Just as well, Rebecca reflected, Meg was a downright child and frank in her observations; it would not escape her that Aunt Edith was exceedingly cross. Tension in the long, low-ceilinged room was as tangible as the hard wood of the window seat under her thighs. Rebecca clutched at the rim of the seat and braced herself against the torrent to come.

Edith selected a button. Not a word, not the smallest movement from Rebecca; only, a moment ago, that, sigh. Little enough for umbrage, but it would serve, it was a starting point. 'Bored?' she inquired with false solicitousness. 'Longing to be gone? Pray don't let me detain you. On the other hand, if you are in need of occupation there is sufficient work here for two.' Pleased with that, a mite relieved by the small discharge, Edith shuffled herself into greater comfort on her chair. Her eyes remained on her work as she awaited with confidence her sister's arrival at the worktable.

But Rebecca made no move. Her eyes, like hands holding a talisman, held fast to the warm yard outside and the blue-green space beyond. 'Put aside the clothes you don't need immediately, Edith. I'll take them home for Daisy or Nurse to deal with.'

'Well! I must say . . . You, a professional needle-woman. . .'

'No.'

'What do you mean, "no"?'

'Not in the sense you mean. I don't do mending. I'm an embroiderer; that's quite a different thing.'

'Oh, I see. I beg your pardon. How nice that you can afford to maintain the distinction. So you intend to hand over our shabby garments to the inestimable nurse?'

'Possibly. Possibly to the girl. I may do some myself. What I meant to say was, I don't do the mending as a rule. There are other things I do better – cooking, gardening, the accounts. You'd be surprised how time-consuming the accounts and the orders can be.'

'Meanwhile, dear Nurse Ballinger attends to your mending.'

'Yes.'

'Well, I'm sure she'll be gratified to handle our poor rags. Did I tell you, by the way, that the good-natured soul saw fit to snub me in Webb's last Thursday?'

'Probably she didn't see you. She bustles so.'

'I assure you, she did. We came face to face, eyeball to eyeball over a bale of Indian calico. "Good morning," I said, with every expectation of a few words concerning the quality of said calico – it *had* been the subject of discussion between the three of us in your very own dining room, if you recall? However,' – Edith paused to bite through a piece of thread – 'I was presumptuous in my expectation. The good nurse scuttled off without a word, leaving me foolishly gaping.'

Rebecca was aroused at last. 'How awful, Edith! No excuse. I'm afraid she's a bit . . .'

'Of a snob.'

'Please don't put words into my mouth. I was going to say, she's a bit confused about her position. I don't blame you for feeling resentful, indeed I don't. It was hideously ill-mannered of her. But do try to understand, Edith; it will make you feel better about it. You see, it's the ambiguity of her position – not a servant exactly, but not . . .'

'Shut up, Rebecca.'

Rebecca flushed and became rigid again on the window seat.

A darning needle threaded, Edith's hand flew. Her body teemed with anticipated release, for she had reached the crux; she saw clearly, with a zealot's indignation, the nature of Rebecca's fault. 'Always known which side your bread was buttered, haven't you? Like Judas Iscariot, you do not disdain to betray your own if your life is made more comfortable as a result. The Ballinger woman insults your sister. Sad. Unfortunately she is indispensable to the smooth running of your affairs. Your sister must swallow her pride, make allowances, understand. . . It was the same with our stepmother. She drove out your sister and ruined your brother, but you saw that you need not be incommoded. A little tact, a few ingratiating smiles, a deferential reticence. . . It always struck me as remarkable how lenient she was with you, Rebecca – considerate, even – setting you up at Jevons and Mellor, buying you a respectable wardrobe. . .'

'For heaven's sake, I was a child when Father died! It was very hard for me. I just tried to make the best of it. . .'

'Exactly!' Edith cried, snapping the thread in triumph. She paused in her tirade to rethread the needle.

Perhaps, Rebecca thought, I should bear this silently without protest; accept it as part of her burden. She prefers to load me with her anger rather than the mending. Well, I am fortunate, I can stand it, I suppose. . . Dear God, she has got on to the Ludburys now. . .

'You never let on how you felt about them,' Edith was shouting. 'Oh no, you played a more subtle game. You overlooked their obnoxiousness, kept your peace and made off with the prize. Very clever. You beat them, didn't you, Rebecca? It all turned out exactly as you planned. How lucky that you ignored my plodding advice to be frank with your bridegroom-to-be. Keep your own counsel, never speak out – that's your policy, and it has certainly paid off. Well done! But I'm afraid I lack your sense of self-preservation. When our stepmother abused Thomas I complained, I objected forcefully, I refused to stand by, I. . . Damn it! Damn!' She had let herself get overheated. She had been diverted from the main path by a plethora of sidetracks. She had pricked her finger. Tears welled. She fought them furiously.

'Edith?'

No answer. Edith was still struggling.

Then, after a minute or two: 'Edith, shall we make it up?'

Silence.

'There may be something in what you say,' Rebecca offered. 'We had a difficult time of it, you, Thomas and I; we cannot be unscathed, it has made us what we are. But I do love you, Edith.'

Edith laid an arm across the table sank her head on it and wept.

'Give it up,' urged Rebecca, hurrying at last to her side. 'Come on, let's go outside in the sun. Bobby's been quiet for ages, I expect he's asleep. Anyway, we shan't go far. Come on.' She took her sister's hand and pulled her to the door.

The sun dried Edith's tears but failed to revitalize her. She was shaken, spent, weighed down by a sour residue of shame. 'I don't know what gets into me, Rebecca. Sometimes I'm so wound up I could burst. Forget what I said. It was wrong, untrue. . .'

'Perhaps it was,' Rebecca said gently.

'George,' Rebecca said, as they prepared for bed. 'How does one set about finding someone?'

'Who?'

'Someone you've lost trace of.'

'Who?'

'Well, my brother, actually.'

'Him? Drank, didn't he?'

'How would one set about it?'

'When was he last heard of?'

'Years ago. He wrote to Edith to say he was going to sea. But he's been seen recently, about two years ago. Edith had a card from our father's clerk. He thought he caught a glimpse of Thomas in Evesham.'

'I know a chap from there. I meet him now and then at the market. I'll have a word with him if you like.'

'Oh thank you, darling.'

'Shouldn't get excited, though. Sounds a bit vague to me.'

'And do you think . . .' Rebecca paused and took in breath before continuing in a rush: 'Do you think you could take an interest in Sam? Talk to him, jolly him on a bit?'

'For heaven's sake, Becky!'

'For Edith's sake, George. I quite ache for Edith.'

A grunt from the region of the floor where George deposited his morning boots.

'Please, George.'

'We'll see.'

6

'Repeat it. Go on. What must you tell her?'

The raggy child clasped one end of the proffered parcel. Finding the other end held fast, he scowled. 'Nart t'froi ut,' he muttered resentfully.

'On no account fry it,' Rebecca agreed. 'But how should she cook it?'

'Slow.'

'Very slow. In?'

'A part.'

'With?'

'A lid arn.'

'Yes. Now mind you tell your mother because I've put her a good deal more than a pennyworth.' She said this as if they had a pact: her generosity for his compliance.

At midday she always tried to be present in the shop, ostensibly to give George and Tom a chance to clear up before dinner, more urgently to supervise the 'pennyworth of bits' that children, home from morning school, were dispatched to collect. As she made up the precious parcels, picking over, selecting, inquiring casually how many mouths the pennyworth was required to feed, she dreaded that the meat's utility would be impaired by slipshod, inappropriate preparation. It was not only altruism that galvanized her and sprouted small homilies in her mind, but a horror of waste, of futility, of defeat when the means for success were at hand. George, who was carelessly generous, had a word for her compulsion: 'Interference,' he declared whenever he caught her at it.

Hearing his voice, Rebecca suppressed an after-thought concerning the addition of vegetables to the pot. 'Off you go now. Hurry.'

The child scurried to the door and collided with George and Tom on the pavement.

'He's in a hurry! Been catechizing the poor little blighter, have you?'

Rebecca flushed and changed the subject. 'Did the ice come?'

'No. And I'd like to know what's happened to it. He's never been as late as this before.' George pulled open the heavy door to the ice well. 'We'll have to shift this lot, Tom, if he doesn't come soon.'

At once Rebecca's anxiety transferred to her own domestic arrangements. They would be late sitting down to dinner. Daisy would be cross, and would claim she no longer had time to take the children to the dressmaker this afternoon. It would fall on Rebecca to take them, to stand by while Meg fumed and accused Miss Horton of attempted suffocation, of deliberately sticking pins in her; to stay calm while Jim's uncontrollable nose dripped all over the new cloth, and Miss Horton lost her temper and vowed never to deal with them again. If the ice man did not appear at once it would be a horrible afternoon.

Around the ornamental tiles that formed a frieze between white-tiled walls and ceiling, cretinous animals gambolled, mocking her brief thought to ask George to come in immediately to dinner, ice man or no. Turkeys sneered, pigs grinned, lambs and calves threw up their hind legs in derision. Of course he would not come; she would do well to keep her agitation to herself. Irresolute, she pushed her fingers against the scarred surface of the chopping block. The child in her womb stirred sickeningly and thrust some sharply protruding part of itself into her stomach. The shop closed in; white tiles loomed, damp sawdust gathered underfoot, and in the mustiness of well-hung meat her hopes of an afternoon in the garden soured. She would leave the men to it, she decided; but then the thought of Daisy, irate among the saucepans, bonded her more closely to the chopping block.

'Hark!' George instructed, raising his head.

A rattle in the street.

'Oh.' Rebecca came to life and hurried to the open doorway.

'That him?' called George from the ice well.

'No.' She had paused before answering. Time had changed gear.

She had seen at once (surely she had?) that the cart careering into West Street from Astly Hill was out of control, that the horses were bolting, that people had pressed themselves for protection against walls and windows; why, else, did she seize fat Martha, standing aghast on the pavement, and drag her into the shop? Minds and bodies were chained to time, and time had stretched to a leaden crawl. For an age the cart sped down upon them, but no one could get to young Billy Deakin, frozen with stupefaction in the middle of the road. The hoop, his merry companion, veered unattended towards collapse in the gutter. A dozen eyes anticipated the child's collapse. The trampling was good as done.

'George! The *child*!' At the last moment Rebecca wrenched the cry from her paralysis. Afterwards she could not recall it.

George remembered it. It rang repeatedly in his head. He remembered it as a dire imperative.

He tore blindly into action; across shop, pavement, into road. 'The *child*!' she had shrieked, and like a well-schooled soldier he obeyed. With arms stiff as bayonets he went for the target, shot Billy Deakin through the air on to the Post Office steps. Then the hunting field saved him, for he had survived

91

hooves before. He cradled his head in his arms and somersaulted, ball-like, through bedlam. There was a crash; then quiet.

A child's wail splintered the shocked silence. On-lookers found they could move, after all. The night-mare, for George, began then.

''E don' look roight ter me. Tha's a narsy cut on 'us 'ead.'

''Us wind's garn. Sut 'um up.'

'Youm best leave 'um be, Arthur Tupput. Mussus 'as sent fer darcter.'

'Please stand back everyone.' (Rebecca's vain plea.) 'Oh, Mrs Williams, what a relief to see you. Tom has gone for Doctor Griffin. Would you go and ask Daisy for a pillow and blankets?'

'Ay 'tus best 'e stays put tull darcter comes. Oi don' loik 'us colour, Mussus Ludbury.'

''E'm troying t' raise 'ussell. You loi quiet, Muster Ludbury.'

'Your man's an 'ero, Mussus Ludbury. No doubt on ut. 'E's an 'ero, roight 'nough.'

'Thart 'e us an' all. Oi quoite thought erwer Bully were funushed.'

Plainly, this could not be allowed to continue. 'Out of my way,' said George.

Pain seared his chest as he attempted to rise, and he fell back with a groan. Protests and exhortations to lie quiet poured over him. He couldn't, wouldn't stand it. His legs, he found, were still strong. Somehow he arrived on his feet – rude hands were on him now – and drew himself up. 'Has someone sent for the constable?' he demanded, using a superior citizen's tone of voice to put a distance between himself and the vulgar throng. And at once they lost confidence in their hold over him. 'Tell the constable that I'll be glad of a word,' he continued as he staggered towards his shop door. 'It's about time something was done about that carrier. He'll kill someone next.'

He was through the doorway at last. 'Bolt it,' he told his wife.

She caught up with him in the hall. 'Oh, darling! Doctor Griffin's on his way.'

'Then you can tell him he's been troubled for nothing.'

With relief, George reached the dining room and his favourite armchair. Watched by his awestruck children, he lowered himself carefully on to the creaking leather, let his head loll back against the elm-wood frame, and passed gratefully into oblivion.

Charlotte Ludbury eyed the cards with suspicion. Rebecca had invited her to admire them. A card from the Castle took pride of place against the mantel clock, suitably flanked by cards from the Hall and Evenly Manor. Cards from lesser mortals decorated the mantelshelf's extremities.

'And Mrs Simmonds from the Hall called personally,' Rebecca rhapsodized. 'The town is full of it. George is a celebrity – and he's grumpy as anything about it, aren't you, darling?'

Charlotte and George exchanged a bleak regard.

On receipt of Meg's breathless letter (Dear Aunt Charlotte, Daddy has performed a brave deed and is wounded, but not mortally. I'm sure Grandmama will like to write a poem about it. It's just the sort of thing . . .) Charlotte had hurried to Mallory House with a full heart, prepared to praise, to exclaim, to go, if it were called for, into raptures. But one look at her brother's face had been sufficient to warn her that there was a peculiarly Ludbury view of the matter, that the cards and her sister-in-law's satisfaction with them were dubious, possibly even seditious. Not a word would escape her lips until she had had a talk with her brother.

'I think I'll take a breather,' George said after some thought. 'Care for a stroll, Charlotte?'

'Darling, do you think you should? Doctor Griffin ordered complete rest to give those ribs a chance to mend.'

George ignored her and turned to his sister. 'Coming?'

Charlotte hurried to collect her hat.

From the drawing-room window Rebecca watched their progress towards Astly Hill. For once she was glad to see Charlotte, for Charlotte, who was so inordinately fond of her brother, would surely encourage him to see his action as heroic. He seemed quite unable to grasp the genuine admiration of the townspeople. 'He is so naturally brave, so instinctively protective,' Rebecca told herself, smiling at his receding figure, 'that he cannot recognize his behaviour as out of the ordinary.'

On the lower slopes of Astly Hill, George rested against a paddock gate. 'There he goes, the beauty. Full of himself again. Hey! Samson! Come here, you blighter!' The stallion turned, contemplated his master, then tossed his head and made off. 'That's right,' George said bitterly. 'He knows I can't get on his back strapped up like this. Dear oh me!' He shook his head at the rottenness of luck.

'George,' Charlotte began tentatively.

He knew what she was after. 'It was a bad day's work, old thing.'

Charlotte caught her breath in grateful relief that she had declined to show interest in the congratulatory cards. 'Oh, George. . .'

'Yes, a bad day's work. Mind you, if it had ended with saving the boy and a few cracked ribs I shouldn't complain. But it didn't. That was just the start of it. I'll never forget it, Charlie, coming to, flat on m'back in the middle of the road, to find m'self surrounded by gawpers – all the riffraff of the town – poking and prodding and talking as if I were a lump of meat on a slab.'

With a little scream, Charlotte covered her ears with her hands. She could hardly bear to hear it.

'There I was, spread-eagle in the street, the subject of common speculation. And I mean "common". Never been so humiliated in me life.'

Tears sprang generously to Charlotte's eyes and spilled over her appalled face. 'George, George,' she moaned.

Her tears gratified him. Here was an intelligent reaction at last. He wrapped his hands around hers. 'I know, old girl. I know.' How different was this to his wife's wilful attitude. He had almost come to hate Rebecca this past week as she discussed him with well-wishers and gloated over cards and flowers. And she had read nothing in his narrowed eyes save an amusing disposition to be unobliging. He had watched her with disgust, obsessed with the thought that *she* was the cause of it all. It was her premonitory cry that had brought shame upon him.

'George,' said Charlotte, who had been thinking. 'You see what it is – the cause of all this?'

He flushed guiltily. 'I daresay she means well. . .'

'The street!' Charlotte cried. 'It all comes of living in a street.'

'How's that, old thing?'

'If you didn't live in a street – where this sort of thing is for ever occurring, I daresay, and where common people are always about – it couldn't happen. There's always a danger of something like this if you live in a street. Why, you haven't even got a front garden to save you from it. You're not *used* to it, George. We none of us are. We Ludburys are used to a decent privacy. If only you hadn't bought this house. It was an *outsider's* influence that led you to think it would do.'

George ignored this reference to his wife. 'Shops are always in streets, Charlie. It stands to reason. . .'

'Exactly!' she cried. 'One cannot, therefore, live in one.'

'I think you're wrong there. Mallory House is a fine house. And the way Rebecca's done up the drawing room, it's considered quite the thing. No. There are shops and shops in my experience. . .'

'But all in streets!'

Irrefutably. He had said so himself.

'Think of dear Meg,' urged the concerned godmother. 'Can it be the right setting for her? A street, teeming with vulgarity, depravity. . .'

This was a bit strong. 'Come off it, Charlie. West Street is hardly Piccadilly.'

'I cannot think that it is a suitable place for a young girl. Young girls are suggestible, they have delicate, unformed minds.'

'Well, I'm afraid Meg will have to get on with it. I can't see us moving again for a few years yet. I'm doing pretty well though, no doubt about it. Who knows where we'll end up?'

Samson, bothered by flies, ambled up to the gate to see what his master thought of them. And it came to George suddenly, as his horse drew near, that behind his resentment and discomfort a more serious anxiety lurked. With an effort he hauled it into full consciousness for inspection.

Yes, he had done it again. First Samson, now Billy Deakin. For a second time he had demonstrated unsteadiness, a tendency to impulsive action. What would that do to his reputation for sound judgment? He could imagine the talk in The King's Head. 'And that's what counts,' he said aloud, much to his companion's surprise. 'A man's reputation,' he explained. 'It's everything in the world of business.'

Charlotte sighed. As a concept, she found the world of business deeply depressing.

George, however, felt cheered. He had faced it. He knew the worst. 'So long as you come right, old fellow,' he told his horse. 'With a bit of luck you and I'll wipe the grins off their faces, come Boxing Day meet. Just wait till I get these confounded straps off. Put you through your paces then, you young beggar. See if I don't.' He turned to his sister. 'Better make tracks. We don't want Becky to start worrying.'

It was a relief to find he could think affectionately of his wife again. One thing was certain about Becky: in the world of business she was an invaluable asset. For a mad moment his mind's eyes replaced Rebecca with Charlotte – on his arm in the High Street, chatting to friends, walking to church, making an entrance at the ball. He almost laughed aloud in relief. Old Charlie had no idea – she lived in another world.

On Boxing Day Samson excelled himself, handsomely vindicating George and rather spoiling the Honourable Peter's day. He had been in form for some time, but George had preferred to test him away from the public gaze. By Boxing Day he was in peak condition and ready to give his master the ride of his life.

That evening in The King's Head the verdict was unanimous: George Ludbury had had the better of Peter Elton – wily old George. The Ram was no less impressed, and late one afternoon George discovered Sam Biggins taking a look over the stable door.

'Evenin', Sam. Fine-lookin' beast, ain't he?'

'Ay,' Sam admitted. 'I hear you had him off Elton for next to nothing.'

'I ain't complainin'. He gave me a damn good ride on Boxing Day.'

'So I heard.'

'Did you, now? Come up to the house for a glass of cider, why don't you?'

Both men were faintly astonished by the invitation. Sam, who had not yet set foot in Mallory House, supposed success had gone to his brother-in-law's head; and George, leading the way glumly to the scullery door, recalled Rebecca's request that he 'jolly Sam along' and cursed her for putting daft ideas into his head.

'Well, well,' said George, wondering whatever they were going to talk about. 'Pull up a chair.' He filled two glasses from a jug. 'Tell me what you think of that.'

Sam drew heavily from his glass, set it down and considered. 'Bit on the sharp side, maybe.'

'Never. Smoothest cider this side of Evesham. Best day's work I ever did, buying that factory.'

'Was it now?' Sam asked – rather unpleasantly, George thought.

'Well, it's nice to take the weight off me feet for a few minutes, but I shall have to go down to the boiling house directly.' And he drew out his waistcoat watch to emphasize the brevity of their intimacy.

Sam topped up his glass. 'I hear baby's due any day now.'

'That's right.'

'You want to watch out, or she'll go the same way as her sister. Can't think what Edith 's about, going in for her sixth.'

'And I suppose you had nothing to do with it.'

'Damn women. They're all the same.' He peered into his cider, wondering whether it would spoil the evening's beer. 'Ay, they're enough to drive you to drink. Drink or worse.' And he dealt George a dark, quick look from under his brow.

'Worse?'

'Religion, for instance.'

George frowned. 'You'll leave that alone, if you take my tip. Dangerous waters, religion.'

'Interesting, though. I heard that preacher from Larchcombe the other night. Made the hairs crawl on the back of me neck.'

'Dangerous waters. You keep away from it, Sam. Religion's all right in moderation – like drink – but best

98

not overdo it. What I always say is' (he tipped back his chair and stuck his thumbs under his waistcoat) 'Church on a Sunday to show proper respect, then – apart from marryings and buryings which can't be helped – give the place a very wide berth. Everything in its place, see?'

'Maybe,' Sam said. He emptied the jug into his glass. For the time being, it seemed, he would settle for drink.

'I'm afraid I shall have to hurry you. Time and tide wait for no man, and the hams'll boil dry if I don't look sharp.'

Sam drained his glass, retrieved his cap, and, without a word shuffled through the scullery door to merge at once with the early evening gloom.

The baby was a girl. George at once detected a resemblance to his second sister, and the name 'Louisa' was added to Rebecca's preference, 'Alice'. After a time another resemblance was spotted. There was nothing the baby put George in mind of so strongly as a rabbit. A frightened baby rabbit. Thus was Alice Louisa condemned to spend her life responding to 'Bunny'.

Some months later George and Rebecca were strolling on the Ludbury side of Astly Hill. Near the summit they paused to lean on a convenient gate and gaze at the small town below. Their town. They picked out sites of Ludbury industry, the shop and the yard and the cider factory, and considered the merits of purchasing the ailing timber yard by the river. Suddenly, their close bond became a heady alchemy rendering all possible, all within their grasp; and the dashing of hope and the ending of life were as unreal and remote as the indefinite, far-distant horizon. They were so safe that they could indulge in self-mockery. They began to vie with one another to invent newspaper headlines of wild pretension: 'Beef baron of Gloucestershire makes offer for Lipscombe Castle', 'Cotswold butcher wins

Cheltenham Gold Cup'. Their laughter rolled over the hillside so that birds poured in alarm from a scrubby bush by the gate, and cattle in the meadow below were put off the cud, lockjawed with amazement. They laughed all the way down the track; eye teased eye over the stile. On entering West Street Mr and Mrs Ludbury were the picture of decorum, but their steps were sprightly, their aura bright.

Summer at The Grange

(1912)

I

Light erupted as they shot from the tunnel. Sound
dissipated like blood down a drain. Mildly stunned,
George hurried to restore air to the compartment with a
jerk of the leather window strap, for it was warm on the
train and would become warmer. They had been glad
to find themselves sole occupants of the compartment,
glad of the chance to spread themselves. He looked at
his daughter in the opposite corner. She had been sitting like that – chin in hand, elbow on armrest, staring
into the distance – since the train had left Cheltenham,
undistracted by looming banks, small stations flashing
by, or the abrupt night of the tunnel. As he looked, a
long curve of the track thrust her into the sun's glare.
She sat up and blinked, then pushed her head back
against the dusty upholstery. Freckles turned to gold
dust, dark curls dissolved in a halo of light. With a
thud, his anxiety returned; a leaden concern for his
gaunt pale angel. But the whole of the summer lay
ahead, he reassured himself, the whole of summer to
laze away the shadows of her illness. Yes, summer at
The Grange would restore his own girl's bloom.

His own girl was preoccupied. Her mind teetered
from exploration of a problem to its suppression. What
was it about Aunt Charlotte? Could it be . . . ? No, this
was nonsense. She wouldn't think about it. She would
concentrate on her holiday, for she loved staying at
The Grange where there was peace and time, where

people ignored her for hours and whole books could be read at a sitting. Perhaps the best thing about The Grange was the absence of small children; at home and at school she was plagued by them, adults were for ever charging her with their care, mindful on the one hand of her fitness (due to her precocity and common sense) and on the other of her inability to refuse (due to her lack of years). Weeks and weeks lay ahead when no irritating demands would be made upon her. Indeed, nothing was required from her at The Grange other than an occasional demonstration of the higher Ludbury talents, and in this it was pleasant to be obliging.

From the moment she had solved the mystery of letters arranged on a page, Grandmama Ludbury's poetry had exercised a particular fascination.

'Are we the favoured Israelites,
God's holy chosen band,
The tribe whom He hath promised
Shall have fair Canaan's land?'

she had asked uncertainly on coming across an open book on Aunt Charlotte's bedside table.

'Meg! My dear!' her aunt had gasped, scattering hairpins. 'Come at once to Grandmama's room. Bring the book. Hurry!'

Then, on the other side of the landing, bursting in: 'Mama! What do you think? Meg can read! She has been reciting your poetry!'

Mrs Ludbury, not yet attuned to the day, peered at them suspiciously from a dingy pillow.

'Shall I draw the curtains, Mama?' Charlotte asked, doing so. 'Now Meg, read it again for Grandmama.'

And Meg repeated the interrogatory stanza.

'Speak up, girl,' the poet instructed the six-year-old.

'"Yes, we *are* British Israelites,"' cried Meg, speaking up,

'And we must valiant be,
All nations we must conquer
To prove our God's decree. . .'

It was thrilling stuff, it rolled from the tongue. Meg
had but a dim notion of their meaning, but the words
were reminiscent of *Hymns Ancient and Modern*;
they had the same inevitability, the same delicious
buoyancy.

Mrs Ludbury was moved. Here was no ordinary
reading, no dutiful, bosomy rendering burdened by
clumsy emphasis; here was the voice of faith, ringing
with the passion of innocence. Inspired, she sprang
from her bed and commenced her toilet – a brief splash
of fingers in the bowl on the wash-stand, a dabbing of
eyes and mouth, a re-larding of the hair with Vaseline,
an exchange of outer garments and she was ready to
face the day. 'I shall write something for Meg,' she
announced. ' "To a clear-eyed vision", perhaps.'

'Oh, Mama! Oh Meg!' Charlotte was beside herself.
'What an honour for the child!'

'Go away,' Mrs Ludbury replied, settling herself at
her desk. 'Send Louisa up with a tray. Two eggs and a
slice of ham.'

Meg's success confirmed what Charlotte had for
some time suspected: her niece was a kindred spirit.
And Meg did not demur. She observed the authority
exercised by her senior aunt and thought it a fine
quality with which to be associated.

For half a decade godmother and goddaughter had
enjoyed a close, untroubled alliance. But now, rolling
towards Birmingham for a recuperative, longer than
usual visit, Meg thought of Aunt Charlotte and frowned. What *was* it . . . ?

George was still watching her; and he saw her eyes –
green as glass like her mother's, but set close together
in the Ludbury way – become divided by a fierce line.
'What's the matter?'

Silence.

'Megs?' He leaned forward and touched her knee.

She looked at him and hesitated.

'Come here.' He slapped the seat at his side.

She crossed over and flopped against him.

'Out with it. Come on. You can tell your old Dad.'

It came out in a rush. 'I don't want to sleep with Aunt Charlotte.'

'That all? Not the end of the world, surely. Don't sleep with her. Sleep with one of the others.' George knew that every female visitor to The Grange was obliged by tradition to share somebody's bed. All beds were double beds – feather mattresses were more easily beaten into shape if they were commodious – and from the time Charlotte, Louisa and Pip had graduated to beds of their own, visitors were expected to climb in beside them. The spare rooms were reserved for Mrs Ludbury's pupils who paid for their laundry. George's old room was kept for visiting gentlemen, Edward and Freddy having not yet achieved the privilege of separate rooms.

'I'd rather sleep with Aunt Louisa,' Meg said.

'There you are then.'

'She won't like it though, Aunt Charlotte won't. I always sleep with her.'

There was silence. Two minds applied themselves.

'How's that cough of yours?' George asked eventually.

'Better.'

'Let's hear it.'

Obediently she exercised the remnants of her formerly prodigious cough.

He squeezed her arm. 'That'll do. Cough like that in front of Aunt Charlotte and leave the rest to me.'

'Oh thanks, Daddy.' Her eyes fixed solemnly on his: she had his promise, they conveyed.

Relaxing, turning her head to gaze sightlessly at the passing view, Meg felt a little ashamed. What a fuss she had made, she who was not given to fussing, and for no reason that her mind could fathom. Aunt Charlotte, it was true, in the privacy of her room voiced her opinions constantly, but Meg had never attended with more than half an ear. The self-righteous tone, sometimes vehement, sometimes disapproving, did not jar her sensibilities. It struck a note which suited her, a familiar drone to accompany the visual pleasures of the room. These were many and inexhaustible: Aunt Charlotte behind the wash-stand screen, fully visible to the dedicated observer, scrubbing every inch of her body (an interesting contrast, this, to Grandmama Ludbury's ablutionary style); Aunt Charlotte at her dressing table, savaging her hair with brushes backed in silver pliable and crackly as thin tin; or picking over her jewellery, always rejecting the black satin neckties studded with brilliants and tiny pearls, the ropes of jet, the beads of amber and the moonstone ring, selecting without fail a giant cameo brooch (present from Mrs Skedgemore); Aunt Charlotte working hair into tight bun, waist into tight corset, fingers into tight gloves; blinking sorrowfully when all was done, suddenly at a loss, a prey to Meg's oft-repeated questions – Who is the man in that photograph? What mountain is Mrs Skedgemore striding upon? Who are the ladies sitting to attention on the lawn? Where? Why? Tell me again. (Another photograph, Meg knew, lay hidden beneath handkerchiefs in the dressing-table drawer, the likeness of Mr Winterbotham who had not come up to scratch; mournfully moustached, spoken of only by Aunt Pip in moments of spite, disappointing, anticlimactic Mr Winterbotham.) Pressed flowers (souvenirs of an Alpine holiday with Mrs Skedgemore) lay uniformly brown beneath grimy glass; a scent puffer (always empty) blew stale gusts reminiscent of eau-de-Cologne; from the looking-glass knob a silver purse, with ring for dainty suspension from little finger, awaited Sunday's collection money; and on a wardrobe shelf a dead fox with cunning eyes waited to insinuate itself around Aunt Charlotte's shoulders. . . The fascinations were endless. She almost regretted giving in to her sudden aversion. By comparison Aunt Louisa's room was barren. Even Grandmama Ludbury's room failed to match Aunt Charlotte's for interest. How Aunt Pip's room compared she could not say, never having lingered there long enough to form an opinion.

It was now very warm on the train; the sunlight, formerly exhilarating, had become sickeningly intense. Upholstery, clothes and skin fused at pressure points. Meg edged away from her father. A small village sped by, a field of cattle, a group of haymakers; but her eyes, darting furiously to keep up with the scene, registered nothing. An inner scenario had seized her attention – appalling and calamitous . . . 'Not Aunt Pip,' she almost shouted. 'Whatever happens I won't sleep with her.'

George looked at her in amazed concern. Clearly she was still far from well.

'I mean it. If I can't sleep with Aunt Louisa I'll put up with Aunt Charlotte. But on no account Aunt Pip.'

'I should think not,' said George, quite put out that she had thought it necessary to make the stipulation. 'You might credit me with a bit of sense.' Everyone drew the line at Pip; it was an established family joke. They had lost count of the girls who had fled from her bed, all those daughters of visiting British Israelites, shrieking fit to wake the dead – loud enough, certainly, to rouse the whole household. But there had been jolly times subsequently, he fondly recalled, usually at the supper table on a winter's evening. ('What *did* you do to that poor little Rosie, Pip? Put a toad in her nightie? Put a mouse in the bed? Go on, tell us. And do you remember the Boscott girl? What a din she made. You must have done something really frightful to her.') While male members of the family speculated and her mother and sisters chuckled, Pip looked from one to the other with quiet pride. Catch one of the family sleeping with Pip? Not likely. 'As if anyone'd expect to do that. Now stop worrying your pretty head. Your old Dad's got the matter in hand.'

Aunts Charlotte, Louisa and Pip were gathered under the portico, flapping and screeching like demented birds. To Meg it seemed that a score of aunts fell on her in the sudden gloom of the hall. Such was the excitement that she required no prompting from her father to exercise her cough; out it came, unbidden, as she tried to respond to a dozen questions at once.

The aunts backed off in surprise. 'Dear, dear,' murmured Aunt Charlotte doubtfully.

George seized the opportunity. 'Troublesome, ain't it, Megs? Not too bad in the daytime, but you should hear it at night. Worse than a mad dog. Might be better if she slept in Louisa's room – furthest way from Mama's. She's been worrying her head off about disturbing her Grandmama.'

'Oh, how thoughtful! What a sensible idea!' Charlotte exclaimed with relief. Taking her niece by the hand she led her through the open door into the drawing room. 'Did you hear that, Mama? Isn't Meg a dear, thoughtful girl? She's going to sleep with Louisa so you don't hear her cough.'

Mrs Ludbury on the sofa twisted her neck and pursed her lips to the side away from Meg to indicate she might be kissed. 'Mmm,' she said as Meg straightened up. 'Getin' too tall, How old are ye now?'

'Twelve and a quarter, Grandmama.'

'Then what are y'doin' in long skirts, I'd like t'know? George?' (She suffered his embrace with impatience.) 'What's the child doin' in a missy's skirt? What's your wife thinking of?'

'She's such a beanpole, Mama. Becky thinks she looks more graceful with a couple of extra inches.'

'Never heard of such a thing. Disgraceful! Charlotte! Do something about it.'

'Yes, Mama.'

'Daddy!' hissed Meg.

But George evaded her eye. 'How y'doin', Mama? Been po'try writin' again? Goin' all right, is it?'

Meg nudged him. 'Dad*dee*,' she growled between clenched teeth.

He winked and leered in a manner that promised great things would be done if only she would leave him to it. 'Go along and unpack with your Aunt Louisa,' he urged.

She dealt him a look that promised dire consequences if great things were not done, and left the room with her aunt.

Louisa could scarcely believe her luck. From the first mention of the revised sleeping plan she had held her breath, sure that her prize would be snatched back. But here she was leading Meg to her own small room. What a prize – with or without a cough – matchless Meg, confidante of her Aunt Charlotte, noticed with flattering frequency by her grandmama! There was something quite thrilling about Meg; that head of curls atop tall angular frame, those fearless green eyes – they put one in mind of a print on the vestry wall, a portrait of a boy angel set for battle against the forces of darkness. 'Here we are,' she intended to say gaily as she thrust open the bedroom door; but no words came. The heat had made her giddy, the heat and the excitement and the unexpectedness of it all. Air. She required air. The window was already partially open, but she ran to it and thrust it as high as it would go, and then stood gulping and gasping, wondering if she would ever speak again. 'Isn't this tremendous?' she got out at last. 'Who'd have thought it? I'm sure I never dreamt. . .' As her tongue loosened, her heart sank. Inevitably it was a foolish utterance, for she knew herself to be an irredeemably foolish woman.

Meg heard not a word. Pale-faced and frowning, she was turning over in her mind the likelihood of her father forbidding his sister to lay hands on his daughter's skirts.

Seeing the frown, Louisa was full of contrition. 'How thoughtless of me! I quite forgot. You're an invalid. And the men are haymaking in the field behind the orchard.' She seized the window frame and brought it down with a thud.

Meg's frown deepened. 'No, Aunt. Leave it open. It's so hot.'

'But your cough, my dear, your dreadful cough.'

'I haven't got a cough. Do open it, Aunt.'

'Not got a cough? But when you arrived. . .'

'Look, it's better. I coughed then because everyone was suffocating me. Daddy made it all up because he knew I wanted to sleep with you rather than Aunt Charlotte. So let's have some air,' she cried, marching on the window. 'There!'

Louisa groped for the bed, found it and sat heavily down.

Meg glanced at her. Blow! She'd done it now. 'I hope you're not going to tell,' she said sternly. 'You don't want Daddy and me to catch it?'

'No, no,' Louisa said wildly.

'Then don't say a word. Daddy was just being kind. You do want me to sleep here, I take it?' she asked confidently.

Louisa nodded.

'Well then, say no more about it. Where shall I put my things?'

Louisa made haste to clear a drawer and make space on the wardrobe rail. That done, she returned to her perch on the bed and clung, as if in danger of drowning, to the black iron bedstead. If she had understood the matter correctly, she, Louisa, had been preferred to Charlotte as bedfellow, and George, dear wise George had condoned that choice – indeed, had gone out of his way to facilitate it. A thrill of pleasure stirred in the pit of her stomach. Her mind leapt to suppress it. It was wrong, terribly wrong. It was deceitful. The pleasurable thrill surged wickedly, and for some moments Louisa struggled to douse it in a cold stream of morality. It was a brief struggle. By the time Meg's belongings were stowed, Louisa had surrendered to the delights of preferment. New to such pleasure, it went straight to her head. 'We must *do* something,' she cried, leaping unsteadily to her feet. 'We must celebrate!'

'What?' Meg asked suspiciously, looking up from a book.

'There must be something. . .' Her eyes flew round the room and came to rest on a drawer dislodged in the recent shuffle of clothes. 'Of course! Meg, do you like secrets?'

'Yes,' Meg said firmly.

'Then I'll show you my special secret, because I know you won't breathe a word. . . You'll be the only one in the world to know besides me and . . .'

'Yes? Besides you and . . . ?'

But Louisa had fallen to the floor and was taking a package from the drawer.

'You and *who*, Aunt?'

Holding her breath, Louisa removed several sheets of tissue paper. At last a small glass jar with a silver lid was exposed. Louisa set it down with care, then unwrapped a second jar and a third.

Meg felt cheated. 'But I've seen dozens of those. People have them on their dressing table; Mama does, and Aunt Charlotte. . .'

'But these were a present – from a very special person.'

'Oh!' Who'd have thought it? Aunt Louisa had a secret admirer!

'Can you guess who?'

'No.'

110

'Three guesses.'

'But I don't know anyone who . . .'

Louisa laughed delightedly. 'Yes you do. You've seen her often.'

Her. Meg felt she might have known. Aunt Louisa was such a *fool*.

'I'll give you a clue. She comes to tea with me every other Thursday.'

'Oh, *her*.' Dowdy Sally Edmunds. Honestly!

'Sally,' Louisa confirmed tenderly.

'Well, what a fuss about nothing. Put them on your dressing table, for heaven's sake. What's the point of hiding them?'

Louisa was shocked. 'But it might cause jealousy. Charlotte only has two, and Pip hasn't any. Besides, it doesn't do to draw attention. . .'

A door on the landing slammed violently.

'Quick! We must hide them!' Her panic galvanized Meg. Within seconds the jars were re-entombed, the drawer closed, and blameless innocence restored. 'We'd better go down now, or they'll start wondering what we're up to,' Louisa said, feeling she had had quite enough excitement to be going on with.

Matters of far greater moment than the doings of Louisa and Meg occupied the others that morning. George and Charlotte had been engaged in a perambulatory tête-à-tête for the past half-hour, watched closely by Pip from the drawing-room window.

'Where are they now?' asked Mrs Ludbury, who was still recumbent on the drawing-room sofa.

'By the monkey puzzle tree,' Pip said.

'But they were there five minutes ago.'

'They stopped.'

Mrs Ludbury considered the significance of this. 'Does Charlotte do all the talking?'

'More or less.'

'Are they heated?'

111

'Charlotte looks hot.'

'And George?'

'Pretty fed up, I'd say.'

At that moment George was thinking that his sister was taking the deuce of a long time to get to the point. 'I suppose,' he got in as she paused for breath, 'the upshot of all this is that Mrs Skedgemore has asked *you* to take charge of her little scheme?'

'Hardly *little*, George. It will be the largest institution of its kind in the country.'

'But you don't know a darn thing about the deaf and dumb.'

'I wouldn't be concerned with *them*. I'd be running the place, supervising the staff, keeping the accounts, exercising overall control. You see, George, Ada knows she can depend on me. Those were her very words. "My dear Charlotte," she said – we're very intimate, you know – "My dear Charlotte, with you in command my mind would be at rest, for I know I can *depend* on you. *You* will be able to manage that frightful little man. . ." And *there* is her problem, of course; the wretched man was imposed on her by the Committee. She had no option. And he actually accused her of interfering! In her own charity! Now you see what she's up against. But with me in charge she'd feel free to come and go – we have the easiest of relationships. And I'd soon put the wretch in his place.'

'I bet you would, old girl!'

'As Ada says, our minds are attuned, we think as one.'

'Well, I'll say one thing for it. . .'

'Yes, George?'

'If a bit of the Skedgemore money rubs off on you it won't do any harm.'

'Oh, George.' She seized his arm on a passion of indecision. 'Where does my *duty* lie? My duty to the family? Would they survive without me?'

'It's only five miles up the road. You'd come home from time to time, I take it?'

'Oh, yes. Ada's very understanding. She knows how they all depend on me. But they're so hopeless, George. I mean, take Freddy and Edward: out till all hours – drinking, I understand – and always causing talk. First Edward and that maid creature, now Freddy and that awful Downs girl. . .'

'The Downs are respectable enough. Old man Downs runs a damn fine stable. One thing, old Fred'd always be sure of a decent mount. . .'

'Mama can't abide the girl. And there's Pip. This nursing business is just an excuse. Ada tells me it's quite a scandal what some of these QV girls get up to. But Mama won't hear a word against it. You'd think she'd be more cautious after the trouble with Augusta.'

'Strikes me, it was Mama made all the trouble there.'

'Mark my words, Pip will disgrace us if this nursing lark isn't put a stop to. Her behaviour is quite . . . quite . . .' Unable to put an adequate word to it, she changed tack. 'And there's Louisa, such a simpleton. . .'

'Louisa's all right. She feeds you all. She practically runs the place. . .'

'She needs constant direction, George.'

'She'll get enough of that from Mama.'

'Mama's becoming frail.'

'Come off it, Charlie. She's strong as an ox. Look here, this place' – he jabbed his finger towards the house, a gesture sadly misinterpreted by the watching Pip – 'could do with a mint of money spending on it. As things stand, I don't know where it's to come from. Now, if you do your pal a good turn she might feel inclined to repay the compliment. See?'

'You mean . . . ?'

'I mean, a good connection won't do the family any harm.'

At once Charlotte's dilemma was resolved. 'Oh, the *family*,' she breathed. 'You think it might serve the family *interest* if I took the position.'

Understanding had been reached in the nick of time, for they were about to be violently interrupted.

'Don't listen!' screamed a figure, leaping from the portico. 'Don't listen to her, George. She tells lies. She's against me.' Pip sped over the grass towards them and hurled herself at her brother's chest.

'Whatever . . . ?'

'You were talking about me. I saw you point. She's trying to put you against me . . . She's failed with Mama, so now she's trying with you. She wants to stop me nursing. . .'

George's guilty look towards Charlotte confirmed it.

'I knew it! Jealous, miserable beast! I hate her! I *hate* her! She's jealous of anyone doing anything she can't interfere with. She makes me sick! And why *shouldn't* I, George. Why *shouldn't* I be a nurse. I'm good at it. I like it.'

'I don't know, Pipsqueak. Come on, Charlie. Out with it. Why shouldn't little Pip do as she likes, put on a nice smart uniform and play nursie? Where's the harm?'

Pip disengaged herself. For a moment she was dumbfounded. But only for a moment. 'That's *right*, Georgy Porgy,' she gurgled. 'Ickle Pip likes it, so where's the harm? And ickle Pip's ever so good at cheering up the poor old gentlemen. Do you know what naughty Doctor Phillip said?'

George chuckled invitingly.

Pip stood on tiptoe and whispered into his ear.

He roared with laughter. 'What a girl!' he cried, slapping her bottom.

The rage boiling in Charlotte exploded. '*Now* you can see. It's plain as a pikestaff. This business has made her . . .'

'Go on,' dared Pip.

'Made her . . .'

'Make the silly cat say it, George.'

'Lewd!' shrieked Charlotte. 'Lewd!' she bellowed again, with such force that the warm air shivered, and the pines at the back of the shrubbery moaned 'lewd, lewd' in reproach.

'Lewd,' Pip retreated thoughtfully when the echo had died. 'Lewd!' she shouted sharply, much taken with the word. Whether it pleased or offended her they could not tell, for she turned her back on them and began to walk carefully over the grass. Her voice – obsessed and mechanical – returned to them: 'Lewd . . . Lewd . . .' until the waiting house swallowed it, and only the drone of insects disturbed the uneasy hush beneath the monkey puzzle tree.

Cautiously, Louisa and Meg left their room.

'It was Pip, your Aunt Pip,' Louisa whispered, nodding in the direction of a bedroom door, from behind which came the sounds of turbulence.

Warily they walked to the top of the stairs.

'Wait a minute,' hissed Meg. 'I think she's calling you.'

'Nonsense,' Louisa said quickly.

'She *is*. Listen. She's calling: "Lou, Lou," over and over.'

'Let's get away, then. Quick!' Louisa caught hold of Meg's arm, and with indecent haste they descended to the ground floor.

Louisa disappeared into the kitchen.

By the front door George was speaking sharply: 'But you shouldn't have used the word. No wonder she's upset. I think Mama's right about this – she's full of energy and she needs an outlet. It seems to me you've got it all out of proportion. She's always been high-spirited, but there's no harm in her.'

With surprise, Meg saw that Aunt Charlotte was the recipient of the rebuke. Good. He was standing up to her. No doubt he had put her right about the inviolability of a niece's skirt. Perhaps he had even warned Grandmama that in the matter of skirt-length, Meg's mother knew best. Aunt Charlotte swept past. 'Daddy!' Meg called softly, running to him. 'You said something to her?'

George, who felt too much had been said that morning and could not, for the moment, identify the nature of his daughter's expectations, played it safe. 'Rather, old thing.'

'Good. Otherwise Mama would have been upset.'

George made a soothing noise, and Meg took his hand. She would not see him again until September, and now was only the middle of June. 'I think Aunt Louisa's a bit dotty,' she confided.

'Aha!' George said, memory stirring. 'Comfy with her, are you? Your old Dad managed that rather well, don't you think?'

'Yes, Daddy,' she agreed, and rewarded him with a kiss.

After dinner, and a gloomy inspection of the dairy herd, George climbed into the dog cart so that Freddy could return him to the station. Now Meg stood with the handkerchief brigade, waving and blowing kisses. George waved his own scarlet square until they were out of sight. Then he used it to mop his eyes, for not until the harvest was good as done would he see his own precious girl again.

2

Perhaps because Aunt Charlotte and Pip were pre-occupied elsewhere, the next few weeks were all that could be desired by a convalescent requiring peace to follow her own inclinations. Aunt Pip appeared most mornings at breakfast radiant in the uniform of The Queen Victoria Institute For Nurses, then absented herself for the rest of the day. Aunt Charlotte, having accepted Mrs Skedgemore's offer, was away for days at a time busy with the affairs of the Deaf and Dumb. Life for those remaining at The Grange slowed a pace or two, was conducted at a lower pitch, and Meg found herself free to do much as she pleased.

Several diversions presented themselves between luxurious stretches of solitude. Small measures of Aunt Louisa's company were pleasant, churning butter or working in the garden. Once Aunt Louisa took a coin from her cache of egg money hidden behind a loose brick in the dairy (Aunt Louisa was perhaps not as potty as she seemed) and the two of them went off to spend it in the village shop. But when Meg shut herself away with a book in Aunt Charlotte's deserted room, or roamed alone in search of botanical specimens, Aunt Louisa was never put out. Even when Meg disappeared on one of Miss Sally Edmunds' Thursday visits she offered no more than a mild reproach: 'Oh, she *was* disappointed to miss you. We searched high and low. . .'

It was during one of her solitary rambles that Meg discovered an unexpected pleasure: the persecution of Uncles Edward and Freddy. Their alarm at her sudden appearance in the hayfield was intriguing. Was it due to Uncle Freddy being presumed at work in Mr Henshaw's office? Or to Uncle Edward being caught recumbent under the hedge? Whatever the reason, her sudden, stern-eyed appearance in field, stable or barn evoked the same interesting response: her uncles were vastly agitated.

She was careful not to overdo things, calculating that a degree of false security would enhance avuncular jumpiness; besides, there were so many other possibilities for diversion. Grandmama Ludbury, for instance, was writing a long and thrilling poem – an exhortation to the nation to pull its socks up: great things, the poet prophesied, lay in store if only the

British would stir themselves. Inspired by these noble sentiments, Meg committed the words to memory as fast as her grandmother could write them. She became a regular visitor to the poet's room. Mrs Ludbury encouraged her to arrive an hour before the midday meal – always a trying time, when concentration was a prey to hunger pangs and a state of panic could be induced by suspicion that the meal would be late. Meg diverted her from this anxiety and gave her strength to endure the pre-prandial vigil. Mutual appreciation proved a robust aperitif: when at last the gong sounded, grandmother and granddaughter descended hungry as lions to the dinner table.

Towards the end of the third week Aunt Louisa made a timid suggestion: perhaps Meg would like to help her clean the church brasses that afternoon.

Meg considered, then agreed. It would be kind to indulge her good aunt. Furthermore, she was fond of churches. After dinner they set out, down the shrubbery-bordered path to the gate, and along the straight exposed drive to the road.

'It will be cool in the church,' Louisa said, recalling her niece's delicate health; though rosy cheeks and a vigorous step suggested recovery was well advanced. As they drew near to the Sheldon house Louisa wondered, as she always did, what she would do if Mrs Sheldon appeared. 'Your dear Mama's home,' she murmured, out of a sense of duty. Fortunately Meg was incurious about her mother's former home. 'Mrs Sheldon, my niece. Your ahem . . . step-grand-daughter,' imagined Louisa, torturing herself. No, she decided, quickening her step, she could never do it. She would feign blindness, loss of memory, an urgent summons. . . Ah, but here they would pause. 'We'll pop along here. Just for a moment.' She steered Meg into a small lane and came to a halt before a gaunt red house.

Meg's heart sank. Home Farm, where Miss Sally Edmunds kept house for her brothers.

But Louisa made no move to go further. 'Watch the window,' she whispered, pointing to one on the second storey. 'Sally will be looking for us, I dare say. I told her we might be along this afternoon.' But the window was as impenetrable as the surface of a murky pond. Suddenly it flew up and an arm emerged. 'Oh, oh,' cried Louisa. 'She's got a handkerchief. Quick, we must wave ours.' Frantically they fumbled for handkerchiefs. 'Wave! Wave!' Louisa instructed, leaping up and down.

Feeling foolish, Meg waved. 'Why don't we just go in, Aunt, as we're here?'

'Oh, no dear. It's not one of our days. Oh, she's gone. All over. Well, well, wasn't that nice?'

'Yes,' Meg agreed politely.

The first call on their attention on reaching the church was Harold Ludbury's grave. Out went last week's dark crimson cabbage roses, into fresh water went this week's dark crimson peonies.

'Oh Aunt, we forgot the shears,' Meg cried in vexation. 'And I meant to tidy the grave.' She referred not to Harold's grave which was immaculate, but to the grave of her maternal grandmother. 'It beats me why Mrs Sheldon doesn't tidy it. She keeps Mr Sheldon neat and tidy.' (Mr Sheldon lay waiting for his second wife at a safe distance form his first, on the other side of the churchyard.) 'After all, she wouldn't be Mrs Sheldon if this one hadn't died, so it seems only fair to keep her grave respectable.

The novelty of this view prevented Louisa from marshalling an argument against Meg's proposed use of shears. Relieved that immediate danger was averted due to forgetfulness, she began to worry about future visits. But as the church door swung grudgingly open, a comforting thought struck her: it was most unlikely that the present Mrs Sheldon so much as glanced in the direction of her predecessor's resting place. With luck, a modest application of the shears would go unnoticed.

Louisa spread a blanket over the vestry table and set out Brasso and rags. From High Altar and Lady Chapel they removed crosses and candlesticks and bore them westwards. 'But they'll be back in a minute,' Meg reassured God, with whom she was on comfortable terms. Saint Michael and All Angels Headley Green was a humble, single-aisle building almost an apology for a place of worship when one considered the lofty porportions of Lipscombe Parish Church. 'But you know, God, this is not a *bad* little church,' she pointed out on the trip back to the east with newly polished candlesticks. 'The stained glass is really pretty. And they keep it spic and span.' These favourable words would, she trusted, inspire Godly content with the facilities in Headley Green.

'There now,' Louisa exclaimed in a loud whisper, standing back to admire their handiwork. 'Doesn't it all look *nice*? But just look at our hands. Try to keep them hidden, dear, until we get to the drive.'

Faint end-of-milking sounds reached their ears as they drew near the house: chains thrown against stone, shouts from the eager to be off, moos from the disinclined to be hurried. 'Nearly tea time,' Louisa observed. 'I hope Polly is seeing to it. Mama hates tea to be late; it ruins her digestion for supper.'

Hope was soon dashed. Snivelling of a sustained and resolute nature came from the region of the kitchen. Louisa ran in dismay to the yard door. Meg ran too, determined to be first at the scullery sink.

Scrubbing noisily at her fingers to signal unconcern with the drama next door, she nevertheless managed to catch the gist of it. 'It's 'er. She's come back. In 'ere all arternoon, catechizing, criticizing, pokin' in 'ere, pokin' in there. . . I shall 'ave to give notice, Miss Louisa, really I shall. . . More than flesh and blood.

. . .' Discreetly, Meg slipped through the kitchen, and tactfully, without a sound, closed the door. So, she thought, placing a cautious foot on the stair, Aunt Charlotte has returned.

'Meg!' hissed that lady from the landing. 'Thank goodness it's you! Come at once to my room. Hurry!'

Warily, Meg obeyed. That uncomfortable feeling had grown in her again, that there was something rather awful about Aunt Charlotte. What *was* it? It was something that made her feel prickly, a bit hot, a bit . . . guilty.

'Meg, dear!' Charlotte, recalling what is due to a niece who is also a goddaughter, smacked her lips against Meg's cheek. 'Sit down.'

'I've been cleaning the church brasses with Aunt Louisa,' Meg said pleasantly, trying to dispel her unease with an easy tone.

But this news did not please Aunt Charlotte. Lines gathered between her eyebrows. 'I am well aware of what has been taking place this afternoon. Even so, I should like you to tell me precisely whom you saw and what you did.'

'I told you. Cleaned brasses. Did Grandfather's grave, too. Oh, and waved to Miss Sally Edmunds if you call that doing something.'

'You saw no one?'

'Only Mrs Neville outside the shop. And Aunt Louisa spoke to an old man by the lych gate.'

'And in the church?'

'No one was there but us. Why?'

Charlotte stared thoughtfully at Meg, and Meg, wondering how tea was getting on, stared back.

'To put it plainly, Meg, I wish to know whether at *any time* you and Aunt Louisa, or possibly just your aunt while your attention was elsewhere, whether . . .'

'Yes?'

'. . . there has been any communication of *any kind* with . . . ah, Mr Jones.'

'Who?'

'The curate,' snapped Charlotte.

'Oh, him. No. Never. None at all.'

'I see.' Charlotte pondered on the pattern of the carpet for a while. 'You see, dear, sometimes things are not as simple as they seem. Sometimes things that appear straightforward are in fact quite complicated.' Dull purple spread over her cheeks. Nervously, she cleared her throat against the back of her fist. 'I want you to promise, my dear, that if ever you *should* see Mr Jones when you are out with Aunt Louisa . . . that you will come and tell me. Because, as I have explained, things that *appear* simple. . .'

Well! Who'd have thought it? Aunt Charlotte jealous of Aunt Louisa and the curate! Not that there had been the slightest hint of anything between Aunt Louisa and the curate – no blushes in the porch after Matins last Sunday, no dropped prayer books when they had shaken hands – but the very prospect was nauseous to Aunt Charlotte. It must be that Aunt Charlotte was 'crossed in love' – a nasty condition, graphically described by the Mallory House maid whose sister had suffered from it with near-fatal consequences. Tact and understanding were called for. 'I'll keep a lookout for him,' she promised sympathetically.

'I knew I could rely on you, dear. You and I are alike. We are the strong ones. But you'll find that a heavy burden as you grow older, for it behoves us to be vigilant when those closest to us, our nearest and dearest, prove weak. We who are strong must be vigilant on their behalf. Do you follow?'

And Meg, thinking of Jim and Bunny, agreed that she did.

'Dear girl! Such a comfort! Now, there is something I should like you to have.'

While her aunt rummaged in her handkerchief drawer, Meg, for one dreadful moment, supposed she was about to be presented with the portrait of Mr

Winterbotham – a gesture of renunciation in favour of the curate. But no. . .

'Here it is. Given to me by *my* godmother, your Great Aunt Josephine – how I wish you could have known her.' She put a leather-bound *Book of Common Prayer* into Meg's hands. 'Take it. Treasure it.'

'Thanks, Aunt Charlotte,' Meg said with relief.

'And remember,' Charlotte called as her niece made for the door. 'Vigilance!'

'Don't worry. I'll look out for him, Aunt.'

In the room she shared with Aunt Louisa she tossed prayer book on to chair and herself on to bed. What a turn-up! Aunt Charlotte and the curate! Then she frowned as a difficulty occurred to her. What if Aunt Louisa, in spite of her happy seeming indifference, was after Mr Jones all the time? (She recalled the hidden egg money and reflected that Aunt Louisa was, on occasion, crafty.) What, then, should become of her promise to look out for him on Aunt Charlotte's account? Oh, bother them all!

She rolled over and pulled an old journal from under her pillow. Turning the pages her attention was taken by 'The Caves of Ramoon – a Visit to the Mummy Crocodiles'. Aunts and curate suffered instant oblivion.

'I shan't get a wink of sleep tonight,' Mrs Ludbury foresaw, piling her plate high nevertheless. (Cost what it may, one did one's duty.) 'I don't know what you were thinking of, Louisa, staying out so late, forgetting all about tea.'

'Polly was to have seen to it, Mama, only she got upset,' Louisa explained for the umpteenth time.

'She'd no business to get upset. Get rid of her.'

'Very well.' Louisa was unperturbed, having ignored similar instructions with safety on previous occasions. Maids were indistinguishable to Mrs

Ludbury, all equally responsive to a firm cry of 'Girl' or 'Mary Anne!'

'And where, pray, are your brothers?' Pip was not expected, but three chairs remained empty at the supper table.

'Edward had to see a man about a horse, Mama.'

'Hmm.' Suspicion crossed Edward's mother's mind. 'And y'say the girl was upset. What about, eh?'

Silence. Meg, who was allowed to stay up for supper during this vacation to increase her consumption of health-restoring food, observed her senior aunt with interest. What *had* upset the girl?

Charlotte saw that a change of topic was required. 'What do you think, Mama?' she cried, as one to whom an enchanting thought has just occurred. 'Ada is to give a soiree at The Hall for all her friends. Lady Jane Bingham will be there; her Grace, too, I shouldn't wonder. There is to be a famous singer, and she has asked *me* to read "England's Might". What do you think of that?'

The author of "England's Might" stuck forefinger and thumb into the farther recesses of her mouth and retrieved a long and elastic piece of gristle. Examining this carefully she said: 'I'd have though Meg'd make a better job of it.'

'Of what, Mama?'

Mrs Ludbury arranged the gristle tastefully along the under-belly of a dragon bordering her plate. 'Of m'po'try.'

Charlotte was incredulous. 'You propose that Meg should do it? *She* should read "England's Might" at Mrs Skedgemore's soiree?'

'Not read it. Recite it. Meg has it off by heart. She does the thing properly. She declaims it with passion' – the point was emphasized with a thrusting knife – 'the pure passion of undefiled youth!'

'Really, Mama,' Charlotte bristled, wondering whether to draw attention to her own maiden state.

But Mrs Ludbury had grown warm. 'Meg's shining innocence allows full rein to the majesty of the words, to their noble vision, their fearless truth. What's more . . .' but here she recalled her duty to the inner woman and it was through a mouthful of cold runner beans that the sentence was completed: 'there's no danger of her losing her place.'

Across the snowy tablecloth, tarnished here and there by ancient jam and gravy droppings, Charlotte contemplated undefiled youth. (It *might* be quite a coup – talented niece on top of famous mother. It *might* be a brilliant success.) Undefiled youth stared back with gleaming eyes. (It *might* be fun – one in the eye for Aunt Charlotte. And of course, Grandmama was quite right: she, Meg, could do the poem justice; Aunt Charlotte, blinking and heaving, could be positively embarrassing. Yes, it *might* be quite a feather in the cap.)

'Have to do something about her skirts, though,' Mrs Ludbury said as an afterthought. 'Couldn't stand up in a missy's skirt.'

'Then I shan't do it,' said Meg.

It was into the subsequent silence, punctuated only by Louisa's sighs and the scrape of cutlery, that Freddy bounded. 'Sorry I'm late, everyone. Old man Henshaw sent me out on a job.' His eyes slid cautiously towards his niece. Fortunately the girl was not attending. 'Glad to see you didn't wait for me.'

'Wait for you?' Mrs Ludbury scoffed.

''Course not. Fine. Good-oh.' He rubbed his hands to express satisfaction. 'What that? The jolly old mutton again? Push it along then, Louisa. Damson pickle, is there?'

'Do be quiet, Frederick,' his mother said. 'I'm trying to think.'

'Sorry, Mama. Shan't utter a squeak.'

Replete, Mrs Ludbury pushed away her plate and wrestled with the problem of Meg's intransigence. The

125

girl wanted to do it, she'd stake her life on it. How to get around her? 'Dear girl,' she said throatily, making a grab for her granddaughter's hand. 'Is it nothing to you that I choose you as my mouthpiece?'

'Oh no, Grandmama. I mean, I think it's very nice.'

'Will you not trust me, then?'

'I do, really. But my Mama knows best about my clothes.'

'In Lipscombe, yes. But did she ever envisage her daughter in the drawing room of Headley Hall, standing before an audience of *titled ladies*?'

'Well. . .'

'She did not. Circumstances change. The unforeseen occurs. You see, m'dear, in this you must trust me, for mine is the poet's voice, the artist's eye. And I tell you, in all sincerity, that there must be *no doubt* as you proclaim those words of your lack of years, of your extreme youth. If doubt is allowed to creep in the effect is ruined!' And the poet flung hands to the ceiling at the mere thought of the ruination. 'Destroyed! Fatally compromised!' She reclaimed her granddaughter's hand and drew it breastwards. 'Remember the Scriptures,' she whispered urgently. ' "Out of the mouths of babes and sucklings. . ." Therein lies the poignancy. Now d'you see?'

'Oh, yes!' breathed Meg in total surrender.

'I'm so glad, so very relieved.' Meg's hand was relinquished. 'See to the skirts tonight, Charlotte. Louisa, I'll take a glass of port wine to ease m'digestion.'

'There's no need to shorten them all,' Meg grumbled from the bed. 'Just take the one I'll be wearing at Mrs Skedgemore's.'

Charlotte ignored her and continued to rummage through her niece's clothing.

Propped up against the bedstead in her nightdress, Meg decided th .t she thoroughly disliked Aunt Charlotte – an altogether more comfortable position than thoroughly disliking herself. The unpleasantness that was Aunt Charlotte was a welcome diversion from a nasty idea crawling about in her mind: that she had betrayed her mother by allowing her head to be turned. She squashed the idea with ferocious concentration upon her aunt's stout back. Diligently, Aunt Charlotte measured skirt against skirt, tossed some on to a chair, smoothed others – the newest and best – over her arm. 'I quite loathe her,' Meg told herself, feeling almost righteous again. Then aloud: 'And if you cut too much off I shan't wear them. I'll kick up such a fuss you'll have to send me home.'

Startled, Charlotte turned. The child's colour was ominously high; the result of too much praise, too late at night. She went to the bed and sat on it, putting out a hand to touch the furrowed brow. 'I hope you're not running a temperature after all that excitement.'

Meg shook off the hand. 'Of course I'm not.'

'Well, then. . .' Charlotte considered her doubtfully. 'Why are you looking at me like that?'

A pause. Then: 'I wonder, has there ever been an attempt to straighten those awful curls?'

'They're not awful. Mama says they're pretty. And you can't straighten curly hair.'

Charlotte rose and made for the door. 'I'll be back in a moment.'

'Why? What for?' Meg shouted, feeling crosser than ever as her aunt departed with the skirts.

When Charlotte returned, with Louisa in apprehensive attendance, her hands were full: hairpins, tape, night cap and a jar of Mrs Ludbury's Vaseline were deposited on the dressing table.

'What . . . ?'

'Sit in the chair, I've an idea. We'll smother the hair with grease, pull it as straight as we can get it, then flatten it down with tape and pins, and tie it all up in a cap.'

'It won't do any good, Aunt Charlotte.'

But Charlotte was determined, and set to. Soon the blameless little room was host to an ugly scene: unrelenting zeal engaged wrathful indignation in bitter battle, and were both further enraged by third-party incompetence. 'Now get into bed,' panted Charlotte when all was done. 'And mind you lie still.'

Meg passed a terrible night. Louisa was able to vouch for this when they were confronted by an accusing Charlotte in the morning.

'I'd like to know how *anyone*'d manage to keep still with all that sticking into their scalp.' Meg, whose head resembled a spaniel's coat after a sticky day's shooting, pointed to the scattering of hairpins over floor and bedding. Of night cap there was no sign – it was thought that it might be recovered from the bottom of the bed. 'I had nightmares. . . .'

'She did indeed,' Louisa confirmed.

'Hardly a wink of sleep. . .'

'Hardly a wink.'

'And how are we to get this horrible grease out of my hair?'

'The copper is lit, dear. Get dressed and come down to the wash-house.'

'And then,' Charlotte said, determined to salvage something from the night's chaos, 'come to my room and try on the skirts.'

Soap fumes and steam engulfed the wash house. Meg leant over the sink and thought she would faint. Alternately lathered by Aunt Louisa and doused by the maid, she gripped the slippery porcelain and prayed that they would soon be done. The throbbing of her temples had reached a piercing, sweat-breaking climax.

'And now breakfast,' Aunt Louisa cried, attacking her with a towel.

'No. Nothing,' mumbled Meg.

This was alarming news. Aunt Louisa and the maid burst into agitated discussion. It was settled – Meg was able only to nod her agreement – that a little something on a tray should be attempted in the peace of the sewing room. 'Just a *lightly* coddled egg on a *whisker* of toast with some *weak* milky tea,' Aunt Louisa declared, confident that this insubstantial proposal should reassure the most delicate stomach.

In the sewing room, sitting where her mother had once sat, nibbling, sipping, letting Aunt Louisa's inconsequential chatter flow over her, Meg felt soothed, almost drowsy.

'My dear!' Louisa cried, as her niece's head, more exuberantly curly than ever after the attention lavished upon it, suddenly drooped. 'Don't forget Aunt Charlotte expects you.'

Meg sat up, blinked rapidly, then groaned.

'Aunt Charlotte is leaving us later on,' Louisa confided, 'for the Deaf and Dumb. Then you can rest. Then we'll be nice and quiet again. So I should go and get it over, dear, if I were you.'

Wearily, Meg wandered through the house, up a flight of stairs, down another, round corners, through doorways, until the main landing leading to Aunt Charlotte's room was reached.

'Come in,' that lady called sonorously.

In silence Meg entered; without a word removed skirt and put on one newly shortened.

Aunt Charlotte was ecstatic. 'Much better. Far more suitable.'

Meg went to the long looking glass to see.

'Much, much better,' Aunt Charlotte gloated, looming larger than life at Meg's shoulder. Her body, like a cloud over the sun, blocked light from the window.

Meg peered. Two anonymous figures, a girl and a woman, waited in shadow. She half-closed her eyes. The image receded; her mind stepped back. Mama had stood with her like this before the long looking glass in Mallory House – lovely Mama, acknowledged throughout Lipscombe as a lady of taste and fashion. ('That *does* look well. I was right to have them made up longer. Much more becoming on you, darling. And how glad I am that we chose the expensive cloth – not a word to your father about that. Doesn't it hang well? Those extra inches make all the difference.') A lump filled Meg's throat. She swallowed painfully and sniffed.

Aunt Charlotte went to the bed and returned with a second skirt. 'Try this one too. Just to be sure.'

With shaking hands Meg changed skirts, then turned again to face her reflection.

This time Charlotte placed herself behind her niece's other shoulder. Light fell unimpeded on the looking glass. 'I hope a lesson may be learned from this in certain quarters,' she said censoriously.

'*In certain quarters.*' Suddenly, with the clarity of the sleep-starved, Meg knew exactly what it was about Aunt Charlotte. A hundred casual remarks with some connection to her mother, heard but never fully considered, joined this last in glaring significance. She knew it. She would voice it. 'You hate my Mama!' she told her aunt's reflection.

There was a moment, brief as an intake of breath, before denials flew and indignation set in, when recognition shone in Charlotte's eyes. Then: 'How dare you?' she spluttered. 'Wicked, wicked girl! You accuse me. . . You are speaking, you understand, of the wife of my own dearly beloved brother. Words fail me. . . I shall never, never forgive you. . .'

Meg collected her skirts, walked to the door and pulled it open. Then she turned back to face her aunt. 'That proves it. What you just said proves it.'

Proves it? Charlotte gripped the bedstead.

'You called her "the wife of my dearly beloved brother"; not "my dearly beloved sister-in-law". 'Cos that would be a lie. 'Cos you hate her.'

Charlotte found her tongue. 'Wait! While I am gone you will reflect . . . on the grave injustice, the grievous hurt. . .'

She was still protesting as Meg, very gently, closed the door.

3

The Leisure Hour: A Family Journal Of Instruction And Recreation. Volume 41. Meg separated the ancient magazine from its fellows and threw herself full-length on to a deep sofa at the far end of the drawing room. Dust flew up and joined a million other swirling particles in tubes of light streaking the cool dimness. It was a good place to be on a hot afternoon, a seldom-used place barely visible from the bright end of the room; indeed, a quick glance in from the doorway might lead an inquirer to suppose the room deserted. She stretched and flexed herself against faintly damp moquette, sniffing its mustiness with pleasure, for it confirmed how unaccustomed was this end of the room to disturbance. And now for the journal. She propped it against bent knees and dislodged page from sticky page in search of a likely tale. 'The Mortons of Morton Hall. Chapter 18: in which the secret of relationship is discovered by Henry and Mary Morton.' Promising. Her hand fell still. For the next half-hour, only the dust moved in the drawing room of The Grange.

Four days had passed since Aunt Charlotte's return to the Skedgemore Home for the Deaf and Dumb, four days in which Meg had been troubled by the memory of her outburst: it slipped into her mind in unguarded moments triggering unpleasant ripples of shame. She did not doubt the truth of her accusation, but upon reflection guessed that similar ill will lodged in her mother's breast – whenever her mother uttered the words 'your Aunt Charlotte' they were invariably accompanied by a small frown of distaste. It was a pity she had brought trouble on herself by drawing attention to their enmity. For this her aunt was to blame. It was her punctiliousness in the matter of the skirts, her obstinacy in the matter of the hair which had led to a sleepless night and an uncharacteristic lapse of good sense. However, she would not brood. She would be magnanimous. She would rehearse 'England's Might' with her grandmother so that Aunt Charlotte would be honoured at Mrs Skedgemore's, and she would exhibit a suitable measure of contrition on her aunt's return. Having settled the matter satisfactorily in her mind, she had determined to banish it and attend to more rewarding concerns.

To croquet, for instance. Startlingly, Aunt Louisa was the family champion, demonstrating, in this one aspect of her life, quiet confidence and a refusal to be deflected. Meg was charmed by this strangely resolute Aunt Louisa and persuaded her on to the lawn as frequently as domestic concerns would allow. Only she, Grandmama and Uncle Freddy had any hope of matching Aunt Louisa's skill. Aunt Charlotte was a poor shot and got cross, Aunt Pip was a cheat and aimed at ankles, and Uncle Edward got over-excited and forgot what he was about. Lately, Meg had practised every day, determined that at the next family tournament she would dispatch her own ball smartly through hoops and her opponents' balls into the shrubbery.

But reading was her favourite distraction. The bookcases at The Grange were stuffed with out-of-date reading matter, and Meg found the antiquated flavour addictive. At this moment she was breathing the air of 1890, and for some time failed to register sounds of an arrival on the gravel outside. When the noise penetrated her consciousness, she looked up and frowned. Uncalled for activity was occurring; some-where in the house, now. She checked her position on the sofa and saw that she was fully enveloped. With luck she would escape detection. A little uneasily, she returned her attention to the doings at Morton Hall.

Some minutes later, the door of the drawing room opened. She held her breath. Someone was behaving unnaturally, creeping stealthily about the room. It could only be . . .

'Boo!' shrieked Aunt Pip, vaulting over the sofa, landing with her knees on its edge. 'Where's Mama?'

Meg was speechless, for in spite of the warning she had given herself she had suffered a nasty turn.

'Made you jump,' Aunt Pip observed with satisfaction. 'Well, where is she?'

Meg shook her head.

'You don't know? U-*huh*.' Aunt Pip eyed her nar-rowly and considered her next move.

Meg's heart sank. Aunt Pip had on her mad look. This, after some weeks of calm when her spasmodic appearances had been uneventful, her demeanour quiet, her eyes dreamy as if drawn to scenes far distant from the dining room at The Grange, was disappointing. Evidently the lull was over. Her eyes, now, gleamed dark and calculating; her body crouched like a cat's.

Aunt Pip sprang.

She snatched *The Leisure Hour* from Meg's hands, leapt backwards to her feet and examined the print-crammed pages. '"Discover the secret of relationship", eh? *I* can tell you a thing or two about *that*, more to the point than that stuffy old thing.' She tossed the journal into a far-flung chair. 'Oh yes,' she preened, smoothing hands over white-aproned hips, heaving breasts high above blood-red sash (for she was still in her nurse's uniform), 'I can tell you a good deal about *relationship*.' She sat carefully down on the sofa's back. 'You see, I'm the sort of girl the men go for; a bit of a lark, jolly good fun. Doctor Phillip finds me quite irresistible.' She giggled fondly. 'Now, where to begin. . .' She thought for a moment and thoroughly licked her lips. 'Kissing,' she said decisively. 'That's generally the first move. One moment you're fooling about, then, before you know where you are, the crafty fellow slips an arm round your waist. . .'

It dawned on a horrified Meg that Aunt Pip was about to touch on a subject much whispered about in secret corners of The Hollies – her sedate little Lipscombe school; furthermore, information captivatingly imparted by her best friend and arch rival, Maisie Littlejohn, daughter of the publican at The Rising Sun, was likely to fall charmlessly from her aunt's lips; worse, might stick revoltingly in her memory for years to come. At all cost her aunt must be forestalled. 'No!'

'No, what?' Aunt Pip demanded, indignant at being put off just as she had got into her stride.

'I don't want to hear.'

'Well! Horrid little prig! You really are like Charlotte – beastly kill-joys the two of you. Well, let me tell you, miss, men don't care for that prissy, old maid sort of thing. They can't abide it. . .'

Undeterred by this news, Meg drew up her legs, placed her feet against Aunt Pip's nearside hip and shoved. As her aunt sprawled on the floor, Meg made for the door, the hall, and the safety of a proper, decent aunt even now descending the stairs.

'Oh, Aunt Charlotte!' she exclaimed, grabbing a virtuous arm, 'I didn't know you were coming home today. But I'm so pleased to see you.'

'Where is your grandmama?' Charlotte asked.

Aunt Pip came running towards them.

'I did push her,' Meg admitted in advance, 'but it was to stop her being rude.'

Charlotte looked suspiciously from flushed niece to panting sister.

A belch exploded gently into the momentary silence.

'Mama!' Charlotte and Pip turned, as one, towards the kitchen.

'There you are. I've been looking everywhere. I must speak to you. . .'

'Don't listen, Mama. She's followed me home to make trouble. . .'

'Mama, I insist. . .'

'She's a sneak. I hate her. . .'

'Silence!' The diminutive figure at the kitchen table proceeded to lick several fingertips and then to polish them on her black serge skirt. She viewed her daughters with annoyance and selected the lesser evil. 'Come, Pip. We'll take a turn on the lawn. I could do with some fresh air.'

From the gloom of the hall, Charlotte and Meg watched them pass into sunlight, down the steps, across the gravel and on to the hoop-strewn lawn.

'I wonder if Grandmama would like a bit of a game,' Meg said thoughtfully.

Charlotte sighed. She patted her pocket so that paper inside it crackled. 'This will have to wait I suppose. But it's most aggravating of Mama. There's no time to lose. Pip's getting out of hand.' She spoke absently, almost to herself, and was taken aback by Meg's stout response.

'She certainly is. She's quite disgusting.'

Correction was due, perhaps; but Charlotte was only human. 'Come, my dear. Come upstairs to my room. I've something for you; rather choice, I think.'

Arm in arm, they ascended.

'Oh, Aunt! It's beautiful! Simply gorgeous!'

It was a green velvet beret with a tassel, and it reposed attractively on the rear portion of Meg's curls. Charlotte was tempted to reveal a further merit – that it was chosen by Mrs Ada Skedgemore – but thought better. Ada, after all, had not paid its considerable price.

'How clever of you, Aunt Charlotte. It's the first hat I've ever really liked. It's so pretty, yet it doesn't draw attention to itself.'

Worth every penny, Charlotte decided happily. She had had her doubts. She had begun to regret confiding in Ada about the child's unruly hair and the undistinguished nature of her Sunday hat, particularly when Ada had propelled her into the ruinously expensive outfitters where little Skedgemores were accoutred. But dear Ada was vindicated. The hat transformed her niece into a child of high quality. 'Say it now,' she breathed. 'Say "England's Might" now, with the hat on.'

Gratefully, Meg hurried to oblige. She took up a position in front of the bedstead, clasped hands before bosomless chest in the manner recommended by Grandmama Ludbury, and began.

She had progressed no further than the third stanza when Charlotte was diverted by a sound on the gravel. 'Hush!' she commanded, darting to the window. 'They're coming in.'

'I expect Grandmama will go and lie down in the dining room now,' Meg said helpfully.

'Yes.'

Only one pair of feet came up the stairs. Only one door along the landing opened, then closed.

'Aunt Pip,' said Meg.

'Yes.'

'If you creep past her door you'll catch Grandmama without her knowing.'

'Yes. You may stay here, if you wish.'

'Oh, thanks, Aunt Charlotte.'

Aunt Charlotte was a very poor creeper, thought Meg, listening at the crack. (It had seemed prudent not to close the door altogether, there being rather too much rattly give in the door knob.) She turned to the looking glass, noting as she turned her head the flick of the beret's tassel. What a jaunty little hat! And soft as thistledown in her favourite shade of deep, dark green. It was really amazingly nice of Aunt Charlotte. No doubt it was a peace offering, a mark of contrition after being so beastly about her hair. Her heart swelled with forgiveness.

Along the landing a door clicked faintly. Meg's heart leapt. Footfalls softer than her heart's beating came nearer. 'Oh no, God. Don't let her be coming here. Make her go into Grandmama's room.' At the last moment she dived behind the wash-stand screen.

The rummaging went slowly at first. Drawers slid cautiously to and fro, their contents shuffled with the delicacy of a mouse in the night. Intermittently there was silence. Noise was the more reassuring, it confirmed Meg as the spy, Aunt Pip as the spied upon; silence bred doubt, the possibility of crazed eyes drawn to the wash-stand screen. Just as the tension became unbearable, Aunt Pip lost patience, and a violent ransacking got underway.

At once Meg fell to considering whether any property of her own was at stake, and her hand flew in alarm to the precious new hat on her head. She seized a towel, wrapped it around the beret, and stuffed the parcel out of sight between the wall and the back of the wash-stand. Relieved as to her personal treasure, she became solicitous for Aunt Charlotte's, and allowed herself a wary peep. It was enough to reveal that Aunt Pip had gone completely mad. The room was a bedlam of disorder. She trembled. Outrage took hold of her, the same indignant outrage unleashed by the delinquency of a sibling at home or the stupidity of an inferior child at school. 'Stop!' she cried, stepping from the screen's protection with the terrible authority of The Hollies' senior monitor. 'How dare you? Just look at the mess! I'm going to fetch Aunt Charlotte at once, and I shouldn't care to be in *your* shoes when she sees this!'

This sudden apparition out of nowhere disorientated Pip. But the offensiveness of the remarks expressed coupled with the memory of recent intemperate behaviour drove her into action. She flew at her niece, sending her backwards on to the bed, then jumped on top and pinned her down. 'You are not going to get anyone. You're not going to tell. Swear that you'll never tell I was here. Go on. Go on.' She jabbed a sharp knee into Meg's stomach.

'I jolly well won't.'

'You jolly well will.' Expertly she wrenched an arm. 'Ouch!'

'Swear! I shan't leave off till you do.'

'Ouch! All right, all right.'

'Swear you won't tell.'

'I swear I won't tell.'

Aunt Pip bounced away. 'And woe betide you if you break your word.'

Meg rolled over and off the bed, and raced for the door.

The landing startled with its innocence – deserted, silent, safe. She looked back into the room. There was quite a gap between herself and Aunt Pip, and now she, who was fleet of foot, had the advantage of a hand on the door knob. How she detested the mad creature by the bed, how she longed to demolish her, to blow to oblivion, to smash to smithereens she who had bested her and was to to escape her just deserts. 'You do realize,' she said coldly, 'that you are mad? Stark, raving mad? Normal people don't go on like that. And you know where you'll end up? In a lunatic asylum. People can't be allowed to go around smashing things up and jumping on people and twisting their arms off. They have to be locked up.'

Aunt Pip shrivelled before her eyes; her head sank, her body sagged. She stood as if rooted, swaying slightly and, it seemed, struck dumb. When at last she moved it was wearily, one foot dragged after the other. Meg stood back to let her pass. There was no danger now. Aunt Pip was a spent force.

'Clear up the mess. There's a good girl,' she said absently, as if she had been baking a cake and left a quantity of bowls to be washed.

'Blow her!' thought Meg, watching her sidle towards her room and shut herself in. The cheek of it! And here was a ticklish problem: on her oath not to give Aunt Pip away and likely at any moment to be confronted by Aunt Charlotte. Suddenly the door at the far end of the landing opened and Aunt Louisa, on her way to change for tea after plucking poultry in the yard, appeared. 'Thank goodness!' Meg called along the length of the corridor. 'Come here quickly, Aunt. Hurry. There's no time to lose.'

Louisa, coming uncertainly along the landing, was not sure that Charlotte would like it, not sure at all. A sight of the room silenced her.

'We must put it straight in two minutes flat,' Meg told her. 'I just hope nothing's broken. You do the chest-of-drawers. I'll do the dressing table.'

But Louisa was unable to move.

Meg drew herself up. 'Jump to it, Aunt!' she commanded.

Louisa jumped and set to.

When Charlotte returned, depressed by an unsatisfactory interview with her mother, all was tranquillity in the bedroom. Only Meg was in possession, looking up from a book with a smile of welcome.

'Hello, dear,' she sighed. ' You know, sometimes I almost despair. Sometimes there seems no end to the wickedness and folly in the world. Yes, sometimes I almost give up. . .'

'I know what you mean, Aunt, but you mustn't. It's no good giving up, or where'd the world get to? It's very aggravating, but we just have to get on with it.'

Warmed by the 'we', Charlotte sat down on the dressing-table stool. In front of her, in its snowy wrappings, reposed the velvety green beret. At least there was Ada's soiree to look forward to. Life was not all sordid goings on and obstinate refusals to face facts. The soiree would be an uplifting experience; and how *nice* that she and Meg were to share it.

4

The great day dawned much as any day. Listening to the mundane sounds of early morning, Meg could detect no cognizance abroad that this was the day chosen by Mrs Skedgemore for her soiree.

Late afternoon was the time appointed – no surprise had been expressed about this by any in Mrs Skedgemore's circle, and Charlotte and Meg, being new to soirees, took the time as a matter of course. Promptly after the midday meal they went to their rooms to change. Half an hour later Meg presented herself in Aunt Charlotte's room for inspection.

'No, no. The hat's not quite . . . Sit down. Now. . .'

'You're pulling my hair.'

'Keep still. There! That's better.'

Meg consulted both wings of the looking glass. No difference could be detected. She hoped her aunt was not going to get into a state.

'You hadn't placed it centrally. Not quite. Stand up and let me see. Over there in the light.'

'You've seen it all before.'

'Yes, good. Wait!' (The last word emitted in a terrible shriek.)

'What now?' Meg asked in a discouraging voice.

'The boots!'

Meg looked down at her blameless boots. 'Polished this morning,' she said indignantly.

'Horrid. Shabby. Black.'

'What do you mean? Of course they're black. We always have black. Black goes with everything.'

'Exactly.' Charlotte moaned, clutching her face in her hands. 'Black gives it away. Everyone will guess you've only one pair. . .'

'But so I have, Aunt.'

'. . . if you wear black boots with a brown skirt and jacket and a green hat. No. You must wear my pair of brown calf.'

Meg stamped her foot. 'Nonsense! Anyway, they'd be miles too big.'

'Polly!' Charlotte bawled on to the landing. 'Bring plenty of brown paper. Hurry!'

There would be no stopping her, Meg saw, sitting down to unbutton the despised black boots. 'But I bet I won't be able to walk in them.'

'You will if you make up your mind to it.'

The toes of the brown calf boots were stuffed with paper and Meg put them on. She was most uncomfortable, her toes squashed, her ankles unsupported.

'More is needed around the heels,' Charlotte decided, cramming in more and more paper.

'I shall never stand it.'

'Persevere, child!'

Mrs Skedgemore's drawing room was magnificent; domed ceiling, fluted pillars, gilded mouldings, and everyone arranged comfortably on satin settees or Regency chairs over a vast expanse of carpet. It was a perfect setting for her recitation, Meg decided. It was all so delightful that she almost forgot the pain in her toes and her fury with Aunt Charlotte; but not quite: a strange manner had overtaken her aunt on being greeted by her hostess and – laconically – by other ladies, a breathy sort of voice and much inclining of head and squirming of shoulders. 'Toadying!' Meg told herself with amazed disgust, and took care to serve the company with stern, straight looks so that no one should be in doubt about *her*. The best ladies, it became clear, were seated centrally on the splendid settees. There was an intermediate rank of less wonderful seating to which Aunt Charlotte, showing herself sensible of the honour, was directed. Meg was shown to a line of hard-backed chairs near the wall accommodating ladies who, in the absence of life rafts, clung to their handbags.

The principal entertainment was provided by a thin young man at the pianoforte and a large female singer with a voice of the deepest profundity. Their performance was loud and agitated, much too loud and agitated, Meg thought, trying desperately to ease her throbbing toes. It was clear that this was a popular view. Surreptitious shuffling broke out, and a degree of shrinking among the ranks closest to the music's source. It was the pianist's fault, Meg decided, he would egg the singer on with his thumping and crashing, making it a battle as to who would produce the most noise. And a foreign noise at that. 'German,' a lady in front of Meg mouthed to her neighbour who wrinkled up her nose in response. She began to doubt her ability to do justice to 'England's Might'. Pain from her feet was now shooting up her legs; and her head had begun to ache, thanks to this beastly racket. But when the musicians disappeared amid grateful applause, Mrs Skedgemore announced the recitation in a manner guaranteed to fire a proud granddaughter with enthusiasm for her task.

'Your Grace . . . ladies . . . as I am sure you are all aware, Her Majesty, the dear late Queen, was moved on numerous occasions to accept a dedication of verse by that well-known poet, Mrs Harold Ludbury. This afternoon we are honoured to have in our midst the poet's daughter and granddaughter. Miss Margaret Ludbury will now recite for us her grandmother's latest inspirational work: "England's Might".'

At once they settled down. This, it soon became clear, was more like it; every word in the dear mother tongue and so neatly rhymed as to be almost anticipatory. Marvellous the way it bowled along, scattering images of glory, and derring-do. This was the stuff to give the troops, thought forty comfortable matrons.

'Well done, child!' cried Her Grace above rapturous applause at the poem's conclusion. She held out her arms. 'Come and kiss me. Sit here.' And an awe-struck silence fell as the ladies watched Meg's elevation to the best settee. Into the silence dropped a further thought from Her Grace: 'What a treat, my dear, after that awful foreign stuff we were obliged to endure!'

A shiver of embarrassment cut the over-heated atmosphere. The ladies, accustomed to echoing Her Grace's every remark, found themselves on this occasion inhibited by the danger of offending their hostess. A lead was required.

Mrs Skedgemore was never discovered at a loss. 'Of course,' she trilled, 'Mrs Harold Ludbury is a genius.' That being so, her tone implied, Schubert could hardly compete.

'Oh, yes. A genius,' the company echoed in relief.

'A composer of music for pianoforte, too.'

'Music, too?' they gasped.

' "The Daisy Polka", for example.'

' "The Daisy Polka"!' They were entranced, for they all knew 'The Daisy Polka' – such a jolly piece, so refreshing, so English. 'Do, do play it for us, Miss Ludbury.'

And Charlotte, blushing and protesting, was led to the piano.

Just a little peeved by this swift shifting of the limelight, Meg watched as her aunt lowered ample bottom to stool, flexed fingers ostentatiously, then threw herself into the performance with light-hearted verve. How everyone smiled and nodded and drummed fingers on knees. Really! 'England's Might' was too good for them. And what a fool was Aunt Charlotte, purple-faced with effort, jigging her head like a puppet. A fool, too, for her simpering and fussing, above all for insisting that her niece cripple herself for nothing. A glance around the floor yielded abundant evidence of black being good enough for the best ladies' feet. And how she cursed herself for agreeing to sit on this low settee. Its lowness obliged her to prop her feet on her heels, and the resulting release of pressure on her toes encouraged the deadened circulation with a pain so excruciating that she feared she would faint.

It was now exceedingly warm in Mrs Skedgemore's drawing room. Sweat broke out on Meg's brow. She dabbed at it in alarm, recalling how perspiration had besmirched the brow of Sir Percy Rawlins in *Tales from the Dungeon*; only Sir Percy had suffered stretching by rack while she suffered compression by boot – an opposite but no doubt equally damaging torture. And then the miseries of Chinese ladies as outlined in *Tales of the Orient* sprang to mind; the poor wretches doomed to a life of hobbling as a result of foot binding. No racing with Maisie Littlejohn for them. Suddenly it was too much to bear.

At the piano Charlotte became aware of slackening attention. In her peripheral vision heads that had wagged in time, hands that had tapped the beat, grew still; interest in 'The Daisy Polka' had inexplicably waned. With mounting anxiety she moved into the coda – a cunning refrain; surely they would notice? But at the final chord there was silence, followed belatedly by desultory applause. Hurt, bewildered, Charlotte turned to confront her audience.

For a moment the mechanism through which her brain made sense of her eyes' reporting broke down. She did not see what she was seeing. It was impossible. It was a nightmare.

It was Meg, the object of all eyes, who broke the silence. Folded over chest on to thighs, her arms outstretched, her hands clasping stockinged feet, she gave a deep and piteous growl. The ladies stirred imperceptibly. They ventured no comment. Suddenly Meg flung herself up and back against the settee, eyes closed, back and neck arched. 'Urrgh! That . . . was . . . simply . . . frightful.' There was another – possibly sympathetic? – stirring amongst the ladies. Meg opened her eyes and looked towards her toes. 'Oh, they moved! What a relief! Do you see? I can wriggle them. I shan't have to hobble after all. A near thing, though, I reckon.'

'My dear child,' murmured Her grace, conscious that no one could make a move until she had pronounced as she found; but her voice trailed away.

'Don't worry,' Meg said kindly. 'I'll be all right. But I'm not going to put them on again like that.' She seized a boot, thrust in her hand, and proceeded to extract a quantity of compressed, rather damp, distinctly malodorous paper. When her boots were empty – and the carved Chinese rug liberally strewn – she cautiously inserted her feet. 'I shall just have to wobble in them. They're miles too big; they're Aunt Charlotte's, you see. Mine are black. She didn't think black would do; but just *look* how many people are wearing black.' (She indicated several pairs of nervous feet.) 'If only,' she sighed wearily, 'people'd keep a sense of proportion. If only they wouldn't *fuss* over silly things. If they'd concentrate on things that matter – Grandmama's poem, for instance – other people'd be saved a lot of bother.'

And then Her Grace saw her way clear. 'A most straightforward child,' she pronounced. 'I do like straightforwardness in a child.'

The ladies gathered their wits and made haste to admire straightforwardness, particularly in a child. Hearing them, Mrs Skedgemore let out her breath and rang for the parlour maid. 'Tea, Evans. But first' – she indicated the balls of brown paper – 'a shovel, perhaps.'

145

Only Evans exhibited any sign of being put out. The ladies became animated, excited by the prospect of food. And Her Grace yelled to Meg above the hubbub: 'Now, tell me all about yourself, my dear.'

Charlotte rose from the piano stool in alarm, prepared to create a diversion at the first mention of the butchery trade; but Ada caught her arm. 'Charlotte, my dear! What a success! You and your . . . charming niece. Do thank your mother for allowing us to hear her masterpiece. I'm sure we all feel better for it. Now, do come and talk to poor old Mrs Chevons for me. Deaf as a post – such a bother – but you're so clever with them, dear.'

So it was a triumph after all, thought Charlotte, feeling sick.

Mrs Chevons, though profoundly deaf, was not dumb. There was a lot to be said for the conditions coinciding, Charlotte decided, thinking of the poor grateful creatures at The Home, as Mrs Chevons bored on at full blast. Nodding absently from time to time, she scanned the room. Across a sea of heads she saw the flying tassel of Meg's beret. Her niece was holding forth, was giving freely of her opinions. Charlotte considered the cringing anxiety in her stomach and faced up to her misgivings. Those very traits in Meg that she had welcomed as evidence of their affinity – her single-mindedness, her stout good sense, her undeflectable strength of purpose – had begun to alarm her; they seemed somewhat exaggerated in her goddaughter. Was this possible? Could too much of a good thing be parcelled up in one human being? Her heart quailed as she thought of Meg gaining years, gaining confidence. But this was faint-hearted stuff! This was reprehensible! Courage! When all was said and done, the child was still a child. Years lay ahead during which she must persevere. As Meg's godmother it was her *duty* to persevere. For dear George's sake – for the sake of the *family* – it was her duty to minimize the tragedy of Meg's maternal inheritance and place her firmly in the Ludbury tradition. Duty. . . . Just thinking the word cheered her up. 'Duty!' she murmured, so that its sweet sound could bolster her sensibilities, which had taken quite a knock this afternoon.

'How's that?' bellowed Mrs Chevons.

5

Meg looked out at the rain. It fell steadily, as if rain were the natural condition, as if there had never been a day without rain. Impossible, this morning, to believe in those weeks of sustained sunlight and dry, warm air, but croquet hoops on the lawn and an abandoned sun hat on the seat by the wall bore sodden testimony. It was Uncle Freddy's hat. Uncle Freddy had sworn at breakfast because of the rain. 'A couple more days was all we needed, damn and blast it! It'll take a week to dry out after this downpour, if it ever stops, devil take it!' Uncle Edward, whose responsibility the harvest was, had been unperturbed. 'Beg pardon,' was all he said, over and over again. It had driven Aunt Charlotte mad: 'For heaven's sake hold your breath, Edward. I shall scream if you hiccup again.' The rain had made everyone tetchy. One could only be thankful that Aunt Pip was not here to add to the gloom. What to do? Favourite occupations suggested themselves unalluringly; it was delicious to creep out of the sunlight and shut oneself away with a book, but melancholy to read while weather rattled the windows like jailors' keys. She spun the revolving bookcase and fingered a volume or two, but sticky pages and musty furniture lacked charm amid universal dampness. The empty grate (fires in August were unheard of) brooded dark and murky as a neglected tomb. Abruptly, she turned and left the room.

But in the hall her sudden purpose fell away; action had not of itself solved anything. She considered the stairs without hope. In their respective rooms, Grandmama Ludbury wrestled with her latest epic and Aunt Charlotte with some tricky correspondence concerning the Deaf and Dumb. Not, her aunt had hastened to make clear, that she wouldn't be delighted to see Meg in, say, an hour. (Aunt Charlotte's goodness to her following Mrs Skedgemore's soiree had been surprising. Meg had a tiny suspicion that if her aunt were disposed to search for it, material for grievance would be found. But no; Aunt Charlotte had been specially nice, had even brought home from Birmingham an illustrated book about missionaries which Meg had found entrancing. How wonderful, she and Aunt Charlotte had told one another, turning the pages chummily, to be a missionary. 'Though one's first duty is to one's nearest and dearest,' Aunt Charlotte had been swift to point out. Agreeing politely, Meg had privately thought how much more pleasing to God – and much more fun – would be the licking into shape of dusky heathens than pale frailties like Bunny and Jim.) For the time being, then, Aunt Charlotte and Grandmama Ludbury were out of bounds. What about Aunt Louisa? When last seen she had been struggling into forgotten weather-proof clothing. Meg considered whether to follow her example. She looked into the kitchen. It was full of steam, and the cook was banging a saucepan vengefully on the range. She withdrew. Irritable with indecision, she stood at a loss in the dank, dark hall.

Suddenly, her attention was caught by a sound in the dining room. The sound came again: glass knocking glass. She could swear that the cupboard, housing Grandmama's port wine and the whisky for visiting gentlemen, was under attack. A muffled curse convinced her. 'Uncle Edward!' she cried, thrusting open the dining-room door.

Edward withdrew smartly from the sideboard cupboard and cracked his head on the handle of the drawer above. His hands, summoned by pain to his skull, relinquished their burden, and a bottle fell to the floor, rolled briskly over the carpet, and came to rest some way beneath the great oak table.

'Aren't you going to pick it up? It's dripping whisky on to the carpet,' Meg cried indignantly.

He stared at her with watery eyes. His mouth attempted a civility – 'How do?' – but gave up halfway, unbiddable, slack, and excessively moist.

Staring back, Meg saw that he was hopeless: feeble, utterly reprehensible, probably tipsy to boot. As always when presented with the weakness of her fellows, she found it necessary to report her observations. Edward listened carefully, interest dawning in his eyes. The voice was Charlotte's – her tone, at least, rehearsing Charlotte's oft-expressed opinions: 'downright disgraceful . . . know perfectly well . . . forbidden . . . too tipsy even to pick it up . . .' – but the shape was not Charlotte's; it was too slight, too weak. It was that girl haranguing him, that girl who kept trying to catch him out. Just a young filly, a slip of a thing. . . Put him in mind of what's-her-name.

'I suppose *I* shall have to get it, then,' she said, meaning to shame him into action.

He was unmoved.

Bristling with angry impatience, she reached down to grope beneath the table.

'Oh-ho!' cried Edward, recognizing a bit of fun when he saw it. 'Got you now, missy. Oh-ho-ho!'

For some moments shock deprived her of volition. The attack was unimaginable. It was also – she became aware with horror as a hand shot under her skirt and invaded the privacy of her drawers – very rude. A brief struggle brought home to her the invincibility of Uncle Edward's grasp. For the first time in her life she tasted helplessness. The smell of him, the damp heat of him, the loathsome, crushing propinquity overwhelmed her, seemed to make her his creature. She broke into great gasping sobs.

'Just you keep still, missy, while I get at you,' Uncle Edward said in unpleasant tremolo against her ear – the most she had ever heard him utter in one go.

Hatred of him, of his assumption that she was nothing, that his hideous pleasure was all, coursed through her like a blast of clear air and restored her to herself. It was unthinkable that he – pathetic and contemptible – should humiliate her; she would never, never allow it. She put her mind to defeating him. Some parts of her body were vanquished – her neck pinned by his chin, her arms and ribs crushed by his arm, her buttock clawed by his unspeakable fingers – but these she would disregard. Withdrawing consciousness from these areas, she focused fanatical single-mindedness upon her free, strong legs. One would support her, the other, an immaculate action, would strike out for freedom. She drew up her right leg, held it still for a second to gather every ounce of strength, then crashed it, heel first, into Uncle Edward's toe.

He roared and slackened his grip. She hurled herself forward, scuttled beneath the table, and rose to face him on the other side. Now she had room to manoeuvre. Now – there was no doubt in her mind – she would outwit him.

Edward perceived that the game had changed. He had played this one before, too. 'I'll have you yet,' he shouted, more excited than ever.

Silently she matched his every move, his every dodge and feint, maintaining a line between them that sliced the table in half. On and on they went, Box and Cox for eternity. With mounting impatience she willed him to make the obvious move. 'Under the table, blockhead!' she all but screamed, every nerve strained in anticipation of a dash to the door; but the wretch, grinning and slavering, continued to dart from side to side.

With an effort, she kept herself calm. Another plan was required, and after a minute's reflection she had it: it was necessary to incapacitate Uncle Edward; peripherally, she saw a choice of missiles, but decided on one of the toby dogs on the mantel shelf – it would be easily seized and should fly through the air satisfactorily if held by the head and hurled at shoulder height. The more she rehearsed it, the more she liked it. Damage would be done. Great trouble would result for Uncle Edward without – she suddenly saw – any inconvenience to herself. 'Oh, thank you, God!' she exclaimed in silent gratitude, recognizing the Divine Hand at work. No wonder the fool had not made a dive for her under the table; God had prevented him, anticipating in His great wisdom that a mere escape would oblige her to report her uncle if he was to be suitably punished. And what a terrible thing describing to Aunt Charlotte and Grandmama Ludbury certain particulars of the assault would be; there was the risk – most unfairly – that she would be tainted with his guilt. This new plan was the thing; it ensured that her head remained high while his had coals of fire heaped upon it. Righteousness nerved her arm and steadied her eye. She seized the dog and took aim.

He was felled in a flash. She had all the time in the world to walk over to where he lay sprawled unconscious and survey the ruin. It was insufficient, she decided, and selected her grandmother's prized Wedgewood urn from the top of the sideboard. As it fell, Uncle Edward groaned. Around him pieces of matt blue porcelain mingled with shiny toby pot. Right. Now she'd do for him.

'Aunt Charlotte! Grandmama! Come quickly!' she bellowed at the foot of the stairs. And, as stirrings overhead began: 'Uncle Edward's drunk as a lord. He's smashed the dining-room china. Hurry!'

'What? Whatever . . . ?' Aunt Charlotte and Louisa arrived simultaneously from different directions.

'In here. Drunk. Smashed Grandmama's china. Spilt whisky all over the carpet. . .'

'Fetch your grandmother,' Aunt Charlotte commanded.

'Oh, Edward, Edward,' groaned Aunt Louisa. 'Must the child get her? Couldn't we. . . ?'

But Meg sped away before Aunt Louisa's soft heart could prevail.

'Dinner already?' the poet asked, looking up from her work. Her hopes dashed, horribly enlightened, Mrs Ludbury descended briskly to the dining room. 'Fetch me a stick,' she snarled on viewing the scene.

'No, Mama. No,' begged Louisa.

Meg rushed to the hall-stand and selected the stoutest stick.

'Wretched, evil man! Take that! And that!' Mrs Ludbury cried, setting about her son. 'Out of the house! To the pigsty where y'belong!'

Edward revived. Catching sight of his niece, he let out a frightened shout. 'Not me! Never!'

'Out!' his mother cried, raising the stick.

'Out!' Meg echoed, pointing the way.

And out Edward ran, stumbling and crashing, into the pouring rain.

6

It was at supper on Meg's last evening at The Grange that Freddy dropped his bombshell.

'Damn good pie, Louisa,' he said helping himself to a second slice. Then, winking lewdly: 'I must say, Bill Edmunds knows what he's about.'

Everyone except Meg and Freddy paused in their eating.

'Explain yourself, Frederick,' Mrs Ludbury said on a dangerously low note.

'Better ask Louisa. Bit of a dark horse, is our Louisa.'

'Well, Louisa? To what does your brother refer?'

'I've no idea, Mama.'

'Come off it, Lou. I was talking to Bill Edmunds only last night. You should have heard him in The Fox, boastin' about your prizes at The County Show. Reckons he's all set up – wonderful cook, expert poultry keeper. . . You're a sly one, Lou, hanging around that dull Sally, and after her brother all the time!'

Cutlery crashed on to plates. Mrs Ludbury rose.

'It can't be true, Mama,' Charlotte urged.

'Silence from you! Louisa! What have you to say?'

'Nothing, Mama. It's not . . . I haven't . . . Sally and I never . . .'

'Mama,' Charlotte urged again.

Mrs Ludbury turned to her elder daughter. 'Well, Miss? I thought *you* were keeping a lookout.'

'But Mama,' protested Charlotte, 'you know very well we thought the danger came from the curate, and I've been to great pains making sure *that* was safe. . .'

'It appears you troubled yourself in vain. Sir!' – she turned on Freddy – 'your sister has been the subject of bar-room speculation. What, pray, did you do about it?'

'Hang on a minute, Ma. It wasn't like that. All decent and above board, weren't it, Edward?'

'Well, Edward?' Mrs Ludbury demanded of the opposite and bewildered end of the table. 'What part did *you* play in this disgusting intercourse?'

Edward leapt to his feet. 'Not me,' he cried, edging craftily towards the door. 'No fear! Never touched her. Gotta see t'the bull,' – with which he darted into the hall.

'It is plain to me,' Mrs Ludbury announced, re-seating herself carefully, 'that the Edmunds are far from desirable acquaintances. You will oblige me, Louisa, by having nothing more to do with Miss Sally.'

'But . . . Ma . . . ma!'

'I require your promise.'

'But Mama, Sally would never . . .'

'Your promise!'

'I beg of you, Mama. I beg of you with all my heart. . . .'

'Promise at once!' shrieked Mrs Ludbury. 'My heart's racing! I shall have an attack!'

'Promise quickly,' cried Charlotte. 'How can you delay?'

'Don't!' Meg instructed her anguished aunt. 'You mustn't promise. It would be wicked. She's your best friend.' Then, to her grandmother: 'It's not her fault if a stupid man says stupid things, and it's not Sally's either. How can you be so mean? Leave her alone!'

'How dare you?' wondered Mrs Ludbury in terri-fying *pianissimo*. Then, gathering her strength: 'Orff!' she roared. 'Orff to yer bed!'

'All right,' Meg retorted, tossing her head. But at the door she looked back. 'Whatever you do, don't promise, Aunt Louisa. They can't make you.'

Hours seemed to pass before Aunt Louisa tiptoed into their room. Meg had lain awake, listening for her in the dark, but she said nothing during the sounds of undressing and washing and hair-brushing. When the bed gave and her aunt eased herself in, she ventured a whispered inquiry: 'You didn't promise, did you?'

'You should be asleep, dear.'

'You did! You promised!'

The bed shuddered.

'How could you give into them? Golly! It makes me sick!' She rolled over in disgust, and was soon asleep.

Some time later she awoke. Surreptitious weeping – small squeaks, sudden snuffles – ruffled the night-time silence.

'Please don't cry, Aunt,' Meg begged, feeling rather guilty. 'I'm sorry I said that. . .'

'I'm just a silly,' sobbed Aunt Louisa. 'Go back to sleep, dear.'

Suddenly Meg had an idea. Her father was coming to The Grange in the morning to take her home. 'We'll tell Daddy about it. *He*'ll know what to do. *He*'ll make them see sense.'

'I don't think we should bother your father. . .'

'But he's marvellous at putting things right. You'll see.'

'Oh, Meg. . . You are a dear.'

George arrived mid-morning and was monopolized by Charlotte until dinner time. During the meal suggestions were made for his further employment. Knowing that they were to catch the three o'clock train, Meg saw that she would have to be bold.

'There's something I want to tell you before we go, Daddy,' she hissed urgently as pudding vanished from plates. Instantly all eyes were upon her.

'Yes?' George invited amiably.

'Not here. It's private.'

George frowned, and Meg understood that a less provocative word should be found.

'I mean it's a *secret*, Daddy.'

His face cleared. 'Aha! Got a secret, eh? Well, I daresay we'll be forgiven if we take a stroll. A young lady does have to whisper in her daddy's ear from time to time. Ain't that so, Grandmama?'

Mrs Ludbury's suspicious grunt was drowned by the violent scraping of Edward's chair.

'Something up, old man?' Goerge asked pleasantly.

But Edward, muttering incoherently, rushed to the door.

'The bull, did he say? Something wrong with the bull?'

'Search me,' said Freddy. 'He's got the beast on the brain these days.'

'I'll take a look at it before I go. Come along then, young lady.'

Mrs Ludbury and Charlotte watched from the window as George and Meg walked over the lawn.

'What's she up to, I wonder?'

'I'm not sure, Mama. I'll have a word with George when they come in.'

Louisa, brushing crumbs into crumb tray, caught her breath.

By the monkey puzzle tree, George nudged his daughter in the ribs. 'Been hearin' great things 'bout a certain young lady. Seems she had no end of a success at old Ma Skedgemore's thingamabob. Yer Aunt Charlotte's been ravin' about it. Good ol' Megs! I always knew y'were a sharp 'un, but I never knew y'could do recitin'. You'll have to give us a performance when we get home – do that Bunny and Jim a bit of good, show 'em how to speak up.'

'All right, Daddy, but listen.' She felt that time was short. 'Something awful's happened.'

'Has it, by Jove?'

'Yes. To Aunt Louisa. She's got a friend, a very dear friend, called Sally Edmunds. Well, this Sally's got a brother, and he's been boasting about Aunt Louisa in a public bar, boasting that she's going to marry him, I think. But Aunt Louisa hasn't the least intention of marrying him. She just wants to go on being friends with Sally. Grandmama and Aunt Charlotte wouldn't listen to her. They were really beastly. . .'

'Hold on, hold on. I've had my ears bent by this one already. . .'

'Then you see how mean they're being?'

'I see nothing of the sort. Damn cheek, I thought, fellow all set to help himself to our housekeeper – made no bones about it, from what I hear! Needs watching that sort of thing. Women like your Aunt

Louisa are easy prey to a man like that. And how'd they get on here, without her, I'd like t'know?'

'She's not going, Daddy. Oh, I wish people'd *listen*. She's no intention of marrying the silly man. She just wants to stay good friends with Sally – you know, have tea with her on Thursdays and that sort of thing.'

'Mmm. Strikes me there's been a bit too much of that. Always leads to trouble, women indulgin' in idle gossip – gets out of hand; and before y'know where y'are the house is a pigsty and there's no dinner for a man when he comes in from a hard day's work. It doesn't do, Meg. . .'

'What *nonsense*,' she almost screamed, stamping her foot. 'Is the house a pigsty? Well, is it? Of course it jolly well isn't. Aunt Louisa works harder than anyone here. Why *shouldn't* she have a friend? Why *shouldn't* she be happy like everyone else? It's the meanest thing I ever heard. . .'

'That's quite enough of that! I'll not be cross-questioned by a slip of girl! You'd better go in. I'm beginning to see what your Aunt Charlotte was getting at – in danger of getting above yourself, she said. Well, I'll have no more of it. Understand?'

'Golly! The sneaky thing! And she's been as nice as anything. . . Well, I've had quite a lot to put up with from her, let me tell you. A load of nonsense about the curate when she wasn't in love with him at all. Tomfool idea about straightening my hair. Chopping great chunks off my skirts – and what's Mama going to say about that, I'd like to know? Forcing me into her beastly boots . . .'

'Not another word, miss! Back to the house! Pack your bags and stay in your room till I'm done.'

He strode vigorously away, purple-faced, beetle-browed. He had no purpose other than the dissipation of anger, but as the cowshed came into view, he recalled that it might be as well to look at the bull.

Through a cobweb and grime encrusted window of the cowshed, Edward saw George approaching. He shot out of the door, out of the yard and was away over the field before his brother could stop him.

'Hey! Edward!' George yelled. But Edward disappeared behind an overgrown blackthorn hedge.

'Blow me if he ain't deaf as well as daft!' George marvelled, turning into the bull's quarters.

They made it up on the train.

George's anger had dissipated in the bull's shed. As he watched the contented beast chewing his way through a manger of hay it suddenly struck him that life was really very simple. Just look at the sturdy fellow tucking in. Why didn't people show similar good sense? They had plenty of good dinners, didn't they? They were warm and comfortable? Yet they would go stirring up nastiness. They should take a tip from Bully Boy, here, and save their energy for the things that mattered. 'I daresay you'll be giving the heifers something to think about soon, you old rogue,' he told the bull, dealing him a comradely slap.

He returned with his new-found philosophy to the house and sought out Louisa. It was time she had a little break, he announced; a little holiday. They could manage without her for a while. She must come to Mallory House. Becky would be delighted to welcome her just as soon as her forthcoming confinement was out of the way. No, Louisa was not to worry. He'd deal with Mama. And before leaving The Grange he had convinced his mother that looking forward to stay at Mallory House was just the thing to keep Louisa's mind off less savoury matters. On the way to the station he advised Freddy, who was driving the trap, to think harder in future before committing himself to speech. All in all, George was pleased with himself as they waited for the train, and burning to acquaint his daughter of his virtue.

The train was quite full. They were obliged to sit side by side. Meg allowed him to take her hand, for she was already inclined to forgive him. There had been a hint of callousness in his attitude to Aunt Louisa which still gave her unease. She recalled one of her mother's pet observations, that Daddy was the kindest of men – any reference to past grievance, such as the violation of the doll, Malakie, was explained away as 'teasing', a thing all fathers liked to indulge in. But teasing did not adequately explain his cursory dismissal of Aunt Louisa's unhappiness. On the other hand, the sight of Aunt Louisa hanging her head like a sinful child had enraged her. Aunt Louisa was simply not worth it. Hang it all, she was a grown-up lady; if she had a mind to be friends with Sally Edmunds she should just get on with it. And in the trap Daddy had given Uncle Freddy a good ticking off, she recalled with affection. Yes, all in all she had decided to forgive him.

'I say, Megs,' he began shyly, his mouth close to her ear. 'What d'yer think? I've asked your Aunt Louisa to come and stay with us at Mallory House later on.' He leaned away from her, watching anxiously for approval to break over her face.

'Oh, Daddy! That *is* kind of you!'

He relaxed. 'Well,' he said modestly, 'you set me thinkin'. They do take her for granted – no doubt about it. The old girl deserves a holiday.'

How good he was. Her mother's opinion was vindicated. She nestled closer.

He raised her hand and dropped a kiss on it. She was his own girl.

And he was the best daddy in the whole world.

Stirring Times

(1912–1914)

I

'This is not my child,' Rebecca told herself, peering closely at the bundle beside her. It was her fifth child. ('Fifth and last,' Doctor Griffin had warned, for it followed too closely the birth of their fourth, a large rollicking boy, baptized Harold after the grandfather he favoured, but popularly known as Harry.) The babe newly born stared back solemnly. 'No, she is not at all what I have been led to expect.' And Rebecca fell back, exhausted, on her pillow.

'Isn't she a beauty?' Nurse Ballinger asked, removing the bundle.

So Nurse had noticed, too. Not a trace of Ludbury. Undoubtedly a stranger.

Then George was holding her hand. 'Becky! You're awake! Oh, Becky!'

With an effort she brought him into focus.

'You've seen her? Incredible, isn't it? Spittin' image.'

She grew alarmed. 'Image?'

'Hasn't she seen her, Nurse?'

Nurse bustled up. 'Sh!'

'Image?'

'Of her Mama, of course. Now back to sleep, Mrs Ludbury.'

So that was it. Well, well. . .

When she awoke George was back. 'Sarah,' she told him in a stronger voice.

'You mean, the baby?'

'After my mother. Sarah.'

'Capital. Sarah. Yes.' His eyes darted calculatingly.

'Sarah Edith,' she said to forestall him.

'U-huh . . . How about Sarah Edith Caroline?'

Oh dear! And she was so tired. 'I suppose so,' she sighed.

'Darling! There's no resemblance this time, I know, but it would be hard on Pip to be left out when we've remembered the other girls.'

She nodded and closed her eyes.

He bent down and kissed her forehead. 'Sarah's a fine name – perfect for a christening. Dignified. And we can call her Sally for short.'

Sarah, to be known as Sally, was born in November 1912. It was not until the following spring that George recalled his invitation to Louisa. 'Wait until the weather is warmer,' Rebecca insisted. 'I shall be strong again in a month or two. There must be no suggestion of her nurse-maiding me. She is the one in need of spoiling.' George took the point and agreed to a postponement.

Then a letter from The Grange, followed closely by a second, banished Louisa from his mind. Freddy became the focus of family attention, exposed in the first communication as a villain, hailed in the next as a hero. Freddy's employer had dismissed him – not unreasonably: Freddy, the truth was now known, spent most of his time on the farm. This had come as a blow to Mrs Ludbury; indeed, Charlotte feared it would be the finish of her. But Freddy – 'The cunning little blighter!' George cried on reading the second letter – had taken himself off and reappeared in the uniform of the Worcestershire Yeomanry. This splendid apparition restored Mrs Ludbury to health and, when it was explained to her that membership of the Yeomanry was reserved for the landed interest, reconciled her at a stroke to agriculture.

'The boy's a genius,' George marvelled, interrupting his reading to relay key points to Rebecca. 'He'll do well; he's a damn fine horseman.' But then, reading on, he discovered that Edward, too, was to join the Yeomanry; Mrs Ludbury was convinced that such an impressive get-up would do wonders for him. 'I've got m'doubts about *that*.'

'About what, darling?'

'About Edward.'

'Well, of course,' Rebecca said, inquiring no further.

1913 was an extraordinary year. Militarism, whether on horseback or foot, became an obsession. Patriotism reached fever-pitch, and Meg knew in her bones that the prophetic vision of 'England's Might' was soon to be realized. From early in the year, Lipscombe Drill Hall quaked under the stamp of hobnailed boots but, as the days lengthened, the Territorials took to the streets under the command of Sergeant Littlejohn, licensee of the The Rising Sun. Townspeople stood in doorways to watch, and children – at a suitable distance – fell in behind. The Terriers became the talk of the town and Sergeant Littlejohn its favourite son.

Naturally, Maisie Littlejohn assumed command of matters military at The Hollies. Nothing pleased the children now but marching, and Meg was obliged to submit. Then the news about Uncle Freddy set her thinking.

'My uncles are in the Yeomanry,' she informed Maisie tentatively.

Maisie played for time. 'What's tha-art?'

'Like the Terriers, only on horseback.'

'Well, we ain't on 'orseback.'

And that appeared to be that.

One bright morning in May – a Sunday, with pavements full of folk returning from church and gossipers idling in the sun – the Gloucestershire

Yeomanry rode into town, halting at The King's Head where their commanding officer, the Honourable Peter Elton, proposed to refresh himself. It was a brilliant assembly; for half an hour the Terriers were forgotten.

'You see,' Meg said, jabbing her friend in the ribs, 'that's what my uncles do in the Worcestershire Yeomanry. They ride about saluting and being brave, just like them.'

All children within earshot were impressed.

'And that's Davy Bennett's big brother on the black horse.'

'And that one over there knows my Dad.'

Maisie made haste to minimize the damage. 'Oi'll let yer be moi deputy, then. Yow can 'elp me drill 'em, loik your Tarm 'elps moi Dad.'

'Your Tarm' referred to George Ludbury's forearm, but Meg knew this was no time to be sniffy about the possessive pronoun. 'Right,' she said. 'Shall we march 'em up Astly Hill?'

From that moment the playground could not contain them. The children marched through streets, back lanes, country roads and meadows; and everywhere the persistent treble rang out: 'One *two*, one *two*, one *two*.' The rougher children from the church school formed their own contingent; and in the gardens behind the tall houses in The Square, little boys home from school could be heard drilling their sisters: 'Smarten up, Lizzie! About *turn*!'

Watching over this admirable activity was the town's very own demon; the ugliest gargoyle on the parish church tower, christened 'Kaiser Bill' by a passing wag. The name stuck at once. Fathers storming full of wrath from public bars, drunk on beer and reports of the latest German atrocity, would seize their children and take them to view the offending masonry. Fists were shaken, jeers offered up. To the children it was clear: God – as the parson had explained – resided in the church amid His many representations; so the devil must live in the tower because his likeness was there to prove it. Young passions rose on a march past the church. 'One *two*, one *two*,' they cried fiercely, daring Kaiser Bill to swoop down.

Hatred of things German found its way into Mallory House. Rebecca, playing her favourite 'Moonlight Sonata', was required to desist forthwith; that miserable German stuff was not wanted. How about 'The Old Grey Mare', or 'The Daisy Polka'? Decent, jolly tunes.

Rebecca closed the piano lid.

'Tell you what,' George cried, 'we were going to hear Meg say that po'm of her grandmother's – the one she said at old-mother-what's-her-name's. We seem to have forgotten all about it. Come on, Meg, let's hear it now. Put on that nice hat your aunt got you. Come along, children, your sister's going to give us a treat.'

From the piano stool Rebecca watched her children arrange themselves – as if it were the most natural thing in the world – about their father; Bunny on one knee, Harry on the other, and Jim on the arm of his chair. Four pairs of Ludbury eyes watched frowningly as one of their own took up her position in front of the firescreen. Upstairs in a cot, Rebecca reminded herself, slept an infant who favoured her mother. Perhaps she would grow up to prefer 'The Moonlight Sonata' to 'The Old Grey Mare'. The thought pleased her. She crossed her legs, leaned an arm on the shelf of the piano lid and waited expectantly.

Meg clasped her hands, cleared her throat and announced:

' "England's Might", by Mrs Harold Ludbury.

'Gird up your loins, ye Englishmen. . . .'

There was a snort from the piano and a rush for the door.

'What's the matter with *her*?' Meg asked suspiciously.

'Heard the baby, I expect. Go on.'

'Yes, go on.' 'Say it, Meg.' These urgings from the children.

'Very well,' she said graciously. 'I'll begin again.

> 'Gird up your loins, ye Englishmen,
> Sound bugle, fife and drum,
> Rise up in mighty multitude
> To the battle, come!
> Stern duty bids you forward
> As England's noble sons.
> Neither shrink nor waver, but
> As heroes, stand to guns.
> Oh, mighty men of England
> We sing your praises high,
> For Englishmen will ever fight
> To conquer, or they'll die! . . .'

'Bravo!' cried George.

'Bravo!' the children echoed.

'That was just the chorus,' Meg pointed out sternly. 'There's a lot more to come.' And returning her gaze to an imaginary far-distant horizon, she proceeded to give it to them.

Rebecca collapsed on to her bed. 'Gird up your loins!' she moaned, wiping her eyes. Oh dear, it was too much. Just wait until she told Edith. How Edith would *scream*. Pity Meg would never share the joke – bit worrying, in fact, that humourlessness of hers. But she could hardly encourage her daughter to see the funny side of her paternal grandmother. George would take a dim view of it. Humour wasn't exactly George's strong point, either. And that awful doggerel they were filling the girl's head with. . . Well, something could be done about that.

She sprang from her bed, left the room and ran down two flights of stairs to the dining room. From a glass-fronted bookcase above a bureau she took down William Wordsworth, Robert Browning, Alfred Tennyson – treasured volumes from her schooldays. She'd be subtle about it, of course, but it was time the Ludbury influence was countered. There was too much of this insistence on Meg taking after her Aunt Charlotte. Meg was a dear, bright girl; there was a whole world waiting for her to explore, wide and varied beyond the imaginings of the Ludburys. It was time her mother pointed the way.

2

'Oh, no!' Louisa leapt to her feet, thereby securing the attention of all in the compartment. The train juddered and swung. George put out an arm to steady her while she enlarged on the difficulty. 'All this way with my back to the engine! I shall be sick as a dog!'

'Change places with your aunt,' George commanded Bunny, then handed his sister into the vacated seat. 'You'll be right as rain now,' he predicted.

After a few anxious moments, Louisa found that she was. 'I think it was caught in time. But one can't be too sure when it comes to train sickness.'

George grinned encouragingly and reflected that his sister was not improving as a traveller; the journey, last week, from Headley Green to Lipscombe (George had been obliged to go and collect her) had been punctuated by her agitation. He hoped that she would soon settle down, for today was a holiday, an outing with the elder children; they were on their way to Warwick to see the Worcestershire and Warwickshire Yeomanry display their skills in the grounds of the castle. The news that Freddy and Edward were to take part had

167

precipitated Louisa's visit to Mallory House so that she could be one of the party. It was a glorious June morning, a perfect day for an excursion. He squeezed Bunny's knee and winked rakishly.

Bunny's scowl vanished. She had been pondering the significance of riding with one's back to the engine, and the feeling had grown that if it was not good enough for Aunt Louisa it was unlikely to be good enough for her. Sickness had been mentioned. She had arranged her features in familiar lines of distaste and prepared to complain. Then came that squeeze of her knee, that roguish look, and at once she saw her good fortune: *she* was next to Daddy; Meg, on the other hand, was at the other end of the compartment opposite Mama and next to a rather horrid fat lady. Bunny, who never thoroughly enjoyed anything unless it was enhanced by evidence that others were less well favoured, smirked and snuggled closer to Daddy.

At the other end of the compartment Rebecca had seen the fat lady exchange a certain look with her companion during Louisa's perturbation. She hoped Louisa would not feel obliged to tell the world of her anxieties throughout the day. From the moment this outing had been suggested, Rebecca had suffered misgivings. It had too large a Ludbury content for her peace of mind – Edward to take part in the display for instance. But George had been sanguine: the Yeomanry knew what they were about and were bound to keep Edward firmly in the background.

Meg leaned forward, tapped her mother's knee and pointed. A mass of scabious covered a stretch of the embankment like a blue, feather-tipped carpet. They watched with pleasure until the sight had gone, then smiled their mutual satisfaction to one another. It was good, at least, to be out with Meg. 'She is such a companion,' mused Rebecca fondly. 'In fact, were it not for that frightful, humourless intensity that gets hold of her now and then' (here 'England's Might' sprang to mind), 'I do believe she'd be altogether perfect.'

'Would you like to change places, Jim, so that you can look out of the window?' Louisa suddenly asked the boy at her side.

There was no reply. Jim continued, mouth agape, to consider the picture of Caernarvon Bay on the wall above Bunny's head.

'The boy doesn't hear,' George said. 'Stay where you are, Lou, and enjoy the view yourself.'

Too late, understanding dawned, on Jim. It was often like that. There were so many noises inside his head to disentangle that comprehension was tardy and frequently coincided with a speaker's impatient dismissal. The effort was exhausting; one might as well give it up, hold one's tongue, think one's own thoughts, daydream a paddle in a Caernarvon sea. . .

'Deaf as a post,' muttered George, feeling irritated. He had pooh-poohed Rebecca's urgings that Doctor Griffin considered a surgeon might usefully examine the boy. Doctors knew nothing. The boy took after his Uncle Edward. And since there was a family pre- cedent, signs of stupidity were confidently expected, despite the teacher's assertion that Jim was quick with figures. 'Sixty minus twelve divided by four,' he barked at Jim one day, quite out of the blue – 'Come on! Make haste!' – and was vindicated by a blank stare and silence. 'Quick with figures, my foot! The boy's a fool. Just like Edward.'

'There's Warwick Castle!' Jim said now, pointing to the window. In the distance, round towers and battlements rose from a green-fringed river.

'So it is,' George conceded. At least the boy's eye- sight was in working order. 'Do you see, Louisa? My, what a setting for it! This'll be a day to remember.'

The Ludburys joined the throng pressing slowly up the narrow tree-lined way to the castle, spread themselves gratefully in the formal gardens below the orangery, then sauntered down a broad green aisle to the vast lawns of the pageant ground. Here, ropes, flags, stands and marquees designated the display area. High up in the central stand, the Ludburys disposed themselves – a giddy height, but forest giants beyond the marquees, cedar, oak and beech, kept things in proportion. A band played cheerily until the stands were packed and there was no standing space to be had along the ropes below. When the music ceased, a wave of silence passed over the crowd. A drum roll brought everyone to their feet. 'God save our gracious King!' they sang lustily. Then, the anthem completed, a roar broke out as the company rode from the marquees, flags flying, leather gleaming, tails like silken streamers; the smartest, shiniest body of men and horseflesh ever to gallop on English turf. To spot one's own among the glorious troop brought a lump to the throat, for a great thing was being done, and one's own flesh and blood was down there doing it. By God, this would give the Kaiser something to think about! 'There's Freddy! There's Edward! Do you see them, children?' Aunt Louisa bawled. No matter. Tom, Dick and Harry – not to mention Uncle Bill and Cousin Bob – were being claimed at full blast from all over the stand.

Smaller groups took the stage now, performing dazzling feats of horsemanship. Then Freddy, with five others, rode on. No one for yards around could have remained ignorant of the whereabouts of Freddy's supporters. 'Is that Freddy, George? I do believe . . . Yes! It's Freddy! Do you see, children? Do you see your Uncle Freddy? Doesn't he look smart? Oh, my! What a clever thing! If only Mama were here. . . George, I do wish Mama could see. . . No! Good Heavens! He can't be about to. . . oh, I can't look. He did it! Oh, Freddy! The brave, clever man! Clap, children. Clap Uncle Freddy!'

'Well done, Uncle Freddy!' yelled a man in the crowd, and a sea of grinning faces turned to where the Ludburys sat.

'Why doesn't George stop her?' Rebecca moaned behind her hand.

'She's excited, Mama,' Meg said. 'And he *was* splendid, wasn't he?'

'One can enjoy things quietly.'

'Not these sort of things. They carry you away.'

An hour later, Rebecca was thinking that one could have enough of a good thing, that there was a limit to the admiration one could summon up for a succession of horsemen doing very similar things, and it was with some relief that she understood the final item to be underway.

Every horseman rode out, the Warwickshires from the left marquee, the Worcestershires from the right, and formed two large circles at the extremities of the arena's diagonal. Swords were drawn and held to noses. Then, at a furious pace, a changeover began, a Worcestershire intersecting with a Warwickshire, horse by horse, until the circles had changed places. The process was almost completed when a hitch occurred. A rider, a short, red-faced fellow, pulled violently on his reins just as he was about to make the intersection. There was a cruel sawing of the horse's mouth, a violent swerving to left and to right, then, when it was already too late, a vicious kicking of the horse's ribs and a hopeless dash for it.

'The horse'll never stand for it,' George said, turning white.

The infuriated animal shot erratically across the arena with one urgent ambition: to divest itself of the irritant upon its back forthwith. It stopped with deadly abruptness and flung up its hind legs.

'Edward! Edward!' Louisa screamed as Edward flew through the air. The horse, well-satisfied, gave a jubilant back-kick and took off on a lap of honour.

Edward, meanwhile, came to his senses and cautiously raised his head.

'He's alive!' exulted Louisa. 'Thank God! He's alive!'

'Hurrah!' roared the crowd.

'Smother her, for pity's sake,' implored Rebecca through clenched teeth.

'Blasted fool of a man!' Meg said. 'Trust *him* to let the family down.'

George was begging Louisa to be calm.

Louisa's alarm was drowned by the enthusiasm which greeted Edward's recovery. He clambered to his feet, recognized (after some thought) his horse, and took off in pursuit – a gallant little figure, his bandy legs going like pistons.

Meg turned to her mother. 'I detest the man. I shall never forgive him. . . Mama! You're laughing! How can you? Think how awful it is for poor Daddy.'

'Heavens, yes.' Rebecca pulled herself together.

Determined-looking men ran into the arena and carried Edward off. The crowd groaned its disappointment.

Bunny started to snivel.

'Stop that at once,' hissed Meg in her most threatening tone.

'In a moment it will be over,' Rebecca promised. 'Then we'll go back to those lovely gardens.'

'Oh, good, Mama,' said Meg.

Bunny turned to Jim. 'Mama says we can go back to those lovely gardens in a moment.'

'What?'

She placed her mouth against his ear. 'The gardens. We can go back to them soon, Mama says.'

Jim's face lit up. All three children looked brighter. Ludbury in feature and emotion though they were, Rebecca's children loved gardens as she did, preferring them most distinctly to horses.

As the final applause died away, Rebecca resolved to make it up to George, poor man. It was a shame his relatives were so frightful, making idiots of themselves in public – and he so easily embarrassed. How thankful he must be to have left all that Ludbury silliness behind him and only be obliged to put up with it on rare occasions. With a rush of wifely protectiveness she vowed to restore his shaken manhood – as only she knew how – at the earliest opportunity.

'What a splendid day it has been,' Rebecca said, putting her hand over her husband's as it lay on the over-used tablecloth. It was dark in the tea-shop. People outside in the sun cupped hands to the window and peered in, hoping to see a vacant table. 'And we were so lucky to get a table.'

'Even luckier if we get served. Miss!'

A waitress hurried by, looking hot.

'It will be our turn eventually.'

'Can't bear these stuffy, poky little places.'

'I know, dear.' She lowered her voice and inclined her head to his before continuing. 'But it's such a treat for Louisa and the children. *Hasn't* she enjoyed herself? It was such a brainwave of yours.'

'I'm not so sure about that. You were right about Edward. . .'

'But *Freddy*. . . Nothing can detract from the brilliance of Freddy's performance. You wouldn't have missed that, George, now would you? And the whole thing was such a spectacle. Then the gardens and the picnic and the dungeon. . . Oh yes, it's been a marvellous day.'

This time the waitress stopped, pencil poised. 'Yes, sir?'

'Er, what d'you think, Becky?'

'Oh, tea . . . a selection of cakes . . . some scones, perhaps, and jam. . .'

'Tea. Cakes. Scones. Jam. For six,' George said with the air of a man who knows how to take a decision. He turned again to his wife. 'So you think – by and large – it wasn't too bad?'

She looked him steadily in the eye. 'It's been an altogether splendid day, George.'

And George began to feel that it had.

3

Germanophobia raged that winter, generating a heat more fortifying to the good people of Lipscombe than many a bright fireside. By spring, the desire for a showdown had grown to fever-pitch. News that the Territorials and the Yeomanry were to engage in week-long manoeuvres came as a relief – perhaps, at last, serious preparations were underway to deal the Kaiser a bloody nose.

George, like many employers, was approached by his foreman for a week's leave. Tom was confident. All Lipscombe bosses, it was felt, would be delighted by the prospect of a little inconvenience while their employees went off to do their duty in the hills; indeed, so great was the anticipated enthusiasm that there was some expectation of half-wages. On hearing this, George narrowed his eyes and carefully picked his nose. Tom, it occurred to him, was in need of guidance. 'Come into the scullery for a minute, Tom. Sit down. Take the weight off your feet. Glass of cider?'

Two cautious glassfuls were set down on the scrubbed deal surface. Neither man drank, but stared hard at the amber liquid. George was thinking of Tom, of how he had taken him on as an apprentice when he had first come to Lipscombe. He had taught him many things – all the fellow knew that was pertinent to making a living – but Tom was now a married man (George had responsibilities here, too, for Tom had courted his wife, the former Daisy Major, on Ludbury premises) and George saw that his education was incomplete. 'Well, now,' he said, looking up with a paternal leer – and then lost his thread, diverted by a trick of the light. Yellow glare from the lamp on a shelf above Tom's head cast hard shadow in the hollows of the young man's face, making it look extraordinarily skull-like. George screwed up his eyes until it was quite definitely a skull between hunched shoulders he saw opposite him in the lamplight. ''Xtr'ordinary thing,' he began, then took himself in hand (he really must guard against this butcher's obsession with the lie of the bone) and cleared his throat. 'I'm not sure you've thought this out, Tom. Have you considered Daisy and that baby that's on the way? These things make a difference, you know. Soldiering's all very well for the single fellows with no responsibilities, but it doesn't do for married men with children. Stands to reason. Where'd the women and children be if we all went off at Sergeant Littlejohn's behest? Answer me that. I know what you're going to say' – he held up a forestalling hand – 'Littlejohn's a family man and so are a thousand others for aught I know. Well, God help their families, that's all I can say. We've seen eye to eye on most things over the years, Tom, so just you mark my words: a man's first duty is to his dependants, for who's to look after them if he don't? And you needn't think it's the inconvenience, Tom. Nor is it the money.' He stopped abruptly, feeling rash as soon as the word was uttered. Quickly he headed for safer ground: 'What I mean is, I'd see Daisy all right. She'd not go short. There'd be eggs, meat, milk; I'd see to that. No, Tom, it's the principle that concerns me. You think it over. And drink up, lad, or we'll not be done tonight.'

In the morning, Tom offered George a communication from Sergeant Littlejohn. George declined to take it. 'We don't need go-betweens, Tom. If your mind's made up, then off you go.'

For six days Lipscombe was subdued. Though the children endeavoured to maintain martial order on the streets, the absence of stamping feet and raucous cries allowed an unfamiliar hush to creep over the town. On the seventh day the Terriers marched back along High Street. Life's normal pattern resumed: parading, speculating, and longing for the day when the Germans would be taught a lesson.

Relief came to Lipscombe in the final moments of an airless, sultry day. Windows propped open to encourage cooling draughts allowed the newsboy's cry to penetrate each home for the second time that evening. Children leapt from their stuffy beds. Their startled parents ran into the streets. 'Echo. Second edition. War declared on Germany.' The boy ran out of news-sheets and panic broke out in West Street.

'Come in here,' George cried, waving his smartly purchased copy. 'All of you. There's plenty of room and a good light here. I'll read it out, shall I? Then we'll know what to make of it.'

Her husband had assumed leadership again, observed Rebecca from the dark doorway between shop and hall. Her thoughts flew back to 1911 and the street parties for the Coronation. George, as patron, organizer and master of ceremonies, had ensured that the party in West Street was the most lavish and the most talked about in the town. And now they looked to him again, these neighbours made one body by the gloom and their common listening attitude – a body under continuous augmentation as children crept like mice from the shadows. 'Mama,' Meg whispered from the hall. Rebecca placed a finger to her lips and motioned her to pass into the shop. From the lamplit centre of the gathering, George's voice rang out – steadily, a little portentously – conveying all that The Evening Echo could reveal about the declaration of war.

When he had done, others found their voices. 'At last!' and 'About time!' were the favourite comments. 'Perhaps they are right,' Rebecca thought. 'Perhaps this will get it out of their systems and make them normal again.' (Though she kept it strictly to herself, Rebecca was heartily sick of hating the Germans; it had become such a predictable pastime and it had gone on for far too long.) The gathering shuffled uneasily, at a loss now that 'At last!' and 'About time!' had lost their freshness. Then the women had a brainwave: they would return home at once to work baskets and ribbon boxes and embellish their children's clothing with red, white and blue, ready for school in the morning. Hearing this, Rebecca's heart sank, for she knew her duty – Mallory House was never outdone. 'Meg!' she hissed. 'Gather up the children's clothes and bring them to me in the dining room.' And soon she was settled by a lamp with needle and thread, and a quantity of patriotic trimming left over from the Coronation.

'Well done!' George commended her, coming in.

'Darling, move! You're in my light. And that was very well done yourself. It would have been awful for the Misses Pogson to mull over the news alone, and some of the poor dears can't read.'

George backed away. 'Does Meg know?'

'Of course – trust her! She came down and I let her go into the shop to listen. I've sent her back to bed.'

He sunk his hands into his pockets and swung back and forth on his heels.

'I shan't be long, if you want to go up.'

'No, no. Not at all. No, no, no.' He watched her busy fingers enviously. Then, almost choking over the words: 'This has been a momentous day.'

'Hmm. Well, I hope people will keep their heads. Life has to go on.'

He considered this in silence, then turned towards the hall. 'I'll just see if she's . . .'

'Oh, don't George. She's got school in the morning. Don't disturb her.'

He was already on the stairs. 'Just say "Goodnight". After all, it has been . . .'

'A momentous day,' she muttered, snipping off red thread, reaching for blue.

'You awake, Megs?' he whispered, thrusting candle-light into the room.

'Yes,' Meg replied cautiously. Her father was not always pleased by her wakefulness, particularly when it involved Miss Angela Brazil. 'I couldn't sleep.'

'So you were down there. You heard all about it.'

'Yes.' She shot up eagerly in the bed, her back as rigid as the iron railings of the bed head. 'I was thinking, Daddy. Today will go down in history.'

At once he felt better; his craving for the right response satisfied at last. 'It certainly will, old thing.'

'Grandmama was right all along. She foresaw this day.'

'Did she, by Jove?'

'You remember, Daddy. In "England's Might":

> 'The mists of doubt will roll away
> On that valiant glory day.'

'See? And she said we should rise up in mighty multitude. Well, now we're going to.'

Pride all but asphyxiated him.

'Gosh! It'll be fine on Sunday. I bet we have a parade with flags and banners. . . Oh, if only I were grown up. . .'

'Whatever for?'

'To rise up in the mighty multitude, of course.'

'But ladies don't.'

She was silent, horrified by the waste, for she and Maisie Littlejohn were the cream of The Hollies fighting force – worth a dozen of the boys who quaked beneath their command. Her eyes flashed defiance in the flickering light.

He took her hand. She had the old girl's spirit, there was no doubt about it. By God! Mama, Charlotte and

178

Meg, what a trio. . . 'But ladies can inspire the men,' he explained huskily.

Inspire the men. . . Yes, she and Maisie were good at that.

'Better get some sleep, old thing.' George leant forward and kissed the frown between her eyebrows.

'Oh, Daddy. . .'

'Come on, or your Mama'll be cross. You'll have a busy day tomorrow, I shouldn't wonder. Night-night, girlie.'

'Goodnight, Daddy.'

Rebecca was still sewing in the dining room. 'Just Jim's to do,' she said as George passed through on his way to the kitchen.

He shut the door. He was up to something. 'Darling,' she called, 'do get off your feet. Your legs will be fidgety in bed if you keep on, and you know how that disturbs me.' No reply; just a faint commotion on the other side of the door. What an obstinate man! 'Remember that you have to be up early in the morning. You are still going to market, I take it?' Silence. Oh well. . .

Five minutes later the door burst open. 'Done it,' he announced, looking flushed.

'Good, and so have I.' She closed her work basket. 'What, exactly, have you done? And what on earth is that?' She looked in puzzlement at the lump of wood in his hands.

He held it out, grinning sheepishly.

'What *is* it, George? Good heavens! It's the bird from the top of the clock. You've sawn it off. Whatever for?'

'It's an eagle. A German eagle.'

'Why German? It's ours. Off our clock.'

'It's a German clock. A regulator. It just occurred to me as I was coming down the stairs. I heard it strike the hour. . .'

'But how *silly*! What does it matter?'

'Don't you understand, woman? This' – he brandished the offensive carving at her – 'is the German national emblem!'

'But who was to know? Really, George, fancy spoiling the clock. . . And such a waste of time – this war business'll soon be over and then you'll have to nail it on again.'

'Nail it on again?' he roared, hardly able to believe his ears. 'I intend to burn it! Now! Right away!'

Her stiff silence, as she gathered up the children's clothing and went into the hall, told him all: she thought him foolish, she was out of patience with him. He ran his fingers over the ridges of the bird's wings and wondered whether to leave the cremation for another day. No, darn it! He'd said he'd do it, and so he would. He'd show her. . .

Later, leaning over the grate, arm and forehead resting against the mantel shelf, he watched his small fire and thought bitterly of his wife. She had made it a furtive, futile thing with her uncomprehending disapproval. If she had but an ounce of their daughter's fine feeling they would have made it a ceremony together. If only Charlotte were with him now, or any of his sisters, come to that. . . By Jove, he was tired! Was the thing burnt sufficiently? He seized the poker and jabbed. A fountain of sparks flew against the sooty chimney breast and clung there, winking. Fresh flames flowered; yellow, vermilion, gentian-blue. A spurting, gaseous jet stung his nostrils and watered his eyes. For a dizzy moment, as he stared into the leaping colour – his eyeballs seared with heat and swimming in tears – his sisters, very far away, danced and writhed in the smoke from an eagle's pyre.

'Fancy missing the market; on beef cattle day, too,' Rebecca said, handing her husband a cup of orange-brown tea.

George was not himself. He had spent a restless night. Twice the jumpiness in his legs had obliged him to leap from the bed and bound about the room. Not a word of complaint had issued from his wife, but there had been a suggestion of 'I told you so' in her long-suffering smoothing of ruffled sheets and weary morning yawn. Damn it! Didn't she understand that everything had changed, that readiness to meet all contingencies was the new imperative? 'I thought it best to stay put today. There'll be things to sort out, arrangements to make. I'll have to see how Tom's fixed now,' he explained virtuously.

Rebecca regarded him in silence, noting his pallor, his hunched shoulders and drumming finger-tips. 'I should take something before your head gets really bad,' she advised, reaching for her own, personal teapot.

Her knowingness did nothing for his throbbing temples.

She poured into her cup a thin infusion of Darjeeling and Keemun leaves, a blend she had devised as an antidote to prenatal nausea and remained faithful to. It was her second pot of the day. Every morning George brought a tea-tray to her bed, for she was a poor riser and required encouragement to face the kitchen range. And every morning, as he set the tray down beside her, he scoffed at the weakness of the brew while his grin betrayed his pleasure in indulging so refined a taste. Now, as she sipped the smoky liquid, she considered his excuse. 'And how do you expect Tom to be fixed?' she asked with sudden sharpness.

'He hasn't been practising to be a soldier these past months for nothing.'

'But surely the regular soldiers. . .' But the sly look he assumed when ill at ease silenced her.

Running feet sounded on the floor above, then Emily's angry shout, and a child's cry trailing quickly into silence.

'George,' she said urgently. 'You must *talk* to Tom. Make him see that Daisy and the baby . . .'

He threw down his napkin. 'Don't you think I have already? Months ago I warned him, told him to give it up, to think of his responsibilities. He wouldn't listen. Off he went with that publican fellow.'

'Poor Daisy! How frightful for her!'

'I told him. I said "a man's dependents come first".'

'We shall have to look after her, George.'

'Of course.'

For a moment their eyes met.

He got to his feet. 'I'd better get on.'

'George.' She stretched a hand towards him.

He walked quickly to her side and put an arm around her shoulders. 'Now don't start worrying, old girl. . .'

Emily bustled in with Harry. 'We ain't 'alf feeling loik it this marnin',' she announced, pushing a truculent-looking four-year-old towards his mother. 'Shall Oi clear, Missus Ludbury?'

George hurried into the scullery, making for the yard.

'Not yet, Emily. I haven't quite finished my tea.' She smiled vaguely at her son, then looked firmly into her tea cup.

Emily understood that Harry was all hers. 'Roight, then, young master, yow'd better come up the garden with me.'

Rebecca sat at the deserted table, picking over her husband's words as if they were clues in a treasure hunt. She had suffered a pang of alarm, she recalled, and had then been comforted. 'I told him. A man's dependents come first. I told him to think of his responsibilities.' She made him say it again and again until she was quite at peace.

Four weeks later the young men marched out of Lipscombe. One final parade, one last bout of cheering and flag-waving and they were gone, and this time they would not come marching back along High Street at the end of the week. 'But they'll be back before Christmas,' the deserted told one another, for, as everyone knew, by Christmas the war would be over.

'Just think,' Meg mused enviously at supper that evening. 'Maisie's father has gone off to war.'

'Ridiculous man,' snapped Rebecca.

Meg was visibly shocked.

Rebecca persisted. 'At his age, with a wife and a sick mother, and how many children? Not to mention a public house to run.'

'Daddy!' Meg cried. '*Tell* her! Tell her it's a fine thing to be doing.'

But George, looking sly, got on with carving the ham.

'I shall call on Mrs Littlejohn,' Rebecca announced after some thought. 'This must be a dreadful time for her.'

'I shouldn't,' George put in swiftly.

'But darling! I know you're not keen on the Littlejohns, but there are times when we should put neighbourliness first. Remember how concerned people were when you were injured after saving that child from a trampling? It was such a comfort to feel people cared.'

George, having carved, sat down and waited as mustard, bread, and vegetables left over from dinner, circulated. How, he wondered, could he put it to her – that he was not, on this occasion, urging social caution, but that he had a strong urge for wariness in matters concerning the mobilization? He would rather not be obliged to voice this particular feeling. What was the matter with her? Her instincts were usually sound. She seemed to have lost her touch over this war business. And now Meg was busy making things worse.

'When, Mama? When will you call? May I come too? I think it's a grand idea – Mrs Littlejohn will be bucked no end.' Meg's enthusiasm stemmed from the sudden hope that difficulties surrounding her friendship with Maisie were about to melt away. 'Answer me, Mama; when will you call?'

But Rebecca did not hear. Her mind had frozen on a memory triggered by her own careless words: George rushing past at her command, out of the shop, into the street, hurling himself under the pounding hooves; thoughtless, heedless, instinctive. . . Abruptly, she rose, pushed back her chair and left the room.

'Well!' exclaimed Meg. 'What's got into her?'

'Just be careful how you speak of your mother!' George exploded. 'You're getting far too big for your boots these days, missy!'

The silent ones at the table watched as their sister turned an unpleasant shade of red. Bunny's foot reached out sideways and hooked itself around Jim's ankle. Under the long damask tablecloth, leg massaged leg in secret gloating glee.

Rebecca's proposed call on Mrs Littlejohn was forgotten. Even Meg found other concerns. She, like other well-grown children, found her labour much in demand as the loss of the most able-bodied from the town began to be felt. With the real soldiers gone there was no time to play at soldiers in the street. Before school and as soon as school was done they were at it: running errands, drawing water, chopping wood, tending animals, cooking, cleaning, hauling, mending. The streets became hushed channels of activity; people scurried through them, calling greetings in low tones. Only outside the Drill Hall was it permissible to linger, as if paying respects at a wayside shrine. Small groups clustered there to exchange news or speculate in the absence of news, eyes drawn to the padlocked doors of the hall, ears only half listening to a neighbour's words, for the stamp of hobnailed

boots persisted in the mind like an optimistic echo.
And there was never a parting without a variation of
the new, talismanic farewell: 'We'll have them home
for Christmas.' 'Ay, it'll all be over by Christmas.'

4

Freddy Ludbury swung along the corridor. On the
other side of the night-blackened window his reflection swung with him. The train lurched. Freddy caught
hold of the brass handrail and propelled himself with
some urgency to the end of the carriage. The lavatory
– praise be – was unoccupied.

Safely seated, he recalled that he had started to
feel queasy with the arrival, three days ago, of those
beastly papers. Since then it had been rush, rush, rush,
not a moment to think, everyone screaming (even his
sleep interrupted by that lunatic Pip raving at the foot
of his bed), horse and tackle to stow, kit to pack,
confusing instructions and this blasted train to catch.
Well, he'd caught it, and it was jolly well making off
with him.

Feeling calmer, he got up and washed. Then, with
some deliberation, he replaced the lavatory lid and sat
down. Things had got badly out of hand. It was time
for a hard think.

George put the tea-tray on the bedside table and turned
up the lamp. 'Time to look sharp.'

Rebecca groaned and pressed her face into the
pillow.

'Come on. I'll pour it out for you. Here. Do sit up,
Becky.'

'All right. Put it down for a minute,' she said thickly,
playing for time.

'Sit up, then.'

She wriggled into a suggestion of a sitting position.

'Shall I put an egg on for you?' (Shudders from the bed.) 'Bit of toast, then? Oh, come on, Becky, or we'll miss the train.' He thrust the steaming cup towards her.

She reached out for the cup and sipped from it to make him go. As soon as she was alone, she returned it to the tray and slipped lower in the bed. Four o'clock, she reflected bitterly, was a particularly vile hour to be woken at. There was something unspeakably harsh about the words "four o'clock" as applied to the morning. One o'clock and two o'clock, looked upon as extensions of the night before, had a charming sound, suggestive of dancing and wine, of love-making and intimate confidings. But the hours between two and six were better not mentioned; one should remain firmly unconscious of them; to be woken during them was misery of a perverse and unnatural kind. She cursed herself. She had been mad to agree to it.

'You haven't moved,' George observed, looking in on his way between bathroom and stairs. 'I shall go without you, mind. I bet the Poulters have set off already. Lord knows what that downpour did to their drive.'

'I'll be down in a minute,' Rebecca said, made alert by this reference to their friends. Molly Poulter could not be allowed to grab all the glory. How she would kick herself at Mrs Webb's tea party on Thursday if she were unable to cap Molly's account of a tearful, quayside farewell to her brother with a dazzling account of Freddy Ludbury's send-off. She must bear her present discomfort – beastly though it was – as an investment. Gritting her teeth, she withdrew her legs from their warm cocoon and thrust them into the early morning chill.

Freddy was engaged in his hard think. There was no doubt about it, he told himself: in the beginning the Yeomanry had been A Good Thing. It had come along in the nick of time when his stock had been on the low side. To be perfectly honest, he'd been up to his neck in it – sacked by the boss, in trouble with the bookmakers, and a kitchen maid casting aspersions. Yes, things had been looking distinctly messy. But the jolly old Yeomanry had worked wonders. Suddenly he was a good chap, mother and sisters pleased as Punch, and old George trundling his brats over to Warwick to watch him put Daisy Dapple through her paces. It was quite funny, when he came to think about it; he'd become a hero for pleasing himself. Life, in his experience, was not usually run along those lines. And what a lark it had been. What a time they had had, he and his hunting cronies. Of course, that had been the trouble: they'd been too busy enjoying themselves to notice that nasty red tape sneaking round them. Deceitful business, though, binding a chap hand and foot before he'd had a chance to squeak 'Whoa! Hang on a minute!' Suddenly all the fun had gone out of it. He couldn't say he cared for the new attitude – 'jump when I say jump without so much as a by-your-leave'. Damn it! Here he was squatting over a lavatory pan in the middle of the night, hurtling off to God knows where, and no one had troubled to ask him what he thought about it. Well, it was time Frederick Ludbury, Esquire, spoke up.

He got to his feet, seized the basin and squinted into the pock-marked mirror. 'D'you know, Freddy me lad?' he asked in tones of dawning resolution. 'I ain't sure I like it.'

Bedlam possessed the quayside; families sought or clung to departing heroes, porters with carts and men with lists shouted and shoved, horses whinnied and clouded the air with their breath. 'There's Daisy Dapple going on,' George bellowed in Rebecca's ear. They had left the Poulters hanging on to Molly's brother in the midst of the Gloucestershire contingent, had pressed on through the Warwickshires and, it now transpired, through the Worcestershires too; but had not yet come across Freddy. 'We'll go back a bit,' George said, pulling on his wife's arm. Where the Worcestershires milled they squeezed round every family group, studied every uniformed man, peered at baggage labels. 'I can't understand it.'

'Perhaps he's gone aboard already.'

'Never. He knew we were coming. I wired.'

'Well, there's no sign of him,' Rebecca said with an air of finality, reluctant to push through the crowds again.

Anxiety crept into George's face.

'Ask him,' Rebecca said, pointing to a man with a list.

'He looks busy,' George objected.

'Ask him.' She gave him a stove.

'Fre-de-rick-Lud-bu-ry,' enunciated the man un-pleasantly. 'Relative of yours, is he, sir? I see. Well, we'd all like to know the whereabouts of brother Frederick. Ticked off all correct at Worcester. Ticked off all correct on the train. Not a smell of him since – if you'll pardon the expression, madam.'

Rebecca backed away.

'All I can say is, sir, it had better be good.'

George looked blank.

'The reason, sir. The reason for brother Frederick's mysterious disappearance. Know what we do with deserters, sir?'

George turned on his heel, caught hold of his wife's arm and steered her rapidly away.

'George! Where are we going? Why don't we wait? He'll turn up. You know Freddy. He's slipped off for a drink.'

'Yes, I know Freddy,' George agreed bitterly. 'Blight-er's done a bunk.'

At that moment Meg was walking down Lipscombe High Street, a laden basket on her arm, rebellion in her heart. It was quite enough, she would have thought, to require Miss Ludbury of Mallory House to deliver provisions to Daisy Paxton's humble cottage, without insisting that she stay 'to lend poor Daisy a hand'. That, in her estimation, was taking matters too far. Yet these were the instructions left by her parents – at present disporting themselves on the south coast – and Emily, Daisy's successor, had been on at her all morning to carry them out. There was never a minute's peace these days. Her morning had been squandered cleaning silver with Bunny, her afternoon was now at their former maid's disposal, and tomorrow, her mother had said, she was to look after the younger children while Emily cooked the Sunday dinner, and take them for an afternoon airing while Emily had a rest. When, Meg thought she would like to know, was *she* to have a rest? It was the same story at school: she was taken advantage of, made to be an unpaid child minder. As for the lessons Miss Foley prided herself on preparing exclusively for Meg (Meg being the only pupil at The Hollies for whom a study of Algebra, Botany and French was considered appropriate), there was never time to give them more than scant attention. Her parents appeared to regard homework as a particularly heinous form of self-indulgence in these days of emergency. Meg was conscious of growing disillusionment. 'The fun seems to be going out of this war,' she told herself grimly, as she arrived in The Square.

A small crowd had gathered there. Meg spied Jim, and advanced on him severely. 'What are you going here? You were told to help old Lewis in the shop.'

'I am. He told me to deliver the vicarage joint.'

Meg looked at the parcel under his arm. 'Better get on with it, then; blood's coming through the paper.' Then, with a lift of her heart, she spotted Maisie Littlejohn. 'Hello, Maisie.'

Maisie nodded curtly.

'My parents have gone to see my Uncle Freddy off,' she informed her friend ingratiatingly.

'Huh,' said Maisie. 'Erwer Dad went weeks ago.'

'I know.' Meg was humble. 'I say, what's going on here?'

'It's they Belgies. Escaped from the 'Un. Darcter's took 'em in.'

Craning her neck, Meg saw a small family group newly alighted from a trap. Doctor and Mrs Griffin were leading them to their open doorway.

'Can't be very brave,' Maisie observed. 'If it was me, Oi'd 'ave stayed and defended me 'earth and 'ome. Oi'd 'ave given the 'Un what for.'

'Oh, so would I,' breathed Meg.

'They're not really little,' Jim reflected. 'The man's quite tall.'

'Wha-art?'

'Oh, never mind him,' Meg said hastily, fearing to be shown up.

'Little Belgians,' insisted Jim. 'Them who we've got to fight for.'

'Little *Belgium*,' Maisie hooted.

Jim, mouth agape, looked up at her, puzzled.

'He's a fool,' Meg explained hurriedly. 'Go and deliver the meat,' she bellowed fiercely in her brother's ear. 'I say, Maisie, are you doing anything in particular this afternoon?'

''Spose nart.'

'Neither am I – 'cept I've just got to deliver this basket. Shall we go up Bailey's Lane and climb that tree that hangs over Doctor Griffin's garden? We could spy on them. You never know, they might be enemy agents. They're foreigners, after all.'

'All roight,' said Maisie carelessly.

'MR AND MRS JOHN POULTER STOP MARINE HOTEL STOP BECKY TAKEN ILL STOP AM TAKING . HER HOME STOP GEORGE – that it?' asked the Post Office clerk.

'Yes,' agreed George, passing over his money.

'Now what?' Rebecca clutched the rim of the counter, feeling that the telegram might well prove prophetic before the day's alarms and excursions were over.

'The station. Quick as we can.'

'I'm running out of speed.'

'You'll get a good long rest on the train. Come on.'

Near the booking hall George studied the list of available trains. 'I think I'd better go straight to The Grange. Will you be all right if I put you on a train at Birmingham and wire Lewis to meet you?'

'No,' Rebecca said firmly. 'That would cause comment. Stick to the story in the telegram – take me home because I'm unwell. In a couple of days you can go to The Grange without anyone thinking anything of it.'

'You're right. If there's a scandal we don't want Lipscombe to hear of it.'

So it was that Meg, squinting over *A Fourth Form Friendship* by the frail light of a midnight candle, heard her parents in the hall below. In the morning she discovered the reason for this premature event: her mother had collapsed among the crowds on the quayside, and so ill was she, and so frantic was her father's anxiety, that no questions concerning Uncle Freddy's send-off could be tolerated. Doctor Griffin was sent for. (Meg thought it prudent to keep out of his way – she and Maisie had been obliged to make a hurried descent from the tree overhanging his garden.) But when the news of his prescription – complete rest and quiet – reached her, she groaned, for peace-keeping at Mallory House inevitably devolved upon her.

Two telegrams arrived at Lipscombe Post Office the next day. One of them went straight across the road to Mallory House. 'HAVE FOUND FRED STOP FIXED EVERYTHING STOP PIP', read George. He hurried with it to his wife's bedside. 'My God, Becky! If Pip's fixed everything, I reckon we're done for! Can't you buck up? I shall have to go over there now.'

'Hark,' Rebecca said, for a muffled bell had begun to toll. 'I wonder. . . You'd better stay until we find out what that is about.'

The second telegram was addressed to Mr and Mrs Webb at their drapery shop. Their son, Gerald, the telegram regretted to inform them, had been killed by enemy action.

'That settles it. You can't go now,' Rebecca told her husband when the news reached Mallory House. 'There'll be a memorial service.'

Two days later a letter from Charlotte absolved George from going at all. 'Would you credit it?' he exclaimed, jolting his wife's breakfast tray as he sat heavily on the side of the bed. 'Young Pip's saved the day. She found Freddy in some disreputable place in Birmingham – Charlotte says we shall have to tackle her about that – and took him off to see a doctor chum of hers. He signed a statement to the effect that poor old Fred was too ill to know what he was about. Ain't she a genius? Couldn't have done better meself. Only one snag, though.' His face darkened. 'The Yeomanry are going to send him to Ireland.'

'That's nice – not having to go abroad.'

'Good God, Becky! He'd be better off facing the Hun. The Irish don't fight face to face; they creep up behind and shoot you in the back.'

'Poor, poor Freddy!'

''Spose it serves the blighter right. I don't know,' he sighed wearily. 'I'll never understand why he did it.'

Rebecca was exasperated. Her husband had protested his lack of understanding too frequently during the last few days. 'Why will you keep saying that?' she cried, crashing her cup and saucer down on the tray. 'It's as plain as a pikestaff why he did it. I'm only amazed that hundreds didn't do likewise. I suppose they felt they were on a sort of treadmill and couldn't get off, poor things. I wonder how many considered where all that jolly marching was leading them? Not

192

many, I'll wager. Even those who had doubts would have found themselves stuck with it – their own families screaming encouragement on the pavements, boasting and trying to out-do each other. What a terrible predicament. . . So, George, complain if you must about the embarrassment Freddy caused us, but don't – please don't – say again that you don't understand.'

Well, this was nice. A lecture, eh? Feeling hard done by, George picked up the tray and left the room.

5

Lipscombe held its breath. A change of scene had been effected in the parish church, mourning colours had replaced patriotic banners, and the organ, abandoning its martial obsession, set a new, contemplative mood. The church was packed. People waited with bowed heads as the Webb family assembled in pews at the front of the nave and choirboys in black cassocks – stick-like and drab without their surplices – hurried from vestry to chancel. No one on that sunless afternoon could tell whether the change was momentary or the herald of a new era; but many were secretly comforted, believing the Webbs' loss made their own less likely. It was as if Gerald Webb was Lipscombe's sacrifice; further sacrifices, unless the town had a peculiarly poor run of luck, were not anticipated. For it was already November and, as everyone knew, by Christmas the job would be done, the Germans punished, and the dear boys home.

The following morning an eye-catching announcement was pasted across the central window of Webbs' drapery emporium: 'BUSINESS AS USUAL', it proclaimed. Lipscombe was impressed; this was just the sort of spirited defiance that would secure the British victory.

'What do you think of that?' Rebecca demanded of George, having hurried home to tell him about it. 'It's a very popular slogan. I'll make a notice for us. Where shall we hang it? Over the door or across the window?'

At once George became stony-faced. 'I'll take care of the business, if it's all the same to you. When I want your suggestions I'll ask for 'em.' He turned his back on her and became busy with meat skewers and string.

Evidently, the Webbs' bereavement had unsettled him. She hesitated for a moment, then walked from the shop into the hall. At the foot of the stairs she paused, her mind too engrossed to give her feet further direction. How on earth would he react if there were further losses – perhaps a more personal loss? Briefly, Tom inhabited her mind's eye. She pushed the image away. Nonsense. The blessed war would be over by Christmas, everyone said so. 'Well, God send Christmas is all I can say,' she muttered vehemently, climbing slowly to her room, for George had turned away from her and she was full of sudden dread.

Stricken Times

(1915–1916)

I

Old Lewis was serving a customer in the shop. 'Miserable sort of day, Mrs Ludbury,' the woman said as Rebecca came in from the street. Rejoinder, the merest response, was beyond her. She hurried through the shop in silence, let herself into the house and closed the door. In the hall she turned towards the stairs.

Meg ran out of the dining room. 'Mama, I thought it would be you. Guess what Uncle Biggins has gone and done. Go on, guess . . .'

Having gained the first landing, Rebecca turned to mount the second flight of stairs. Emily was on the top landing, sorting through a drawer of the tallboy. She looked up as her mistress approached but her greeting was stillborn. Forbiddingly, Rebecca carried her air of profound preoccupation past the maid to the door of her own room.

Shutting herself into the room's privacy, she relaxed a little, expelled the sour air at the bottom of her lungs – the residue of shallow, frightened breathing – and pressed a hand over her heart to encourage a more measured beat. After a time she began to remove her gloves – slowly, pinching up each finger tip until the tight kid tubes could be drawn easily from her hands – then smoothed them into shape and placed them in a dressing-table drawer. With equal thoroughness she undid the many buttons of her ankle-length coat, shook out the coat and hung it in the wardrobe. Finally

195

she dislodged hat from hair and placed it in the deeper drawer at the wardrobe's base.

All being done, the window drew her. The street was empty, there was no hint of comings or goings; even so, her eyes stared fixedly at the Post Office steps where at any moment the telegraph boy might appear, leap on to his motorbike and blaze away with another missive of doom. She was anxious to witness as many of these sudden exoduses as possible, for each dispatch reinforced her recent discovery that life's experience hitherto amounted to nothing. The more numerous the telegrams – and they came thick and fast these days – the more urgently was this startling knowledge impressed upon her. (Of course, if she missed the flight of the telegraph boy she would soon know about it, for the church bell would begin to toll.)

Life, she had long believed, was largely what one made of it. She was conscious of having turned most of its challenges and trials to her own advantage. And she had shown courage – she would have given George up if he had not broken free from The Grange. It had been easy to think these thoughts: life had turned out well and proved her comfortable philosophy sound. But now, steeling her eyes to further supervision of the Post Office steps, she wondered at her appalling simplism. She had failed to imagine farther horizons. She had been as a louse under a stone, believing the dark patch of earth inhabited by herself and her fellows to be the world, happily oblivious of passing, careless feet capable of exposing them to undreamt-of terrors. She shivered and gripped her forearms, for it was terrible to discover helplessness where autonomy and striving to good effect were felt to be the general order. Once, she reflected, before the days when telegrams loomed large, she would have sworn that, on occasion, rational beings change their minds, alter their action in the light of new experience. Well, she had been mistaken. To change course was treason. 'But we didn't know it would be like this,' she protested silently to the unimpressed street. 'It was to have been brief . . . remote . . . glorious . . .; not this drab, endless, insatiable slaughter. So why can't we stop? Why is it impossible to call a halt?' Shaking, she dragged a basket chair to the window and sank among its cushions, thinking of the day she had first become aware of omnipresent helplessness.

It had been a day soon after Christmas. She had been at this window, watching the speedy departure of the telegraph boy, when Emily had knocked on the door to say that Missus from the Post Office was downstairs and wanted a word. Rebecca had instantly guessed the nature of that word. 'The telegram was for Daisy,' she told her startled visitor.

'Why, yes! It went off just two minutes ago, Mrs Ludbury. I thought I should let you know at once – not that I can tell you anything, of course. But with you and Mr Ludbury having had so much to do with Daisy and . . . er . . .'

So it was already difficult to speak his name. 'Tom. Yes. Thank you. I shall go to her at once.'

Daisy, in her small kitchen, sat sprawled in a chair; her face bloated, stupid with shock. Already one of her sisters had arrived and was crouched, crying, over baby Tom. Questions were unnecessary: the telegram lay on the table. Looking at it quickly, spotting the words 'regret', 'Lord Kitchener', 'killed', it was 'nevermore', a word she had not read, that rang with hollow finality in her head. Looking at Daisy, who was now gasping and tearing her hair, Rebecca saw that it was 'nevermore' that had leapt at her from the scrap of buff-coloured paper.

'Go at once to Doctor Griffin's,' Rebecca commanded, dragging the widow's sister to her feet. 'Tell him to come at once. Explain that your sister has received bad news. Say Mrs Ludbury wishes him to come.'

Much later, Rebecca had thought of George. She found him in the scullery of Mallory House, sitting at the scrubbed deal table, staring into space. 'You've heard.' She could see that he had. 'I've been with Daisy. I had to get Doctor Griffin to her. I told him to send us the bill . . . George, it's cold out here. Come into the dining room.'

'Let's have Daisy and the child here,' he said suddenly, without moving from the table. 'We've plenty of room. We can keep an eye on them, take an interest in the boy . . .' He choked on his mention of the boy.

Rebecca sat down and stretched a hand towards him over the table top. 'I'll put it to her, as soon as she's able to take stock.'

He held her hand in a fierce grip, but avoided her eye. 'Doesn't seem five minutes since *he* was sitting there, where you are, and I was here, looking at him, thinking what to say, wondering how to talk him out of it. Do you know, Becky, I reckon I had a kind of premonition that evening? The daylight had gone, I remember; there was only light from the lamp up there. It did strange things to his face: for a moment I could have sworn his face was a skull – it really did look like a skull opposite me in the lamplight. What d'you make of that?' Briefly, he looked at her. Then he became angry and thumped the table. 'Dear God, if only I'd really laid into him, not just about his duty to Daisy and the baby, but to himself . . . If only I'd made him see the terrible waste there might be of *him*, *Tom Paxton*. But, of course, I never dreamt . . . none of us did . . . And it was only a trick of the light. Oh, Becky!'

'Oh, George,' she said helplessly, watching a tear run down the side of his nose and hang there hesitantly before dropping to the table.

Daisy had preferred to remain in her own home, close to her parents' cottage. She was visited daily by someone from Mallory House: George with a parcel of meat, the children or Emily with provisions, Rebecca with something she had just baked or a present for baby Tom. Huddled in her basket chair, Rebecca recalled that she had been returning from Daisy's cottage this afternoon when . . . (No. She would not think about it yet. She was still too raw, still too shaken.)

'Mama!' called Meg from the landing. 'Can I come in?'

'Yes.'

The door opened briskly. 'Emily says . . . What's the matter? You look frozen.'

'Emily says?'

'Are you coming down, or should she pour?'

'Good Heavens! Is it as late as that? I shall come down. Oh, poor Emily. I must pull myself together.'

'If you're poorly I could light you a fire in here, Mama.'

'No, darling. It's just that I had a rather trying afternoon.'

'With Daisy?' Meg asked, surprised.

'No, of course not. Something unpleasant occurred on the way home.'

'What?'

'Later, perhaps. Now, tell me what your Uncle Biggins has gone and done.'

'So you *were* listening. Well, he's gone and joined up. Attested, or something.'

'Oh, Heavens . . .'

'Daddy says they won't have him. The army won't want a religious maniac raving on about Judgement Day. It would put them right off their fighting.'

'I'd better call at the farm tomorrow.'

'Anyway,' Meg said authoritatively, 'Uncle Biggins is far too old.'

Apart from the occasional sigh and the soft crackle of firewood, now and then a rustle of paper and squeak of pen, a companionable silence pervaded the dining room. Rebecca and Meg shared the table, one studying accounts, the other atlas and textbook. The younger children had long ago gone to their beds, Emily was elsewhere enjoying well-earned recreation, and George, his business woefully understaffed, was still in the shop. When the German regulator chimed in the kitchen, Rebecca closed her books. 'Heavens, ten o'clock! You should be in bed, Meg.'

'Nearly finished.'

Rebecca locked the account books away in a bureau drawer and pulled up a chair to the fireside.

Meg sighed and closed her books. There would be trouble if she worked here any longer; she had better continue by candlelight, out of parental sight. She thought enviously of schoolgirl heroines – no errands, no washing up, no small children to attend to – forever grumbling about prep. Chance would be a fine thing! 'I do wish I could go to a boarding school,' she sighed – not for the first time.

And Rebecca gave her customary reply: 'But you have a family, dear,' – implying that only girls who lacked that blessing were sent to boarding schools.

'I know I have,' Meg said nastily.

Guilt smote Rebecca, for she had frequently observed to herself that The Hollies compared unfavourably, educationally speaking, with Miss Hyslop's establishment. 'When this war is over we'll talk to your father about it. There are good schools in Cheltenham. I don't see why you shouldn't go by train every day like Bessie Poulter. But we can't worry him at the moment. He's worked to death.'

'By the time the war's over I'll be too old,' Meg forecast gloomily.

'What a thing to say!'

Meg knelt by the fire and gave it a poke. Flames shot up with new energy. Heat lulled them. 'Mama . . .'

'Mmm.'

'You haven't told me yet.'

'Told you?'

'What happened. This afternoon.'

'Oh . . . that.'

'Well?'

'Well . . . a woman shouted at me in the street – keep it to yourself, I don't want to worry your father.'

'Of course. But how *awful*, Mama.'

'It was rather. And there were quite a few people about, which made it worse. She grabbed me by the arms, screamed into my face . . .'

'Who?'

'Mrs Truscott.'

'Oh, *her*. But she's batty. Everyone knows.'

'Poor thing! Widowed – three years ago was it? – and now lost both her sons . . . This war is so cruel . . .'

'But you must have felt horrid.' Meg put her arms around her mother's shins and sank her head on to her lap. 'Poor, poor Mama!'

'Yes, I did. Everyone was staring, or pretending not to. And someone – I don't know who – made an unpleasant remark which I'm sure I was meant to hear. . . . Darling, it's late. Goodnight.'

Meg got to her feet. She took her mother's hand and kissed it before applying the customary goodnight kiss to her mother's cheek.

Alone, feeling comforted, Rebecca allowed the demented woman's words to sound again: 'What's your man doin' about it? Hiding behind yer skirt, that's what. Why should you lart get arff scart free, dunnin' us with your 'oigh proices – us as makes the sacrifoices? Vultures, the lart o' yer!' And then that anonymous comment: 'These shirkers make me mad.'

'George,' she ventured when her husband at last sank his weary body into the high-backed armchair, 'you haven't pressed anyone, have you? I've been going over the accounts. I see one or two of them are

201

behind. We agreed to let the hard hit ones go . . . Mrs Truscott, for instance . . .'

He rolled his head against the back of the chair until he could see her beneath half-closed eyelids.

She was daunted by his scrutiny. 'I just wondered. There's been so much sacrifice lately . . .' Her voice trailed away uneasily.

'Why?' he asked.

'Nothing in particular.'

'Someone been gettin' at yer?' he sneered.

'Oh, no.' The denial was too prompt.

He grunted disgustedly. Then, after a long silence: 'Sometimes I wonder if it's worth the aggravation.'

'What aggravation? What do you mean?' Alarm coated her voice with uncharasteristic shrillness.

Then it came to her. People were getting at him. If unpleasant things were said to her, what, in heaven's name, was said to him? And he had to call at their homes, walk in their streets . . . 'Oh, George,' she cried, almost groaning with sympathetic comprehension. 'Oh, darling . . .' She reached forward and touched his knee. He made no move towards her. 'George?' she asked, unable to find the words to put her question.

'I'm going up,' he said roughly. 'I'm done in.'

And then she understood. They would never discuss it. It was impossible.

She knew what it was, she decided, some hours later as she lay staring into the dark, sleepless beside her tossing, dreaming husband. He could not admit to being hurt, to vulnerability – at least, not to her, for she was the motherless one he had comforted all those years ago. George the protector, Rebecca the protected – that was the way it had to be. But how lonely he must feel keeping it all to himself; the hostility, the barely veiled rudeness, the snide remarks purposely loud enough for him to hear.

George groaned and turned and flung out an arm. She lay very still, the weight of his arm across her stomach, hearing his breathing become deep and measured, fearing to disturb his sudden peace. Would he ever allow her to comfort him? She could not imagine it. Was there anyone in the world he could confide in? She doubted it. Then a memory flew into her mind – George and Charlotte walking on Astly Hill, she and Meg dawdling and laughing some way behind. George and Charlotte had their heads close together, their voices were low and earnest. Charlotte . . . Could he, would he unburden himself to Charlotte? Rebecca lay beneath her husband's arm and wondered.

2

Mrs Harold Ludbury was having a splendid war. Air raids threatened that summer of 1915, parts of London had been hit and it was rumoured that the Germans now set their sights on Birmingham. Newspaper reports were cagy – details left to amateur speculation. In the villages surrounding Birmingham, opinion became quite clear on the matter: though a chunk or two of the city might be lost without a qualm, no part of their respective parishes was expendable. Mrs Ludbury determined to be vigilant. She spent hours on the summit of Grange Farm's closest approximation to a hill, scanning the skies for Zeppelins, a pitchfork propped against a nearby gatepost so that hers should be the upper hand in the event of a German leaping from behind a bush. Edward – who had acquired a motorcycle – was instructed to be constantly alert for his mother's signal (red handkerchief waved vigorously overhead accompanied by blast on tin whistle), on receipt of which he was to race to the nearest police station. While she had eyes in her head, this portion of The Sacred Isle, if not inviolate, should at least be forewarned.

Edward, too, was enjoying himself. The motorcycle was a distinct improvement on the horse, having no will of its own, and with Freddy banished to Ireland there was no one to remind him of his duty to the farm. The old cowman and a boy did their best to keep things going, Louisa sorted out the money, and his mother was content that all reference to the farm had ceased.

War had brought a quiet revival of happiness to the third full-time resident of The Grange. After her enforced renunciation of Miss Sally Edmunds' company, Louisa had suffered miserably. On the Sunday following her mother's proscription of their friendship the most horrible event of her life had occurred. Matins being ended, she, her mother and Charlotte had shaken the parson's hand and proceeded along the church path to the lych gate; and there hovered Sally, waiting to exchange their customary greeting. Louisa often relived that walk in nightmares, her feet scrunching on the gravel, the bodies of mother and sister pressing hot warning on either side, and Sally, oblivious, waiting . . . Then she awoke, her dreaming self shying from that irrecoverable moment. But the conscious Louisa was bent on self-flagellation. She sat up, clasped her knees, stared into the dark and remembered. ('Step, step, step . . . Go on, draw level now . . . You know what happened then, what your eyes did . . . slid blankly across her face, stared straight ahead while your feet carried on . . .') Night after night she impaled herself upon her memory's bed of nails, seeking atonement through pain for her unforgivable cowardice. Then, in the spring of this year, Sally's brother (he who had boasted of capturing Louisa's fancy) died of his war wounds. Prayers were said for him at morning service, and Sally rose promptly after the blessing to hurry home. Louisa rushed prematurely from the Ludbury pew. 'I'm sorry, so sorry, so very sorry,' she said over and over again, catching and holding her friend's arm in the porch. They walked, one babbling, the other silent, into the sun. Mrs Ludbury brushed the parson aside and hurried after them. Seeing her approach, Louisa at last found the courage to face maternal wrath. 'I am expressing my condolences to Sally, for she is my dearest friend, and I don't care what you and Charlotte may say . . .'

'My *dear* Miss Edmunds,' shrieked Mrs Ludbury, interposing her agitated body, 'how brave of you to come! How I feel for you! Let me embrace you! Your brother was a hero, one of our nation's gallant defenders. Remember that. Let that knowledge bear you up in this hour of grief. Now then' – her tone indicated that she was coming to the point – 'you must come to The Grange very soon and tell me all about it. I wish to hear every detail – his wounds, his sufferings, his final agony – for I intend to compose a poetic memorial. Arrange it, Louisa. Walk home with Miss Edmunds and fix a day. Charlotte and I will go on. Come soon, my dear, while it is still fresh in your mind.'

It dawned on Louisa that a dead brother was a different kettle of fish. She glanced at her friend, then remembered that Sally was ignorant of the reason for their estrangement.

Sally never found time to fulfil Mrs Ludbury's invitation, but she invited Louisa to visit her at Home Farm, and their relationship began to recover. There were moments of deep embarrassment (an occasional unfortunate reference to an event that had occurred during their estrangement, resulting in blushes and confusion), but common enthusiasms put their friendship on a different plane with less dependence on their former girlish intimacy (an intimacy still secretly mourned by Louisa). Together they became stalwarts of The National Egg Collection For The Wounded (patron: HM Queen Alexandra, Louisa hastened to reassure her mother), working a joint shift at the local receiving depot and becoming hearty protagonists in the cause of the Rhode Island Red against the Irish Leghorn faction.

'Do you ever wonder if we are doing enough?' Sally asked Louisa one day. 'I do. I really do. So many young women have proper war work, I mean, take your sisters . . .'

'But we could never do what they do!' Louisa cried, thoroughly shocked. 'Charlotte and Pip are not *ordinary* girls. Besides, I don't think Edward could manage without me on the farm with most of the men gone now. Whatever would Mama say if she knew what I get up to? But I rather like leading the horses . . .'

'I suppose people do have to eat . . .'

'And we can't all be nurses . . .'

Charlotte and Pip were the jewels in Mrs Ludbury's diadem of patriotic motherhood. 'Give your sons!' the Mothers' Union exhorted. Well, she had given Freddy, and welcome to him they were. (The army might help itself to Edward, too; it was not *she* who had decided the farm had prior claim on his services.) She had also given two daughters, and Mrs Ludbury had no doubt which gifts were most becoming to the nation. Freddy, certainly, was doing a splendid job – he and a thousand faceless others – but Charlotte and Pip were leaders in their respective fields, expert, sought-after and dedicated.

Charlotte was a big noise now. Mrs Skedgemore had recommended her talents to the illustrious committee formed to accommodate the wounded. While titled ladies and retired military men squabbled among themselves, Charlotte got things done. She shuffled the Deaf and Dumb into closer quarters to make room for beds for soldiers, and persuaded her patron to give up a wing of the Skedgemore residence. Soon all the best houses were accommodating convalescent soldiery. She pursued her licence to advise, hector, upbraid and overrule with unflagging zeal, scarcely giving a thought, these days, to that perennial anxiety, the family interest. The wounded interest absorbed her: it had the merits of straightforwardness and immediacy. Furthermore, she reflected, blushing over a rather fulsome report of her doings in *The Birmingham Gazette*, it was refreshing to be thanked for one's pains.

Of course, Charlotte kept an ear open for news of Pip. This was not difficult, for Pip was now a senior nurse at the Birmingham Hospital and had achieved a measure of fame for her tireless, innovatory work with the more terrible wounds and injuries. Charlotte was reassured: if the reports were reliable her sister could have no spare energy for the kind of escapade that had so nearly besmirched the Ludbury name, and it was particularly gratifying to learn that a certain doctor – a certain married doctor – had taken his surgical skills to the battlefield.

Suddenly, at the beginning of November, the newspapers were full of Nurse Edith Cavell's execution. Within days Charlotte's complacency was shattered. 'Isn't it wonderful news about your sister, Miss Ludbury?' the senior nurse at the Home for the Deaf and Dumb enthused. 'I can't tell you how much I admire her. I'm afraid I lack that sort of splendid courage. But she really is an example of what Mr Asquith was saying in *The Times* – you know, that there are thousands of brave women none of us know about . . . I wonder if other nurses from here will follow her?'

With admirable self-control, Charlotte retired to consult the infallible Mrs Skedgemore, who in turn hurried to see the matron of the Birmingham Hospital with whom she was well acquainted. Mrs Skedgemore returned, breathless, with the news. 'Your sister's resigned. She's joined the Red Cross. She goes to the Front in a week.'

They regarded one another.

'Mmm,' Mrs Skedgemore nodded. 'And we know what *that* means. She's going after him.'

Charlotte lost no time. She claimed a week's compassionate leave forthwith, and set off for the The Grange.

'GRAVE NEWS STOP COME AT ONCE STOP WIRE ARRIVAL STOP CHARLOTTE' George read aloud to his wife. 'It's come from Headley Green, so she must be at home. Good God! Do you think it's Mama?'

'Could be Freddy,' Rebecca suggested.

'I shall have to go. But I don't see how I can. There's not enough help around here.'

'Of course you must go. At once. We'll manage. Edith's boys are only too glad of extra work. Don't worry. Just go.'

'Thank heaven for that,' she told herself, watching his departure. He had become so withdrawn, so white and strained, that this summons away from Lipscombe seemed to come as a godsend. So long as Charlotte's grave news was not too terrible. And then she surprised herself with the further thought that if George found he was able to confide in his sister she would be glad of it, for he was in urgent need of consolation.

Charlotte was waiting at the station. By the time she and George arrived at The Grange, he knew all: knew that Pip had abandoned the wounded in her care to follow her lover to the Front, knew that it was the talk of Birmingham, knew that it was up to him to take a firm line and save the family interest from further erosion.

Pip was touched to see him. 'George! All this way to see me? Isn't it good of him, Mama? I'm sure things are just as hectic in Lipscombe as they are everywhere else these days. And from the look of you, my boy, you're working too hard. Get more rest, George. I mean it!'

He was taken aback. Young Pip was changed. She was thinner, paler; above all, she was authoritative in a mild sort of way.

Mrs Ludbury was unchanged. 'Isn't it thrilling? Aren't you bursting with pride for your sister? Careless for her own safety, thinking only of our fallen warriors, she marches bravely forward in the footsteps of poor Miss Cavell. She is a heroine . . .'

'You're never going behind enemy lines?' George cried in alarm.

'Silly! Of course not.' Pip linked arms with her brother and led him towards a settee. 'But all the reports about Nurse Cavell set me thinking.' She spoke earnestly, craning her body towards his. 'They made me wonder what I'm doing here where there are so many to help – all these volunteers to back up the nursing staff. What am I doing here when there are not enough nurses at the Front? And, you know George, I'm really rather good at it. Nursing's the one thing I do that makes me feel totally in control of myself. I know I'm often scatty and excitable – it's worried me; I've sometimes wondered whether I'm barmy – you know, a bit mad!' She peered at him watchfully. 'But this is something I can throw myself into. It makes me calm; it makes me purposeful. My fingers are so nimble, so light and quick' – she looked down at them with surprise – 'they know just what to do when my heart sinks into my boots and my mind goes blank at the terrible sights and the ghastly smells . . . Of course, it's often too late. I'm always thinking: if only I could have got to the poor man straight away. So I'm going, George.'

He could see the old Pip now, eyes wide and gleaming, but not with malice, not with that trying mischief of hers. He swallowed, feeling quite overcome. 'Pip, old girl. I hardly know what to

209

say. But Mama's right. You *are* a heroine. Good luck to you!'

'George!' bellowed Charlotte. 'You know perfectly well what to say. Tell her we know what she's up to, that she'll stop at nothing to get after that man. Why, a friend told me that his poor wife fainted when she heard Pip was going out after him! It's immoral! It's disgusting! It can't be allowed! Tell her, George. We shall all be dragged down if she goes. Tell her she *must not* go!'

'You . . . creature!' Mrs Ludbury snarled in her senior daughter's face. 'You nasty, jealous creature! It's a pity *you* don't show a spark of gallantry instead of hobnobbing all day long with your gossiping, nosy-parkering, high and mighty cronies. You haven't one iota of your little sister's courage.'

'Ignore her, Mama. I always do. So long as I have your blessing and George's good wishes . . . Though I should go just the same without them.'

George stood up and kissed the top of Pip's head. Then he turned to Charlotte. 'I think we'll go for a walk. Come along, old thing.' Firmly, he led her away.

'I've had enough,' cried Charlotte, stumbling over a molehill. 'I'm at the end of my tether. This eternal worry about the family . . .'

'Do give it a rest, old girl,' beseeched George, steadying her. 'Let's enjoy the peace and quiet. I could do with a bit of peace, I can tell you.'

At once she was on to a new scent. George was in trouble, she knew it in her bones. Her tongue was stilled as her mind raced in new directions, each ripe with potential for anxiety.

They reached the spot where their mother watched for Zeppelins. George filled his lungs with good air. Marvellous, rolling country! You could see across to Herefordshire. 'Good Lord! Ain't that Louisa leading the horses over there?'

'Where? I can't see.' She followed his gaze short-sightedly. 'Surely not, surely . . .'

'Course not. Silly of me!' He turned to lean over a five-bar gate facing away from where the ploughing team toiled. 'Just look over here, Charlie. I reckon those are the Malvern hills in the distance.' She joined him, as he had known she would. 'This doesn't change. Whatever else goes on in the world, nothing disturbs this. This – the fields and hills and copses, the wind in the beech over there, and hundreds of birds you can't see singing their hearts out – this all goes on forever.'

Briefly, the concerns and frustrations of the present evaporated. Their minds, halted in their agitated tracks, became uninhabited. Only their senses soared, bombarded by the certainty that this vista, this soft polyphony, this rushing, fragrant breath across their skin, amounted to the only eternity they were ever sure to know.

Thought crept back insidiously, but warmer now and bent kindly on the other, for they were conscious of shared sensation.

She is good, thought George. Charlie is a good old stick. It was not her fault that she had developed an obsession for the family interest. *He* knew all about that, in fact he suffered from a touch of it himself. Like his siblings, he had imbibed the pre-eminence of the family interest with his mother's milk. Charlotte had taken it most to heart, that was all. And there was no great wonder about that. Charlie had grown up in Gussie's shadow – Gussie the favourite, the one expected to gratify every maternal ambition – and look what had happened to Gussie. Total banishment! No wonder Charlie had learnt her lesson well. He, like Gussie, had kicked over the traces, but his punishment had been temporary. Perhaps, as a male, he had promised, and so disappointed, less. But Charlie had gone the other way; no hint of rebellion in her, just unswerving adherence to their mother's line until she had become its chief exponent. George wondered if this irritated their mother, for he was sure she was not fond of Charlotte. Certainly not as fond as she was of Pip. What a shame that had been just now, that putting down of Charlotte's activities. Deceitful, too, for their mother was so proud of them that she had sent a copy of *The Birmingham Gazette* to Lipscombe so that Charlotte's famous doings should not go unremarked. But people like himself and Charlotte, working hard in the background, were easily abused these days. Those who struck out for glory were the ones who counted. Pip was lucky; she wanted something from this war and she was going out to get it. How he envied her autonomy. Yes, that was it. Being deprived of volition was driving him mad! Look, he had never shirked hard work – the harder the better – so long as he was his own man, in charge of his own destiny. He had a feeling, a fearful dread, that he was becoming a prey to circumstance, to the whim of others. Dear God! He must do something! He couldn't go on like this . . . 'Charlie!' he cried, choking back a sob. 'You've got to help me. You're the only one I can turn to . . .'

As if dreaming – for these were words desired beyond hope – Charlotte took his hand.

' . . . the only one. I daren't say a word to Becky. Her eyes follow me around as if I were a ghost. I can't stand the look in her eyes! I think she's sorry for me! Damn it, I can't have that! I'm the one who looks out for her, not the other way around! Of course, I know why she looks at me like that . . . . Do you know which two words haunt me in Lipscombe? Go on, have a guess.'

She made no attempt, just gazed at him in dumb, piercing love.

'All right, I'll tell you. "Shirker! Slacker!" They're the two words I hear without fail whenever I'm about in the town. "Something ought to be done about these

212

shirkers." "It makes me mad seeing these slackers getting away with it." That's the sort of thing I hear all the time. And I'm meant to, that's the point. How do you like that?'

He saw that she did not. Two fat tears burst from the wells of her eyes. He squeezed her hand. 'You were right all along. You warned me – remember? – about living in a street with common folk. I remember that day so well . . . We were leaning over a gate like this on Astly Hill, me with me ribs still strapped up from that trampling. I was watching Samson, poor old boy. (I often wonder whether I did him a service. Might have been better if I'd let Elton's vet put him down. I had to send him off, you know; he was commandeered. Didn't half upset me watching the old fellow go . . .) But I had me eye on him that day when you said I should get a proper house to live in, a farmhouse – put a decent distance between us and other folk. Oh Charlie, if only I'd listened to you. Poulter and Hawkins are all right, tucked away on their farms; nobody bothers them; and I've noticed they rarely set foot in the town these days. But I didn't listen to you. I was too full of the new businesses I was setting up. The cider factory was one of them. Well, I've had to shut it down – no one to work in it, and no one to drink the stuff. And I might just as well stop trading as a butcher; I've made a loss for the past three months – can't pass on the price rises without being slandered. It can't go on, Charlie, it can't go on. I'm so tired I can hardly think. Charlie, what am I to do? Oh, Lord! I've got to get away from the place.'

Charlotte knew her moment had come. Slowly, deeply, she drew in breath. 'Of course you must get away. At once! Away from those dreadful people. I shan't rest, I shan't go back to the Home until we have found somewhere suitable.'

'You're the best sister a fellow could have . . . But how shall we set about it?'

213

'I wonder if Ada could help us?'

'No. It can't be around here, old girl; it's too far to move the stock. You can't get a decent removal service these days. It'll have to be close to Lipscombe, but tucked away. And it'll have to be cheap – I'll never sell the business at the moment; I'll let it if I can and sell up after the war.'

'I shall come back with you, George. We'll go in the morning. I shall hire an agent.'

'Charlie!' He placed a kiss on her knuckles. 'But it might be better if you put up in Cheltenham. We don't want to alarm Becky before we have to.'

'Quite right, George! Much better keep her in the dark until we've settled it. That way there'll be no argument.'

'Dearest girl! Where'd I be without you?'

'You know you'll always have me, George.'

Arm in arm, invigorated with new purpose, they walked back to the house.

George found Louisa sluicing her boots in the scullery.

'George!' she beamed. 'What a lovely surprise!'

'Been busy, Lou?' he asked, winking broadly.

She stood there, letting water drip on to the floor; made as if to speak, then thought better of it.

'Never mind, Lou. Shan't breathe a word. And you're doin' all right. That was as straight a furrow as I ever saw.' He slapped her jovially on the rump. He was feeling better; quite his old self. 'Time for tea, Lou, ain't it? Time for a nice bit of tea.'

3

'Christmas is an abomination,' Rebecca decided, observing her husband on the other side of the fireplace. He sat up straight in his high-backed chair, knees spread and braced, Bunny astride one thigh, Harry astride the other. 'One is obliged to be jovial, which is all very well when things are going nicely . . .'

' "Ladies go: trip, trip, trip," ' intoned George, bouncing the children delicately.

'Just look at him. Determined to be jolly at all costs . . .'

' "Gentlemen go: trot, trot, trot." '

The children, bounced more vigorously, tightened their grip on his knees.

'. . . Determined, however sharp his anxiety, to make them laugh . . .'

> ' "But the old man stays behind
> To have a glass of wine . . ." '

The children squealed and braced themselves.

> ' "And . . . then . . . he . . . goes . . .
> Gallopy, gallopy, gallopy, gallopy,
>   gallopy!" '

Jigged hard enough to make their teeth rattle, the children shrieked and begged for more.

'. . . Perhaps he *is* enjoying himself,' Rebecca wondered hopefully. He certainly deserved to be. If only *she* could shed her misery for a moment, but it seemed to have taken root like a new and troublesome organ somewhere in the region of her stomach. However hard she tried – producing delicacies from the pantry, treats from the sideboard, presents from the bottom of the wardrobe – Christmas could not lift her spirits; rather, she resented it as a tyrannical imposition, a particularly cruel test of endurance on top of everyday desolation. The worst of it was that it made one hark back to other Christmases: their first Christmas in Mallory House (what a celebration of confidence in the future that had been!), and last

Christmas, the first wartime Christmas, when war was to have been over and done with. Last Christmas had been a brutal feast – so many ghosts at the table, so many hopes mocked. There had been many more ghosts at this year's Christmas tables, but hopes had long since gone. Prayers were most urgent now for the cessation of thought and the pacification of feeling.

'Down you get. Sally's turn.' George divested himself of Bunny and Harry, and held out his arms to his three-year-old daughter.

Sally, lolling against her mother's knee on which she had placed a rag book, appeared doubtful.

'Go on; darling,' Rebecca urged.

She approached her father cautiously, to be swept high in the air before being placed carefully upon his lap.

' "Ladies go"?' he inquired.

She nodded and grabbed his waistcoat for support. Soon she was bouncing and laughing in helpless delight.

Bunny, watching with a dark scowl, pulled a hank of hair across her mouth to gnaw on.

'Get out the cards, Bunny,' Rebecca suggested.

Bunny obeyed with the air of one behaving well about the booby prize.

Rebecca rose and went to the table where Meg sat over a book and Jim sat dreaming by a bowl of marshmallows. 'Come on, you two. We're going to play rummy.'

'Who's Daddy's pretty baby girlie?' George sang merrily to Sally.

'You deal, Bunny,' Rebecca said hastily. 'Give them a good shuffle. And I hope your hands aren't sticky, Jim.'

Jim obligingly licked them.

Meg shut her book with as good a grace as she could muster. Harry wove his toy train in and out of their feet. And Bunny cheered up; she would probably win; she usually did – she enjoyed a game of cards,

216

and her pleasure was doubled by the knowledge that Meg did not.

A sense of well-being stole over Rebecca; the room felt comfortable, so very normal. 'Perhaps, after all, things will turn out well,' she told herself with a resurgence of her old faith. 'This time next year we may be sitting here, playing cards, laughing with the children, and be truly carefree. Who knows, by then it really may be over . . .' 'Do get on with it, Jim; you're holding everyone up,' she cried snappily, superstitiously annoyed with herself for having briefly entertained hope.

4

January 1916. This month's effort in aid of the wounded was to be a sale of work with tea and biscuits at Lipscombe Hall, by kind invitation of Mrs Simmonds. The Lady Amelia Elton had promised her presence, a beneficence rarely bestowed since the death, last October a the battle of Loos, of her son, the Honourable Peter. As Rebecca folded tissue wrappings over her embroidered tablecloth she wondered which of those two great ladies would succeed in purchasing it. Their genteel battle to acquire pieces of Rebecca's needlework had become quite a joke among Lipscombe ladies; Lady Amelia was reckoned to be ahead with a set of tray-cloths, pillow cases and a mantel drop to Mrs Simmonds' cushion covers and chair backs.

Time slipped back for a while at Lipscombe Hall. The women busied themselves in familiar ways; laying out stalls, setting out tea things, fingering contributions, exclaiming over coveted items and casting politenesses over the rest. Rebecca felt at ease, the graceful occupant of a particular niche in Lipscombe society, pleasantly acknowledged by all with the appropriated degree of condescension, friendship or deference. The quality of her tablecloth was acclaimed: hers was a valued contribution. Mrs George Ludbury, for a time, relaxed.

The tablecloth was snapped up by Mrs Simmonds. There was no contest; plainly, the Lady Amelia had no stomach for battle that afternoon. Some surprise was expressed about this – *sotto voce* – behind the tea urn, for the Honourable Peter had been famous for his ability to arouse a hearty maternal contempt. 'Well, well, well . . .' 'It just goes to show . . .' 'When all's said and done a mother's still a mother . . .' But there was no cause for alarm, it was decided; the Lady Amelia was too high-spirited to be cast down for long.

It was as the ladies were clearing up, that the familiar, easygoing atmosphere was disrupted. Rebecca was helping Daisy to fold the huge sheet that had covered their stall, when a sudden draught caused heads to turn towards the doorway. Mrs Dancey, who was known to have left half an hour ago, stood there, brandishing a copy of The Gloucestershire Echo. Her breathlessness indicated that she had returned with speed. 'It's . . . official,' she gasped. 'Compulsion.'

'At last!'

'No! I thought they'd never make up their minds to it.'

'About time!'

'I should say so! I'm fed up with these shirkers.'

'Well this'll sort 'em out. Up to what age will they be compelled, Mrs Dancey?'

'Forty-one . . .'

(And George, thought Rebecca, clutching her throat, was only forty.)

'. . . all the unmarried men under forty-one.'

Rebecca's breath escaped noisily. She glanced about her, but no one had heard, they were too busy protesting.

'What rubbish! Why should the married ones get away with it?'

'It's an insult to the widows.'

'Just look at all the married men who've gone . . .'

'Mr Littlejohn, Reggie Farlow . . .'

'Daisy's Tom . . .'

'At least you've the comfort of being able to hold your head up, Daisy . . .'

Daisy, with a horrified glance at Rebecca, turned away.

An embarrassed silence fell.

'Oh dear!' the last speaker wailed. 'I'm sure I meant no offence, Mrs Ludbury.'

Nothing personal, no offence meant at all, they assured her; and then fell over one another in their haste to pack up and be gone.

Mrs Simmonds moved in to restore the tone. 'I have always held,' she proclaimed loudly, 'the airing of unsolicited opinion to be most unfortunate. In fact, I thoroughly disapprove of it. Now' – she turned to Rebecca with a gracious smile – 'tell me, Mrs Ludbury, how is Mr Ludbury? How well I recall his courage in saving that wretched boy . . .'

'Do, please, be silent,' Rebecca's eyes implored. She resolved to leave at once.

Rose Slatter, who knew how to take a cue from her betters, called after her: 'Wait for me, Rebecca. I'm coming too.' And she seized Rebecca's arm in ostentatious affection.

For the length of Hall Lane, all along High Street until they reached Slatter's grocery shop, Rebecca was obliged to endure an intimate perambulation. Fortunately, Rose Slatter's flow of inconsequential chatter was endless, for Rebecca, when the time came to say farewell, found herself speechless.

It was late; it was time to be thinking of bed. George reached with a poker towards the fire and battered the last burning log into fragments. 'Gave you a hard time this afternoon, did they?' he inquired – apparently of the shattered embers.

Rebecca, who had been silent for much of the evening, rushed to deny it. 'Oh, no! Not at all! It was a very successful afternoon. My cloth was particularly admired. Mrs Simmonds bought it.' She watched the look she disliked – a cunning smirk, laced with disbelief or disdain – develop around his mouth and eyes. Blow! She had let an opportunity slip there. If her reply had been honest, the unspeakable might have been spoken at last and the chasm between them bridged. 'Well,' she countered herself, 'they could not be said to have given me a hard time exactly; nothing *personal* was intended, but you know what that lot from Castle Lane cottages are.'

He shifted uneasily and lowered his eyes for a moment to the newspaper on the stool at his side.

She swallowed, clasped her hands and gathered her courage. 'Remarks were made, and I must say I became rather uncomfortable. How I detest these words that are bandied about indiscriminately: you know, "shirkers", "slackers"; they are so unfair . . .' Seeing him wince, she let her voice trail away.

'I suppose,' he said at last, '*this* brought it on.' He jabbed with his forefinger at *The Gloucestershire Echo*. 'I daresay they didn't like it, that the married men are let off?'

'Oh, George . . .'

'For the time being, that is.'

'What?'

'Let off for the time being – the married ones.'

'But you don't think? Surely it won't come to that? Anyway, you've almost reached the age limit; by July . . .'

Her alarm seemed to amuse him. 'Poor old Becky. Put you through it, didn't they? What a shame, when there are so many married men who can't wait to join up. Ol' Sam Biggins, for instance – I wonder how long before they're reduced to taking the likes of him? Anyway, I bet nothing's said to Edith, with Sam attesting and showing so keen. That's an idea – maybe I should offer myself to spare you the embarrassment. Is that what you'd like, Becky?'

'What are you saying? You can't be thinking of it?'

'Can't I?'

Dear God, he was teasing her! Softly, she began to cry.

He came to his senses. 'For heaven's sake! Do you really think I'd do it? Do you think I've such a poor opinion of myself that I'd let a brainless pip-squeak like Elton tell me what to do?'

'He's dead,' she whispered.

'There are plenty more like him. They're the ones running the show. Good God! No wonder there's carnage. The Honourable Peter Elton, leader of men!' he went on in a quieter tone. 'Another thing, Becky; I don't believe in family men goin' off to fight. I told Tom that, and I meant it. Fightin's for soldiers. I'm a patriot, you know that, but I know where m' duty lies, and it ain't on the battlefield. I know what's best for me. I know what's best for my family. And I shall darn well see that we do it.'

Relief rushed to her head like wine. 'Darling!' she cried, going pink. 'Oh, darling! We're going to stick it out! Of course we are! I should have known! From now on I shall close my ears to the nastiness. Now I know where we stand I shall be strong – it was the not knowing, the never talking about it that made me uneasy. Sooner or later it will come to an end and things will get back to normal. Then we'll start again, pick up the business, lick it back into shape, see all our friends again, be happy again . . .'

'Are you mad?' he roared. 'Are you a complete fool? Business back to normal with half our customers dead or destitute? Can't you see straight, woman? And what friends have you in mind? Friends? I tell you I never want to set eyes on these damn townsfolk again . . . once we get away from here.'

So that was it. Ice froze her heart but cleared her head. So there had been something to fear after all; the churning dread of the last few months had had a solid foundation. But she had not foreseen this. 'Get away from here?' she asked with deceptive calm.

'It's settled. We leave this place at the end of the month. I've taken a farm.'

'Where?'

'Knoller Knap.'

'Knoller Knap?' she repeated incredulously. 'You mean *on* Knoller Knap?'

'The house is about halfway up. The farm covers the west side of the hill – the top two thirds, more or less. Ridge Farm.'

'Ridge Farm. *Ridge*,' she repeated with bitter emphasis.

'It's an ideal spot, don't you see? Right out of the way. No one'll bother us up there. There's only a dirt track and that gets too steep near the top for any but determined callers. We'll be all right there, Becky, snug and cosy and private, hidden from the world until this war blows over. The important thing, I reckon, is to be self-sufficient. It's not bad land, I should be able to provide us with a living single-handed. That's how it's got to be: just us, no workers, no maids, no hangers-on; no reason for anyone to interfere with us.'

'You can't mean it.'

'Of course I mean it,' he bellowed. 'How much longer do you think we can go on like this? It's grinding us down – the hostility and the worry – and it's not as if we're making a proper living; you know that as well as I do.'

The room appeared to lurch. She gripped the chair-arms. 'Surely . . . Emily . . .?'

'I said *no hangers-on*. No paid help for me and none for you. The girls'll have to do their share. It's only a small place . . .'

222

She no longer heard him, heard instead Doctor Griffin's serious words uttered only a month or so ago: 'You're doing too much; that's why you get breathless. Slow down. Get another girl in. You do understand what I am saying? It's vital that you take life more easily.' But she couldn't repeat them now, not when George was so agitated; it would seem like an excuse, enrage him further; he had always been scornful of doctors and their opinions. Perhaps, if moving to this place were only a temporary measure. . . . 'George,' she said, interrupting him, 'you haven't sold Mallory House?'

'I've let it. And Sam can make use of the land on Astly Hill for the time being.'

'So we can move back here when the war's over?'

He cursed furiously and leapt to his feet. From the sideboard he took whisky and a glass.

'This is our life,' she pleaded. 'We built it together. We've been so happy, so successful. It's us, George, this house, this business; don't throw it all away.' She stretched a hand towards him. 'So long as we've got each other, darling . . . George, look at me! Let's be brave! Let's stick it out!'

He drained his glass and turned to her. 'You've no idea,' he said bitterly. 'No . . . i . . . dea. After all I've been through you'd have me crawl here on my hands and knees, begging custom from those who've slandered me.' His voice grew loud. 'You'd put me through that, so that you can go on with your tea-parties. Damn it, woman' – he was shouting now – 'you'd let your husband be made a fool of, so long as everything went on just as you like it.'

'No, no,' she protested, wringing her hands.

'Oh, yes. Fine wife you are. It's lucky for me I've a sensible sister. She doesn't snivel and whine, she gets on with it. She found Ridge Farm. She took time off from her own concerns . . .'

223

'Charlotte? You mean *Charlotte* found this place on Knoller Knap?'

'That's right. Put up in Cheltenham for two weeks. Sorted everything out for me . . .'

'Behind my back! How *dare* she? What's it to do with her?' Rebecca was shouting now.

'Everything. She cares about me. She'd rather I didn't have to face those foul-mouthed women every day of my life. If only I'd listened to her years ago. She warned me about shop-keeping and living in a street; she always said I should get a proper farm and live respectably . . .'

'Damn and blast her! Damn and blast your detestable sister! She's been out to wreck us from the start – and now she's done it! Scheming, spiteful, sour-faced witch! Devil . . . take . . . her!'

'Well!' The scales fell from his eyes. '*Now* we're hearing it. *Now* we're getting the picture. Mama always said you Sheldons were a nasty, common lot, and wasn't she right? Look how you all turned out: sister a downtrodden slattern, brother a penniless brawler, and you shoutin' and cussin' like a barge woman . . .'

'What do you know about my brother?'

He laughed unpleasantly. 'You asked me to find him, didn't you? Well, I found him in a Gloucester doss house – lost him again pretty darn quick – didn't want to hurt your feelings. That's rich! You ain't so particular, are yer? You don't mind cussin' a lady. You're no better than the rest of your family. You're nothing but a . . . shop girl!'

'Shop girl?' she repeated, bewildered.

He sank down on his chair. Suddenly he was confused, couldn't think, for the life of him, why he'd used that particular epithet. He knew he was tired, though, by Jove. 'Look,' he said quietly, 'get to bed. I'll sit here for a bit. We're both overwrought – better if we forget what's been said. The main thing is, we're getting away from here. Start thinking about

224

the arrangements tomorrow, will you? Perhaps your Mrs Simmonds will take Emily on – you said she complimented you on training her so well. Anyway, we've just over a month to settle up.'

Rebecca stood up on shaking legs and left the room.

Meg, who had been drawn by raised voices to listen on the stairs, scampered up to the top landing. From the shadows she watched her mother pass and enter her room. She shivered there for a while, chewing her knuckles; then, losing patience with herself, crossed the landing and rapped on her mother's door. There was no reply. She opened the door and walked into the room.

Rebecca, at her dressing table, had removed her hairpins: a single thick hank of hair snaked down her back. She was motionless, as if hypnotized by her own reflection.

Meg came and stood behind her. Her heart ached, and she longed to ease it by performing some daughterly act. 'I'll brush your hair for you, Mama,' she said, and took up the silver-backed hairbrush. 'I'll brush it fifty times like you always do.' She sank the yellow bristles into the black peak at the top of her mother's forehead – though it didn't look so very black tonight – and pulled it slowly over and down so that the thick hank spread and became a fine, cloudy mass. 'One . . .,' she chanted, raising her arm again, 'two . . .'

The Hill

(1916–1918)

I

Wind was king on Knoller Knap. There were days
when it hummed peaceably about the hillside, others
when it moaned and whined; and there were bilious,
roaring days when dogs were worked up to howling
frenzy and humans so battered that the stoutest efforts
of lung and larynx were instantly annihilated. The terrain was wind-swept and scrubby. Looking down, the
view was of tree tops in thick clusters and a scattering
of roof tops in a greener, softer land. The ascent to Ridge
Farm began along a narrow, winding, tree-lined lane;
then came a steep curve and the earth veered towards
the vertical. At this point horses hesitated and engines
faltered, but the knowledgeable walker pressed on:
soon the lane would swing sharply to the right and
peter out into rough farm track running horizontally
around the hill.

There was treasure in the hillside, a spring of liquid
crystal gushing from a rocky channel immediately
opposite – and above – the farmyard. The water was
well known in the locality for its ability to restore
fading eyesight, and in all but the roughest weather
its devotees climbed the hill to fill their water bottles.
'You see what we have here?' George gloated whenever
a pilgrimage to the spring was sighted. 'Pure, wonderful water. Water folks'll climb all the way up here for.
We shan't hurt drinking it – be able to see in the dark
before long, I shouldn't wonder. I tell you, it's better

than anything that ever came out of a tap.' (A fortunate attitude, for there were no taps at Ridge Farm.) His enthusiasm fired his children – with the possible exception of Jim, whose duty it was to fill water pails night and morning – and they drank and raved over the water as if it were vintage champagne. Rebecca, as had become her custom, forbore to comment.

George was a new man. Escape from Lipscombe had released new energy and optimism. Setbacks and difficulties were swiftly revealed as providential. The removal cart was unable to get up the steepest part of the hill, but, by great good fortune, the farm stock had been brought over the day before and it was a simple matter to hitch up a horse and cart and ferry the stuff to the house. And the absence of a cooler in the milking shed was but a temporary drawback; with ice-cold spring water close by, all that remained was to apply a little ingenuity. Everyone, save Rebecca and Sally, spent the first evening in the cowshed, busy by lamplight, passing up hammer, nails, pieces of rope, holding things in place, hanging on to the ladder for George, who fell at one point and gashed his head, but continued undeterred, head bound tightly in a towel to staunch the bleeding. When the job was finished he milked the complaining cows. Daddy, the children decided with swelling hearts, was truly marvellous, and they could not admire the cooling system enough.

It was as well that George's enthusiasm was infectious, for life on Knoller Knap depended heavily on the children's labour. Jim was not only water hauler for house and yard, but assistant cowman, pigman and yard sweeper. Harry, too, learned to make good use of a broom and to fetch and carry for animals and workers. Bunny became the poultry keeper. Meg had declined this role; poultry – their quivering pink bits, jerking heads and swivelling eyes – disgusted her, and she dreaded their tendency to become, without warning, a squawking, wing-batting flurry of feathers, beaks and claws: the sooner live poultry became dead poultry the better for her peace of mind. Instead, she became her father's right-hand man in field and barn, devoting the daylight hours after her return from school to the horse team and the mangle.

Late one afternoon, about two months after their arrival at Ridge Farm, Meg was returning there from school. She sniffed the air in the lane appreciatively. May blossom. At once a scene evoked by the Principal Mistress during that morning's Assembly came back to her: May morning at St Ursula's College in Chelsea, a group of fair maidens rouse an even fairer maiden from her bed, enrobe her in a wondrous gown stitched by an army of other – possibly less fair – maidens, garland and crown her with blossoms, lead her across the dewy ground to a throne of flowers where, before an assembly of students, staff and illustrious visitors, she presides over the May ceremony – the whole event devised by that artistic genius, Mr John Ruskin, who took such a kindly interest in the college maidens towards the end of the last century. This year, the Principal told an attentive school, the position of May Queen was filled by one of their own, a previous Head Girl of Cheltenham High, chosen by her peers as the truest, fairest and best among them; it was to be hoped that a proportion of the girls now sitting cross-legged on the floor beneath her would aspire, in due course, to emulate their distinguished sister. 'I shall!' Meg now cried as she rounded a bend in the lane. 'I shall train to be a teacher at St Ursula's, and in my final year I shall be May Queen.'

'What?' yelled Jim uncouthly, sliding down a bank on his bottom and landing, dishevelled, at her feet. 'What yer say?'

She ignored him; simply registered the fact that once again her brother had not been to school but had spent the day dawdling in the hedgerows and now proposed to accompany her home as if he, too, had recently alighted from the Cheltenham tram. Lazy blighter! But it suited her to let him get away with it; for one thing, it was a hold over him that might come in useful, for another, it would fall to her to deliver him each day to the Boys' Grammar School should their parents become aware of his truancy. There were too many inroads into her time already; and it was clear that she had a lot of academic ground to make up. On her admission to Cheltenham High School for Girls her learning had been diagnosed as patchy and she had been placed in a class of girls younger than herself. From this her new school mates deduced that she was an idiot, a deduction she swiftly demolished with a display of sharp wits in the classroom and fearsome play on the hockey field. 'Oh well *played*, Margaret Ludbury!' the games mistress was heard to scream whenever the Lower Fourth took the field. Before half-term, Meg was invited to play for the school. 'I'll show them,' she vowed into the wind. 'I'll be put up into the Upper Fourth next term, I'll be Hockey Captain, I'll be Head Girl, and I'll get to St Ursula's.'

They had reached the steepest part of the climb, but Meg was unaware of increased effort. Silently, she rehearsed her good fortune: if she had remained at school in Lipscombe she would have stood little chance of reaching the standard required for entry into a teacher-training college – not that such a possibility was ever entertained at The Hollies. What a pathetic little place that now seemed. She was glad to have escaped; glad, even, to have parted with Maisie Littlejohn. Now *there* had been an embarrassment – Maisie had returned to school after last summer's long vacation transmogrified into a coy, simpering ninny, deferring to the very boys she and Meg had ruled over so strictly for so long. Meg's bewilderment had obliged her to reconsider her father's estimation of the Littlejohns; perhaps they were rather low sort of people after all, and doomed to inexplicable acts of vulgarity. Happily, the heroines of Cheltenham High seemed unlikely to turn into oglers of inadequate boys.

Of course, one had to take the rough with the smooth, Meg reflected as the lane swung to the right and disintegrated into rough farm track; the move to Ridge Farm had been instrumental in securing for her a superior education, but the farm itself took a great deal of her time. Never mind. It was a pleasure to help Daddy who was so cheerful, so resourceful, so *enthusiastic* – unlike another person she could mention – and it would do no harm to instil in him a sense of obligation. Daddy, of course, would be called upon to pay for her extended education. She had a suspicion that her ambition would cause him some surprise – not altogether welcome surprise. It would be prudent to keep quiet about it for the time being and be as obliging a daughter as any hard-pressed father could wish for.

They were close to the farm buildings now, sounds indicating milking in progress could be heard between wind gusts. Bunny came running towards them, a hen tucked under her arm. (Bunny and Harry attended the village school and had arrived home an hour earlier.)

'What are you doing with that?' Meg demanded, eyeing the hen.

'Silly broody thing! I'm waiting for Daddy to wring its neck. I don't want it to put the others off laying. Daddy's going to show me how to pluck it.'

Meg received this information in silence. Gratifying though it was to learn that something alive and offensive was soon to be rendered dead and inoffensive, a rather horrid keenness in her sister's manner encouraged the suspicion that the fowl's mistress anticipated an active role in the execution. She could not bring herself to inquire whether this was so; instead she strode on with her nose in the air, thinking gratefully of the content of tonight's homework – the works of Pythagoras and Tennyson.

'On either side the river lie
Long fields of barley and of rye,
That clothe the wold and meet the sky; . . .'

'Its very rude to ignore other people and talk to yourself,' objected Bunny, running after her. Meg frequently passed her over as a conversation-alist in favour of a monologue, and it was very irritating.

'She's always doing that,' Jim confirmed before breaking into a run as the back door – affording access to the pantry – came into view.

'Just wash and get out to the milking,' Meg yelled after him. 'No need to stuff yourself, it'll soon be tea time.'

'Very, very rude,' muttered Bunny, going off with her hen.

From the scullery door Meg heard a breadknife attacking a loaf, then her mother's harsh cry: 'Don't make crumbs! I've just swept.'

'And don't, please, trouble yourself to say "hello" to anyone,' Meg commented silently. Aloud, she said loftily: 'He's hungry.' Then, turning towards Jim: 'Do hurry. Tell Daddy I'll be out directly, just as soon as I've changed my clothes.'

'Meg!'

That hateful snappy tone again. Ignoring her mother, Meg made for the stairs.

Rebecca returned her attention to the kitchen floor. Having swept it, she prepared to scrub it – George had made a biting remark about its condition this morning. From the range she took a saucepan of hot water and emptied it, with a sprinkling of soda into a pail. She took scrubbing brush and kneeling pad, hitched up her skirt and sank awkwardly to the floor. As she scrubbed, the thumping began again – the noise of her heart in her ears – and her chest was squeezed in an iron grip, reducing her breathing to short, painful gasps. Cold sweat broke from every part of her body.

Meg clomped back down the stairs in her working clothes. As she came into the kitchen, Rebecca reached out and seized her arm and used it as a lever to haul herself to her feet. 'Here!' she said hoarsely, fearing she was at the point of collapse. 'Finish it!' She pressed the scrubbing brush into Meg's hand, stepped over a damp patch of floor and sank into a chair. She could not explain. Words cost too much, drained energy from resources already exhausted.

Meg observed her, tight-lipped. 'Very well' – she tossed her head contemptuously – 'since you ask so nicely.' She got down to it, set about the floor with vigour, anxious to be done, anxious not to keep her father waiting.

Rebecca failed to hear the footstep in the yard; it was a darkening of the doorway that galvanized her. She cast herself to the floor, pushed her daughter aside and grabbed the brush. 'Go!' she hissed.

Meg saw how it was: her father was not to know the reason for her delayed appearance in the yard; her mother must receive full credit for the well-scrubbed floor. She got to her feet, extended a toe and caught it under the handle of the bucket. 'Then see how you like *that*, madam!' she cried, as the pail toppled and its contents rushed over the floor.

Rebecca, on her knees in the water, looked up at George.

He ignored her. He ignored the flood. Keeping his eyes strictly on Meg he asked: 'You coming, or what?'

'Yes, Daddy. Sorry I'm late. I was kept.' She picked her way towards him.

'Time to cut a bale or two before tea, d'you reckon?' They went out into the yard. 'I say, Megs, guess what old Glory did this afternoon . . .'

Their voices faded, but a sudden shout of laughter and an 'I say!' from Meg were borne backwards by the wind to reverberate with hollow spite in the sodden kitchen. A passion of weeping filled the room, an explosion of crying broken only by harsh, gulping intakes of air.

'Mama . . . don't . . .' Sally's command was laboured because of the effort required to pull her mother's hands from her eyes. 'Please, Mama . . . don't . . . don't.'

With an effort Rebecca controlled herself, panted quietly for a minute or two, then drew the solemn-faced child close. 'We're wet through,' she told her superfluously. 'Two drowned rats.' They laughed weakly with relief. Suddenly Rebecca came to a decision. She pushed the child gently from her. 'Go quickly, darling, and fetch Harry and Bunny.'

She made no attempt to stir herself until Harry appeared, and then she startled her son with the first smile he had received from her for weeks. 'Harry! Will you get this mess up for me, dear? There's a cloth under the sink. And Bunny . . . whatever are you doing with that bird?'

'Waiting for Daddy to kill it.'

'Well, when he's done it will you get the tea for everyone? Not for me – I'm going to lie down. I feel rather ill.'

Tea began as a jolly affair. Bunny was allowed to preside over the teapot, for, as George pointed out, they had her to thank for a well-stocked table; it was thanks to her, too, that they had a chicken dinner to look forward to on Sunday.

'Change from rabbit, I suppose,' Meg mumbled.

Flushed by flattery, Bunny became animated. 'You should have seen Daddy kill it. He was so quick! He just grabbed hold of its neck like this . . .'

'Not at the table!' roared Meg.

'Bit squeamish, are we?' smirked George.

'Certainly not! But if you want me to help you in the hayfield after tea you'd better let me eat it in peace.'

'Mama always cuts up a whole loaf,' ventured Jim.

Meg considered the matter. 'So she does. Cut it all up, you silly girl. We're hungry.'

George sighed. 'How long do you suppose your Mama's going to keep this up?' he asked his eldest daughter.

'Sulking, you mean? Heaven knows. If she's not sulking she's snapping our heads off.'

'She *not!*' Sally objected forcefully. She was regarded with some surprise. 'She . . . poorly.' The final word was a small explosion. Tears began to roll down her cheeks. Knuckles were pressed into eyes. 'She vewy poorly . . . She *fwightened.*'

'Come here,' George told her, holding out his arms. 'Come to Daddy, little Sal.'

She wriggled from her chair, rushed to him and collapsed against his chest.

'There, there. Daddy's best baby girl mustn't cry. Daddy make it better – you see.'

At the breadboard, Bunny forgot what she was about. Knife poised in mid-air, her eyes flew to the hands pressing Daddy's best baby girl to Daddy's capacious chest. Lovely hands – squeezing a podgy knee, caressing the back of a babyish neck. Clever hands, too – twist, snap, done! Her memory busily replaced the neck of a broody hen with the neck of Daddy's best baby girl. She swallowed. Her throat was dry as dust; a crumb lodging at the back of it moved with explosive effect. ('Not all over the loaf, for goodness' sake!' Meg shrieked.) Bunny ran, choking, through the scullery and into the yard.

George was still crooning over Sally. She was calm now. He set her down. 'Now then,' he said, lifting her chin with his hand so that their eyes met. 'Tell you what we'll do. We'll make your Mama a pot of that nasty weak tea she's so fond of, shall we? And take it up to her.'

Sally nodded eagerly.

Meg, Jim and Harry got on with their tea.

The room was dim. 'You all right, Becky?' he whispered, putting the tea on the bedside table. He peered at the eiderdown mound.

'No, George,' she said distinctly.

He turned to the child at his side. 'Daddy's going to stay and talk to Mama. Go down to Meg, there's a good girlie.'

Obediently, she left them.

He sat on the edge of the bed and thought. After a time he said: 'It's too much for you.'

'Yes.'

'You should have said.'

'Oh!' It was a scornful sound.

'I know. I should have seen. It's far too much. And it's not as if you've done half these things before.'

'No.'

'And having little Sal took it out of you . . .'

She turned her head away from him.

'I *am* sorry, Becky; truly I am. Look, we'll get a daily woman. How'd that be? There's no room here for a maid, but we could get a woman from the village to come up every day. Tell you what: keep Bunny home for a day or two until I've fixed something up. You need a good rest.'

'I think I'll go to sleep now.'

'Drink your tea, old thing. It's your special sort. Come on, I'll help you sit up.'

Propped back against the bedhead, she took the cup and drank. He watched her, feeling tender. 'I'll bring you a coddled egg later. You've got to get your strength back. Oh, Becky, I'll make it up to you.'

236

She passed him the empty cup. 'Send Sally back to me, please.'

'Right you are. Snuggle down.' He re-arranged the eiderdown, kissed her forehead and went away with the teacup.

She lay on her back staring at the undulating strip of light between curtains and window top – poor scraps of stuff, the curtains, hurried makeshifts suspended from rings on a rod, with no redeeming fullness or pelmetting. What was she doing in this oppressive little room where the wardrobe, wash-stand and chest of drawers pressed close as vigil-keepers at a death bed? This room knew all about death – what bedroom in an ancient house did not? But this room lay in wait for it, hushed with expectancy. The noise of life could be heard; from outside, the sounds of animals and humans about their business and the wind buffeting the windows and moaning on the hillside; from within, the sounds of eating done with, the faint clatter of crockery, hurry of feet, slam of a door. Yet this small chamber was a core of silence. She was not here willingly; let there be no mistake about that. She had been placed here . . . There had been another time: her first night at boarding school, lying in one of a parade of beds lining a long, narrow room, watching the moonlight through a crack in the curtains, crying inside herself: 'What am I doing in this alien place, why am I here?' Shameful, at her age, to be susceptible to schoolgirl emotion. Too bad. She was too tired to care. This room with its dingy walls and stained, sagging ceiling, could have her . . .

A noise in the little dressing room next door where Sally slept – a room hardly more than a cupboard – awoke her. Just George, she decided; George getting Sally ready for bed, for there was no sound from the other side of the landing where Meg and Bunny occupied one of the two remaining rooms and Jim and Harry the other. Soon George came in, Sally –

nightgowned and smelling of soap – in his arms. 'Here's the little lady, all ready for bed. And Bunny' – he added proudly – 'told her a bedtime story.'

'But I didn't like it, Mama,' Sally whispered when he had gone. 'There was a wicked witch who gobbled up little gels.'

'What a pity, darling. Let me think of a nice one.'

By the time the nice story was done, Sally was asleep. Rebecca raised herself on an arm and gazed down at her child, at the heart-stopping wonder of her. There she lay, her limbs spread and limp, her lips moist and slightly parted, breathing sweetly – dark lashes curled on shiny cheeks, dark hair curled thickly over the pillow. Her skin felt buoyant and rubbery, Rebecca found, touching cheek and arm. Oh, she should stay like this for ever! She could not be improved; she was perfect! Then, with a stab of fear, her eyes fell on the faint blue tracery of veins at temple and throat . . .

'We are so fragile,' she thought, 'yet we imagine we can move mountains, survive an artillery barrage, emerge, unscathed, from a thunder of hooves. The evidence is overwhelming . . .' And she recalled long lists in the newspapers, whole pages given over to a recitation of names: the dead, the missing, the wounded. She thought of her husband clambering on the cowshed roof in the dark and of blood seeping through a towel binding his head. But he did not contemplate his fragility; the move had invigorated him, for the war was not the stuff of everyday life on Ridge Farm; here, there was only the challenge of securing a living for them all on this wind-battered hill. Nevertheless, George was not in his pioneering youth, the work was hard and he had become susceptible to injury, particularly late in the day when he was tired and jobs remained to be done. She thought, then, of herself, hag-like in her mind's eye, and recalled Doctor Griffin's parting instructions to her. 'You'll have to be sensible – Mr Ludbury does understand that, I hope. Pace yourself, do nothing strenuous or taxing – stop at once if you feel taxed . . .' Ridge Farm was certainly taxing. Would she survive Ridge Farm?

At her side, Sally stirred. 'I ought to put her to bed,' Rebecca thought, knowing that she would not. She had become a procrastinator, a self-deluder, of late, forever telling herself that she would do this or that – find the summer frocks still packed away in a trunk and stored, like so many of their belongings, in the barn; teach Sally to sew, to play the piano, to make a flower garden; the very things, she now saw, that make the difference between a life worth living and a drudge of a life devoted to mere survival – knowing full well that she would do none of them for she had insufficient energy. Well, somehow, she must conserve energy for them, for Sally's sake, for these were Sally's precious years. 'If only we get away from here in time,' she cried under her breath; and her hand became a bracelet running up and down her daughter's arm. 'If only I can last out. There are so many things we can do together, Sally and I. We must get away from this blasted hill.'

2

Mrs Maule was unable to oblige on a daily basis, but agreed to devote five days a week to the Ludbury household. This proved relief enough – 'a life saver', as Rebecca fervently remarked, and Mrs Maule appeared to endorse this view of her favours, for she was by no means humble. Rebecca, who had employed women to 'do the rough' for many years, was puzzled by this omission of deference. Was it due to the lack of a housemaid as intermediary, she wondered, or to the tradition that Ridge Farm did not run to servants? Or was it a consequence of George's presentation of the situation – he it was who had found and employed the woman; did he give her to understand that his wife was a poor, incapable thing? For whatever reason, Mrs Maule did not trouble to disguise her low opinion of her mistress and her satisfaction with her good self. Rebecca tried to put a distance between them, but found it difficult to maintain, working, as they so often did, along similar lines and in close proximity. And her craving for adult female company got the better of her. Soon her overriding concern was that Mrs Maule should think well of her, should understand that, though physically incapable of a comparable application, her ambitions for the household were commendably high and that she was grateful beyond measure for Mrs Maule's contribution to their realization – as, indeed, she was. A satisfactory relationship evolved, one in which Rebecca deferred to Mrs Maule in matters domestic, and Mrs Maule learnt to view Rebecca's taste for time-wasting pursuits – fancy cooking, fancy needlework, fancy gardening, book-reading and tinkering on the piano – with a fond, indulgent eye.

At this very moment Rebecca was wasting time – lying on her back, staring at the ceiling, listening to the wind spitting rain against the window and to Sally murmuring a story to herself – but it was with Mrs Maule's urgent blessing. 'Yow'm got thart narsy blue look about the mouth again. Yow'm havin' one of your bard days,' she had said accusingly, with a head-on-one-side scrutiny and an arms akimbo no-nonsense-will-be-tolerated stance. Rebecca admitted it at once. 'Oi knew et!' came the triumphant cry. 'Yow shud never 'ave done all thart cukin' this marnin'. Toim fer your rest now, anyway. Go arn up, an' don't let me cartch you book-readin' when Oi come up with your tea. Get some prarper rest. Leave young Sally down 'ere with me.'

'No, no. She soothes me . . .' And so she does, Rebecca now reaffirmed, listening to the child soliloquizing at her side, throaty and tender as a pigeon at dusk. She reached out and gently stroked the child's cheek. Sally smiled, but continued her sing-song narrative. 'She likes her own stories best,' Rebecca thought fondly.

Every afternoon she retired to her room with Sally, leaving Mrs Maule to clear the aftermath of the midday meal from the kitchen and to set about the ironing or other afternoon chores. Usually Rebecca read for an hour then got up to work in her garden or to sew. But there were days like today when fatigue sang through every nerve in her body, when she could weep for the spent force she had become and she aspired to nothing but unconsciousness. Well, she had slept for an hour and a half. Any moment now Mrs Maule would come in with the tea. She must take care not to become animated during these waiting moments; Mrs Maule would be disappointed if she failed to discover her lazy with sleep.

Footsteps on the landing. The door was pushed open. Rebecca stretched and yawned as the tea tray rattled into place on the bedside table.

'Moi! Yow 'ave slept well! And yow'm a much better colour. There now, and Oi shud stay where you are when yow've drunk et . . . Yow can't go gardenin' en *thes'* – indicating the weather at the window. 'Oi'll take the little 'un – Oi'll be 'ere another 'our yet. Yow doze arff again.'

'No. Sally and I are going to play the piano in a moment. But thank you so much, Mrs Maule. Whatever should I do without you?'

'Oi don't know.' Her tone became grim. 'Fool'ardy, it were, bringin' a lady of your delicate nature up here. Et's the wenter as worries me, when this place gets cut arff from below. What're yow t'do then, Oid loik t'know, when Oi can't get up tow gev yow a hand?'

'Oh, don't, Mrs Maule,' begged Rebecca, who had already been treated to several accounts of the rigours of winter on Knoller Knap. 'At least I've got you now, and I feel a hundred times better for it.' She gave Mrs Maule's hand a grateful pat.

When Mrs Maule had gone, she sipped her tea and reflected that her last remark had been no exaggeration. Life on the hill prior to the coming of Mrs Maule had receded into scarcely believable nightmare. How could she have allowed George and Meg to bully her into a self-destructive round of toil? She had lost all self-regard. It was as if she had concurred with their contempt for her and had set about grinding herself into extinction. It was ironical that as soon as her strength and spirits began to recover – because she was no longer the chief house worker – George had found he could spare any amount of his precious time to indulge her. He had brought a piano tuner over from Cheltenham so that Sally's one-fingered rendering of 'Twinkle, twinkle little star' should ring out good-humouredly. He had dug over a plot chosen by Rebecca for a garden and built a rockery with the unearthed stones. He brought plants and flower seeds home on market days, and embroidery silks for her work box. 'To him that hath shall be given,' mused Rebecca. When she had had nothing – no strength of body or mind, no hope or joy in her heart – he had given nothing, he had trampled on her. Heavens! This would never do! She sprang from the bed and pulled a shawl around her shoulders.

A low whistle, cattle lowing – sounds made artificially loud then cut off by the wind: she went to the window and peered out. Heavy-uddered cows lumbering by. A couple of dogs, sleek, wet, black but for their white-blazed foreheads, running low-bellied up and down the track. Then George, dejected because of the rain – he had hoped to finish harvesting this week. Was the harvest home, she wondered, on Astly Hill? With a pang she recalled that she had not seen her sister for months. Determination seized her; she wrestled with the catch and flung the window wide.

'George! Will you take me to see Edith when harvesting's done? Will you, George?' but the wind blew the words back in her face.

'Wha-at?' he bellowed, gesturing hopelessly.

She shook her head and smiled to show that it was no matter.

Autumn was in the air. Smelling it a few days ago, Rebecca had been smitten by dread of the coming winter. But today, rattling along towards Lipscombe, she sniffed the indefinite odour of stagnant foliage without a qualm. Today was to be spent with Edith on Astly Hill, and on the way there she and George would halt in Lipscombe – she had made sure of this by loading the trap with gifts. 'All this for the Bigginses?' a surprised George had asked, indicating three laden baskets. 'Oh no,' she had hastened to reassure him. 'One is for Nurse and one is for Daisy. We can hardly go through Lipscombe without calling on them.'

The news had filled him with gloom. He felt let down, and began to recall how very good he had been to her of late – got her a daily woman, encouraged every sign that she was coming out of her long sulk, even agreed to take a whole day off to visit her dreary sister. 'And blow me if she doesn't expect me to hang about in that awful town,' George marvelled, his irritation with his wife resurfacing fast. 'Well, she'll have to look sharp or we'll have all those foul-mouthed women clustering round.'

Rebecca, one arm around Harry, the other around Sally (the older children had been left behind to tend the animals), experienced a surge of exhilaration. Ahead lay the town where she had been happy, buoyant, a success. Those days had not long gone and would come again. A sense of travelling with purpose and of imminent arrival filled her with optimism. She saw that her present weakness of body and spirit would pass – who, after all, had not been enfeebled

243

by this war and its encumbering sorrows? – and she would be as she had been before, a little older, perhaps a little slower, certainly a little wiser, but essentially confident and fulfilled. And if not here, then elsewhere – there were other Lipscombes, no doubt. The children felt her excitement and looked up into her face. 'We used to live here,' observed Harry. 'I liked it.'

'So did we all,' cried Rebecca, giving them a joyful squeeze.

George could hear nothing but the wind, the hooves, and the rattle of the trap. Grimly, he watched High Street, with its possibilities for horror, run joltingly to meet him. He had foreseen a brisk trot through the town, he had planned it all in his mind, rehearsed the exact point at which he must pull up the reins so as to take the corner into West Street at a safe pace. But *she* was not satisfied with that, being taken to visit her sister was not enough. Come to think of it, if visiting one's relatives was on the cards, The Grange should have had first call on his precious time, for The Grange now housed Freddy, discharged as unfit for further military service after being damn near blinded in a Dublin street battle. That incident had occurred at the end of April and it was now the middle of September. He had been neither to the hospital where poor old Fred was patched up, nor to The Grange. He must go there soon, before the days grew too short. Meanwhile *this* business had to be got over. 'Whoa,' he called, preparing to take a right turn into Castle Lane.

'Harry will hold the horse, darling,' Rebecca called gaily. 'Come and see Nurse.'

'I'm staying here,' George said firmly. 'Make haste about it. We don't want to attract attention.'

'But, George . . . Oh, I see what you mean.' A small cloud slipped over her bright conception of the day. 'Nurse, dear! We can't stop. Well, just for a moment . . .' Her voice disappeared with her body into the stuffed interior of the tiny dwelling.

It was Sunday. With luck – George pulled out his watch – church would not be out for another half-hour. Come on, Becky . . . At the window of the adjacent cottage a curtain twitched. Higher up the lane a woman came to her gate and put up a hand to shield inquisitive eyes from the sun. George recognized her: shoulder of lamb alternating with shin of beef every Saturday, sausages every Thursday. Come on, for heaven's sake . . .

'. . . miss you too, dearest Nurse, I can't tell you how much. But we'll come again soon. Won't we, George. I've been explaining to Nurse that we'll come back one day when we've more time.'

'That's right,' George confirmed briskly, gathering the reins. 'Whatever did you go in for?' he asked as they moved off. 'For pity's sake just drop the things on Daisy.'

'I can't . . .' But her protest became inaudible. Back across High Street, past the church – yes, he thought there'd be a gathering in the square; always was a gossip-ridden place – and into Old Lane.

Near Daisy's cottage children were playing hop-scotch in the dust. A sullen lad, lolling against a tree, looked on.

'Gawpers already,' observed George. 'Get a move on, will you? That lot in the square had a good look at us, too.'

'Surely you'll come in to see little Tom?'

'Another time. Do hurry, Becky.'

Before Rebecca had reached the door it was pulled open. 'Missus Ludbury!' cried Daisy, bursting into tears.

George shifted uneasily on the hard seat and transferred his attention to the hopping children.

'Billy,' cried one of them, 'ain't thart the butcher?'

'Dunno,' said the lad by the tree, dealing George a rudely candid stare.

Billy. George pondered the name. Could this, by any chance, be the self-same Billy he had once saved from a death by trampling? If so, he told himself bitterly, it just went to show where impetuosity got you.

'Won't yow come in fer a minnut, Mist' Ludbury?' Daisy called from her doorway.

''Tis the butcher!' yelled the vindicated child.

'Tarm's garn to 'es Granny's but Oi cud send erwer Madge fer 'em ef yow'll wait.'

'No, no, Daisy. Got to be getting along. We'll come and see the little chap when we're not so pressed. Here,' – he reached into his pocket for a half-sovereign – 'take this for the lad. Mind he saves it, now.'

'Oh, 'ee shudn't, shu'd 'ee, Missus Ludbury? 'Tes koind, though. Oi dun't 'alf miss yow, all of yow . . . We wus so 'appy en the old days, yow and your fam'ly, me and Tarm . . . Dear Lord, Oi cud croi t' think 'ow 'appy we all wus. Oh, Missus Ludbury!'

Rebecca brushed a tear from her cheek and silenced Daisy with a hug. 'We miss you, too. Goodbye, Daisy dear.'

In the square the gathering had grown – that was George's impression – and a dozen unsmiling eyes pursued them – he was sure of it – as he gee'd up along High Street then reined in to take the West Street turn.

Mallory House jigged near, jigged by. The bareness of the shop (the tenant occupied only the house) gave it a faintly seedy air. For the first time Rebecca saw it as a stranger might, as Charlotte Ludbury no doubt had: simply, a tall dwelling over a shop. To anyone unfamiliar with its elegant interior it must always have seemed thus. The thought startled her and threw other rosily remembered prospects into new perspective. Life in pre-war Lipscombe: had it been ridiculous rather than fun – the Sunday supper parties, the tea parties, the glittering balls in the grubby, rickety Town Hall? And pathetic rather than significant – what, after all, had become of that vaunted network of friendship when the young men failed to march back into town? With relief, her eyes fell upon Astly Hill – the worn stile, the footpath along a flower-sprigged bank, the patchwork of gold stubble, freshly turned earth, and cattle-strewn meadow; it was lovely, whether viewed with her new-found detachment or recalled as the scene of many a companionable stroll.

They drove on, past the farm track on the Ludbury side of the hill, and on towards the Biggins homestead. The climb became steep, and George sprang from the trap calling for Harry to do likewise. Rebecca and Sally were motioned to stay put. A lady, explained George for the benefit of his children, might remain seated, but a gentleman always showed consideration to the horse. 'Well done, old lady. There'll be a long rest for you and plenty of good hay when we get to the top,' he encouraged the mare, who put her ears and her best feet forward.

The kindest of men, thought Rebecca. And sometimes the unkindest. But not thoughtless. Oh no; kind or unkind, he knew what he was doing.

'Lord!' cried Samuel Biggins, scraping back his chair and springing to his feet. 'Lord, why hast Thou cast Thy servant among the ungodly?' And he surveyed his companions at the table with marked distaste. 'Though Thy servant partaketh full well of Thy bounty, oh Lord . . .'

A bit thick, thought George, getting a second dose like this. They had been obliged to wait while the Almighty was harangued at the onset of the meal, and he was not at all sure if the medicine wasn't easier to take on an empty stomach than on one distended by Edith's treacle pudding. She had a heavy hand, had Edith.

'. . . Thou setteth me down among the heathen and it turneth my bread to gall.'

247

Heartburn, diagnosed George. Served the impudent fellow right. Nice thing, weren't it, saying grace in order to abuse the guests? He just hoped the Almighty could put up with it – probably came in for plenty of this sort of thing. Well, the Lord was a better man than George Ludbury, Esquire. Deeply pained, George turned to catch his wife's eye.

Rebecca's two eyes, however, were fully engaged by the pattern of the tablecloth – they had been so engrossed from the moment Sam called upon the Lord, for during the pre-prandial grace her eyes had caught those of her eldest nephew (Teddy was a lively, intelligent youth) and the amusement shimmering in the exchange had very nearly erupted into laughter. Now, she told herself, she must think sad thoughts; it was time she overcame her childish disposition to giggle.

'Succour Thy servant, for he must depart. He must deliver Thy Word to the ruffians, to the scoundrels, to the loose women of Lower Buddington – a hard task, oh Lord, a weary travail!'

'Be gone and make haste about it,' George urged in silent anguish. Lower Buddington's misfortune would be his blessed relief. Poor old Becky seemed to be struggling with a coughing fit. He rummaged in his pockets – he had some fishermen's lozenges about him somewhere.

'. . . But Thou, oh Lord, art my shield and my salvation. Praise be to the Lord! Amen!' With a final glower at the company, Sam took himself off, it was presumed to Lower Buddington.

'We'll go and look over that land, Uncle George,' said Teddy. Everyone became animated. Suggestions for the afternoon's employment flew to and fro.

Rebecca and Edith were anxious to embark upon an intimate conversation and generously banished the children from the scullery for the duration of the washing up. 'There!' Edith said, as Harry and Bobby were dispatched to follow George and Teddy to the fields, and Edith's girls went off with Sally to view the piglets. 'Peace at last!'

'You're looking very well,' Rebecca told her.

'*You're* not,' Edith replied tartly.

'No. Well . . .' Rebecca gave her attention to polishing the glasses.

'You were looking bad enough before you went away. I expected you to have recovered, filled out a bit, got some colour back, once you'd made yourselves safe, so to speak.'

'I can't think what you mean.'

'Darling! I don't blame you. I would have done the same thing in your shoes. You must have been worried to death about George being sent for. I think you did right, persuading him to move into full-time farming.'

Rebecca returned a plate to the sink. 'Still some gravy on that.'

'I myself have been frantic about Teddy – he'll be of military age next July. I was quite distraught. But Doctor Griffin has made it all right – oh, he *is* a good man; it was he who arranged our Annie's job at the cottage hospital, and when she's finished her stint there he's promised to get her into the Birmingham Hospital where she'll get a good training. Anyway, he wrote to the Board to tell them how hopeless Sam is – though I expect they knew that already, he's appeared before them, you know, trying to join up – and making it clear that we're absolutely dependent on Teddy. I'm sure they won't send for him now; after all, we've doubled our grain quota, and you should see the vegetables we've got coming – all Teddy's doing, and he's farming your land as well! Do I sound as if I'm boasting, Rebecca? I can't help it. I'm so proud of him.'

'I should think you are. He's a wonderful boy. No wonder you're looking so much better. But Sam seems pretty much the same?' Her voice made it a question, diffident in tone.

Edith rushed to correct her. 'No. He's quite different. Religion suits him: he's less moody, more controlled, and, of course, drink is quite out of order.'

'He enjoys it, then, all this preaching and so on. Does he make many converts?'

'None at all, as far as I can tell.'

'That doesn't sound very rewarding.'

'I can see I shall have to explain.' Edith tipped a pile of tureens into the sink and took a deep breath. 'Well. There is a precise number of places available for The Elect in heaven. Did you know that? The precise figure escapes me, but it includes the standing room. In other words, there is a limit on the number of available heavenly places. Do you follow?'

As her sister's face was perfectly straight, Rebecca confined herself to murmured assent.

'It would not, therefore, be reassuring to Sam if he made a great many converts. There might be no room left for him. And another thing: every time someone rejects the Word, Sam feels quite bucked because it proves the truth of the prophecy about the small number of The Elect. He does his duty, you see, by taking the Word about.'

'And are you . . . one of The Elect?'

'Lord, no!' screamed Edith, and the sisters collapsed over the sink in gales of laughter. 'Blow it!' Edith tossed a roasting tin into the water. 'Let's leave it to soak. Come on, we'll go and look at our lovely hills.'

Neith, Honnington and Bowery sparkled against the sky; skirts billowed, hair streamed, a skylark soared then dipped out of sight, blue butterflies rose from a clump of wild thyme where small bees hovered. It was the territory of the airborne, the top of the world. But not quite, thought Rebecca, raising her eyes to a distant purple-grey peak. Knoller Knap was biding its time. 'What makes you think it was I who persuaded George to leave Lipscombe, rather than the other way around?' she asked suddenly.

Edith raised her eyebrows. 'Well, wasn't it? I assumed you'd do anything to keep George at your side. I mean, George has always been your safe haven, hasn't he?'

Rebecca, still squinting at Knoller Knap, shrugged.

'Well! When you came up here that day to tell me you were moving, you certainly implied that it was your idea.'

'Oh, no.'

'Very much a joint decision, then. You were cool as a cucumber about it. It was all for the best, you said.'

Alarm had sharpened Edith's voice. Rebecca hurried to reassure her. 'And so it has been. Just look at George – quite his old self again . . .'

'But what about *you*?' Edith cried, seizing her arm.

'I'm happy,' Rebecca said firmly. 'I'm happy here . . . now . . . with you. Look!' She extended an arm towards the view. 'Today is one of those forever days – do you know what I mean? – a day never to be forgotten. These moments will flash into my mind years hence. I shall be here again. I know it. Why does one select some moments and not others, I wonder? Is it something to do with the intensity of the light? Or do we fasten on those rare moments when we are content just to *be*; when the past is irrelevant and the future needn't even happen?'

'Look here, Rebecca,' Edith said, giving her a gentle shove. 'I want to know what's up. "The future needn't even happen"? What are you talking about? Planning and dreaming about the future has been a way of life for you and George. And I must say, your dreams had an irritating habit of coming true – very galling to me when everything here seemed so black and hopeless. Sorry, dear. All over now. What I'm trying to say is, you were the one who viewed the future with confidence. You made quite a religion of looking on the bright side. So what's happened? Is something wrong? Or is it just the war?'

Four red-faced girls charged by. Little Sally hung piggy-back over the largest girl's shoulders. Shrieking, they collided and collapsed in a sticky heap. The smell of crushed grass filled the air.

'Nothing is wrong,' Rebecca said thoughtfully. 'I've changed, I suppose, grown middle-aged. I'm not always looking ahead. Nowadays I try to find happiness at my feet . . .'

'I should just think you do!' Edith cried, holding out her arms to a sprawling Sally. 'Come here, you crumpled little angel!' And over the laughing, grass-strewn child they exchanged fond smiles.

They started back to the house, Sally hand in hand with her aunt, the older girls running ahead to get the tea ready. Rebecca dawdled a little way behind, considering whether or not to tell Edith about Charlotte's role in the move to Knoller Knap. The thought of Edith's indignant sympathy was tempting, for the way George and Charlotte had plotted behind her back as though she were no more than another item of furniture for transportation when the time came, still festered like an unlanced boil. But why cast a cloud over today? When all was said and done her hurt feelings would weigh lightly in the balance of universal misery inflicted by the war. Hers was just another war wound. If the war had not undermined their life in Lipscombe, Charlotte would not have gained the upper hand. No. She would keep it to herself. There was, however, that scrap of news about their brother. 'Edith!' she hurried to catch them up. 'I must tell you: George has seen Thomas. I don't know when exactly, it might have been before the war started.'

Edith looked startled. 'You never said,' she began sharply.

'I didn't know. George didn't tell me until recently. Apparently he was horrified by the state he found Thomas in, and kept it to himself. Don't be angry!

If George and I hadn't quarrelled I wouldn't know now.'

'You quarrelled about Thomas?'

'No, no. About something quite unrelated. George threw this at me to score a point. I'm still in the dark because I can't bring myself to refer to our row. But we'll ask him about it, if you like.'

'Certainly. If George knows something about Thomas's whereabouts, I insist he comes out with it.'

'Of course. Perhaps it would be better if you spoke privately to him. Leave it to me. I'll make sure you get the chance before we go.' She took Edith's arm and tried to ignore the stiffness of her sister's body. But as they drew nearer to the house, Edith relented and pressed Rebecca's arm into her waist.

George came back with his arm around Teddy's shoulders. He was impressed. If he hadn't seen what young Teddy had done with his own eyes . . . all those crops coming right after a fine harvest, and the fences and walls in good order, and the ditches kept clean – mind you, he'd given the lad a few tips about the dairy herd – but the sheep were doing fine, and really, he had to hand it to him. In fact, George didn't mind who heard him say it: he doubted whether he could have done any better himself with that acreage and such miserable labour. All credit to the boy! He was a farmer after his own heart! Then, over tea, George grew confidential. With much tapping of the nose, he promised that when the time came for him to dispose of the Ludbury acres on Astly Hill – and he was in no hurry, mark you – Teddy would have his chance. Industry such as George had seen today should not go unrewarded. Just let the boy keep careful records for a year or two, and if old Chadwick at the bank wasn't impressed, his name wasn't George Ludbury. And, it went without saying, he'd see that his nephew did nicely out of the deal; they had his word on it.

'Do you hear that, Mama?' cried Teddy with shining eyes.

This was handsome of George, thought Rebecca. She glanced at Edith and wondered whether she was still determined to interrogate him. 'George dear,' she said tentatively, when the exclamations over her husband's magnanimity had died down. 'I think Edith would like a quiet word . . .'

'No, no,' Edith put in hurriedly, turning pink. 'Another slice of cake, George? More tea then?'

But George had done very well, thank you, and – Good Lord! – it was ten to five; time to be getting along.

They were waiting for them in the square. Lookouts must have been posted all day at the corner of West Street, waiting for the Ludbury trap to come back down the hill. From the lanes off High Street they hurried to congregate – cottage women, children, girls, youths. George urged the horse on. 'Shirker! Slacker!' they screamed. 'Arter be ashamed! They'll send fer yow yet, Mister Ludbury!' A stone struck his shoulder a glancing blow.

Rebecca turned to gaze at the crowd. Behind the mob, a well-dressed couple stood watching in amazement – the Webbs, on their way home, no doubt, from taking tea with the Slatters. For a heart-piercing moment their eyes engaged with Rebecca's.

The dogs, frustrated by a day's captivity, were barking frantically when the trap turned on to the Ridge Farm track. In the yard the children were waiting. A great din broke out: greetings, questions, commands, shouts to the dogs, exclamations over presents from Aunt Edith. George handed Rebecca down and put his mouth against her ear. He spoke in an undertone of fierce *staccato*. 'Don't ever ask me to go near that blasted town again. Not for anything.'

Rebecca took Sally's hand and followed Meg and Bunny into the house.

Winter on Knoller Knap proved every bit as terrible as Mrs Maule had predicted. It came suddenly, without warning, taking George's weather eye by surprise. On Christmas Eve Rebecca and Meg had taken the tram into Cheltenham. George had met them later with the trap. They returned laden with small gifts for everyone – the sort of things that were beyond his shopping imagination. (And how irksome, Rebecca had suddenly understood, to have become dependent on her husband for purchases; how she missed ready money in her purse and the convenience of shops on the doorstep.) Then, when they awoke on Christmas morning, the world had changed. For confirmation they rushed to look out of windows, but the hush that had disconcerted their ears on waking had told all: the farmhouse now stood in a sea of snow, white cliffs rose up on one side, on the other a white bank slipped down to a white valley. Tree tops poked through the snow like small bushes. 'To think: if it had come yesterday morning, we'd never have got back home,' marvelled George to himself. Then, aloud: 'The animals! All hands to work!' It was not until late in the evening that Rebecca had time to reflect, and then she thought with an ache for past innocence of how, last Christmas, she could not have foreseen anything as dreadful as Ridge Farm on Knoller Knap.

Mrs Maule, of course, was prevented from ascending to her duties but, with the children unable to leave the farm, Rebecca did not go without assistance. Bunny became her mainstay – Meg was needed by George. She had no compunction now, however, in demanding more muscular help with the heavier tasks. Even so, fatigue crept up on her, and with it a reluctance to waste breath conversing. Determinedly, she stuck to her afternoon rests, pushing a chair against the bedroom door to discourage intruders, and covering her head with the eiderdown to smother the noise of constant activity and the smell of damp clothes and stale snow.

Coming softly from her room one afternoon, she overheard Meg airing her feelings. Meg, the kitchen was given to understand, had had enough of people who cleared off in the middle of the afternoon, who failed to pull their weight, and were short to the point of rudeness.

'I have something to say to you all,' Rebecca announced later at the tea table. She was regarded with some surprise. 'If I am short with you' – and she looked directly at Meg – 'it is because I am exceedingly short of breath. Talking is frequently painful. And I speak with emphasis because I dread your eternal cries of "What?" I cannot bear the thought of having to repeat myself. As to my afternoon rests: I am not robust; I am no longer young; the work I am obliged to do is taxing and is something I have not been used to; quite simply, I cannot do without them. Perhaps you would prefer me to drop dead and have done with it?'

Murmurs of dissent, ranging in tone from horror to embarrassment, rose up around the table. 'Mama?' Sally cried timorously, her lower lip trembling.

'It's all right, darling. Mama has no intention of dropping dead, that is why she will continue to take her afternoon rest and ask for assistance when she requires it.'

'Quite right!' George declared roundly, recovering rapidly from his astonishment. 'Do you hear, you children? You're to show every consideration to your Mama. She's not strong. We must take care of her.' He darted a swift look at Meg – it was not missed by Rebecca. 'So they have discussed me,' she thought.

'Is there anything we can do for you at the moment?' George asked solicitously.

'No thank you. I simply wished there to be no misunderstanding.'

The thaw came at the end of January. Snowfalls, though less heavy, persisted throughout February and March. Mrs Maule came when she could, and slowly life became less of a siege. But even the return of warm weather did not rejuvenate Rebecca and George. One summer evening in Rebecca's garden, as they admired the first flowering of a rose bush, the eyes of each fell upon the other, noting gauntness, greyness, hard lines and shadows. 'We're both worn out,' Rebecca said eventually. His eyes fell away at once, but not before she had seen in them a gleam of recognition.

During the summer holiday of 1917, Meg received an invitation to the home of her friend, Edna Mayfield. Theirs was a friendship highly flattering to Meg, for Edna, the elder by a year, was Head Girl elect, destined for St Ursula's College, and considered the most glamorous girl at Cheltenham High. Furthermore, being taken up by the Head Girl elect was a strong indication that Meg would succeed her. Their attachment – an alliance of the two most imposing pupils, both stunning in looks and achievement – was admired throughout the school. Their fellow seniors thought it chic, the more sentimental of the mistress thought it romantic, and in the junior school the concept of 'Edna and Meg' was regularly swooned over.

George was not sure that Meg could be spared; there was still some haymaking to be done, and before they knew where they were they'd be harvesting. He didn't see why she should go gallivanting when there was so much to be done at home.

'For three days!' cried Meg. 'You mean to say you can't do without me for three days! Then I should give up. One of these days . . .' But here she bit her tongue. 'Look, I'm going and that's that. Don't try and stop me or you'll be sorry – I daresay you're banking on me for the rest of the holiday . . .'

'I think she should go,' Rebecca put in hastily. 'She's looking tired. A break will do her good.'

At this, George felt obliged to give in. Secretly, he had been vastly impressed by the Mayfields' address, and he mentioned it now to get back in his daughter's good graces: 'Regent Square, eh? You'd better look out your best bib and tucker.'

This plunged Rebecca into a tizzy over the worthiness of Meg's clothes – dismissed loftily by Meg. Edna, they should understand, was not worldly, and Meg had every confidence that the Mayfields as a family would prove equally high-minded.

Soon after her arrival in Regent Square, Meg discovered that she had not understood the true nature of Edna's unworldliness. The Mayfields – Mr and Mrs Mayfield were blunt where Edna had talked sweetly but ambiguously of 'Friends' – were Quakers. The shock was severe. At the same time, Meg was not sure that shock was a suitable reaction. Until this indigestible mixture of emotion had settled down she decided to assume nonchalance.

Meg was a poor actress. Confronted with her look of an animal at bay, the Mayfields decided that she was out of her depth, socially speaking. They went out of their way to put the young person at ease, for theirs was a democratic household – why else had they sent Edna to Cheltenham High in preference to Cheltenham Ladies' College if it were not to rub shoulders with girls from the commercial and agricultural classes? At the same time, they were careful to demonstrate all the blessings of a professional background – familiarity with things artistic, concern for social problems, an ability to discuss matters of controversy without getting heated – for they understood that this friend of Edna's was clever and likely to enter a profession herself. It was felt in number 18 Regent Square that the young person was 'brought on' by her visit, and she was urged to repeat it soon and often, for her social progress promised to become an interesting feature of the radical dinner parties for which number 18 was renowned.

For her part, Meg considered she was more than fair to her hosts. She repressed feelings of having been misled, and was as friendly as could be to Edna – arm in arm in the park, chatting and laughing about school; or sprawling on Edna's bed, enjoying her vast collection of books. But at the Mayfield dinner table she was sorely tried. Here, for the first time in her life, she encountered differentness, and found it terrifying. Her eyes grew large and staring, and a grin, not unlike that favoured by her father in moments of stress, distorted her mouth. She could not take it in. How was it that nice-seeming, respectable people could disparage the Archbishop of Canterbury, ridicule Mr Bonar Law, speak kindly of the wicked Keir Hardie, and enthusiastically of Home Rule? – worse: sit calmly at an elegant table and announce in everyday tones that, of course, they thoroughly disapproved of the war. Meg had assumed one could be shot for less. On the whole, she felt she coped well with the outrage, and was confident that she allowed no trace of her profound disapproval to show.

On the homeward tram she saw that her greatest difficulty lay ahead: how to present this to her parents. To dissemble, or to confess and abuse her hosts, were both courses she could not entertain; both would mean the end of something – of what, she could not, in her hot confusion, make out. She was sure of one thing: to have her own fears voiced loudly and enlarged by her father would be intolerable. She resolved to drop the bare facts casually and show by her amazing composure that they disturbed her not one whit.

*

259

'So,' George cried, coming in from the yard. 'She's back.'

'Yes,' Rebecca confirmed from the kitchen.

'Well, well, well,' he cried joyfully, washing his hands at the scullery sink. He came into the kitchen and joined his family at the tea table. 'Where's the society lady, then?'

'Oh, Daddy!' protested Meg, running in from the hall. She planted a kiss on his proffered cheek and sat down.

'Tell us all about it, then.'

'I had a lovely time. They couldn't have been kinder. And such a beautiful house!'

'Oho! You passed muster. Clothes didn't let you down. Your Mama's been worrying her head off about that darn in your skirt.'

'Mama! I told you. They don't care about things like that. They don't stand on ceremony – well, they wouldn't, really, being Quakers.'

Silence. Then, with a roar: 'Quakers! Do you hear that?' George demanded superfluously of his wife.

'Yes, dear. How nice. How interesting.'

'It was,' Meg said, her voice very matter-of-fact. 'They were interesting about lots of things: music, politics, social reform – especially of prisons, because, of course, Edmund Mayfield (that's Edna's brother) has had personal experience of prison.'

'Has he, by Jove?' George asked carefully.

'Is he in the prison service?' Rebecca asked hopefully.

'Oh no. He was in prison, for being a conscientious objector.'

Rebecca braced herself.

George choked. Jammy crumbs shot over the table-cloth.

With false calm, Meg took a mouth-stuffing bite of bread and butter.

'Conchies! She's been staying with conchies! You hear that? These fine people are conchies!'

'Well of course they are, George. Quakers don't fight.'

'How you can sit there calmly . . .' Words failed him for a moment as the reason for his wife's equanimity hit him and took his breath away. Of course! she was tarred with the same brush. An outsider. Hadn't he always known it, deep down? Conchies, Quakers, jumped-up factory owners, nasty usurping foreigners. . . . Needed standing up to, that sort of thing. Damn it! Wasn't that what the war was all about? With a thump of the table he turned on Meg. 'You didn't know about these people before you went, I trust?'

This could be tricky, Meg saw. 'No,' she said, considering. 'I can't say I did.'

'Then why on earth didn't you come home the moment you found out? Not stay there enjoying yourself and come waltzing home as if nothing had happened. Tell her,' he instructed his wife, with a sneer, 'tell your daughter how she should behave to conchies.'

'Politely, I trust.' Rebecca got to her feet – this was likely to go on for some time. 'If you must bellow, I suggest you go and do it in the cowshed. I am far from well today; I shall go and lie down. Sally, dear, you may join me after your tea.' So saying, she left them to make of it what they would. After all, it was a peculiarly Ludbury row.

Meg, always a practical girl, decided it was time to restore her father's equanimity. 'Mama's right, you know, Daddy. There's no point in getting excited. Getting excited's the worst thing you can do when you're dealing with people like that. The thing is to keep a cool head and stick to your guns.' (As a silent observer of tactics at the Mayfield dinner table, she had learnt this lesson well.) 'And,' she added stoutly, 'you needn't worry about me.

261

They're not likely to change my opinions, thank you.'

Oho! George understood at once. She'd given it to them good and proper, the downright little madam! He could just see her putting them in their place with her school-marmy manner and her I'm-standing-no-nonsense-from-you tone of voice. 'You're a clever'un, Meg,' he cried huskily. 'Cleverer than your old Dad by a mile.'

Meg, who could read him like a book and knew just where his train of thought had led him, had the grace to blush. It was time to get off the subject. 'How's the hay coming?' she asked pleasantly.

'Done! I was determined to get it finished so that we could enjoy your first evening home.'

'Heavens, Daddy! I've only been gone three nights.'

'Three too many, my girl. What do you say to a stroll round the cornfields? They're coming along nicely. We'll be harvesting in a fortnight if the rain keeps off.'

'Lovely. I'll just get my boots.'

4

Rebecca moved through the quiet house. Mrs Maule had gone home and the children had not yet returned from school. Sally was upstairs in bed, asleep at last after a night and a day of listless wakefulness. Perhaps George was right: sound sleep would restore her vitality. But Rebecca knew that if this were Mallory House and not Ridge Farm she would have sent for Doctor Griffin days ago. Something was wrong with Sally. Ironically, it was George who had this very day gone to Cheltenham in search of a consultation. Last night he had fallen from the barn loft onto the mangle below. 'Damn me if I ain't cracked me ribs again,' he exclaimed, staggering into the kitchen with a ghastly countenance. Rebecca and Meg, following his instructions, had bound him tightly in bandages, but after a rough night he conceded that he required professional attention, and announced that he would seek it in Cheltenham. Surely, Rebecca had objected, some person could be found in the village who would drive him to Lipscombe to see Doctor Griffin. Between bad-tempered instructions to his children, awkward attempts to dress himself and a hasty dash at breakfast, he had disabused her; he'd manage under his own steam, thank you, the last thing they wanted was nosy-parkering around here – hadn't she learned anything? – and if Griffin were the only doctor on earth he wouldn't go back to that blasted town, not if he were dying. So she had watched him saddle up without comment, understanding vaguely that to set off on foot would put him at a disadvantage: without a horse between his legs George Ludbury was less than the man he preferred to present to the world. But now – there was no doubt about it; the grandfather clock in the hall was as adamant as the pendulum clock in the kitchen – George was unaccountably late. She repulsed a faint alarm and attended with conscious effort to her surroundings, wandering, as if for the first time, from room to room of the quiet house.

This little parlour, for instance, where she and Sally came to play the piano – why did it feel so daunting, so tomb-like? It was no good going to the window and peering out at the purple aubretia in the rockery; view or no view, she was uneasy in this little room. And here, on the other side of the hall, here was another neglected room – the dining room, used chiefly by Meg as a study. Why did they never eat in here? Because life had changed, that was why; the kitchen was reassuringly close to the yard, and at Ridge Farm it was not felt possible to stray too far from the job in hand. Her eyes dwelt sadly on the mahogany table with its fat, carved legs, and on the long bow-fronted sideboard topped by an enormous soup tureen. They were overbearing in this mean room. The only thing to be said for them now was that they gave Mrs Maule pleasure; polishing these fine pieces was the treat of her week.

In the hall she put a hand on the banister, listening. No sound from Sally, no sound at all except the wind's hum. Just a minute, though . . . She hurried into the kitchen, then into the scullery and was just in time to see Jim disappear into the yard. 'Come back! Come back at once!'

Jim, cramming the remains of a tart into his mouth, returned cautiously to the back door.

'You're home early. Where's Meg?'

His eyes narrowed cagily.

'You haven't been to school today, have you? Where have you been? Why didn't you come in? – there was enough to do, goodness knows.'

His face was scrupulously blank.

'Wipe your nose.'

He searched in his pocket with a weary air. When his handkerchief emerged she saw that it was a sodden ball.

'Another cold!' she cried accusingly, for it had been one cold after another all winter, and now that spring had finally established itself, it was too bad of the wretched boy to start off another round. 'That's what comes of hanging around in the wet. Well, just keep away from the others; Bunny's only just god rid of hers. As you're here, why not start the milking? Your father will be fit for nothing when he gets back.'

He turned and trudged away across the yard. A pang of guilt struck her; it was such a weary walk. He disappeared round the side of the house on his way to collect the cows from their pasture, and he stayed in her mind, and when the cows clattered into the yard she went outside to watch. George urging cattle into their stalls made quite a fuss, shouting, banging, stick-waving; but Jim, she saw, moved quietly round the great beasts, dropping chains over patient necks, shoving a shoulder here or a rump there.

'Is that difficult to do?' she asked as he began to milk.

'What?'

'Let me try,' she said loudly as he changed cows.

Nothing. Not a trickle however hard she tugged.

'Let me show you. You'll soon get it.'

'Never mind. Can Meg do it?'

'No. Bunny can, though.'

'Why can't Meg do it?'

'Scared.'

'Surely not.'

'Scared of animals. They don't do as she says. She likes things to do as she says.'

'But she's good at leading a horse.'

'Yeah, with bit and bridle on, so she's the boss. Cows are different: you have to *persuade* 'em.'

Rebecca laughed, and Jim, glancing up in surprise, laughed too.

'Do you feel very poorly?'

He nodded.

'Look, I can't let you off the milking because of Daddy's accident, you'll just have to do it for him for the next few days; but you needn't go to school, and you can rest in the warm in between. I'll give you some hot milk and rum before you go to bed. As soon as Bunny comes I'll send her to give you a hand.'

Returning to the house, she thought how debilitated they all were. The winter – their second on Knoller Knap – had not been severe, but it had been lowering; days on end of wet, chilly mist. No wonder George had been careless; he, like the rest of them, was severely out of sorts. And where, in heaven's name, had the man got to?

*

'That'll be him,' said Rebecca, hearing the dogs. 'Quickly, Bunny, run and see if you can help him.' She went along the hall to the dining room. 'Meg, I believe your father's home. Go and help him with the horse.'

Some minutes later George came in. 'Where is he? Where's that dratted boy?'

'Why, dear?'

'It was a mistake going in on the horse. I passed out on the doctor – you never heard such a fuss – made me lie down for an hour and sip brandy. Anyway, thought I'd better not risk it, better take the tram home and let the boy ride the nag. Do you know, I stood outside that blessed school for over an hour? Not a sign of him . . .'

'He's in bed, dear. Ill.'

'Ill? I'll give him ill!'

She put up a forestalling hand. 'Really ill, dear. Running a temperature. So you see, he had come home – I daresay they sent him. But he managed to milk the cows, you'll be pleased to hear.'

This staunch defence of their elder son took the wind out of his sails. 'Huh,' he said, his purpose collapsing.

'Sit down while we get you your tea – or would you prefer an early supper?'

'Just as you like. To tell you the truth, I ain't hungry.'

'What did the doctor say?'

He grinned. 'I'm to take a complete rest.'

'Oh!'

'Fools – doctors. I've always said so. How can anyone take a rest with a war on, I ask you? Oh yes, that reminds me . . . Take a look at this.' He drew a sheet of newspaper from his pocket. 'It's old – from the twentieth of last month. I found it lying about in the coach house at The Lamb.'

She took it dubiously. The headline, dramatically enlarged, printed in the blackest of ink, screamed:

'FLUSH OUT THE SLACKERS!' In the paragraph below readers were urged to write to their Member of Parliament demanding an end to shilly-shallying. Conscription should be extended at once.

'It'll come, you mark my words. Things are looking black. Folks are losing their nerve. Oh yes, it'll come.'

5

It came.

May 1918 was a dismal month, a succession of dreary days when rain or the threat of rain cast a gloom over the out-of-doors and impenetrable shadow in the corners of rooms and barns. Spirits were low; it was felt that the worst of all worlds was more than likely to occur. 'Here it is,' George said grimly, waving an unopened buff envelope at the breakfast table. 'This'll be it.' And so it proved. In accordance with the extension of the call-up to all men under fifty, he was summoned to present himself at once to the tribunal.

'Are they mad?' Rebecca cried. 'What are they trying to achieve? A world full of widows? – for there'll be no men left alive between twenty and fifty before they're done. What a prospect! Can you imagine – a generation of women struggling on alone? Frankly, there comes a time when life is simply not worth the candle.'

George narrowed his eyes. He was incapable of empathy with the plight of his prospective widow, not because his own predicament absorbed him, but because his capacity for feeling had suddenly gone. He was empty: a hollow man. Of course, he had a contingency plan for his dependants – they could not survive without him on Knoller Knap – but for the moment he was unable to speak of it; there would be time later on, he supposed, to go into that. 'I've no doubt we shall see what we shall see,' he said enigmatically. 'Meanwhile, I'd better get ready. I'll go in on the tram with Meg. Jim had better stay here to keep an eye on things.'

Rebecca remained in the deserted kitchen – chin between fists, elbows rucking up the crumby table-cloth. Some other, more significant emotion lurked beneath her anger – before long it would have to be faced – but for the moment she luxuriated in rage: rage at the crassness of war, rage at the crassness of men. Outside, dogs barked and ran on their dragging chains. There would be trouble from *them* today – always was when George was away – on and on they would bark, heedless of shouts or threats, making themselves, and everyone within earshot, frantic. Their present excitement signalled the approach of Mrs Maule, no doubt.

'Marnin,' a voice duly announced from the scullery. 'Oi'm late, but et cudn't be 'elped.' It was a pugnacious beginning. 'Oi 'ad to call on moi sister fust, to make sure as Oi cud come 'ere today, what with 'er expectin' any mennut . . . Wus thart Mr Ludbury Oi saw steppin' arn to the tram? Cudn'ave been, cud et? But 'e were weth Meg, who ever he wus.' She had come into the kitchen and now stood, hands on hips, waiting for an explanation.

Rebecca sighed as if aroused from sleep. 'You can clear this away' – she indicated the table – 'then get on with the wash. I'll go and dust upstairs.' But she continued to sit while Mrs Maule, exuding umbrage, removed the débris from around her.

'Have to move yer elbows, then,' it was pointed out severely. Rebecca moved them and sank against the back of her chair. She must face it: the real cause of her fury was that today, the day that George had been called away, was the very day she had earmarked for an assault on his unwillingness to take her to

Lipscombe. She had better think it over – not in here with Mrs Maule making her presence felt, not upstairs either, for there she would encounter the object of her anxiety; she would go out into the garden and pull a weed or two from the rockery.

Crouching over purple and gold mounds of aubretia and alyssum, she was suddenly overwhelmed by her inadequacy. Dear God, it was the health of her dearly loved child that was at stake! Why had she not asserted herself? In the circumstances, George's refusal to take her to Lipscombe was self-indulgent nonsense – she should have overruled him. Instead, last week, she had been almost grateful (grateful!) to him for taking them to see his Cheltenham doctor – the very man he had ridiculed for prescribing complete rest. A fool, George had called him. Evidently it was better to consult a fool than risk a few rude shouts in Lipscombe. To be fair, the change of diet prescribed by the Cheltenham man had, at first, done Sally good; her stomach pains had subsided and her appetite improved. But the improvement had been transitory, and Rebecca had at last understood that she would have no peace of mind until Doctor Griffin's advice had been obtained. Last night, kneeling by her daughter's restless bed, she had promised herself: 'In the morning I shall tackle him. I shall impress him with my calm determination. I shall be obdurate, completely implacable.' If only she had been so when Sally first became unwell. If only . . .

She got to her feet and began to pace the small patch of lawn between rockery and herbaceous border. It was no use going on like this – paralysing herself with regret – she must act *now*. Mrs Maule would probably know someone in the village who could take them to Lipscombe. Mrs Maule must be propitiated at once. It had been a mistake to ignore her query about George – a woman in Rebecca's position could not afford to stand upon her dignity; her hopes, fears and misfortune must all be open to inspection when those upon whom she depended demanded to pick them over. She would go in at once and explain that her earlier distant manner had been due to anxiety over Sally. And she would offer the coveted information: George had indeed stepped on to the Cheltenham tram, having been summoned on urgent business – no need to go into details . . .

A rapping from above distracted her. Mrs Maule was instantly forgotten.

Sally, kneeling on the oak chest below the landing window, waved and smiled at her mother in the garden below.

Rebecca raised a hand, but forgot to wave. The pane of glass was uneven and green – dappled, silent, fathomless, like still water on a dull day. Moist lips moved in the depths behind the dimly transparent screen, depths too remote to allow the transference of sound. She ran into the house and up the stairs. 'Darling! I thought you were still sleeping. You had such a restless night.'

'Did I?' The child seemed puzzled.

'You did, darling. In fact, I had just made up my mind to take you to see Doctor Griffin in Lipscombe. Daddy's gone to Cheltenham today, but I thought Mrs Maule might know someone who could take us.'

'But Mama, I feel lots better, I really do. I want to read that book Meg gave me today. Can I have some porridge?'

Could she have some porridge! 'You must be feeling better, dear! I'll get it at once. Or shall I stay and help you to dress first?'

'No, get it, Mama. I'm starving.'

'Well! I'll send Mrs Maule up with the water,' Rebecca cried, seizing a jug from the wash-stand. 'Put on clean clothes, dear.' For this, she felt hopefully, promised to be a new beginning.

*

On shaking legs, George ran down the steps to the pavement and turned to walk up The Parade. He needed a stiff one, he judged.

In the gents' at the back of The Lamb he locked himself into a cubicle and took a piece of paper from his pocket. 'Classification Certificate', the document proclaimed: George Ludbury, having been medically examined, was categorized 'R' – rejected and therefore exempt from military service. 'Bloomin' doctors,' George marvelled, recalling the pummelling of his chest and the tapping of his skull to much gloomy wonderment. ('D'ye suffer a lot from headaches, mon? Well, if ye'll tak ma tip ye'll get yoursel' a pair of specs. It's nae wonder ye've had a few wee accidents. . . .') Just let the fellow come out to Ridge Farm, thought George, he'd soon see then who was fit and who was not.

In the best bar George settled down with a glass of the best whisky. His head cleared; after a few sips, irrelevancies vanished from his mind, exposing the glorious, salient fact that he was a free man, free to do as he damn well pleased, wherever he damn well chose. He experienced a sudden longing to jump on a train to Birmingham, but resisted it. Becky would be worrying her head off. A letter would suffice.

'Dear Charlie, old thing,' he wrote – the barman having been prevailed upon to produce notepaper and envelope in exchange for a tip:

How are you? I've got some rum news for you, old girl. I've just been up before the army chaps and their doctor pronounced me unfit to be a fighting man! In other words, they've no use for me – yours truly is free as a bird! Now then: how about our little plan? There's nothing to wait for now. Trouble is, though, it'll take me a while to realize the cash for the business and the two farms – and I've made a promise about the Astly Hill land which may slow things up. So how about you doing as you suggested – broaching the matter with your good lady friend? Just to tide me over, of course. Are you still keeping your eyes skinned for a likely place? Write back at once and tell me what you think. I'm sick to death of this hole-in-a-corner existence. Can't wait to live decently again, and, as you so rightly say, the nearer to The Grange, the better for all concerned. Tell you what; I wouldn't say 'no' to farming on Drifton territory, though there'll be no hunting until this wretched war is over, I suppose. Mind you write back straight away.

Your loving brother, George.

'Unfit?' Rebecca repeated, her mind reeling. They were standing on the track. She had been listening all afternoon for his return and when the bored noise of the dogs turned to barks of frantic joy she had raced across the yard and down the track to meet him.

'That's right. I'm not good enough for them. Suits me. I can do as I please now. I'm a free agent.'

'But unfit . . .' Tired, overworked, strained, perhaps. But unfit? The word denied the very essence of George Ludbury.

'Cheer up, Becky. Anyone'd think you were disappointed.'

'Oh, my dear! I'm so relieved. I can't tell you how thankful I am.'

'That's more like it.' He drew her arm in his and they walked briskly towards the house. 'Always take a doctor's opinion with a pinch of salt – that's my motto. But this chappie today did me a good turn. There's no need for us to hide away up here any more, there's no reason for anyone to take the slightest interest in us now.'

'You mean we can move?'

'Exactly.'

272

'Oh, George!' she gasped with surprise and the effort to keep up with him.

'Those blasted dogs! Quiet!' he bellowed, striding into the yard.

The noise ceased at once, and the dogs writhed at the end of their chains, torn between the requirements of obedience and the urge to convey rapture.

'Well, well! Look who's here!' He fell into a crouch and extended his arms towards the running child. 'My little girl's better, if I'm not mistaken.' And he swung Sally on to his knee. 'She's got quite a good colour,' he remarked over his shoulder.

'Yes, but . . .'

'And do you know what? Little Sal's going to live in a great big house. Daddy's goin' huntin' and Mama's goin' to be a fine lady again. And little Sal can have a pony of her very own. Would she like that, d'you think?'

The child nodded solemnly.

'A nice little dapple-grey, or a brown and white piebald like Meg used to ride?'

'One like Meg.'

'One like Meg! That's the spirit!' He set her down and turned towards his wife. 'She's right as ninepence again.'

'Well I hope so.'

'Mrs Thing still about?'

'Ironing in the kitchen.'

'Blow! I'm parched after that climb. Bring some tea into the parlour, will you?'

The little parlour imposed formality. Smelling of polish and damp, it had the starchy air of a room unaccustomed to people taking their ease. They sipped their tea with care.

'Well, we have something to celebrate at last,' Rebecca observed timidly. 'I suppose it's too soon to consider where we might go.'

George stared thoughtfully into the empty grate. 'I'll set a few wheels in motion . . . make inquiries . . . let it be known in the right quarters . . .'

'What, exactly, do you envisage?'

'Oh . . . a large farm – all our eggs in one basket this time, I reckon – a good spacious house, well set up with a garden for you and stables for me . . . A respectable sort of place, somewhere nicely situated, somewhere you'll feel at home . . .'

'I felt at home in Mallory House.'

(A brief hesitation indicated that he had heard, and chose to ignore, her tasteless interjection.) '. . . with nice people about for you and the children to know. Spot of hunting for me . . . You know, it's been hard going these past few years, it's time we had a bit of a let-up.'

'What about finance? I thought one of the reasons for taking this poor place was that we couldn't lay our hands on the money. It's tied up in land and property, isn't it?'

He looked cagy. 'There are ways and means. Now that there's no question of the army having a claim on me, I've become a proposition again. See? It's a matter of speaking to the right people. I'll get an agent to study the market and find buyers when the price is right. Don't you worry about it. And I shan't forget my promise to young Teddy. I'll hang on to Astly Hill till he's ready. I can afford to. It's amazing . . . I set out to keep us ticking over on this place – to feed us, clothe us, send the children to school – but, d'you know, I've made a tidy profit? I checked the figures today.'

'That's marvellous! Oh, I should like to see them!'

'See what?'

'The figures. You know how I enjoy going over the accounts. Do show me. How wonderful to see in black and white that it's not been entirely pointless! – working so hard on this hill, I mean.'

After a pause he said, gruffly: 'You don't want to worry your head with figures and such like.'

'Worry my head? Over figures? The idea! Please recall, George, that it was I who kept the accounts throughout our years in Lipscombe – very successful years . . .'

'And I don't know that I should've let you.' It was an impulsive observation. Having made it, he avoided her amazed and furious eyes.

The hypocrite! she thought. Shouldn't have let me, eh? I'd like to know how he'd have managed to run a farm and three businesses *and* take days off to go hunting if I hadn't done all the book-keeping . . .

Words were not racing in this fashion through George's mind; his mind was full of shadows. His impulsive remark had been prompted by a sudden surge of feeling – revulsion for past activity and what it had led to, and an uneasy nostalgia for a dimly remembered sense of rectitude concerning what is and what is not of proper concern to a gentlewoman. Images of mother and sister stole across his inner eye. His throat swelled, so that when he spoke – half to himself – it was huskily: 'Not the kind of thing to concern a lady.'

Was he mad? Had the strain of the day turned his mind? But no, his eyes were watching her with sharp cunning. Wonderful! He had simply changed the rules! And at this late stage in the game! Very well, she would show him where playing it this way led. 'I see. Book-keeping is no longer part of my competence. I trust you agree that the children's health remains within it?' As he made no sound, she continued with exaggerated confidence. 'Good. For I must tell you that I am far from satisfied with the advice we obtained last week concerning Sally. I have decided that Doctor Griffin, who has known her from her birth, should examine her at once. Will you be good enough to take us to Lipscombe in the morning?'

George clambered to his feet – she sprang to hers to minimize the disadvantage – and addressed her: 'You're obsessed. You're determined, come what may, to get me back to that town. Well it won't work. And, I must say, I'm surprised you stoop so low as to use the child to further your schemes.'

'You're the one who's obsessed,' she retorted. 'I've been up night after night with Sally while you've slept on undisturbed. Night after night, out of my mind with worry. Sally should see her own doctor, the one who knows all about her. That would be plain to anyone who wasn't blinded by an obsessive dread of a little unpleasantness . . .'

'Out of my way. I shan't listen to you any more.'

'Oh yes you will!' she shouted, catching hold of his arm. 'That child will see Doctor Griffin if I have to pay someone to take us.'

He dislodged her hand with a violent thrust and snatched the door handle. Then he paused and turned back. 'You do that' – he spoke quietly, with menace – 'and I'll never have dealing with anyone in that place again. Think about it. No dealings with Teddy, no dealings with Chadwick at the bank. I'll hire an agent to sell Astly Hill to the highest bidder.'

'Why?' she whispered.

'You know what they're like, how they put the nastiest interpretation on everything. It'll be all round the town that Ludbury's wife had to get someone else to take her sick child to the doctor. How do you think I'll like doing business with Chadwick after that, eh?'

'So you admit the child is sick.'

'Don't try and catch me out! The child is better. We agreed on that back there in the yard. The Cheltenham chappie was on the right track – I saw that as soon as he suggested a milky diet. It made sense . . .'

'Oh, well . . . if George Ludbury saw the sense of it it must be all right.'

Silence fell between them. Both began to lose heart in their anger as the first depressing pangs of anticlimax foretold the remorse to come. It dawned on Rebecca that she had done her daughter a disservice. She started to shake, and grabbed the back of a chair for support. She must retrieve the situation. But how . . . how?

George, who had opened the door, stared glumly into the hall. Had he been entirely straightforward? There was that letter of his to Charlotte . . . He dismissed the thought. His wife was unworthy of confidences. It was clear as daylight that she was out to manoeuvre him. The more firmly he dwelt on this, the surer of himself he became. 'I meant what I said,' he muttered darkly, before setting off down the hallway. He needed air, fresh air, blowing as hard as it cared to blow.

In the yard he slipped the dogs from their chains, then strode up the track whistling superfluous encouragement. He scrambled up a bank, legged it over a gate – the dogs slithering underneath – and climbed towards the top of Knoller Knap, where the wind whipped his face and blasted thought from his head with a zealous, ear-splitting whine.

6

Rebecca slept fitfully that night. Sally slept soundly; even so, Rebecca resolved to keep a close eye on her during the day in spite of a longing, the moment she was dressed, to return to bed. She supervised breakfast with a fragile grasp on reality. People ate, talked, then disappeared about their business while she steeled herself to put food in front of them and attend to what was said. When only she and Sally remained in the kitchen, she sank into an easier chair and tried to compose an appeal to Mrs Maule.

'Good morning!' she called with feigned cheerfulness when the lady's step was heard in the scullery.

Mrs Maule came to the kitchen doorway and looked in. 'Uhuh! We're feelin' better, then,' she observed archly. 'We wus roight arff et yesterday.'

'Was I grumpy yesterday, Mrs Maule? Sorry. I suppose I was out of sorts. Much better this morning, just rather tired.'

'We all 'as erwer arff days, Oi suppose. And, of course, yow dow 'ave your partic'lar troubles . . .'

Oh dear! Her quarrel with George had obviously reached the kitchen. She had better get straight to the point. 'I've something to ask you, Mrs Maule. Do sit down for a moment. Sally, dear, run outside and play for a little while, will you?'

Mrs Maule lowered herself gingerly on to a hard chair. 'Yes?' she inquired suspiciously.

Rebecca attempted light-heartedness. 'Nothing too earth-shattering – just a little favour: I need someone to drive me into Lipscombe – tomorrow, if it can be arranged. I want to take Sally to see a doctor.'

'Her saw a darcter only larst week.'

'Yes, but I'm still not easy. I'd like her to see our doctor in Lipscombe. Mr Ludbury is frightfully busy at the moment, otherwise he would take us, of course. That business he had to attend to yesterday – I did tell you about it, didn't I?'

'Nart really.'

'Oh, it was to do with the accounts – that sort of thing's much better left to the men – I'm afraid Mr Ludbury got quite impatient with me!' (Mrs Maule gave a loud sniff.) 'Anyway, it's put him right behind with the work and he'd rather not spare the time to go to Lipscombe. Do you know of someone who could oblige me?'

Mrs Maule looked doubtful. 'There's old Joe Greaves, maybe.'

'Will you ask him for me? I'm so very anxious about Sally.'

Mrs Maule clapped hands on to knees and launched herself. 'If yow ask me,' she began, with misplaced confidence, 'yow marlly-carddle thart choild. Hers forever hangin' arn to your skirts, endoors or out adoors, even upstairs when you're supposed to be takin' your arternoon narp. 'Taint natural. A choild of her age shud be at schowl – they'd sown learn her there nart to be such a Mama's baby. Her puts it arn deliberate. Her knows et upsets yow. That's what hers arter – your undivoided attention.'

Rebecca looked hard at Mrs Maule's feet. Then, as if bracing herself, she shot up her head with a false smile. 'Mrs Maule, you have been a valued support to me during the last two difficult years, and I shall be eternally grateful. You won't fail me now? You will help me in this?'

'Oi'll dow moi best. Oi can't prarmise, moind, what with erwer Marlly bein' so poorly and upset . . .'

'Of course! How is your sister?'

'Well, they just says any day now. Her always has a bad toim, and weth her husband messen' since Chrestmas . . .'

'If there's anything I can do,' Rebecca murmured sympathetically.

'Yow look as ef *yow* shud be laid up – them black marks under your oiyes again, and your mouth all blue.'

'Perhaps I will go and lie down.'

'Well, yow leave thart choild down 'ere weth me.'

'She's got a jigsaw laid out in her room. I know she's anxious to get on with it. Sally, darling!' Rebecca called, going to the door. 'You can come in now. And you'll do your best about a lift, as soon as possible?' she reminded Mrs Maule, unable to put the matter out of her head.

Lying on her bed – Sally just inside the communicating doorway – Rebecca thought how much she detested Mrs Maule. Only the knowledge that they would soon leave this place allowed her, at last, to admit her detestation. While her eyes traced the cracks and patches in the ceiling plaster, she confessed it thoroughly. How dare the woman put her right about Sally! Of course, Mrs Maule was jealous of the child, that had suddenly become plain down there in the kitchen – she resented Sally's continual presence. Thank God the end was in sight!

The next day, as Rebecca awaited her with particular eagerness, Mrs Maule failed to arrive. The postwoman, half an hour late, arrived as Rebecca came out to scan the track. 'Do you know whether Mrs Maule's sister has had her baby, by any chance?' she asked.

'Oi dunno, moi duck. There ain't 'alf a carry-on at Barn Cottage, ef thart's anything to go boi.'

'The poor woman! Let's hope it's over quickly.'

Taking the proffered letter, she noticed absently that it was from Charlotte. She retraced her steps, her mind chasing the problem of getting Sally to Lipscombe. If her sister was now giving birth, perhaps Mrs Maule would be back in the morning with news of a lift. She might even have arranged for someone to take them to Lipscombe today. 'Letter from Charlotte,' she called at the entrance to the barn.

George dropped what he was doing at once. His eagerness for the communication made her curious, and she paused to dislodge a tuft of weed from the cobbles.

'I shall have to go over there at once,' he said, when his reading was completed. 'I'll stay overnight and be back by tomorrow evening. If I hurry I can be in Birmingham by midday.'

'Is something wrong?'

'Far from it. This could be just what we want. Old Colonel Beacham, who farmed at Priors Grendon, died a few months back. His place is to be auctioned on Friday. I'd better take a look at it right away.'

Only five miles from the Grange, she silently noted. Aloud, she asked: 'Is it possible to arrange finance by Friday?'

'That's another thing. It'll all have to be gone into. I'd better get on with it. Keep Jim home tomorrow to see to the animals, and make sure he gets on with the milking as soon as he gets home today.'

Her mind raced. She hurried after him. 'George! Just a minute!'

He turned impatiently.

'I can't let you go without saying how sorry I am that I introduced Sally into our argument yesterday. It was very wrong of me. It gave quite the wrong impression. Please believe me, George: I had no motive other than a profound anxiety for Sally's health.'

He softened at once, seeing that she was not about to prevent his departure, just trying to put things right between them. 'That's all right, old girl. We both got overheated. I know you've been worried about Sally. So have I. As a matter of fact I thought of asking Charlotte to find us the best physician in Birmingham so that we can get an appointment as soon as we've moved over there . . .'

So, it was a foregone conclusion; they would move to the Birmingham area.

'. . . But there's no urgency, Becky. You must allow she's better?'

Rebecca nodded. Relief that they were at one in concern for their child stole over her. She began to mistrust her recent agitation. George was so sensible. 'As long as she doesn't deteriorate – as she did that time before we went to Cheltenham. That was so alarming . . .'

'Trust me, old girl. I know a sick animal when I see one. She's not off her feed – not altogether; as long as she's taking something she can't be far wrong. No

281

harm's going to come to her in the next twenty-four hours, and the sooner we get ourselves settled into a decent home, the better for all of us, specially for little Sal. I'll have a word with Charlotte. We'll get the best man money can buy. Trust old George.'

'Oh, thank you, darling! And tell Charlotte how very grateful I shall be if she can recommend someone.'

He was pleased with this. 'I will! I will! Now, I really must get a move on. Best bib and tucker for Priors Grendon!'

The sun came out as Rebecca stood at the scullery sink washing the breakfast plates. Sally stood on a chair at her side, busy with a tea cloth. 'We're moving, we're moving,' Rebecca's heart sang. George had departed full of confidence. How reassuring he had been! 'Trust old George.' Well, she had been trusting old George for more years than she cared to remember – no point in stopping now. She turned and grinned at Sally. Good heavens! She felt happy! She was simply bursting with joy. The surprise made her laugh out loud.

'What, Mama?'

Rebecca shook her head helplessly; and Sally, finding the hilarity infectious, flicked her mother with the tea cloth and broke into peals of laughter.

On the train, George went over his sister's letter.

Dearest George,

What splendid news! And coming at such a time – for Manor Farm, Priors Grendon, is to be auctioned this coming Friday! (Poor Colonel Beacham died in March. Do you remember Pip telling us about his funny ways when she used to nurse him? The dear old boy!) Anyway, George, it is not *just* the place? Such a fine residence – more so than The Grange, even. So convenient, too – you'll be able to keep a very close eye on things from there. Do come at once and have a look at it. I've had a word with Ada and she is quite willing to assist. One thing, though, dear: she prefers to acquire the property herself and let to you as her tenant. This seems to her a more suitable course than a loan. Now don't be put off, [at this point, Charlotte correctly foresaw an ominous drawing together of eyebrows] Ada is so very good, I can assure you there would be nothing unpleasant in such an arrangement. Think of it! Manor Farm, Priors Grendon. Now *there* is an address. And there has always been a distinguished tradition with The Drifton from that house – the stables are bound to be a feature. You will have to make haste, mind. Come at once. Wire me from Cheltenham.

Your loving sister,
Charlotte

Rebecca awoke with a feeling of surprise. She had embarked upon this night without George at her side with trepidation, afraid that the isolation of Ridge Farm would prey on her mind in the small hours and kill all hope of sleep. It was still early, of course – there was an experimental note in the birdsong at her window – but duty had been done and she could now doze without obligation until it was time to get up. Thus, benignly, deceitfully, began the day she would recall in obsessive detail for the rest of her life.

She wandered in and out of sleep, heard the house stir and Meg call to Jim: 'Time you went up for the cows.' Dear, reliable girl! Some distance away a cow lowed, and a dog began to complain. The sounds travelled smoothly; evidently the wind was lying low this morning. Then, in the middle of a warm hole of silence, a shocking noise shattered her complacency. Retching, a strangled cry, more retching: the noise was close as the next breath. Before she had breathed it she was out of bed and through the communicating door.

Vomit lay in pools on the bed and in far-flung splashes on floor and wall. For a moment Rebecca gazed at it, noting items from the small meals they had rejoiced to see Sally eat. 'Oh darling! Poor darling!' The child clung to her, then thrust herself away, arching her body in painful spasm. Her skin burned to the touch. Her breath was sour.

'What's up?' It was Meg in the doorway who, taking in the scene, gasped: 'Golly!'

'Get some hot water and soap and towels.'

'There's a kettleful already. I'll put a pan on to heat and bring the kettle up. And you can come and help.' This last was to Bunny who had arrived silently and remained, staring dispassionately, after Meg had flown.

'Fetch Sally's face flannel,' Rebecca said sharply, disturbed by the unmoved spectator. Alone again with Sally, she began to panic. What was she to do? Meg returned, breathing heavily. 'Oh Meg, what are we going to do?'

'Get Daddy back,' Meg said decisively.

'Yes!' Rebecca cried. 'But how?' (Was it at this point, she was to ask herself in days ahead, that Meg's decisiveness and her own weak longing diverted her from a more effective course?)

'Send a telegram,' said Meg.

'Of course! You can catch the Cheltenham tram as usual and be at the main Post Office the moment it opens. Send it in your name, dear – "Come home at once, Sally very ill, Meg" – something like that. Money! We need money!'

'He keeps some in his writing box.'

'It's kept locked.'

'He puts the key in his waistcoat pocket.'

They exchanged looks of dismay.

'He wore his best suit!' Rebecca almost screamed.

Meg raced to the wardrobe in the main bedroom and felt inside her father's everyday tweed. 'Got it!'

She raced downstairs to the dining room. In a moment she was back with a coin. 'This'll do.'

'Good. Send the telegram to The Grange. Then go to Doctor Smalley's in Bath Road – you know where that is? – and ask him to come at once. Remind him that we brought Sally to him about ten days ago. Impress upon him the urgency.'

'I'd better get ready.'

'Tell the others to stay at home today. And hurry home yourself,' she called after her. (Later she thought that it should have been doctor first and then telegram. Or if she had sent Meg to the village to discover who the local doctor was . . . or to beg some local man to come up at once and drive them to Lipscombe in the Ludbury trap . . .)

Meg was pleased with her mother's instructions. She intended to carry them out with speed and efficiency, for she was fond of her younger sister, and then call at her school, for heaven only knew when she would be allowed to go to Cheltenham again. Little Sally looked very poorly indeed, and her mother was sure to need her at home for the next few days. The trouble was, exams were not far off: if she could collect some books from a sympathetic teacher or two, all might not be lost.

The hours dragged by for Rebecca. The departure of Meg, and the hope that Mrs Maule would arrive, buoyed her up for a while. Then Sally was again violently sick. By the time she had washed her and seen her slip into feverish unconsciousness, it was virtually certain that Mrs Maule did not intend to climb up Knoller Knap today. She crept from the room and called Bunny, who hurried up with an eager face. 'I want you to go to the village,' hissed Rebecca, pulling Bunny into the bedroom so that she could keep an eye on Sally through the communicating doorway. 'Find Mrs Maule – she may be at home, she may be at her sister's cottage on the main road; Barn

Cottage, that is – and tell her that Sally is very, very ill and we need help. Perhaps a lift to Lipscombe, or a visit from the nearest doctor. Beg her to do what she can. Explain that your father is away from home. Can you do that?'

Bunny nodded, straining to see into the sick-room.

'Hurry, then. Do it and come straight back. If you don't find her in either of those places, ask around. I'm sure she's well known in the village.'

Waiting time loomed again. Hope and despair rose in turn. A feeling of accomplishment after Bunny's dispatch soon ebbed, and was replaced by a tide of futility, for she was still alone, still cut off and isolated from urgently needed assistance. Then, her notions of a lift to Lipscombe and a visit from a local doctor, which had entered her head only as she had voiced them, assumed the stature of well-thought-out strategy, more appropriate and more likely to come to pass than a call from the Cheltenham doctor or George's prompt return. Rocking backwards and forwards on the edge of a basket chair in the communicating doorway, she willed Bunny to succeed.

It had gone quiet on Knoller Knap. There was no sound at all it seemed to Rebecca, other than harsh breathing from the narrow bed. When barking broke out, indicating an arrival, she flew from the house, across the yard and on to the track. It was Bunny, running on tired legs – just Bunny. Rebecca could not wait. 'You found her? What did she say?'

Puffing, Bunny yelled back: 'No . . . I couldn't . . . they wouldn't let me . . .'

Rebecca bit on her knuckles and waited for Bunny to draw level.

'They were all at Barn Cottage. A horrid old man shouted at me through the window. Then a lady came out of the next cottage and said their Molly had just died and she didn't think Mrs Maule would come out. Then the old man came running out shaking a stick at me. It was awful, Mama, I was really scared . . .' But her mother was already running back to the house.

There was no change in Sally. Rebecca assured herself of this and returned to the kitchen, arriving as Bunny trudged in from the yard. 'Go upstairs and sit in the basket chair in my room. Watch Sally, but don't disturb her. If she wakes, or shows any sign of distress, shout for me at once. Do you understand?'

Bunny nodded and went off to do as she was bid.

'I must think clearly about this,' Rebecca told herself, striving to quell her mounting panic. 'I'll drink some tea . . . eat a slice of toast . . . I've become too weak to think.' Ponderously she moved about the kitchen preparing her first nourishment of the day. The tea slopped as she poured it. 'Oh, damn!'

'I'll do it. You sit down.'

She had seen Jim come in without really registering his presence. As he handed her a properly filled tea cup she saw that his eyes were grave. 'Thank you, dear. Sit down. You have some too.' She sipped and nibbled, then moved from the table to sit in George's high-backed armchair. Her head fell back against the padded leather. For a few moments she closed her eyes. When she opened them, Jim was standing over her. 'I expect you're hungry after all that hard work outside. I'll send Bunny down in a while to make a cold dinner.'

'I can do that. Shall I boil some potatoes to have with the meat?'

'Yes, if you like.' What a surprising boy he was. Later, when he had put a saucepan of peeled potatoes on to the fire, she asked: 'How did you learn to do that?'

'Watching Emily.'

A thought sprang to her mind. 'Jim, can you drive the trap?'

'What?'

'Drive the trap. Could you drive it, do you think? You've watched your father often enough.'

'Perhaps. As long as he got the horse down the steep bit.'

The steep bit. She recalled George thrusting his shoulder against the horse, leading it diagonally across the steepest part of the descent, urging that carefully did it, that it should be taken nice and slow . . . Yes, the steep bit was treacherous, even for George. She saw now that the hill itself was the cause of her predicament. The doctor from Cheltenham would not arrive – 'Ridge Farm, Knoller Knap?' she made him scoff; it was not a reassuring address. She might as well face it: only Meg and George would come up Knoller Knap today, and no one other than George could get their sick child safely to the bottom. (But she should have got Jim to try, she would insist when it was all too late. Or, instead of wasting Meg on a fool's errand, she should have persuaded Jim and Meg together, early that morning, to try and get the horse and trap down the steep bit . . .) 'If only your father would come,' she groaned. 'Oh God, make him come!'

Jim stared at her sadly. 'I expect he'll come soon. I'll lay the table now.'

Upstairs, Sally awoke and put out her hand to the tall shadow leaning over her. The tall shadow was unresponsive. 'Mama?' she managed, dislodging, with difficulty, her tongue from the roof of her mouth.

'She's not here,' said Bunny.

There was a pause. Then the bed began to shake as the sick one heaved and spluttered – and all the time, Bunny observed, the heavy-lidded eyes clung to her own in fearful fascination. 'Got you! You've given in!' she exulted. Aloud, she remarked: 'You're awfully smelly.' The bed became still, but the hoarse breathing quickened and the eyes widened splendidly. Bunny tried for an even greater effect. 'And you're ever so, ever so poorly. "Very, very ill", Mama said. She told me to tell Mrs Maule.' The eyes became so huge that they seemed to fill the face – it was quite, quite thrilling. 'Mrs Maule's sister died this morning.' Bunny put her head on one side and added, watching her victim with care: 'I expect you're going to die . . .'

With a cry, Sally thrust her face to the wall. The spell was broken.

Prudently, Bunny hurried to the stair head. Had the cry been loud enough to carry? 'Come quickly, Mama! Sally's awake.' Then, as her mother rushed up the stairs: 'I think she's had a nasty dream,' for a worrying thought had occured to her. But all was well; though her ears strained for some minutes they detected no mention of dying or of being very, very ill. Her mother was doing all the talking: 'I'm here now, darling. Mama's got you. Have you been dreaming? Never mind. Take a sip of this. Just a tiny sip. Good girl. Lie back – no, I shan't go. Shall I tell you a story? Let me think, now . . .' Reassured, Bunny went softly downstairs.

At that moment Meg was walking along the track. The dogs gave her presence away, and she hurried into the first barn to hide a bundle of books in a secret corner. A precautionary measure; her conscience was perfectly clear, for she had spent but a small portion of the morning on her own affairs. But there was no point in asking for trouble. Some people, that wretched Bunny for instance, were bound to try and make something of it if she walked into the house bearing books.

Bunny and her brothers were eating their dinners at the kitchen table. 'Goody!' cried Meg. 'I'm starving. Is Mama with Sally? I'll just go and see her.'

Rebecca, having heard sounds of an arrival, had crept from the sick room to the landing. 'Well?' she hissed.

'I got a telegram off first thing. Then I went to the doctor's. He wasn't there, but the housekeeper sort-of-person said he was at the hospital because a lot of wounded came in during the night. She said she'd give him the message. I really told her, Mama, about how urgent it was and everything. To make sure, I went to the hospital and left a message for him there . . .'

'That was clever of you, darling!'

'Then I went to the station to find about trains arriving from Birmingham. There's one in at half-past two, which I reckon Daddy could catch. If he does, he'll be home by half-past three. How's Sally? Is she still bad?'

Rebecca nodded. 'Go and get something to eat.'

'Right-oh. Then I'll come and sit with her for a bit.'

Rebecca felt suddenly cheered. (Quite irrationally, she would point out to herself later, recalling this moment.)

Meg rushed to the dinner table and piled her plate high. 'Gosh! I'm ready for this!' Then, having tasted a mouthful: 'These spuds are unusually delicious.'

'I beat cream and butter into them,' Jim said proudly.

'You made them? Well done!' She looked at Bunny, who stared back balefully, her small helping of food hardly touched. 'What've *you* been doing, then?' Meg's practised eye notice a small red spot develop in the centre of Bunny's sallow cheek. 'You've been up to something!'

'No, I haven't.'

'Mmm. Eat your dinner then. Waste not want not. Hang on a minute, Harry, leave some potatoes for Mama.'

George, as his daughter had predicted, arrived in Cheltenham on the two-thirty train. The telegram had been opportune. A deal had been concluded with Mrs Skedgemore, and Charlotte had borne him back to The Grange for a celebratory luncheon. But George had been anxious for a little peace in which to think. Doubt had crept over him. Had the undeniable attractions of Manor Farm, Priors Grendon, and the need to come to a swift decision so that Mrs Skedgemore could put in an offer and get the auction cancelled, softened his judgement? Had he – perish the thought – allowed a fast-talking, toffee-nosed woman to put one over on him? Charlotte, with her breathless deference, had not helped matters. He had been turning these uncomfortable thoughts over in his mind when they pulled up in front of The Grange, and there was Louisa tumbling from the portico, shrieking and waving a telegram. With relief he had instructed the taxi driver to return him at once to Birmingham. On the train his misgivings were discovered to be groundless. Mrs Skedgemore's agent had been a sensible sort of chap, and it was him, not Mrs S., he'd be dealing with. By the time he reached the Ridge Farm track, George was feeling chirpy. Of course, there was this business with poor little Sal ahead of him . . .

Rebecca was in the kitchen when she heard the particular note of canine joy she had been listening for. She ran until she could hurl herself into his arms. 'George! George!' It was bliss to lean against his chest, bliss to hear the confident voice that had once soothed the harsh grief of motherlessness, bliss to believe that all, now, would be well. (Fool! Fool! she was to scream in her head down the years.) 'Thank God you're here!' she cried, raising her eyes to his face. 'She's so ill. Her stomach's hard as a rock. She's got a raging temperature. You should have seen the vomiting, it went everywhere, right across the room . . .'

'I'll run on and take a look at her. You catch your breath.'

They met again on the stairs; she about to ascend, he running down with a frightened face. 'Wrap her up. I'm going to rig up the trap. We'll take her straight to the hospital.' His voice rose to a shout as he passed her. 'I want that child looked at *immediately*.'

He was rehearsing for what lay ahead, she understood. Meg, who had been sitting with Sally when her father arrived, came out on to the landing. 'Mama?'

'Just look after things here.' It was to be the last thing she said to anyone for days.

There were no farewells, no waving hands, as Meg, Jim, Bunny and Harry gathered in the yard to watch their parents and sister depart. They wandered diffidently on to the track to watch until the trap passed from sight at the bend where the track joined the lane.

'Daddy's got to manage the steep bit now,' Jim said.

Meg shivered. 'The wind's getting up. Let's go in.'

7

The wind grew more vehement as evening and night progressed. Meg sent the others promptly to their beds, then sat with her books in the kitchen, continually distracted by elemental bluster. The wind teased her ears so that she often rose in anticipation from her chair; but no one came along the track, and the dogs, if indeed they had spoken, were instantly mute. At midnight she gave up the vigil. Leaving the yard door unbolted, she went upstairs, undressed in the dark and got into bed.

'Can you sleep, Meg?' whispered a wakeful Bunny.

'Yes – if you'll keep quiet,' lied Meg, for her ears could not stop straining for sound and she was too exhausted to be firm with them. The trap would not return until daylight, she reasoned, becoming more and more agitated over her inability to sleep. The hall clock chimed away the small hours. A bird at the window called a single, interrogatory cheep. Daybreak. She would never sleep now.

She awoke to be immediately disorientated by unusually comprehensive sunlight.

Its significance dawned slowly. 'Bunny, wake up! We've overslept.' In their room her brothers were still dozing. 'Get up, you lazy pair! It's nearly eight o'clock! The milking should be done by now, and the water fetched. We'll be for it if they come home and find nothing done.'

Milking was done, the house orderly, and breakfast underway by the time the dogs became excited. The children left the table and huddled in the yard doorway. Soon the trap swung into the yard. Their father sprang to the ground, then turned to assist their mother. She rose, put one hand on his arm while the other gathered her skirt. Empty-handed. The watchers took note of this and returned at once to the kitchen. 'Don't say a word,' Meg commanded superfluously. They sat at the table and waited.

Over cobbled yard stone, over flagged scullery stone, tapped quick, light feet. Their mother entered and passed through the kitchen without a glance in their direction, without a word. On went the footsteps, through hall, up stairs, along landing, until a door closed and their ears could detect nothing but the wind's whoop and fall. The children gazed at one another. 'I wonder if Daddy needs a hand,' Meg said; but no one was inclined to move. Eventually, Meg went into the scullery and peered cautiously through the window overlooking the yard. When her father emerged from the stable, he ignored the dogs' ingratiating squirms and strode quickly towards the track. 'He's gone straight up the field,' she reported. 'What's more, he's gone without the dogs.' This unlikely behaviour attached them even more firmly to their chairs. It was difficult to know how to proceed with the morning. 'I vote we keep our heads down,' Meg said at last. 'Each find a job to do – a quiet one – and keep out of their way.'

Their parents remained in hiding. The children prepared and ate the midday meal alone.

'Do you think . . . ?' Bunny began.

Meg cut her off. 'No I don't. I don't think anything at all.'

Harry began to cry.

Meg relented and put an arm around him. 'Look, I'm as much in the dark as the rest of you. Obviously something's up, but until they tell us about it, all we can do is keep our minds on other things. Now then, what are you going to do this afternoon?'

'Help Jim,' said Harry.

'Jim?'

'Tidy the yard. Sluice the cowshed. Milk.'

'Bunny?'

'Clean out the hens.'

'And I'll make some jam tarts for tea.' But first she would apply herself to the French Revolution – some point must be given to this aimless day.

In the dining room, she arranged her books on the table, took up a pencil and began to read. Faintly, the noise of the dogs reached her, their cries muffled by the bulk of the house and deflected by the wind. Was that little wretch, Harry, tormenting them? Or was someone on the track? But after a while she could only hear the wind rattling the window in its frame. Suddenly, there was a disturbance near at hand, an urgent knocking on the door to the garden. She stood, her mind reeling with the improbability of this event, for no one ever called at the Ridge Farm front door. The summons came again. Apprehensively, she went to the door and opened it a crack. A man in black stood there, a pale young man, with a top hat covered in flowing black crepe much agitated by the wind. She opened the door further to reveal herself. At once, the man whipped off his hat and put if to his chest.

He bowed. 'The coffin, Madam.'

'Oh,' said Meg.

'Instructions to come to Ridge Farm.'

No response came to mind.

'Where, Madam?'

'Where?'

'Where would Madam like it placed?'

Her eyes searched his for clues. None were found. 'I don't *know*,' she cried, clasping and unclasping her hands.

He regarded her for a moment. 'Perhaps you would care to consult . . . ?' He indicated the interior.

'I can't . . . There's no one . . . Well, I daren't disturb her, and he . . .' her voice trailed away in despair.

His manner yielded a degree. 'The parlour is the usual place,' he confided. 'Shall I look?'

'Oh, yes!' She ushered him in, and the wind snatched the door so that it slammed behind him. 'Would in here do, do you think?' she asked, opening the door to the small, damp, seldom-used parlour. As he passed, she saw that he limped grotesquely.

They stood together in the centre of the room, turning, looking about them, visualizing it as a waiting place for the dead. They made small adjustments – he eased a chair nearer the wall, she closed the piano lid – moving with smooth decorousness as if in time to slow music.

'Perfect,' he murmured.

She sighed.

'Perhaps?'

She read his mind. Both reached a hand towards the curtain and drew together. As curtains met, eyes met, met and slid away.

He limped quickly into the hall. 'Would you?'

'Of course.' Using her body as a door stop against the pushy wind, she braced herself and waited.

The procession came awkwardly down the bank, steadied, then came solemnly along the garden path. The young man led the way, clutching hat to bosom with an air of inexpressible sadness. A great lump formed in Meg's throat. She saw that his limp was embellishment, that he was a prince among undertakers (for the coffin bearers were elderly and coarse of countenance); enough could not be done for him, she felt, busying herself with doors like an over-anxious footman.

The coffin was settled with military precision. 'Open or closed?' inquired the pale young man.

'Closed,' Meg said hastily.

They left with little more ado. It was a dream, thought Meg, staring at the closed front door. Then she turned and saw the coffin through the sitting-room doorway. Suddenly, she was angry. It was too awful. *They* should have been here to receive it. It was monstrous of them to leave it to her – without warning, too.

'Is it *her*?' hissed Bunny.

Meg's heart leapt. 'Don't creep about like that! Yes, I suppose it must be.'

'Shall we look to make sure?'

'No!'

'But the man said "Open or closed?" I heard him. So we can look if we like.'

Meg surveyed her with distaste. 'We *don't* like.' Firmly, she closed the sitting-room door. 'Do the boys know, by the way?'

'We watched from the top of the yard.'

'That's that, then.'

'But what about *them*?'

Meg shrugged. Parents were beyond her comprehension.

Aunt Charlotte arrived the next day.

'What are you doing here?' Meg asked.

In view of the tragic circumstances, Charlotte decided to overlook this piece of rudeness. 'Your father wired me to come,' she explained in tones of suitable gravity.

'Well, he'd better say where you're to sleep, then, for I'm sure I don't know.'

Charlotte's eyes narrowed, but she spoke forgivingly: 'Some little nook . . .'

'There isn't one – unless you propose to sleep under the dining-room table. The coffin's in the sitting room, and father slept in here last night' – they were in the kitchen – 'and may well do so again. There's no spare room and no spare bed.'

'There's Sally's,' Bunny pointed out.

Meg dealt her a furious look. '*That* is hardly large enough for Aunt Charlotte. It isn't a proper-sized bed,' she explained to her aunt. 'It's such a tiny room that Daddy had to build a little bed into it . . .'

'But *I'm* quite little.' Bunny squeezed herself up to show. 'I'm the littlest one now.'

'There you are! Bunny can go in poor Sally's bed and I will sleep in hers. Otherwise you two girls will have to share Meg's.'

Meg suddenly saw the merit of Bunny's suggestion. 'We did put clean bedding on it – we thought she'd come back.'

'That's settled, then,' Charlotte said comfortably.

As afternoon merged into evening, Meg's misgivings about the sleeping arrangements deepened. It was not as if she could consult anyone. Her father, perhaps reassured by his sister's presence, had come to the table at teatime – his first appearance there since the tragedy – but his utterances had been sparse and monosyllabic, and his demeanour did not encourage questions. Of their mother there had been no sign, though it was thought she had been downstairs in the night. Aunt Charlotte, who had mounted the stairs with confidence, calling: 'Rebecca dear, it is I, Charlotte. May I come in? Do allow me to console you, my dear,' had been answered only by silence.

'Not eaten for two days!' Charlotte now moaned. 'You know, George, she ought to keep up her strength.'

George thought he would take a turn outside.

'I'll just get my stout shoes,' Charlotte cried. But too late: he was already gone, the yard door closed pointedly behind him.

The controversial bedtime arrived. 'Up you go, and don't make a sound,' Meg said sternly to Harry and Bunny. 'You must be particularly quiet, Bunny. Whatever happens, don't disturb Mama.'

They promised complete noiselessness. Jim thought he might as well go up, too.

'Good!' said Charlotte, drawing her chair closer to Meg's. 'Now we can have a proper talk. Tell me all about it. Unburden yourself, my dear.'

'Nothing much to tell. She was off-colour. Then she was violently sick. Then Daddy came home and they took her to hospital. No one's said a word about why she . . .'

'Peritonitis,' hissed Charlotte.

'How do you know?'

'Your father said so in the telegram.'

'Well, that was nice . . . I didn't even know she was dead until the coffin arrived.'

Charlotte sighed. She studied, with rapt attention, her hands clasped prayerfully in her lap. She sighed again, heaving high her considerable bosom. 'Meg, dear,' she began without raising her eyes; then paused.

'What?' Meg prompted suspiciously.

'I wonder . . .' As her voice hesitated wonderingly, her clasped hands rose and nestled at her throat. 'I wonder whether you have considered the funeral, dear?' Her eyes now sought and held Meg's.

'No. I can't say . . .'

'I have. I have given the matter much thought. And I find myself posed with a problem: should not the burial service for an innocent child contain some special mark of that innocence? Can it be fitting that coarse men should handle our angel-child's remains? Ask yourself, Meg. I think you will conclude – as do

298

I – that our innocent darling should be borne to her rest by unsullied hands, by youthful hands. Do you follow me, dear?'

Meg wondered whether Aunt Charlotte would be reassured to hear about the princely nature of the pale young undertaker.

'Think!' commanded Charlotte, making Meg jump. 'I'm sure you and Bunny have a few intimate friends, some sweet-natured girls, who would support you in your solemn task. Two sisters and four friends should suffice – the coffin can be no weight at all. Six pure maidens in white, their only adornment a ringlet of laurel leaves . . .'

'No.'

Charlotte blinked.

'I'm not getting togged up in laurel leaves to make an exhibition of myself at my sister's funeral. Neither is Bunny. And that's that.'

Charlotte thought rapidly, her eyes darting from side to side. 'I should have thought,' she said at last, 'you'd wish to make it a truly memorable occasion, for your poor little sister's sake, for your grief-stricken parents' sake.'

'Well there you're wrong. I don't want to remember her funeral. I want to remember her alive, running about, singing her songs, jiggling on Daddy's knee.'

Charlotte had one last try. 'Then you oblige me to take the matter up with your father . . .'

'I shouldn't if I were you, Aunt. I don't think he'll like it either. And as far as I'm concerned, you can talk until you're blue in the face: I shan't change my mind.'

Looking at her – at the fierce eyes and determined mouth – Charlotte knew she would not.

George came in. 'Time you two went up.' Evidently, he intended to spend another night in the kitchen.

'Come on, Aunt,' said Meg.

Preparing for bed, aunt and niece found little to say to one another. They were soon asleep, Meg at once, Charlotte a little later owing to the strangeness of the bed.

Thin rays of early morning were glinting through the curtain crack when Meg awoke. She held her breath. Had she dreamt it, or had someone shrieked? Cautiously, she raised her head and studied Aunt Charlotte. Nothing the matter there – dead to the world. But even as she looked, her aunt sat bolt upright, and she herself was propelled from her bed by a fearful commotion. 'Out! Out!' screamed a voice thick with rage. Meg rushed on to the landing.

Her mother was there, gesticulating in the manner of a vengeful oracle. At her feet cowered Bunny. 'Wretch! Demon! Singing like that! Singing that song! You're possessed! Never, never go in there again. And keep away from me, keep away . . .' Her voice became a wail, and she lunged into her room and slammed the door.

Meg seized her sister's arm and dragged her into their room. 'What have you done?' she demanded, flinging her on to the bed.

Bunny shook her head. She would deny all, she appeared to indicate.

'I know what you did. You put on Sally's voice. You pretended to be *her*. Didn't you?' Meg shook her violently. 'What a fright you must have given Mama, you little beast!' Without more ado, she turned her sister over and applied several hearty slaps to her bottom.

'Should you be *quite* so vigorous with your sister, dear?' Charlotte inquired from her bed.

'Sister, be blowed! She's an evil little runt!'

Charlotte, who knew only too well how necessary was the suppression of sisterly evil, yawned. 'Well, it *is* rather early. You had better both get into that bed. You can sleep top to toe.'

The prospect of Bunny's toe near her own top galvanized Meg. She was not having it. Enough was enough. She marched across the landing and rapped on her mother's door. 'Look here, Mama. Be fair. Father invited Aunt Charlotte – quite unbeknown to me; but it was I who had the trouble finding somewhere for people to sleep – I've had the trouble of just about everything. Well, I need some sleep if I'm to go on. So will you please allow Bunny to go back in that room? I've given her a jolly good hiding and I can guarantee she won't do it again. I'm tired, Mama . . .'

The door opened. 'Sorry,' said Rebecca. 'As long as she keeps quiet . . .'

Her ravaged face was utterly disconcerting. 'Oh, Mama!' Meg whispered.

The door closed at once – but gently, this time.

Meg was eating her breakfast with the stolid application of one whose mind is elsewhere. A most arresting dialogue had occurred at the commencement of the meal. When, Aunt Charlotte had inquired of her father, did he think of moving? Not that dear Ada was impatient – she understood perfectly how involved and time-consuming was the planning of a remove from one farm to another. And she herself would acquaint Ada with the recent tragedy which could not help but delay matters . . . Not at all, interposed her father. Come what may, they'd move to Worcestershire the moment harvest was in.

Meg's jaws chomped rapidly on toast and bacon as if bent on keeping pace with her flying thoughts. After the first pangs of shock and indignation, self-interested calculation set in. Next school year, her final year, was to be the triumph of her career at Cheltenham High, for she was Head Girl elect and destined to excel in the Higher examinations and secure a place at St Ursula's College. It was planned, it was written, and nothing was going to prevent it. Somehow she must get into school and seek help. Against the combined cerebral resources of herself and the Senior Mistress, the works of George Ludbury were unlikely to prevail. But when could she escape to Cheltenham? Not today. And the funeral was tomorrow. Perhaps the following day would present her with an opportunity. Unable to sit in patience once eating was done with, she rose, muttering a vague excuse, and strode from the house.

On the track she met Mrs Maule who was carrying a letter in her hand. 'Oh, I'm glad to see you,' she cried, thinking of the disorder of the house and the mountain of dirty linen in the wash-house.

'Well, moi poor sester was buried yesterday, so Oi thought as Oi'd come and geve poor Mrs Ludbury a hand – seein' as how we're sesters in grief, yow moight say. How's her takin' et?'

'Badly, I think. I caught a glimpse of her this morning and she looked pretty rough. I say' – she indicated the letter – 'is that for us?'

'For your mother. Oi saved the post a step.' She continued to hang on to it. 'Oi'll take et to her when Oi goes up for moi arders.'

'Indeed, you will not!' cried Meg, snatching the letter. 'She won't even let us into her room. And if you want to know what to do, just take a look in the wash-house.'

In the kitchen only Charlotte and Bunny still lingered at the table.

'This is Mrs Maule,' Meg announced.

'G' marnin',' said Mrs Maule challengingly.

'I see,' said Charlotte to Meg, who understood by this that her aunt saw Mrs Maule and was not encouraged by the sight. 'I shall go into the dining room and write a letter.'

Meg was about to follow her aunt from the room, when the uneasy suspicion arose that, between them, they might have offended Mrs Maule – a grave error in the circumstances. 'I say,' she called in the direction of the scullery where that lady's back was still visible. 'Mama will be bucked no end when I tell her you're here.' The broad shoulders unstiffened a degree.

'A letter for you, Mama,' Meg called outside her mother's door.

There was a pause, then her mother called: 'Come in.'

She was sitting in the basket chair by the window from which the curtains had been drawn.

'Oh, Mama, you're looking better!'

Rebecca smiled.

'Can I bring you some breakfast?'

'Tea would be nice. My special.'

'And a slice of toast?'

'Oh, very well. Where's my letter?'

'Here. From Aunt Edith, I think.'

'Good! I sent her a wire when . . . Wait and hear what she says.' She read rapidly, then put the letter in her lap. 'She'll be at the church just before ten. Teddy's going to bring her. Then they'll come up here for dinner and stay for the afternoon. Thank Heaven! I need to talk to her . . . Oh . . . ! Charlotte's here,' she recalled, and turned her head to stare out of the window. 'Charlotte,' she repeated in a small, bleak voice. Then, with an air of fierce decisiveness, she turned again to Meg. 'Get rid of her for me. I don't care what you say – just make her go. I won't put up with it. Not now. If I see her – all false sorrow and hard eyes – I might come out with it – that if it wasn't for her interference we wouldn't be here on this blasted hill, and Sally . . . Sally . . .' Sudden tears choked her.

Aunt Charlotte's interference? Her mother was overwrought.

'Mama, please don't . . . I'll think of something. . . . But it'll be a bit difficult getting her to go before the funeral – I suppose that's what she's here for. She's already tried to turn it into a production – me and Bunny and some other girls to be pallbearers, all decked out in laurel leaves. I soon squashed that. I told her I wasn't having it.'

'What a sensible girl you are! Well, let her stay for the funeral – I can keep out of her way until then. But she's to go directly afterwards. I must have some time with Edith.'

'All right. I tell you what, Mama' – Meg had seen her chance – 'I'll go with her into Cheltenham as soon as we come out of church. It'd be polite, and it'd make sure of it.'

'Wonderful!' Rebecca caught Meg's hand and laid her cheek against it. 'You are a dear. Whatever should I do without you?'

This was disturbing. 'I dare say you'll manage – when I leave home, that is.'

'Leave home?' Rebecca was bewildered.

'I've tried to tell you. I'm going to be a teacher. I shall go away to college, then goodness knows where I'll end up.'

Rebecca sat very still for a moment. Then she dropped a kiss on to her daughter's hand and let it fall. 'Of course. And I'm very pleased for you. I'm just so glad to have you with me now, for I doubt my need of you will ever be so great again.'

'I do love you, Mama.'

'I know. Now, can you look out a hat for me for tomorrow? Find that black one with the veiling I wore to the Webbs' memorial service. It'll be in the trunk with the hat boxes in. And I thought I'd wear that black crepe frock with the purple-lined pleat over the knee. Take it out of the wardrobe and give it a press. Oh, and make sure the children are decent.'

'Right-oh. Mrs Maule's back, by the way.'

The delicate colour vanished from Rebecca's cheeks. Even her lips turned pale.

'Why? Whatever is it?' whispered Meg.

Rebecca pressed a hand over her heart and shook her head.

'It's a good job she's back, isn't it? With all the washing to do, and Aunt Edith and Teddy coming to dinner tomorrow?'

Rebecca nodded.

'Well then, buck up. I'll go and make your tea.'

'Meg!'

Meg turned in the doorway, surprised by the harsh tone. 'Yes?'

'You bring it. Don't let . . .'

'Of course not, Mama. Don't worry, I shan't let anyone disturb you.' Carefully, she closed her mother's door.

Charlotte's were the only tears shed at Sally's funeral. They were noisy tears, and Meg hoped they would not discomfit her parents. But the perceptions of George and Rebecca were not lively that morning.

George observed – from frequent checks of the fob watch clutched in his hand – that time was getting along nicely. The parson was a man after his own heart: having awaited the cortège as if under starter's orders, set a cracking pace in the introductory prayers, cut in ruthlessly on congregational sluggishness in the responses, galloped hard through lesson and psalm, he had begun his sermon with a promise to be brief. Quite right, too. It was a very brief life to sermonize upon. Brief and spotless. Who could doubt that her journey to heaven would be swift, straight and thornless? Shouldn't wonder, the clerical chappie seemed to imply, if she'd already arrived and settled in nicely. Well said, lad, thought George, taking another peep at his watch. Yes, time was getting along pretty well, all things considered.

She is not here, thought Rebecca, sliding her eyes along the small coffin in the aisle. That night when she had crept down to take a look, she had seen at once that the still, cold shell was not Sally, did not contain Sally. Sally had gone. And now, staring up at the breathless individual in the pulpit, she longed to point out that Sally was not in heaven, either. The man was mistaken. Sally was up on the hill, with the wind beside the stream, on the track, in the garden, or chanting a tale to herself in the quiet of a shadowy barn. And that is where I should be, thought Rebecca; not in this dank church performing an empty rite. This is form without substance: up there is the heart of the matter. Her eyes closed. Her breathing became light and rapid.

When his wife failed to rise for the hymn, George was not surprised. Feeling wonky, he surmised; it was not to be wondered at. He grasped her firmly when it was time to follow the coffin to the graveside, and held her close during the committal. The pale young undertaker stepped forward and let a handful of earth trickle reluctantly through his fingers; it spattered briefly, shockingly, on to the coffin below. It was over. It was done.

'That's that then,' said George, looking about him, all at once feeling bleak. 'I suppose we can all go home.'

But not Aunt Charlotte, thought Meg, taking hold of her aunt's arm. 'Come on, there'll be a tram along shortly.'

'It seems heartless to rush off,' objected Charlotte, gazing after her brother.

'I told you: she wants to be alone with Aunt Edith. And it'll cheer Daddy up to show Teddy the farm.'

'Well, I suppose we could get a bite to eat in Cheltenham . . .'

'Good idea, Aunt – if there's time before your train.'

Great things were achieved in Cheltenham once Aunt Charlotte had been dispatched. Meg and the Senior Mistress put their heads together and came up with a water-tight plan – all contingencies allowed for, any possible objection overruled in advance. Meg returned to Knoller Knap well-armed for battle. During tea she rehearsed her opening move. The moment came to make it as she stood by her father on the track, waving Aunt Edith and Teddy out of sight. She put a hand on his arm. 'Let's go and see how the corn's getting on, Daddy.'

'Gracious me! I've been traipsing over the fields with Teddy all afternoon.' But her suggestion pleased him, nevertheless. 'There's a cow I want to take a look at.'

'Good. I'll come with you.'

'Me too,' squeaked Bunny, running up.

'No. Scram. I want a quiet word with Daddy.'

There was no point in beating about the bush. In her best matter-of-fact voice she told him: she would continue her studies at Cheltenham High and would lodge during term-time with the Senior Mistress; a year hence she would become a student at St Ursula's College in London. It was all settled, all worked out; there were no conceivable problems as far as she could see . . .'

George, who had never heard the like before, saw one at once. Where, he would very much like to know, was the money to come from to pay for all this? For he was sure he hadn't an idea.

'From you, of course,' Meg burst out indignantly. 'Blow me! I've been housemaid, nursery maid, errand boy and farmhand for as long as I can remember. I've jolly well earned it!'

George spluttered, made one or two false starts, then began to shout.

'It's no good shouting,' Meg enunciated sternly into his face. 'I can't hear a word when you bellow.'

George took a grip on himself. A new tack came to him. 'What about your mother? How is she to get on without you? Fine daughter you've turned out to be — all set to leave her at a time like this!'

'You're the one all set to leave,' Meg retorted. 'If you'd troubled to discover how a move might affect me, we wouldn't be standing here arguing the toss. And it is, you didn't even bother to tell me about it when you'd settled it all up.'

More brass-faced cheek! He supposed she was too old for a thrashing. Just the same, for two pins . . .

'And don't look at me like that. Are you going to cooperate or not? Because you'd better understand that I shan't give in. If you spoil things for me at school I shall get a job as a pupil-teacher and darn-well pay for my education myself. Think it over. By the way, I shall go back to school on Monday, come what may. Exams start next week.' With this, she turned and strode smartly away, leaving him confounded on the dusty track.

Rebecca was in her garden. Seeing her, Meg decided to enlighten her, too, as to her plans. This was an easier job. Her mother listened calmly, quite understood that Meg's studies could not, at this stage, suffer an interruption, thought it amazingly kind of Miss Devlin to offer her accommodation, only . . .'

'Only what, Mama?'

'Only your father will make such a fuss.'

'He already has. He'll get over it.'

Yes, but will I? Rebecca asked herself, returning wearily to the house. In the kitchen she sank into the high-backed chair. She had intended to retire after one last look at the garden, now she thought it prudent to wait and have a word with George. Her head fell back. Her eyes closed. She thought of Edith, of the weeping they had done that afternoon, of the hand-holding during long silences. There had been small need for words; Edith understood the nature of her sister's loss, she had made no attempt to minimize it or suggest that its impact would pass.

Her understanding had brought Rebecca a measure of relief. But there was one thing Edith had failed to grasp: Rebecca's remorse. Good. Her remorse was too fearful a thing to allow anyone to guess at; she must keep it hidden like an offensive deformity. It would be her secret, to be examined in private, to be fed, stroked, and revitalized by endless recitals of maternal failure.

'You here?' George said, coming in. 'I thought you'd have gone up. What a day, eh? Think I'll go up myself before too long.'

Their daughter being buried and done with, he could return to the marital bed, Rebecca observed to herself. Aloud, she said: 'About Meg.'

'Been pestering you with her wild ideas?'

'Hardly wild, George. Listen a moment. If you fight her, you'll lose. You'll lose the battle, you'll lose her. You don't want that. Now, if you let her finish her schooling at Cheltenham and then go to this teachers' college, you'll keep a very dear, grateful daughter. Think carefully, George.'

As was his custom in times of crisis, he began to search his family history for signs and omens. It was not a fruitless search. 'Of course, the girls had their little jobs – Pip her nursing, Charlotte her Deaf and Dumb . . . I bet I could fix Meg up with a job at the village school when she's done with this college business.'

One battle at a time, thought Rebecca. 'There you are, you see. Now go and make it up with her. She's in the dining room.'

He sauntered down the hallway feeling pleased with himself, opened the dining-room door and looked in with a sheepish grin. 'You'd better ask this good lady of yours how much she wants for your keep.'

'Daddy!' She rushed to administer a proper reward. 'There! And don't forget I'll be home every holiday.'

'Saints preserve us! We'll be sick of the sight of you if we're not careful.'

Rebecca heard their pleasantries and yawned. Now she could go to bed. She longed for oblivion. Perhaps, tonight, she would keep her mind from going down a certain path.

Meg awoke with a start. She lay in the moon-streaked room wondering why her heart had jumped, why her ears were straining, for only the wind disturbed the night-time hush. She got out of bed – saw that Bunny was sleeping soundly – and went to the window. A river of light flowed between the banks of black shadow thrown by the house and barn. Suddenly, fleetingly, a white-clad figure darted across the top of the yard, making for the track. The sighting was so brief that Meg, with her penchant for common-sense, was inclined to dismiss it – it could have been anything, a sack whitened by moonlight and tossed by the wind, anything. Even so, she went to the door and looked out on to the landing. The door to her parents' room was open; from within came the sound of her father's strenuous breathing. Pausing only to collect shoes and coat, she hurried downstairs. Moonlight shone in the space normally filled by the yard door; the wind had pinned the door back against the wall – perhaps it was the sound of that collision that had awoken her. She pulled on shoes and coat, and ran swiftly to the track.

The fleeing figure was revealed brilliantly by the moon. Meg set off in pursuit, her eyes on the erratic weaving of the ghostly one ahead. Then a sound reached her, so terrible that her pounding legs lost their stride. As she hesitated, it came again: an unearthly shriek, a despairing descant to the wind's roar. She stormed ahead, on and on until, drawing level, she was able to seize a handful of billowing nightgown and pull her mother into her arms.

*

'Sleepwalking – or sleeprunning, I should say,' Meg hissed. 'Driven by a nightmare, I should think.'

'Poor old lady,' whispered George.

They were standing near the bed in which Rebecca was still sleeping at ten o'clock in the morning.

'It's her feet I'm worried about. I cleaned them as best I could, but they're badly cut and there's grit under the skin.'

'Don't disturb her. She's exhausted. If need be, I'll get a nurse to come up later.'

'Telegram, Mr Ludbury,' Mrs Maule yelled ominously from the bottom of the stairs.

They looked at one another. '*Now* what's to do?' whispered George.

'Shall I get it and bring it up?' She knew that he would be put off by a hovering, inquisitive cleaning woman.

'Go on, then.'

Meg duly retrieved the telegram, and George went to read it by the superior light of the landing window.

'Well I never! I say, Meg, just listen to this: "Mama and Pip go to Buckingham Palace tomorrow. Pip to receive Royal Red Cross Medal. Writing. Charlotte." I wonder when Pip got home? But to the Palace! Great scot! The old lady'll never get over it.'

Meg, whose faculties were a little shaky after her broken night, uttered the first words to arrive in her head. 'She'll die happy, then – Grandmama will. At least *one* of you managed to turn up trumps.'

Affairs of the Heart

(1921–1923)

I

Stealthily over the Axminster, under cover of a hanging tablecloth, a large, smartly booted foot slid sideways and came to rest against a foot of more slender proportions in a pointed shoe. After a pause a little pressure was applied, and then – encouraged perhaps – the booted member slid behind and around the pointed shoe until foot locked on foot, ankle rubbed ankle, and with exquisite thoroughness calf brushed lengthily along calf. Despite appearances to the contrary – his eyes engaged his hosts' with laconic intelligence as if, at any moment, he would summon the energy to put an opposing point of view, and hers clung to her plate with the consuming interest of one bent on the gratification of greed – Karl Bruchstein and Meg Ludbury were totally absorbed in their surreptitious footwork.

'Darling, you go on and on, and it is plain that Karl disagrees with every word. I think you do it to provoke, and just as we were about to decide what to do about tomorrow. Isn't that so, Meg?' demanded Gussie Beale, nee Ludbury, of her niece. 'Were we not about to pin him down? Really, he is the most exasperating man.' And she pulled a face at her husband to indicate the fond depths of her irritation.

Meg sat up and drew her legs together. 'Yes, Aunt Gussie.'

'There! You see? Meg agrees you are quite beyond it.'

'No, no. I mean, yes, we were about to decide about tomorrow.'

'Well, dear one, are you going to allow Jackson to drive us or are you not?'

Doctor Beale frowned. 'Not, I'm afraid. I can't put off Dulwich tomorrow. Why not leave it until Thursday when all my appointments are here? Your excitable sister is probably jumping the gun again. I seem to recall your mother being at death's door before.'

'That was Charlotte's doing. This has Pip's authority, and Pip is a darn good nurse. Oh Ronnie, you *are* a mean man.'

'Go by train. Jackson can drive you to Paddington and collect you in the evening.'

'I'm much too fat to clamber on and off trains – in this heat, too. It's going to be a *beastly* day anyway ... '

'I shall drive you,' announced Karl. 'I have to call at the Birmingham Hospital sooner or later, it might just as well be tomorrow. I'll drop you both off and pick you up on the way back.'

'You darling boy! See how obliging some men can be, my dear!'

Meg jumped in quickly. 'The trains are awfully good, Aunt Gussie. There's plenty of room in them to move about. I shouldn't wonder if it weren't cooler by train than by car.'

'But if Karl's going anyway, and if it's no trouble to him ... '

'No trouble at all. In fact, I shall enjoy the company.'

'That's settled, then. Early start I suppose. What do you think? Seven o'clockish?'

Karl turned to Meg with his amused look – 'supercilious' was her private description of it. Annoyed, she looked hard at her plate. A most disagreeable scene loomed in her mind's eye in which she was obliged to present Doctor Karl Bruchstein to Miss Charlotte Ludbury. It quite put her off her pudding, which was a shame, for the primary purpose of her frequent visits to the Beales was to fill all the corners of her long, gaunt frame that remained unfilled due to the ladylike régime at St Ursula's and the stinginess of the allowance from her father. She took up her spoon and pulled herself together. Karl Bruchstein would be her aunt's concern tomorrow, for he was Doctor Beale's colleague and protégé, and he found it convenient to convey Aunt Gussie and herself to The Grange because he was soon to take up an appointment in Birmingham. That was all. He was nothing, her detached demeanour would make clear, nothing whatever to do with her.

'A little more, Meg?'

'Yes please.' As she passed her plate she decided she could even afford to hint that she disliked him, for it would not be far off the mark. The man enraged her, he was so . . . superior. And his opinions were diabolical – atheistical, anarchical, mechanistic. What particularly infuriated her, she thought, making rapid headway through her second helping, was the way he assumed she was an idiot. He was an arrogant, condescending poseur – and a foreigner and a Jew to boot. These last she could have overlooked were his other attributes less hideous. As it was, he made her blood boil. And if he thought she was about to take that miserable little job arranged by her father, just to be near him in Birmingham, he had another think coming. No. She would take the job she had been offered at the slum school in Sheffield, a school suitably eager to employ her, a school – it had been made plain to her at the interview – where promotion prospects were good.

'Why don't you two young things take a stroll in the park?' suggested Gussie, smiling significantly at her husband. 'We'll have coffee later. It's such a beautiful evening.'

Meg was not fooled. Her aunt and uncle hoped for a romance. It was quite disgusting. 'Right-oh,' she said, getting promptly to her feet. And Karl unwound his long body from the chair and offered her his arm.

'The thing I find so fascinating about you, Meg Ludbury,' he said some twenty minutes later as they stood pressed together behind a screen of laurels, 'is your fanatical single-mindedness. It is so totally at variance with your vague appearance. Short-sighted, are you not?'

She wished he would keep quiet and get on with it. 'We'll have to start back in a minute,' she pointed out. Obligingly, he put his hand inside her blouse. She closed her eyes.

But he was in the mood for titillation. 'You know, my dear, your May Pageant was my undoing. Gussie, thought I would find it amusing – typical English understatement. I salute your Mr Ruskin! He was a man of genius. But he should have lived to see Queen Meg, a queen beyond his wildest hopes, a mediaeval dream of queen! What a spectacle! – so much green everywhere (such a succulent colour, is it not?): green eyes, green gown, green coronet in your loose frizzy hair . . . Oh, my dear, what would Rossetti have made of you in your clinging gown, and those silly, prancing girls crushing flowers into the slimy grass with their great white feet . . . ?'

Meg, who generally held that kissing diminished rather than enhanced the pleasure, put her mouth over his to silence him.

'You will have to sit in the front.' Gussie said. 'I need the whole of the back seat to spread myself.'

Meg climbed in. Karl helped Gussie to stow herself behind, then got into the driver's seat. 'Ready, Miss Ludbury?' he asked with mock solicitousness, his hand at a provocative angle on the gear stick.

'Quite,' she said shortly, fixing her eyes on the road ahead.

'You can chat quite freely, you two,' bawled Gussie after a while. 'Can't hear a thing back here.'

'We can chat,' observed Karl.

Meg turned to look at the houses, row upon row of them, on her left.

'Today I shall look for a house in Birmingham,' he announced, noting the direction of her eyes. 'Near to the station, perhaps – you are always so against wasting time.'

He was counting on it, the impudent fellow! Worse, he was making fun of her again. How she relished the thought of disappointing him. It would give him quite a jolt when she took herself off to Sheffield. Which she would. They were very clear at St Ursula's as to Sheffield being a better prospect than the two-class school in Priors Grendon. And she had never had any intention of returning to live under her father's wing – she could just imagine how he would interfere; already he had got himself elected chairman of the school managers. No, it would never do. She sighed.

'More air,' he suggested, lowering the window another inch.

She glanced at him, at the springy shock of hair brushing the roof of the car – he was such a giant of a man – at the large-featured face, the affected bow-tie, the elegant, manicured hands. It was a pity he was so impossible, she told herself, thinking regretfully of points in his favour, points she might miss in Sheffield. She would not miss them, she contradicted herself. Certainly not. Once out of range she would never give him a thought. Life had been perfectly satisfactory, by and large, without him. The round of lectures, society meetings, school visits, games practice, later night gossips, and blissful early morning services in the college chapel (incense, vestments and plainsong; the chaplain was very spiky) had

317

completely fulfilled her. During her first term she had been elected to the Ursulanian Society – a rare honour for a fresher – and her popularity and success had lately been crowned during the May Day ceremony. (The formerly wonderful Edith Mayfield had been denied a similar success, having been snubbed for her Quakerism by the High Anglican voluptuaries of the Ursulanian Society. Meg Ludbury was the old girl raved over, now, at Cheltenham High.) Karl Bruchstein had been discovered towards the end of her first year when, driven by hunger, she had sought out her affluent relatives in Kensington. Though she had loathed him on sight, she had been unable to ignore him; indeed, to some extent she had pursued him, determined to find out what exactly it was that his sardonic manner hinted at and her own heart leapt at as if already privy to the secret. Well, she had found out. It had been quite a revelation. But her famous common sense had allowed her to compartmentalize, to keep a sense of proportion, to get on with the job; and during the many-faceted life of college she put him firmly out of her mind. And so would it be in Sheffield; she would shrug him off, snuff him out, forget him.

Out of the corner of her eye she watched his left hand move the gear stick and his right hand perform an elaborate signal through the open window. A pang smote her – she did so hate waste. However, she had already learnt that there was no changing him, having tried on numerous occasions to make him understand what a desirable thing was a decent, English, God-fearing outlook. He had thought it a joke.

'Right at the crossroads,' boomed Gussie, sticking her head between the front seats. 'Help! I've got the collywobbles. Wish I'd waited for the funeral. Slow down, Karl, it's somewhere along here on the right. That's it!' She thrust a pointing finger across the driver's face, then sank back with a groan.

Only Aunt Pip hobbled down the steps as the car drew up in front of the house. For a moment Meg was nonplussed – arrivals at The Grange were always greeted by a clutch of noisy aunts – then she recalled the purpose of their visit and supposed that Aunts Charlotte and Louisa were keeping vigil at Grandmama Ludbury's bedside. Aunts Gussie and Pip fell upon one another. They were very alike, Meg saw, except that one was overblown and the other emaciated.

'What have you done to yourself, child?' screamed Gussie. 'You're a skeleton.'

'Never mind me. What about him? Who is he?'

'My paramour, of course.'

'Rubbish, you fat hag! But isn't he nice? Introduce me.'

'This is Doctor Karl Bruchstein,' confessed Gussie. Then, to Karl: 'My sister, Miss Caroline Ludbury, RRC.'

'An honour!' Karl said, with a bow.

'A doctor! Oh, I think doctors are lovely! Are you Meg's? Is he Meg's young man?'

'Certainly not,' said Meg, speaking for the first time since their arrival.

'More fool you!' said Pip.

Meg turned haughtily towards the portico, but as she moved she saw Aunt Gussie give Aunt Pip a poke. Aunt Pip yelled in triumph. 'He is! He's Meg's young man. The lucky beast! She doesn't deserve him. You do know,' she cried, catching hold of Karl's arm, 'that she's a horrible prig? I shouldn't bother with her, if I were you. Now, when I was a young nurse . . . '

'A plague on you, Aunt Gussie,' Meg said under her breath, and hurried into the house.

At the top of the stairs Charlotte was waiting to brief the newcomers. 'Where's Augusta?' she hissed as Meg appeared.

'Being silly with Aunt Pip.'

'Oh.' Charlotte's look said it all: there was no occasion too solemn to inhibit the silliness of certain sisters. 'But thank God you're here, Meg. You've meant so much to your Grandmama; you epitomized some of her finest work.' And she clapped her niece damply to her bosom.

'How is Grandmama?' asked Meg, extricating herself after a decent interval.

'Near the end, I fear. But she may be spared long enough to take comfort from your presence. And, my dear, I am so *thankful* we have a chance to talk today. I've a great deal to say to you' – she grabbed Meg's forearms and gave her a small shake – 'of the *utmost* importance. You are needed at home; your father requires proper support and, as I have explained before, your poor Mama isn't quite up to it . . . Ah, Augusta . . .'

Gussie arrived breathlessly on the landing. 'In time, are we?' she inquired.

Charlotte frowned. 'Augusta, I am sure Mama would wish you, too, to be at her side at such a time, but if she should show any sign of distress, I must beg you to withdraw at once.'

'In here, I suppose,' Gussie said, making for the door.

Charlotte hurried to precede her.

Hesitantly, Meg followed her aunts.

The room came to meet her, wrapped itself around her so that she felt she had done nothing, been nowhere since she last breathed the stale, dust-laden air. Its changelessness was impressive – the desk beneath Grandpapa's portrait, the little-used washstand, the tin of hair grease in pride of place on the dressing table, the half-decayed, half-drawn curtains, the odour of jerry, camphor and grime; everything was exactly as it always had been. It was only yesterday that she had stood at the foot of the high bed reciting the latest dollop from her grandmother's pen: at any moment, Meg felt, a sharp voice would snap from the pillow-mound at the bedhead: 'Head up, girl! Speak out!' But something was missing, she saw as she approached the bed; there were no pinpricks of light gleaming like demons in the gloom. Grandmama Ludbury's eyes were shut.

A sob shuddered into the silence. 'Meg! Augusta!'

'Shh,' Charlotte admonished Louisa.

With the air of one who has seen it all before, Gussie felt for her mother's wrist and put an ear to her mother's chest.

'What do you think?' asked Pip from the doorway.

Gussie shrugged.

'She'll rally suddenly, then go,' predicted Pip. 'There's no point in us all hanging around. As long as one of us stays to call the rest.'

'Come on, then,' said Gussie, taking her arm. 'I want to know what you've been up to, why you're just skin and bone.'

'Oh dear,' Louisa said sadly when they had gone. 'Perhaps I should see about dinner.'

'Yes, go on. Meg and I will keep watch.'

Oh Lord! I can't stand it, thought Meg looking across the bed at Aunt Charlotte who was eyeing her purposefully; not all that again about being a dutiful daughter and coming back home to poor Daddy because Mama is completely useless . . . 'I'll be back in a minute,' she mumbled, hurrying after her humblest aunt before an objection could be raised.

Louisa, having heard her, awaited her on the landing with tremulous joy. She seized Meg's arm and drew her to her own room at the end of the corridor. 'Come in, dear. I remember how you always loved my little room – so much so, that we once told a naughty story because you wanted to sleep in here instead of Aunt Charlotte's room. Weren't we *wicked*?'

Meg, who couldn't think what her aunt was talking about, muttered: 'Were we?'

'Yes dear, you remember. And to celebrate I showed you my secrets.'

Meg sat on the edge of the bed. Clearly, Aunt Louisa was off her head. In another room Grandmama Ludbury lay dying. Aunt Pip was thin as a stick – a bent one at that . . . Were the inhabitants of The Grange disintegrating?

'And now,' said Louisa, 'she's dead.'

'Who's dead?'

Louisa sank into the basket chair and fixed wide eyes upon her niece. 'Sally is, dear,' she said reproachfully. 'We are talking about Sally.'

It was time someone took a firm hand with Aunt Louisa. 'I hardly need you to tell me that. She's been dead for three years now, we can't dwell on it for ever.'

'Three years?' Louisa's eyes raked the room for an explanation. 'Oh, no, not your little Sally. My Sally, my dearest friend, Miss Sally Edmunds.'

'Oh, her.' A faded summer rushed back in fragments, vague, troublesome memories full of warring aunts and wicked uncles. 'I'm sorry for that,' she said, speaking more kindly. 'Young to die, wasn't she? What happened?'

Louisa became agitated. She clamped a hand to her mouth as if fearing the escape of an indiscretion. 'It was something we ought not to mention,' she ventured at last. Then, as tears began to flow: 'I'm afraid poor Sally died . . . shamefully.'

'What are you on about? Must you keep talking in riddles? I'm going to have a fearful head. Look, do you want to tell me or not – I presume you brought me in here to say something?'

'Oh, Meg! She died in childbirth. Unmarried,' she suddenly blurted. 'No one knew a thing about it. She didn't breathe a word to me, just went away. She wrote to me on a picture postcard from Sussex saying she was living on a farm and they all favoured Irish Leghorns down there . . . How *could* she? Without a word of explanation to her dearest friend . . . '

'I'm not surprised,' Meg said stoutly. 'Fat lot of use *you'd* have been in the circumstances. I mean, if you can't even mention the matter, what on earth would have been the point of confiding in you? Really, Aunt Louisa . . . ' Then, as time was getting on, and Aunt Louisa appeared to have taken root, hands gripping chair-arms, mouth agape like that of a hooked fish, she stood up and said: 'I say, what about dinner? Hadn't you better go down and see to it? And there'll be a nasty atmosphere if I don't go back to Aunt Charlotte.'

In the doorway, Meg hesitated. 'You are coming, Aunt?'

'Oh . . . yes . . . ' Louisa assented vaguely, still rigid in her chair.

At dinner, Pip let the cat out of the bag. 'When is your young man coming back?' she demanded of Meg across the table. 'Will he be here for tea?'

'No,' said Meg quickly, and was then covered in confusion.

'What's this?' Charlotte asked.

'Meg's young man brought them in his car. He's coming back for them later.'

'Who is this man?'

'Doctor Karl . . . How was it?'

'Bruchstein,' said Gussie.

'Sounds foreign,' Charlotte commented ominously.

'Jewish, I should think,' said Pip.

Silence. Thoughts raced through over-heated minds; comments and questions rose to the surface to be rejected pending further consideration. The fevered speculation was broken by Pip, whose words revealed the nature of her own particular train. 'Interesting thing about Jews,' she mused: 'they all have the end of their John Thomas cut off. We found that quite useful when it wasn't known what a chap's religion was. Of course, you do come across other chaps with

323

a trimmed John Thomas, but if you've got a fellow about to expire and he's all intact, you needn't waste time looking for a rabbi . . . ' Her reflections continued in silence.

The immediate concern of the other ladies present was to discover whether masculine sensibilities had been affronted. Eyes flew to the top of the table. Fortunately, Freddy was absent, it being his turn to keep watch at the deathbed, and Edward's attention was elsewhere. 'What's that?' he cried jumpily, as sisterly eyes turned upon him. Thanking heaven for small mercies, they looked away.

Gussie hastened to change the subject. She turned towards Charlotte. 'George will be here this afternoon, I think you said. I haven't seen him for years. Is he liking his new place, do you know?'

An urgent need for peace and quiet came over Meg. Announcing that she would relieve Uncle Freddy and that she did not require pudding, she rose and left the room.

Uncle Freddy was mightily glad to see her. He sprang to his feet, placed a hasty peck on her cheek, and hurried away to his dinner.

Meg could detect no change in the occupant of the bed, except that the breathing sounded more rasping. She went to the window and started out across the lawn, beyond the monkey puzzle tree, over the dwindling fields to the purple-hazed horizon. Families, she reflected, were the very devil: nosy, interfering . . . she couldn't put up with it. Thank heaven for Sheffield. But in the meantime she had a term to complete at St Ursula's and several summer weeks to go through at home. She had better try and intimate to Aunt Charlotte, before anything could be said to her father, that Aunt Pip had been talking through her hat.

Wheels squelched over the gravel below; there was a last-minute application of brakes. Pressing close to the window and looking down, she saw that it was her father's big black Morris. He was a dreadful driver, given to yelling 'Whoa' and pulling on the steering wheel before recalling that it was necessary to depress the brake pedal. Aunts swarmed from the portico and buzzed around him. Attempts were made to lead him indoors, but Charlotte succeeded in drawing him on to the lawn. She waved her sisters away, and began to lead her brother, their heads inclined at a confidential angle, towards the monkey puzzle tree. Here we go, thought Meg, now he'll hear all about it. She closed her eyes and prayed that there need be no mention of rabbis or John Thomases.

Gussie entered. 'Here!' hissed Meg, indicating the window. She pointed to the conference on the lawn. 'See what you've landed me in? I told you we should take the train.'

'What does it matter?' asked Gussie airily. 'What can they do?'

'Make life jolly uncomfortable.'

Gussie thought for a moment and discovered the truth of this assertion. She put her arm in Meg's. 'Sorry! Look: when Karl comes back we'll just clear off. No need to hang about. We'll have done our duty.'

Glumly, they went closer to the bed and sat on two straight-backed chairs. Long minutes went by. They were joined by Louisa, then Pip, then Charlotte and George. George nodded bleakly to his daughter across the bed. Then, at last, Grandmama Ludbury opened her eyes.

'Quick, get the boys,' hissed Charlotte.

Meg sped away, and returned a minute later with two reluctant uncles. She crept nearer to the bed.

Mrs Ludbury's eyes roamed with disfavour over the assorted faces at her bedside. The watchers almost forgot to breathe, so great was their sense of awful expectancy. At any moment, it was felt, the dying one would bequeath her final message to the world.

Would she bid each one farewell? Would she salute Gussie with the hand of forgiveness, or Miss Caroline Ludbury, RRC, with the kiss of consummated rapture? ('Quick, Pip, go and get the medal in case she wants one last look at it.') Might she, at long last, acknowledge Charlotte's staunch defence of the family interest? Would the sight of her granddaughter inspire a valedictory couplet, or the sight of George trigger memories of Harold – would her dying breath be expended on a request to gaze for the last time upon the likeness of her spouse . . . ?

'Where is she?' Mrs Ludbury snarled.

She? Which she? Several she's jostled and pushed, stepped forward and back, offered themselves or another.

Mrs Ludbury was getting cross. Her mouth trembled with impatience. 'Louisa!' she got out at last.

Louisa? It was too improbable. Eyes turned incredulously to the favoured one, who edged forward fearfully. 'Yes, Mama?'

On the threshold of eternity, Mrs Ludbury delivered herself: 'I'll have it up here on a tray. Mind you slice it thin, and don't forget the mustard.' Whereupon, her head fell back against the pillows, never more to rise.

Her grandmother's timely demise saved Meg from further embarrassment. When Karl arrived, she and Gussie hurried to shut themselves in his car, and those watching their departure were obliged by the recent nature of their loss to keep a discreet and reticent distance. Earlier, Aunt Charlotte had taken Meg aside and begged her, in the family interest, to go home with her father until after the funeral. Meg had scotched this emphatically: she had a viva with an external examiner in the morning, so it was imperative that she return to college tonight.

Gussie, in the back of the car, now recalled this. She leaned forward. 'I say, Meg, you will have dinner with us tonight before you go back?'

'That would make me too late. I'd rather go straight back, Aunt.'

'I'll take you,' Karl offered. 'We'll drop Gussie off and pick up your things, then go on to Chelsea.'

'All right. Thanks.'

Gussie sank back, too exhausted to press it.

Half an hour later, the occupants of the front seats were dismayed by sounds of weeping in the back. Meg was startled. Aunt Gussie had been a pleasant discovery; easy-going, jolly, interested in one's doings but not inquisitive, undoubtedly the best aunt of the bunch. She had been pleased to detect an independent edge to Aunt Gussie's character. So what was she thinking of, blubbing like a ninny over the death of a woman who had had more than her fair share of life, and who had spent much of it making the lives of dissenting others thoroughly uncomfortable?

Her disapproval – evident, perhaps, in the stiffening of her back and the sudden turn of her head towards the side window – was conveyed to Gussie, who heaved herself forward and placed her head between the seats. 'You needn't think I'm crying for *her*,' she protested hotly. 'I'm crying for *me*. I'm crying for all of us, for the whole darn shooting match: for the confounded impossibility of ever getting things right between us. I mean, what was so wrong, what was so wicked about going one's own way? It didn't hurt anyone, did it? We can't all be the same – some of us don't want to be the same. Why can't people live and let live instead of being so hard-faced, so *condemning*? And don't look like that – you might feel the same one day. You wait and see . . .'

Well! What a scene. And in front of *him*, who was tickled pink, Meg would wager. Cautiously, without moving her head, she peeped at him out of the corners of her eyes. But he was expressionless, intent on the road ahead.

On arrival in Kensington, Gussie hurled herself on to her husband's breast. 'Ronnie! It's been a horrible day. Yes, she's dead. But I was a silly on the way home and they're annoyed with me.'

'Certainly not,' murmured Karl.

'Prove it then. Come to luncheon on Sunday. Both of you. We're expecting quite a jolly crowd.'

'Delighted,' said Karl, turning inquiringly to Meg.

Meg decided to be forgiving. 'Of course,' she said, placing a kiss on the tear-stained cheek.

'Straight to Chelsea?' Karl asked as they drove away.

Meg considered.

'Well?'

'Perhaps not *straight*, necessarily.'

'To my rooms, then. For a cup of tea.'

'So long as we can have milk in it and not that beastly lemon.'

Meg pushed against the door (it opened smoothly, with great weight upon its hinges) and stepped inside. A small red glow in the chancel, a token of the sacrament, was the only illumination; but after a moment her eyes grew accustomed to the gloom and she was able to proceed confidently to a pew halfway down the aisle. The stale, incensed quiet lapped over her, and the pulse of the place – the unaccountable creak and rustle of an unpeopled building – became her pulse. She always felt at home in this chapel dedicated to Ursula, princess, saint and martyr, leader of English virgins. During the past two years, contemplating the Burne-Jones portrait of the saint in stained glass above the altar, she had often wondered whether she, too, was Called. It was not unlikely, bearing in mind the special relationship existing between herself and the Almighty, their easy, conversational intimacy, the overwhelming evidence that He and she thought as one. However, her biology being as He had ordained it, the priesthood was not her destiny. What, then, could be His purpose but a nunnery? Arrival at this conclusion invariably let to unease concerning the vow of obedience: it was one thing to swear obedience to God who could be relied upon to see things her way, quite another to submit to a mere earthling whose spiritual antennae might be imperfectly tuned. On the other hand, it struck her as highly probable that mothers superior were of similar clay to principal mistresses, with whom she had always got along splendidly.

Thus had her thoughts run on. But now God, in His wisdom, had presented her with Karl Bruchstein, and at once the vow of chastity became the obstacle. God, it was plain, did not intend her to be celibate, though why He had chosen Karl Bruchstein to bring this truth home to her, rather than some nice upstanding Christian, was not plain. Why choose an atheistical Jew? she silently asked the likeness of Christ, dimly visible on the rood screen Cross. All at once she was answered. God intended her to convert the man. She sat very still, allowing the enormity of this to sink in, for it was a tough nut to crack, almost as tough as those encountered by missionaries in darkest Africa. . . . 'Oh!' she gasped aloud, as the workings of Divine Intelligence were further illuminated. 'A missionary!' So that was His purpose for Meg Ludbury. Well, well. . . . She had to hand it to Him; it made sense: within a month she would be qualified to teach, a qualification she could take anywhere in the heathen world. But first, advised God, let her sharpen her wits on the heathen doctor. Oh, she would, she would! So Sheffield was not to come to pass. It would be Priors Grendon, after all; just a few miles from Birmingham where her quarry was soon to reside. She slid on to the kneeler and embraced destiny with a joyous Magnificat.

Tenderly, St Ursula looked on.

2

'Blasted, interfering so-and-so! I tell you, I can't put up with it.' He brought his fist down with a thump.

As the cutlery bounced, Rebecca thought she would go to her room. They had been through this before, for Mrs Skedgemore was forever doing what George could not put up with, and it always proved noisy, lengthy and exhausting.

'I mean, what does she think she's about? I pay the rent don't I? What makes her think she can come poking her nose into my business without so much as a by-your-leave? I blame Charlotte, she got me into this with her "Ada is so good" nonsense. I'll give her Ada is so good! When I found that woman large as life in the dairy, I saw red. I let her hear about it . . . '

'We know. We could hear every word in the house. Try and put it out of your mind, George, or you'll have frightful indigestion.'

It was summer. At Manor Farm in Priors Grendon the entire family was seated at the table. Meg sat at her father's right hand. She had completed her course at St Ursula's and was waiting to take up her appointment at the village school. Opposite Meg sat Harry, who was home from his expensive boarding school. (George had been taken with the desire to make a gentleman of his younger son.) Jim sat at his mother's right hand. He had done with school and now worked fulltime on the farm. He had become such a part of the work force that he referred to and thought of his father as 'the Guv'nor', though he carefully refrained from calling him anything at all to his face. Privately, Jim dreamt of Canada, egged on by Meg in whom he had taken to confiding. She brought him geographical magazines full of articles about pioneer farming, which he hid under his boots at the bottom of the wardrobe. Sometimes he thought he would show them to his mother – she was always so interested when he spoke knowledgeably of distant places – but he could never quite gather the courage. This was strange, for he was close to Rebecca; they had discovered a mutual delight in the cinema, and once a fortnight he borrowed the Morris to take her to a picture house in Birmingham. At Rebecca's left hand sat Bunny, ready to jump up and remedy any shortcoming on the part of her mother or the maid. Bunny had one aim in life, which was to make herself indispensable to her father. She stuck grimly to house, garden, hen coop and dairy, ignoring all her mother's hints about training to do this or that in Birmingham or some other disgraceful place. And her father *was* pleased with her, she could tell from his fond manner, his winks and his pattings of her head, all proclaiming how very satisfactory he thought it to have a dutiful daughter at home.

The pudding had been eaten. The talk had turned to the afternoon's activities when it was cut short by the sound of a car drawing up outside and a toot of a horn. George went to the window to investigate. 'Pip,' he announced. 'Funny time to come, ain't it? Go and let her in, Bunny; I dare say Beattie's got her hands full in the kitchen.'

After a few moments he went into the hall to greet his sister. 'Something up?'

'Edward and Freddy are up,' said Pip, leading him back into the dinning room where she collapsed into the nearest chair. 'They're at it hammer and tongs, and this time it's serious; they've taken a shotgun apiece and shut themselves in the barn. Charlotte sent the men off in case of a scandal, then sent me here to collect you.'

Rebecca was not sure she liked the sound of this. 'Really, they are two grown men. I should leave them to sort out their own affairs.'

'Trouble is,' said Pip, 'if they sort 'em out by blasting each other's head off there'll be a bit of to-do. I daresay we'd think it a merciful release, but there might be talk of murder . . .'

'I'm coming. But I'll come under my own steam if you don't mind.' (He was not the man to allow a woman to drive him.) 'Coming back with me?'

'No. Go on your own if that's your attitude. I'll be along when I've caught my breath. I've got something to show Rebecca.'

'Take care, George,' Rebecca urged.

Pip watched from the window as George backed the Morris from a barn. 'Hopeless,' she commented.

'What do you mean?' Rebecca was indignant. It was one of her favourite treats to motor out with George exploring countryside and town, and to stop for a meal at a good hotel.

'He hasn't an idea about motors.'

'Well, really! I think it's marvellous how quickly he took to one, and I always feel perfectly safe with him.'

'Of course you do, dear,' said Pip. 'Never mind him. Where can we talk?'

A maid came in with a tentative air. 'Yes, do clear, Beattie,' said Rebecca. Then to Pip. 'We'll go into the sitting room.

They sat in opposite chairs and looked quizzically at one another.

Pip felt in her pocket. 'Had a letter yesterday from Tony Benton, you know, the one who lost a leg . . .'

Unexpectedly, a friendship had sprung up between Pip and Rebecca. Soon after their arrival at Priors Grendon, George had persuaded Rebecca to accompany him to The Grange for tea. As they approached the house she had thoroughly cursed herself, foreseeing a very hard time ahead. Charlotte and Louisa had greeted her in the drive, one stiffly, the other tearfully. Entering the enormous, well-remembered sitting room, where she expected to find Mrs Ludbury lying in wait for her, she was startled by the sight of a younger, paler, spent-looking woman lying on a great settee. She had started forward, full of an instinctive concern, and her greeting had been largely an exclamation of surprise as realization dawned. 'Hallo . . . oh, *Caroline.* I'm afraid I didn't quite . . . But how nice to see you . . . '

Afterwards she wondered what had made her use Pip's baptismal name: perhaps it was Charlotte's frequent reference to 'my sister, Miss Caroline Ludbury, RRC', or perhaps it was the lack of any resemblance in the ill-looking woman to the fiendish adolescent of her memory. Whatever the reason, Pip had been pleased. 'Well I must say, it's nice to be called Caroline again. Makes me feel I'm with friends instead of blasted relatives.' Many times during the afternoon Rebecca felt Pip's eyes upon her, and when Pip suggested that she accompany her to her room to look at her souvenirs, Rebecca readily followed, ignoring Charlotte's attempts to prevent her. The war souvenirs, each one inspiring an amusing anecdote or poignant memory, had enthralled Rebecca; and Pip at last found someone, unique among her relatives, who was ready to listen to her. And there were no cries, accompanied by hands flying to cover ears, of 'Stop, Pip, I can't bear to hear it; please don't mention such things.'

Now Rebecca laughed over Pip's letter from Tony Benton. 'It's delightful. He should write for a magazine. I wonder if it's occurred to him.'

'Gosh, that's an idea. I'll write and suggest it. He must get dreadfully fed up, poor dear.'

A companionable silence developed. 'Caroline,' Rebecca said after a while, 'I'm worried. Will you drive me to The Grange?'

'They wouldn't like that. Much better if you keep out of it. I'll go back if you like, in case they need a nurse.'

'Oh, heavens! You really think they might . . . ? Caroline, I insist you take me. I can't sit here waiting and wondering when George . . .'

'But he wouldn't want you, Rebecca. He'd hate it if you turned up. So would they all. This is a family matter.'

'But I'm his wife.'

'Exactly. Not one of us. Look, if the family's getting up to a bit of fratricide they'll want to keep it strictly to themselves. The last thing they'll want is an in-law turning up.'

The in-law submitted with a shrug. 'Very well. You go, then. But please bear in mind that I'd like my husband returned to me in one piece.'

'I shouldn't worry about George. He's the sort who knows how to take care of himself.'

Shots rang out – opinions varied as to the number.

'Drat!' cried George, seeing an hour's sweated toil go to waste. He had cajoled and argued, made threats, made promises, all, it now seemed, in vain. Charlotte and Louisa, whom he had banished to the house, came running, wringing their hands and wailing their dismay.

At that moment Pip arrived. 'What happened?' she asked, discovering the excited group outside the barn.

'Shots,' George said, and then there was an argument as to how many.

'Haven't you been in to look at them?' Pip interrupted.

'The door's bolted.'

'Then it'll have to be broken down. They can't just be left to rot.'

George looked as if he was none too sure of this. 'I suppose we could try the window.'

They were about to act on this suggestion when the sound of a bolt sliding back arrested them. Freddy peeped out.

'Trust *you* to get in first,' Pip told him.

'Edward! Oh, Edward!' screamed Louisa, rushing into the barn. The others, except for Freddy, followed her.

Edward was found to be alive, but more than usually dazed. His left leg was pitted and bleeding. Pip announced that he would live. 'But we'd better get him to a doctor.'

'Couldn't you . . . ?'

'No. I'm having nothing to do with it. Come on, get him into the car. I'll sit with him in the back.'

'We'd better say he had an accident. Shot himself.'

'They'll believe it. As soon as he's reasonably compos I'll din it into his head that Freddy's presence was a figment of his imagination.'

Freddy was looking nonchalant in the sun. 'All right, is he?' he asked as they staggered out with Edward.

'We'll see. Meanwhile, give us a hand.' And when Edward had been stowed in the car, George added: 'Stay in the house with Charlotte. I'll have something to say to you when we get back.'

In the small waiting room of a cottage hospital, George sat glumly with Pip. This was where Charlotte's urgings to 'keep an eye on things' had led him, to this smelly little room through which a nurse marched from time to time, glaring at George as she went. 'Thinks *you* shot him,' Pip explained, before turning her attention to a print on the wall depicting a surgical operation without benefit of anaesthetic. He received her opinion in gloomy silence and wished himself a million miles away. Becky was right: Edward and Freddy should be left to get on with it, and if that meant blowing one another to kingdom come, so be it. If only he hadn't parked himself on their doorstep where folk were bound to think of him as one of the Ludbury brothers. He groaned aloud at the thought.

Pip shot him a look, then moved on to another print.

Once again, he reflected, Charlotte had misled him. She had been certain that, as eldest son, the major interest in The Grange would pass to him. 'So it's imperative you live as near as possible to keep an eye on things – we don't want Edward and Freddy to ruin the place.' Well, the old girl had confounded their expectations by handing on The Grange and all its works to those in residence. Viewed dispassionately, it was a sensible arrangement, after all, he and Gussie were both comfortably off, whereas the others, with the possible exception of Charlotte, were dependent on the place. To George had come his father's bureau and writing desk, to Gussie the hiccupping ormolu mantel clock, with which bequests the two deserters were formally dismissed from further interest in the ancestral home. Even so, Charlotte had commented, it was a blessing that George was at hand to counsel the boys, for who else would they listen to? A fat lot of listening they had done this afternoon! He had worn himself out pleading with them to listen, and now he was obliged, as usual, to clear up their mess. Their feckless, drunken feuding could go on for years, he reflected, putting his head in his hands. Then, remembering the nurse, he raised it again; there was no point in *looking* guilty . . .

'Right atrium, right ventricle,' Pip said out of the blue. She was squinting at something on the wall above his head. She came tapping over the thin linoleum and propped herself against him while she took a closer look. 'That's right, the valves go in there . . . Bet that's where the trouble is, you know; bet that's what's making her so blue . . .'

Of course, George acknowledged, this feuding was hard lines on the girls; poor little Pip, worn out by the war, and good old industrious Lou, and Charlotte with her Deaf and Dumb – he'd bet his last shilling that the wonderful Mrs Skedgemore would drop Charlie like a stone if there was a scandal . . .

'I don't know why you don't take her to see a heart man, George. Don't say I didn't warn you.'

George took out his watch. 'Takin' their time, ain't they? Thought you said they were only surface wounds.'

'I've warned you and I've warned her. Neither of you take it seriously. Daft old Pip, that's what you think . . . '

'Do shut up, old girl. I'm trying to sort things out. It can't go on, you know . . . '

'That's what I keep telling you. Short of breath, pain in the chest, swollen ankles, turning blue . . . You should do something, George. It's no good expecting her to do anything, she doesn't care enough – at least, that's what I think; she'd rather leave it in the lap of the gods . . . '

'What the dickens are you on about?'

'Rebecca, you stupid man.'

'For Pete's sake, Pip, stick to the point. Could you have been wrong about him, do you think? Could he have conked out on the operating table?'

'Nothing the matter with *his* heart. It's liver with him.'

'Is it now?' he asked, becoming interested. 'Likely to take him off in the near future, d'you reckon?'

'Mr Ludbury, you might as well go home,' announced the nurse, bustling in. 'You, too, Miss Ludbury. Doctor thinks your brother' – she mentioned the relationship reproachfully – 'ought to stay here overnight – just for observation. Come for him about ten tomorrow.'

George looked at her sheepishly. 'Doin' all right, is he?'

'His condition is satisfactory.'

'That's the ticket. We'll trot off, then. Come along, Pip.'

Charlotte and Louisa came running over the gravel. Their screams shrilled above the engine's noise. 'George! George!'

For once, George remembered the brake pedal. He depressed it.

'Damn you, you fool!' cried Pip, removing her head from the dashboard. 'Why can't you put it down *slowly*?'

'It's Freddy,' shrieked Charlotte. 'He's gone. We couldn't stop him.'

'Where?' asked George, climbing out of the car.

'We don't know. He took off over the fields.'

'With a suitcase,' added Louisa. 'Oh, whatever shall we do?'

'Nothing,' said George. 'He's runnin' true to form; doin' a bunk. Well, as far as I'm concerned it's good riddance. One less to worry about. Louisa and the men'll make a better job of the farm with both blighters out of the way. Let's hope it lasts. I'll have a word with you about that heifer, Lou, before I go.'

3

'Someone's been reading my correspondence,' cried Meg, bursting into the sitting room in great wrath.

Rebecca looked up from her embroidery: she was sitting in her straight-backed sewing chair at the window. 'Surely not.'

'I'm quite sure of it. It was the letter that came for me this morning. I read it in a hurry then put it under the prayer book on my bedside table. When I came in just now I found it lying there on top of everything.'

Rebecca recalled an incident that had occurred

when the letter arrived that morning, but made no comment.

'I'm absolutely certain someone's been to my room on purpose to read it.'

'You've only yourself to blame if they have,' observed Pip, who was spending the afternoon at Priors Grendon. 'You should have locked it away.'

Meg was scandalized. 'One shouldn't have to. People shouldn't read other people's letters.'

Pip shrugged. 'I've no patience with "people shouldn't". "People do" is what counts. You've lived long enough to have discovered what people do and to take account of it, I should've thought.'

Meg turned her back on Aunt Pip. 'Mama, let me make myself clear. I will not stay in this house if my correspondence is to be interfered with.'

'Rubbish!' cried Pip, quite unimpressed by the excluding back. 'If you leave letters lying about, people'll read 'em. Fact of life. Don't tell me *you've* never had the odd squint at someone else's letter . . .'

'Indeed I have not!' cried Meg, going red, for she had suddenly recalled an occasion when, finding herself alone in Karl's room for half an hour, a letter poking out from a pile of books had proved too much for her curiosity. 'I wouldn't dream of such a thing. And my letter had not been left "lying about" as you put it. It was in my own room.' She moved closer to her mother and spoke between clenched teeth. 'Might I have a private word with you, do you think?'

'I'm off, anyway,' announced Pip, getting to her feet.

'Oh Caroline, are you? I thought you would stay for tea.'

'Not today,' said Pip, giving Rebecca's ear a friendly tweak. 'And don't bully your mother,' she advised her niece.

'Come again soon,' called Rebecca.

Meg waited until her delinquent aunt had gone. 'Why do you encourage her, Mama? You know she's bats, and thoroughly wicked.'

Rebecca ran her needle into the line and put down her embroidery. She looked up at her daughter, at the small frown between her eyes, at her pursed lips, and general air of having been affronted. Meg, who supposed her mother was about to speak, waited; but for some moments the only sound was that of an angry fly on the window pane.

'Haven't you *anything* to say about it?' Meg demanded.

'Caroline is neither batty nor wicked. Where do you get these ideas? No' – she waved a tired hand – 'don't tell me . . .'

'It's not just Aunt Charlotte's opinion. I've seen the evidence with my own eyes. Golly! – once she nearly throttled me . . .'

'I don't want to hear. I find it too depressing – these labels you and your Aunt Charlotte stick on people; it's a way of writing them off, dismissing them. Perhaps, when you've lived a bit longer you'll learn to be less judgmental. Caroline is startling because she's direct. I find her directness attractive. I've become very tired of maintaining convention and propriety at all costs . . .'

'Indeed! Well, I hope you're not too tired to distinguish between right and wrong.'

Rebecca sighed and turned to watch the thwarted fly. 'You know, a different outlook to one's own is not necessarily wrong. It may merely be different – that's always worth a thought.'

'Mother! I begin to think you're as bad as she is. I begin to think you're losing your grasp of the essentials. There *is* such a thing as wrong-doing – you know perfectly well – and it's no good making excuses for it. Heavens! If you insist on talking like that I shall lose confidence in you. I shall start to wonder – since you think it such an innocuous thing – whether you, or you and Aunt Pip together perhaps, went up to my room to rifle through my correspondence.'

Rebecca rose. 'Please do not raise your voice to me. There is too much voice-raising in this house as it is. I shall go into the garden and do some weeding until tea. And by the way, if living in this house is at all irksome to you, please do not remain on my account.' Quietly, she let herself out of the room and went to the garden door.

Meg thought for a moment, then grabbed an old journal from the book stand, marched to the window and swatted the fly. Its inert body on the windowsill afforded her some satisfaction. Soon her mother appeared on the garden path, carrying gloves, fork, trug and kneeling pad. She placed the pad on the flat stones between path and flower border and carefully knelt down. Her movements were slow and deliberate. The sun shone on the shiny mauve silk of her frock and the shiny white silk of her hair. Meg caught her breath. She had never registered it before – the fact that her mother's hair was totally white. She felt a sudden surge of shame, and hurried out into the garden, going more slowly as she approached the kneeling one. 'I say, Mama, I'm awfully sorry. I didn't mean that, you know. Not for one moment did I seriously think it was you who . . .'

Rebecca put up a hand. She had been thinking over the rather surprising incident at breakfast when the letter in question had arrived. As Meg had not yet come down, she had put it beside her plate. Seeing this, George had flown into a rage: all letters, he declared, should be placed on his desk for his perusal and for him to distribute in his own good time – was he head of the household or was he not? Rebecca had quietly ignored this hitherto unheard-of regulation, and Meg had come down and pocketed her letter before further objection could be made. Nothing more had been said, but the incident now made Rebecca uneasy. 'Meg, my dear, I think your father finds it hard to appreciate that you are a grown woman. You have always been his particular favourite; I think he feels it rather, your independence, your new life . . . Do you see what I mean?'

'Oh yes,' said Meg. 'I suppose I shall have to be more careful.'

Rebecca lowered her head and stared at a small mound of campanula, thinking how dreadful it would be if she were to grin at her daughter's sudden capitulation; but the dome-shaped mass of violet bells and frilly leaves rising sweetly from the cleaned earth tugged at her attention until she was all admiring scrutiny.

'It's perfect,' Meg said, voicing her mother's thought.

Rebecca smiled. 'You know, dear, I was most surprised when you agreed to take the job your father arranged at the village school, but I'm so glad you did.'

Meg thrust her hands into her pockets: one of them slid against Karl's letter – she would have to find a safe place for it . . . What on earth had her father made of it – if indeed it was he who had sneaked into the room to read it? But perhaps Bunny had been the intruder. On the whole, recalling certain excesses of expression, she rather hoped it had been Bunny.

'And that's a very nice coat,' Rebecca remarked, watching her.

'It's a blazer,' Meg corrected her. 'Aunt Gussie bought it for me as a reward for getting a distinction on my teachers' certificate.'

'How nice of her!' (Rewards had not occurred to anyone at Priors Grendon.) 'How kind she has been. I hardly remember her. What is she like?'

'Oh . . . big, fat, jolly, noisy. Everyone likes her. Their house is always teeming with people.'

'Well!' Rebecca tried to picture it. 'I know your father was pleased to think of you visiting her . . .' But her voice trailed away as she recalled that the thought of those visits had become displeasing to George of late – another totally inexplicable Ludbury mystery. She returned her attention to the weeding.

As the maid withdrew, Charlotte exchanged the arrangement of her features proclaiming 'matron of the home' for one illustrating her more pressing role of distraught sister near to breaking point. 'George!' She clasped him to her bosom. 'Thank heaven you've come! But we must speak *quietly*.' The instruction exploded unpleasantly in his ear.

He freed himself and backed away. 'Thought they were all deaf in this place.' Looking round, he found the one and only easy chair and sank into it, closing his eyes in anticipation of trouble to come.

'It's Freddy,' she hissed, dragging the chair from her desk to his side.

'Lord, I thought we'd done with him . . .'

'Married! Special licence! To that unspeakable woman at The Green Man!'

George, who was unaware of an unspeakable woman at The Green Man, looked stunned. 'The Green Man at Headley Cross? But that's Ernie Fanshaw's place – good-class establishment; they do a jolly fine sirloin, and the roast lamb's pretty good . . .'

'*Was* Ernie Fanshaw's. It belongs to his widow now.'

He whistled. 'Poor ol' Ernie. You mean Freddy's married the widow?'

Charlotte's grimace expressed an affirmative of some significance.

'Well I'll be blowed. Mind you, bit of money there. Oh yes, that place brings in a bob or two, I'll wager.' His eyes suddenly narrowed. 'Owns it, does she?'

'Owns it, runs it and, from what I hear, is not above working in it when the mood takes her – behind the bar!'

George pondered this. 'Big strapping woman as I recall. Bit loud. Well, I'll tell you one thing: she'll keep him in order.'

Charlotte grew impatient. 'The point is, what are we going to do about it? How can we get him out of it?'

'We can't, old girl; not if he's married her. No doubt about that, is there?'

She shook her head sorrowfully.

'Have to make the best of it, then. Look at it this way: Mama's not here to kick up a stink, he'll be out of Edward's way so there'll be a bit of peace on the farm, and his wife'll keep him fed, watered, and too busy to cause trouble. Shouldn't wonder if she lets him keep a decent hunter if he plays his cards right. I tell you, Charlie, it's been at the back of my mind for some years now that Freddy'd get into a really big scrape – end up in jail, even. Think of the trouble I had smoothing over that corn merchant he diddled . . . No, all in all this mightn't be such a bad turn up . . .'

'But George!' cried Charlotte, getting to the crux of the matter. 'What if he brings her to The Grange? Supposing he expects us to *know* her?'

It was a ticklish one and took some minutes to consider. At last he had it. 'I'll drop in at The Green Man one dinner time and have a quiet word with him. I'll point out that it wouldn't be the thing . . . unfair to embarrass his sisters.'

Charlotte heaved a sigh of relief. 'You'd better do it straight away, George.'

'And now' – George straightened a leg so that his hand could reach into the depths of his trouser pocket – 'perhaps you'd care to help me sort out this little facer.' And he passed her the hasty copy he had made of a letter that had arrived that morning addressed to his daughter from one signing himself 'Karl' and announcing his address to be '22, Bonnington Terrace, Birmingham'.

344

'It's from *him*,' shrieked Charlotte. 'That awful foreigner! Heavens! He's asked her to go to his house! George, we must stop her!'

'Any ideas?' George asked.

Karl was waiting for her at the ticket barrier. They did not wave to one another to attract attention. Head and shoulders above the crowd, he was well aware that she could not miss him, she reflected, fixing her rather short-sighted gaze on the high swept-back hair, the sardonic grin, and the floppy wine-coloured bow-tie safeguarding him from the indignity of being taken for an Englishman. He took her hand and put its fingertips to his lips, then tucked it under his arm. Over his other arm he carried a mackintosh. 'We'll walk,' he said, 'as it is such a delightful day.' She smirked, pleased to note that his lack of faith extended to the weather.

They passed shops and offices and eventually came to the hospital.

'Shall I show you my consulting room? I could practise my new technique on you: sit you down, look into your eyes and ask a very ridiculous question. Overcome by embarrassment for me, you would be propelled into instant garrulousness – the English are obligingly prompt with their embarrassment . . .'

'No thanks.'

'No? Well then, we will progress across the park and thus into Bonnington Gardens, Bonnington Square and Bonnington Terrace, descending the social scale as we go – by a whisker only, you understand; we should have to go on for another half-mile before we were thoroughly sunk.'

'How are Aunt and Uncle Beale?' Meg asked, fed up with this silly talk. 'You've seen them since I left, I take it?'

The conversation became safely domestic, which prompted Karl to mention his mother. 'You must tell me frankly what you think of my little house. At the moment it lacks this and that. I shall make purchases. You will give me your opinion, perhaps? You see, I hope very much to persuade my dear, obstinate mother to give up her apartment in Vienna and join me here.'

'I didn't know you had a mother.'

'It's quite usual, I understand.'

'You never mentioned her before. What about your father?'

'Alas, dead. Only mother and two sisters remain. Anna lives in Prague, Hélène in Paris.'

'Oh.' News of these relatives put her out; she wondered whether they would help or hinder the work she had to do on him. Mother-love did not fit in with her conception of atheism: perhaps this concern for an aged parent should be seen as a chink in his free-thinker's armour.

'So, you will advise me?'

'Yes, if you like.'

'But have I not said that I like?'

'All right, then.'

Number 22 was one of the more superior houses in Bonnington Terrace by virtue of its end-of-terrace position and extra four feet of garden at the side. It was of traditional Victorian design: front door leading to hall with doors off to two large rooms, staircases ahead and narrow passage to breakfast room and kitchen beyond. The two large rooms were square, high-ceilinged and well-lit, the front room having bay windows, and the rear room french windows opening on to the garden. In this rear room – the room Meg pronounced to be the dining room despite Karl's insistence that dining would take place elsewhere – he had piled books and placed a desk, a sofa and easy chairs. The front room was bare and awaited a grand piano, for Mrs Bruchstein, Karl explained, could not be expected to take up residence while the house lacked such an amenity. Other prerequisites for his mother's comfort were touched upon which quite destroyed Meg's confidence in her ability to advise him. 'I don't know,' she mumbled in response to his worries about morning and afternoon light. 'She sounds a bit airy-fairy to me. If I were you I'd buy the bare essentials, stick up some curtains and leave the rest to her.'

The garden cheered her up. About shrubs and rose bushes she was well qualified to advise.

'But my dear Meg, I do not propose to become a gardener.'

It struck her that his character was more seriously flawed than she had supposed. 'You'll have to employ one, then. But it's a shame; fresh air and exercise would do you good, and you'd *enjoy* it once you'd got the hang.'

'No doubt it can be paved,' he said, waving a hand about vaguely.

She frowned. 'You'll have the whole neighbourhood up in arms if you do. It would make it slummy.'

'Was it a mistake to come here?' Karl wondered. 'After all, Mother has no interest in gardens, except in their proper place, of course, in public parks and so on.'

'Well, I give up,' Meg cried. 'You're *lucky* to have such a nice garden.'

'Let's eat,' he said.

It was not the wine, for she had drunk less than half a glass. She did not care for wine; not, that is, for the thin sour stuff drunk during a meal by the likes of Aunt Gussie and Karl. Wine, as she had known it from childhood, was brown and sweet and was taken before dinner on Christmas Day and those other occasions when it was suitable to get a little giddy. Today she had allowed Karl to fill her wine glass on condition that he also provided her with a glass of water. To please him she sipped the wine from time to time, but a great deal remained in her glass. No, it was certainly not the wine. What, then, was the cause of her light-headedness? The sun on the back of her neck? The way his eyes caught hers between mouthfuls? There! It had happened again: a collision of a scrutiny, making her stomach contract and her mouth too dry to dispatch her food. She took another sip from her wine glass, then a mouth-filling gulp of water to remove the rather sickening taste. Of course, she reflected, they had all afternoon before them – *all afternoon*. She dropped her knife at the thought of it. Heavens, she was giddy enough to have swallowed a glass of her father's best sherry in one go! 'Come here,' he said suddenly, pushing back his chair. She almost ran to the other side of the table.

On his knee, his hands at her thigh and breast, hers beneath his jacket, she sank her nose into his hair and breathed in pleasurably. He put his mouth against her ear. 'The sofa, perhaps?' She was on her feet at once, had taken his hand, was drawing him after her. And then, in the lofty room where the smell of sun-warmed book-dust mingled with garden scents drifting in through the open french windows, they were heart to heart on the accommodating sofa.

After a time articles of clothing arrived on the floor like discarded skins. Meg was happy; all was right with her world. And if God was looking down on her it was with an approving smile, for, as Common Sense made plain, God would not have equipped her as He had if He had not intended full and grateful use of her several components. Which reminded her: later on she must attempt that introduction between God and her lover, her mission must not be neglected. Meanwhile, she would express her appreciation in other ways. She took Karl's head in her hands and kissed him fulsomely.

In happy ignorance of the further munificence to come, Karl was moved by her present warmth. 'Darling!' he whispered, caressing her. She closed her eyes, and the world shrank to a pinpoint of sensation.

A hair – his or hers? she wondered – had become lodged in her mouth. It intruded into her pleasure. She put up an impatient hand and turned her head to one side in order to fish it out. As she did so her eyes opened involuntarily and focused imperfectly upon the face of Aunt Charlotte who was standing at the open french window. Rapid and vigorous blinking failed to disperse the vision; indeed, Aunt Charlotte became an ever more solid feature of the scene.

'What is it, darling?' Karl murmured, sensing her disengagement.

'Aunt Charlotte,' said Meg.

He thought about this for a moment, then raised and turned his head.

There was a long, three-cornered stare.

Karl broke the silence. 'The front door is the usual thing, I believe. Perhaps you would care to present yourself there in about an hour. As you see, we are rather preoccupied at the present.'

Charlotte, who had been as immobile as a petrified rabbit, now leapt forward, eyes gleaming. 'Swine!' she bellowed, whacking Karl with her handbag. 'Filthy, treacherous swine! My brothers shall hear of this. You'll be horse-whipped within an inch of your life! As for you, hussy . . . !' At this point she was obliged to devote her breath to the greater exertion of pulling her niece from the villain's encumbering body.

Meg did not care for this handling. 'Let go, Aunt,' she cried, scrambling to her feet.

Her niece's unorthodox appearance disconcerted Charlotte for a moment – long enough for Meg to gain the upper hand. But Charlotte recovered swiftly, and soon the floor was sprinkled with hairpins, and the sweet afternoon air made fetid by the spittle and sweat of combat.

Youth, in the end, proved victorious. Aunt Charlotte and her handbag were hurled in swift succession through the french windows. 'For God's sake, help me!' cried Meg to the man behind her, as she strove simultaneously to close the glazed doors and prevent her aunt from re-entering. No assistance came. There was nothing for it, Meg saw, but an almighty shove. Making ramrods of her arms, she drove at Aunt Charlotte's shoulders and sent her flying backwards into the Michaelmas Daisies, where her aunt, too – because of the awkwardness of her fall – revealed a great deal of underwear. 'Phew! You might have given me a hand,' Meg said as she pulled the doors together and turned the key. Accusingly, she turned to confront her lover.

The reason for Karl's non-cooperation became clear at once: he was slumped against the back of the sofa, incapacitated by mirth. Since he could neither utter a word nor clearly see her face, he offered her a shaking hand.

She ignored it, just stood gazing down at him, breathing hard. Then, with the resolve of one to whom the truth stands all too clearly revealed, she snatched up her clothing (put on the skirt, but stuffed various underpinnings into her handbag to save time), strode into the hall, grabbed blazer from hat-stand, opened the front door and closed it behind her with sufficient force to make the house and its occupant quake.

She did not look to see whether Aunt Charlotte was lurking in the laurel bushes or limping down the street, simply lowered her head and broke into a hockey captain's sprint which was rewarded by an arrival at the station just in time for the three o'clock train. Blowing hard, she sank into a seat and returned curious glances with blank equanimity, for she was scarcely aware of her travelling companions, being too taken up with the memory of Doctor Karl Bruchstein laughing himself sick at her expense. Well, he could go to hell, and certainly would now that she washed her hands of him. 'He just wasn't worth it,' she reported heavenwards, scowling fiercely at the man opposite, who drew his legs in smartly and tucked them under his seat. And God bowed, with a sigh, to her superior judgement. 'There must be hundreds more deserving than him,' she reasoned; and God concurred at once by putting Sheffield into her mind. Of course! It was not too late; there was a desperate shortage of qualified teachers in the industrial north. And to think she had almost squandered her talents on a dozen slow-witted farm children! What a blessing she had seen the wicked waste of that in time!

The train's rhythm soothed her. The image of her offensive lover dissolved, and was replaced by a sea of urban slum children. 'I'm coming,' her newly resolute heart promised, and the scruffy urchins glowed in an amethyst beam of hope.

'What are you doing?' cried Rebecca, coming suddenly into the room.

'Packing,' said Meg.

Rebecca sat down on the bed. It was too much. First Meg had flounced in and shut herself in her room, then George had come home in a terrible temper, now this. 'Why?' she asked, striving to keep calm.

'Because I am leaving this house for ever. First thing tomorrow morning. I shall take a suitcase with me and send for my trunk when I've found somewhere to live.'

Rebecca tried a new tack. 'Your father is furious with you, it appears. I don't know why. He was making so much noise that I only caught a word here and there. He's gone out to storm at the animals.'

'He's been spying on me. Or, rather, he sent Aunt Charlotte to spy on me, having discovered, from reading my private correspondence, that I would be visiting a friend today.'

Of course: the letter. So that was it. 'A man friend, I take it.'

'Yes.'

Rebecca watched as Meg threw piles of underwear into the trunk. 'Why did you not bring him home?

she asked at last. 'We'd have made your friend very welcome. Instead, you make a mystery and annoy your father.'

Meg sank back on her heels. 'I see. So Doctor Karl Bruchstein would have been made very welcome.' She paused to allow the name to sink in.

Rebecca was enthusiastic. 'A doctor! How nice! And how right for you, dear – I mean, someone clever! Oh, I *am* looking forward to meeting him!'

Her mother was as obtuse as ever. 'Never mind the title, Mama; concentrate on the name. *Bruchstein.*'

Rebecca thought. 'German?' she asked. And then, recalling the difficulties she had experienced over 'The Moonlight Sonata'. 'But the war's over now.'

'Jewish, too.'

'Oh . . . well . . . look, I admit your father can be trying – it's fear that does it, fear of what he doesn't understand. But don't worry; leave him to me.'

'No need. I've finished with Doctor Bruchstein.'

'But *why*?' Having steeled herself to brave her husband's wrath, Rebecca was loath to relinquish the young man.

'Because he's insufferable, if you must know. There were things about him before . . . but after this afternoon . . . It was the most humiliating experience of my life. Aunt Charlotte burst into the house yelling the most frightful obscenities, walloped him with her handbag, then set about me – I mean, literally *set about me*. I had to shove her into a flower-bed and lock her out. And do you know what the blessed man did?'

'What?' asked Rebecca, putting a precautionary hand to her mouth.

'Laughed. Laughed himself silly.'

Rebecca went quickly to the window, but her unbidden mirth died on the way as the pity of it struck her. How may times over the years had she mourned her daughter's lack of humour? And the young man sounded quite delightful. 'Darling,' she said sorrowfully, turning to face her, 'darling, don't be too hasty. Think it over calmly when you've stopped feeling cross. You know, I bet it would seem jolly funny to an onlooker . . .'

'If you don't mind I've a lot to do. When I've finished this I've a letter to write . . .'

'Of course. But, dear, some people are quicker to see the funny side than others . . .'

'Mama! It was me he was laughing at. Me and her. He put us both in the same boat.'

Rebecca returned to the bed and sat down. 'Stop that for a moment. Listen to me.'

Meg slammed down the lid of the trunk. 'Well?'

'This young man . . . Karl – now you will hear me out? – I know he's annoyed you this afternoon, but putting that aside, I can't help feeling he could be a very good friend for you. He's from a completely different background; educated, clever, with a sense of humour – and do be fair about that, your Aunt Charlotte is rather funny when you come to think of it – he could broaden your outlook, help you to see other points of view . . . Do try to keep an open mind. Try and get on with all sorts of people. Now, there must have been something about Karl that appealed to you – give it another chance; it might turn out to be wonderfully rewarding. You really must not allow people like your aunt to blunder in your life with their fears and suspicions . . .'

'Will . . . you . . . shut . . . up?' asked Meg between her teeth.

Rebecca put a hand to her heart.

'Sometimes,' Meg continued darkly, 'I really see what it is about you that so infuriates Daddy. You never get the point. You have to have it explained to you. You can't be relied upon to take the right side. You're not . . . sound. Mad as I am with Daddy for interfering, I can see why he did it – the wretched doctor was bound to become objectionable sooner or later because he's an outsider, he doesn't know what's what. In fact, part of me's furious with myself, because Daddy was right and I was wrong. You don't begin to understand, do you? It's the same with this Aunt Pip business – calling her "Caroline" – honestly! Everyone who has anything to do with her can see she's as mad as a hatter. But not you. You know better. You *encourage* her. No wonder Aunt Charlotte's always had a down on you. I bet she didn't want you to marry Daddy in the first place – because you *don't fit in.*'

Rebecca rose. 'I see. Well, would you mind telling me where you intend to go in the morning?'

'To Sheffield. That job I was offered. I was mad to have turned it down. If it's gone there'll be others – they're crying out for properly trained teachers in the north.'

'Have you enough money?'

Meg shrugged.

Rebecca left her and went along the landing to the room she shared with George. From the back of a drawer she retrieved a box full of coins, then returned with it to Meg. 'Here you are. Take as much as you think you'll need to tide you over. You can pay your poor mother back when you're a woman of means.'

Meg took the box. 'I'm sorry,' she muttered, staring at it.

'It doesn't matter. As long as you're doing what you really want to do – what you feel is right.'

Meg put her arms around her mother. 'You are good – not trying to stop me.'

'But I'd never do that,' Rebecca said, holding her daughter at arms' length and gazing steadily into her eyes. 'Perhaps it's because I don't "fit in" with you Ludburys – as you put it – that I'd never try to prevent my grown-up daughter from doing as she wishes. You might think about that.'

'Oh. Mama . . .'

'Off you go to Sheffield and become a jolly good teacher. And if you meet people there with a different outlook to your own, just try and enjoy it. One thing, though: keep in touch. I don't doubt your ability to look after yourself – and perhaps this is as good a time as any for you and your father to make a break – but we shall miss you; promise to keep in touch.'

'I promise. And I shall miss you, too, Mama.'

Going slowly downstairs, Rebecca suddenly felt overwhelmingly tired. She should not have gone up to see Meg – Caroline was forever warning her about the stairs. ('Go downstairs in the morning and stay down. Don't go up for anything. Get yourself organised. If you need something send Bunny up for it.') Oh dear! What would Caroline say if she could see her like this, hanging on to the banister rail for dear life, fighting to get her breath? And she had done no good speaking as she had to Meg. 'The trouble is I've grown old,' she told herself; and was then immediately cheered. Looking on the bright side (and Rebecca was still inclined to do this) there was something to be said for getting on a bit: defeat was no longer a catastrophe – simply an inevitable ingredient of life.

4

All night the wind raged – there was no let-up, no brief dying fall – higher, shriller for hour after hour in sustained, shrieking crescendo. Such was the wind's blast against the house that Rebecca felt the shock of it through her body; she juddered and jarred under rapid and regular assault, the breath beaten out of her. On and on went the hammering. She endured it helplessly like a leaf in a gale.

Suddenly the night was over and the wind had gone. Her eardrums, absorbing silence, swelled. The bed trembled. Little Sal scrambled up to lie beside her. *How she longed to turn her head, to put out a hand to touch warm, pliant flesh; but she could not, there was no strength in her. Later she would. And it was easy to visualize her companion, lying on her back gazing up at the ceiling, limbs spread and limp, for Sally always lay like that. She would be thinking of a story, preparing to begin. Yes, here it came, in breathy sing-song, a story Rebecca had heard many times before:*

'And the wind said to the little girl: "Come with me. I'll teach you to fly. Come, come along with me, to the top of the golden Hill".'

'Scram!' said Aunt Pip, flapping her arms as if scattering fowl.

Bunny held her ground.

'Clear *orf!*' Aunt Pip advanced threateningly, obliging Bunny to relinquish her foot over the threshhold. 'I'll let you know when she's ready for visitors – not that *you'll* be top of the list, not by a long chalk, missy.'

Deflated, Bunny backed away, and the door was shut in her face. She looked at it for a moment, then turned and walked slowly down the corridor to her own room where she sat on her bed, hands pressed between knees, shoulders hunched, eyes drawn together in thought. There was only one person who could shift Aunt Pip. It was time that person was summoned home. She went downstairs, listened in the hall for a minute, then went to the telephone stand. She found the number in the book and unhooked the ear-piece.

'Exchange and number?' a blasé voice inquired.

Bunny replaced the ear-piece in fright. She had never put through a call herself, though her father had often called her to the telephone to speak to an aunt. 'Here, Bunny,' he would urge, holding out the new-fangled toy. 'Have a word with your Aunt Lou. Hang on there, Lou. Bunny's coming. Now speak up you two, and watch out for the pips.' In dread of the pips the two women offered inanities to one another, while George stayed close by to encourage the dialogue.

Bunny steeled herself and waggled the hook. This time she managed to say the number. After much whirring and clicking, a Mrs Appleyard answered. Meg, it seemed, would not return to her digs until five o'clock. 'I might telephone then,' mumbled Bunny ungraciously, then hung up with a trembling hand.

Five o'clock was impossible. Tea was at five, and it was not until six that George set off on his evening tour of inspection. At a quarter past six Bunny thought it safe to try again.

Meg answered this time, and did not sound pleased. 'Oh, it's you. I told you only to ring in an emergency.'

'It is an emergency,' Bunny protested hotly. 'Mama's had a heart attack.'

'Golly! when?'

'Yesterday.'

'How bad?'

'Hard to say. It was a matter of her going to hospital or staying here and getting a nurse. Daddy said we'd get a nurse. Guess who he got?'

'Not her?'

'Yes.'

'He must be mad!'

'I know. She's had a bed put up for herself in Mama's room and she never leaves her. She won't let any of us in; not even Daddy. Gives out her orders at the door. Just imagine how Mama must feel – at the mercy of a mad woman!'

'I warned Mama not to encourage her.'

'She was just being kind.'

'Well, Daddy must be off his head. What does the doctor think?'

'He thinks it's wonderful. Daddy went on about her winning the Royal Red Cross medal until the doctor

357

thought we were getting a marvel. Of course, he doesn't know what she's really like . . . Meg, you've got to come home. You're the only one who can fix her.'

There was silence.

'Hello! Are you there?'

''Course I am. It's jolly inconvenient. I don't know that I can.'

'You must! For our mother's sake!'

Into the silence broke the dreaded pips. 'Meg!' screeched Bunny. 'The pips!'

'Don't yell in my ear! All right. I'll come tomorrow.'

It was not Mrs Maule bending over her after all. It was Pip – Caroline – Rebecca saw. 'Hello,' she said, and her voice seemed far away.

'You've slept. I'll give you a wash.'

This surprised Rebecca, and yet it did not. It was strange that Caroline proposed to wash her; on the other hand it was not entirely unexpected. She hovered indecisively between a dream of Knoller Knap and a bleaker reality. The dream beckoned promisingly – could she rely on it not to take a treacherous turn? The other course wearied her, she was not sure she could bear it. Then a warm, wet flannel invigorated her, and she decided to let the dream go. 'I've been ill, I suppose.'

'Heart attack. And don't say I didn't warn you. You'll get over it, though, with care. From now on I'm going to make sure you take care. Comfortable?'

'Very. Caroline?'

'Mmm?'

'I'm so glad it's you looking after me.'

Briefly, Pip's busy nurse's attention faltered.

The door opened smartly and Meg came into the room. There was an air of challenge about her.

'Another time knock first,' said Pip.

Meg ignored her and went to the bed. 'Hello, Mama.'

'It's a good job she's awake, or you'd have had a piece of my mind. As it is, you can have five minutes.'

'Then I'll have them in private,' Meg said, drawing herself up.

Pip looked at her patient, who smiled. 'All right. But let her do the talking,' she instructed Rebecca.

Meg pulled a basket chair to the bedside. Her mother looked ghostly in the bed, white hair spread over white pillow, the skin of face and hands almost transparent. Meg reached for the nearest hand. 'Poor Mama.'

'Nice of you to come.'

'Thought I'd better come and rescue you. I see it's true' – she nodded in the direction of a narrow iron-framed bed. 'With you day and night. Don't worry, I'll soon get rid of her, I'll make Daddy get proper nurses in, a day nurse and a night nurse. I know he can't stand strangers in the house, but putting *her* in charge is ridiculous! Oh Mama, has it been awful?'

With an effort, Rebecca withdrew her hand. 'I'm *glad* of Caroline.'

'For heaven's sake . . .' Meg recalled that she was dealing with an invalid. 'Look, Mama,' she continued, her voice artificially gentle, 'I know you feel sorry for her, but at a time like this you must put yourself first. The woman's not up to it. It's all very well having her to tea and so forth, but to be shut up with her like this is asking for trouble. Both Bunny and I have seen her go completely off her head when we've been staying at The Grange. She's not safe.'

Rebecca closed her eyes.

For a while Meg sat in uneasy silence; then she went to a table set up by the window to house Aunt Pip's equipment. This was not a battlefield, she told herself grimly. This was a lady's sick-room where a decent standard of order was required. She raised the muslin dust-sheet and peered critically underneath.

'What do you think you're doing?' Pip cried, darting in. 'Out!' Then, seeing her patient: 'Whatever is it, Rebecca?'

'I must speak to Meg.'

'Yes, Mama?' Meg returned eagerly to be bedside.

'Please don't interfere with us here.'

'Well!' This was rich – and in front of Aunt Pip, too. 'I'll have you know I left a class of fifty ten-year-olds to hurry home to make sure you were all right . . .'

'Then go back to them, dear.'

'What?'

'Go back. We're quite all right here as we are.'

The garden was perfectly still. Leaves lay here and there across the lawn, but few leaves had fallen yet, and none would fall in today's unmoving air. Flat, brown chrysanthemums on rigid stalks jutted at a permanent angle from the border, and clumps of purple aster and pink phlox were fixed eternally among the drab, spent foliage of earlier-flowering shrubs. Without movement there is no time, Rebecca thought, gazing down at the arrested moment. She, too, was immobile, erect in a wicker chair drawn close to the bedroom window. If she breathed she was unaware of it. She, the garden below, and the unseen room behind were locked in timelessness.

It was a bird that nudged them forward, by flying, with disturbing abruptness, out of a mountain ash, leaving quivering red-berried clusters indignant on the branch. Painfully, a single leaf drifted downwards, and Rebecca drew in new breath. Time, with a lurch, moved on.

George came into the room. She knew he was there, and felt a spasm of irritation, for this was her precious time when Caroline took herself off for an hour leaving her to savour solitude. Invaded, she gave up the garden and leaned back in her chair. George came to stand behind her. He put his hands on her shoulders. She felt him searching for words and braced herself to bear the tone he would use.

'Becky, old thing!' He sounded broken. 'Nice to see you out of bed. There was a time when I thought . . . Oh, Becky.'

She sighed and raised a hand to cover one of his. Encouraged, he moved to the side of her chair and knelt down. She observed him with reluctance.

'Sometimes I think I'll never forgive myself. Pip must have warned me a score of times, but it never seemed to sink in; there was always so much going on . . . And when I think back to those years on the hill – how you struggled to keep going . . .'

'Stop!' she said sharply. Then, more gently: 'I'm glad you thought of Caroline for me, George. I should never have made a good recovery with a stranger, or in hospital.' She shuddered at the thought. 'How wonderfully lucky we are to have such a nurse in the family!'

He brightened at once. 'We certainly are! Pip's one in a million!'

Silence, not altogether easy, grew between them.

'How are things on the farm?' Rebecca asked, not really caring to know.

He frowned. '*She* turned up this morning. We had words.'

'Yes.' Rebecca had heard them, and Caroline had darted to the window overlooking the yard to make a gleeful commentary on the scene below.

'I don't know that I can put up with it much longer . . .'

'Poor George. Darling, I'm rather tired.'

'And I shall have it out with Charlotte. Do you know, she tried to pass the woman off as a regular caller? Introduced her to Bunny. She'd have had her in the house if I hadn't been quick.'

'George, help me back to bed, will you?'

Concerned; he leapt to his feet. 'Don't try to get up. I'll carry you.' He lifted her easily from chair to bed. 'I'll get Pip.'

'No. I shall sleep now.' But their eyes had met. She read fear in his, fear of her feeble condition, and fear, she supposed, that he, too, might one day come to such a pass. He read reproach in hers, for had he not sworn to look out for her forever? When her eyelids drooped, he bent down to drop a kiss on to her forehead; then, with relief, he hurried away, back to the business of life.

Bunny lay in wait in the hall.

'Daddy!'

''llo, Bunny-rabbit!'

He seemed preoccupied and would have walked straight by if she had not darted at him and clung to his arm.

'Daddy, I want to speak to you. Aunt Charlotte explained everything to me this morning . . .'

'Did she, now?' His eyes narrowed.

'About Mama. How she won't be able to take up the reins of the house again because she's an invalid . . .'

An invalid. He liked the word. Yes, 'invalid' was very satisfactory; it conjured a pale, delicate gentility. 'Afraid my wife's an invalid,' he heard himself explain to a reverent audience. And there was more: 'invalid' had a note of destiny about it – hadn't her mother been an invalid before her? Of course! The condition ran in her family. It was bred into her, preordained, and there wasn't a darn thing he or any other mortal could have done to forestall it.

'Are you listening, Daddy?'

''Course I am. It just struck me, that's all.'

'What?'

'That your Mama's an invalid.'

'But you mustn't *worry* about it. That's what I'm trying to tell you. You've got me. Aunt Charlotte made

362

me see it this morning, that *I* must run the household now.' (Aunt Charlotte had intended her to see nothing of the sort: of the firm opinion that Bunny was scarcely fit to run a hen coop, she had declared that the family's survival hinged on the return of Meg, and directed Bunny to write at once to her sister begging her to return. Bunny, however, was not one to let an opportunity pass her by.) 'I want you to know that you can rely on me. *I'll* never leave you, Daddy.'

'Nonsense,' George said teasingly. 'Some nice young man'll come along one of these days and take you right away from your poor ol' Dad.'

'Never!' Bunny hurled herself against his breast. 'I shall stay with you forever, Daddy!'

Her words hurt him, for his mind deceitfully put them in the mouth of his elder daughter. Gently, he pushed Bunny away. 'You're a good girl,' he murmured, searching for something encouraging to say. 'Tell you what, if *you're* in charge now . . .'

'I am. It's settled.'

'. . . Just you make sure that Mrs What's-her-name stirs the custard properly in future. If there's one thing I can't abide it's lumpy custard.'

'Oh, I *will*, Daddy,' she promised with shining eyes. 'From now on I'll make sure everything's perfect.'

At the door to the yard he paused and turned back to her. 'By the way, if your Aunt Charlotte tries to bring that woman to the house again, have nothing to do with her. She's not the sort of person we want calling. Know where her money comes from?'

'Where?' asked Bunny, holding her breath.

'Boots. Her husband was nothing more than a glorified cobbler.' He nodded as his words sank in. 'Worse, in fact, 'cos he turned 'em out by the million in factory. Yes, that's where Madam's money comes from – a boot factory. How do you like that, eh? You see, Bunny-rabbit, you have to be careful.

Folks like to give 'emselves airs and graces, but they ain't always what they seem.' And he touched his nose sagely and went into the yard, leaving Bunny gulping with horror at the narrowness of her morning escape and with admiration for his far-seeing wisdom. She'd be on her guard from now on, she vowed. She'd present a poker-straight face to all comers in the future until Daddy had given her the nod.

George walked quickly, anger churning his stomach. Meg . . . Damn the girl! And damnation take himself for letting her jump into his mind like that. 'I'll stay with you forever, Daddy!' he repeated mockingly to himself. Huh! And then he clutched his chest where a dull, sad ache had grown. Oh, when the thought of their times together . . . of their comradeship . . . If it was all to come to nothing, what on earth had it been *for*? For 'nothing' was the state of their relationship now. She'd had nothing whatever to say to him on that last flying visit. Not a word. Oh, Megs . . . And to think he'd set it all up so nicely – little job for her at the village school, nice long holidays giving them plenty of time to spend together . . . It was all Charlotte's fault. She'd worked him up about that foreign doctor fellow, worried him to death, and then barged in on them and made a scene. If there was one thing Megs couldn't be doing with, it was a scene. And he'd bet Charlotte's account of it had been exaggerated – silly old maid. Meg had shown the fellow a clean pair of heels, hadn't she? She was in Sheffield and he, by all accounts, was still doctoring in Birmingham. So there couldn't have been much in it. 'Damn and blast you, Charlotte!' he cursed under his breath. 'Damn you for driving her away.' Then, as a farm hand appeared on the track: 'Hey you, come here! I want a word with you!' ('That's right, Daddy, take it out on the man!' Meg said knowingly in his inner ear.)

*

364

The garden was perfectly still. It should not have been still, for up here the air moves constantly, but it was still. Nothing here is real, Rebecca warned herself, stepping out along the garden path. There was not far to go – it was such a small garden. At the rose bed she stopped and took secateurs from her pocket. Snip, snip, snip; dead heads fell to the ground. But a few blooms still shone in the autumn sunlight; indeed, here was a bud, tight and green, beginning to split and show thin strips of red. Would it come to full bloom so late in the year? Would it, a few days on, show a face as wide as this one? Rebecca cupped a frilly head in her hands. Bending over the rose, she knew she was watched. Soon she straightened up and shaded her eyes to peer up at the landing window. Yes, there she was, looming and receding in the shadowy, pool-like depths. If I run in she will be gone, Rebecca thought, resolving to remain in the garden, content to feel her presence. But her feet were impetuous – perhaps this time they would be faster – and her heart raced to keep pace with them. 'Sally! Sally!' she cried. 'Wait for me!' But the landing, when she arrived there, was deserted. No child knelt on the chest beneath the window. Sally had gone.

5

'What are you doing?' Rebecca called from the bed.

Weeks had passed and Rebecca was stronger. On good days she spent her afternoons downstairs, but today she had felt tired and heavy, too fatigued even to read by lamplight for an hour before settling down to sleep. 'It's too early,' Caroline had warned. 'You won't sleep right through.' And so it had proved. In fact, Rebecca thought, raising her head, it was doubtful whether the night proper was yet underway.

At the far end of the room a candle flickered. Squinting, Rebecca made out Caroline seated at the dressing table, her dressing gown undone and hanging loose, one arm raised and crooked behind her head which craned towards the looking glass.

'What are you doing?'

Slowly the raised arm fell, but Caroline did not turn round.

'Caroline?'

There was a deep sigh. The flame leaped. Caroline got up, gathered her gown tightly to her body and knotted the girdle. At last she turned. 'I told you you wouldn't sleep.'

'But what were you doing?'

She came nearer, her face invisible in the shadow.

'Well?'

'Putting ointment on scar tissue, if you must know.'

A full minute passed while Rebecca considered this. 'A breast,' she said eventually.

'Both breasts.'

'Oh, *Caroline*!'

Caroline shrugged and began to walk about the room, her arms crossed and pulled in, her shoulders hunched – she had held herself like this for the past three years, Rebecca suddenly remembered, all rounded back and body-hugging arms.

'When?'

'Couple of months after I came home.'

'Is that why you came home?'

'No, no. Because of exhaustion . . . and *these*.' She stopped pacing and thrust out hands. The thin candlelight lit the side of her face; her eyes were staring, the pupils hugely dilated.

'Your hands?'

'Arthritis. See? Look at the knuckles. Doesn't matter so much here, but it certainly did there. Got clumsy, slow, dropped things, hurt patients. I hurt too, by jingo; they throbbed and throbbed, nearly drove me

366

mad.' She put her hands against the concave hollow of her chest and began to rub them alternately, palm over back. 'I always prided myself on my hands; they were so quick and accurate . . .'

'And then, later, you found . . . in your breast . . .'

She blinked as if startled and sat on the edge of the bed. 'You mean a lump. I found one, I thought. He found the other. Said he'd have to operate immediately.' Disconcertingly, she began to grin.

'But it's been a success? The disease hasn't spread?'

The grin grew wider. 'Nothing to spread.'

Rebecca's flesh crept unpleasantly. 'What do you mean?'

'It was a mistake. Wasn't cancer at all. Of course' – Caroline put her head on one side and looked cunning – 'it might not have been a mistake, might have been deliberate, a way of seeing me off.'

'I don't understand.'

'Well, it transpired that my surgeon, Sir Peter Orum – a very venerable man but a century behind the times – and I had no choice, all the younger surgeons were busy with the war – was her Godfather. Christopher's wife's Godfather. What do you think of that?'

'Your Christopher's wife?' (They had shared several night-time confidences).

She laughed and nodded. Her pale cheeks glistened with excitement, and her eyes became loose as a blind woman's, swivelling and turning with her racing thoughts. 'As soon as the war was over he was going to ask her for a divorce. We were going to get married – after all, we'd been together for six years. Well, he arrived home to find I'd had 'em cut off the day before. When he heard Sir Peter had operated, he went berserk, turned the place upside down, threatened people, harangued them, then swore the operation was unnecessary. He actually blamed me for not waiting! Good God, I'd been petrified; the man had said I'd be dead in six months if he didn't go ahead. And how was I to know Chris was on his way home? What a nightmare! Sir Peter threatened to sue, which would have finished Chris professionally, of course. In the end I just sent him packing.'

'Why?' whispered Rebecca, desperately reminding herself that the mad-looking creature on her bed was not Pip, but Caroline.

The grin and exhilaration vanished, and a beaten woman hung her head. It seemed there would be no explanation, and by the time Caroline spoke, Rebecca had already guessed how it had been. 'He was horrified by the thought of the mutilation – I could see it in his eyes – because it was *his fault*. He was determined that it was *his fault*. Hopeless. Do you understand?'

Rebecca flung herself forward and pulled Caroline to her.

'No, don't. Why are you crying? I never have. Not once.' She pushed Rebecca firmly down on to the pillows. 'I'll go and get us some hot milk.'

'You can't manage – not with a candle in one hand.'

'I'll get Bunny. It's only just ten, you know.'

Light swung across and out of the room, leaving Rebecca staring into blackness. In the wood below the garden an owl hooted in confiding, well-modulated tones; minutes later a small creature's screams destroyed the ease of would-be thinkers. 'Oh, stop, stop,' moaned Rebecca, stuffing eiderdown into her ears; for she needed to think, being full of the conviction that a tragic mistake had been made and that she, with her particular experience, could point the way to salvation. She sat up eagerly when the door opened.

Bunny bustled in and put a tray on the bedside table. 'Mama . . .'

'Not now, dear. Go to bed.'

'You heard,' said aunt to niece, indicating the door.

'Now, Caroline,' Rebecca began as soon as the door had closed. 'I've been thinking . . . You must give him a chance. Think how he must feel – eaten with remorse and no chance to do anything about it . . .'

'He doesn't want a chance.'

'But Caroline, it's hell on earth when it's too late, when things are past mending, I *know* . . .'

'We are not all the same,' Caroline said sternly. 'Drink up.'

Rebecca caught her breath. 'We are not all the same.' But she knew that, she knew that too well; to think that a Ludbury should remind her of it! She put a hand over her eyes. 'Sorry – rushing in like that – knowing all the answers. Sorry.'

'Drink it up. As it happens, I gave him the chance he wanted – which was to forget all about me. He's doing rather well in America, I understand – with his wife.'

'Sorry . . .'

'Shut up, Rebecca – you sound like a parrot.' Her snappy tone was belied by her hand which reached out to cover Rebecca's. 'It's nice having someone I can tell, though.' She snatched back her hand. 'But I shouldn't have, should I? Look at you! You're upset! What in heaven's name am I thinking of – upsetting a patient?'

'I'm not just a patient. I'm your friend.'

'My friend.' Caroline thought about it. A shame-faced grin spread over her face. 'Funny thing, that. I used to hate you. We all did. You were the beastly sister-in-law. The shop girl. Funny how things turn out . . .'

'Did you say . . . "shop girl"?'

'Yes. That's what Mama called you. "That shop girl".'

'But why?'

'Didn't you work in a needlework shop or something? I don't know. It doesn't matter. It was all silly nonsense.'

'But did *George* ever hear her call me that?'

369

"Spose so. Yes . . . we all did. She said it, then I took it up: "shop girl, shop girl . . ." Wasn't that *horrible* of me? But I hated you long before that – right from the start. I wonder *why*?' She screwed up her eyes, considering. 'It was as if it was *expected* of one: "Rebecca Sheldon is beyond the pale so you can jolly well set about detesting her." I say!' Her eyes widened. 'That's pretty awful when you come to think about it. Gosh! – perhaps we ought to be cagy about every attitude we take – because there might not be a good reason for it – someone might just have popped it into our heads. Help! What a thought! Makes one scared to breathe, almost.'

Rebecca closed her eyes. 'Well, at least we sorted it out for ourselves – how we feel about each other. Bit late in the day, but we managed it.'

Pip jumped to her feet. 'Look at you! I've done it again. Time I gave up nursing. Going off my head. Always thought I would in the end.'

With great effort, Rebecca reopened her eyes to reassure her. 'Nonsense. You're a marvellous nurse. And you don't need nimble fingers to nurse heart cases like me. When I'm better I'm sure Doctor Parry'll want you to look after other patients.'

'Perhaps.'

'But keep plenty of free time to spend here.'

'And you're almost better, anyway. We'll have to let old George back into his bed soon.'

'Not yet. His feet jump about in the night. Wait until I can sleep right through.'

'That'll be when you spend every afternoon downstairs. Then I shall go back to The Grange to plague Charlotte and Louisa.'

Rebecca yawned lengthily. 'Dear me! I think I'm already asleep.'

Caroline climbed into her narrow iron-framed bed and blew out the candle. 'Rebecca?'

'Mmm?'

'I couldn't allow Chris to make a victim of me. You do see? I couldn't allow that.'

On the verge of sleep, Rebecca recalled that she had stopped her ears, not against the owl's call, but against the scream of its prey. 'Because that's what cannot be faced – the possibility of being a victim, the idea of being someone's prey.' The trouble is, she decided, as certain of Caroline's words resounded in her head, the danger of it looms as soon as we form a relationship. We are all of us one another's victims – parents, children; wives, husbands; brothers, sisters; friends, lovers; and of course, unwelcome sisters-in-law.

6

The house was full of the scent of sweet peas, Rebecca remarked to herself, walking slowly downstairs – sweet peas and sun-warmed polish, she amended, pausing to sniff. On the hall-stand, on the cabinet by the dining-room window, on the Pembroke table in the sitting room, were bowlfuls of purple and white blobs swathed in feathery greenery which she had picked and arranged on the previous day. Descending in the faintly buzzing quiet, Rebecca seemed to float in honeyed well-being.

The smell of polish made her think of Bunny, who was an inexhaustible house-groomer, preferring to rub floors and furniture herself so that she could gloat over the shine and cry triumphantly to the sluggish maid: 'See? *That's* how it should be done!' Bunny had an unfortunate away with servants, particularly with cooks: they had been through a couple of cooks since George had confirmed Bunny as the one in charge. Bunny was a comfort to George; he was forever wondering how they would have got on without Bunny-rabbit. However, George and Meg had at last made it up. Rebecca, taking pity on her husband, had written to Meg expressing a longing to see her; and Meg had duly arrived, laden with gifts for everyone. Their reconciliation was sealed when George got up from the tea table to begin his evening tour of the farm, and Meg jumped up to accompany him. Still, some weeks after her departure, George liked nothing better than to regale them with what Meg had thought about this and that.

Rebecca arrived, now, at the green baize door. She pushed it open and went through the rear hall to the kitchen. 'Well?' she inquired of Bunny, who was bustling between scullery and kitchen range. 'Everything under control?'

'Wud be if Oi was left to get arn with et, Mum,' said the cook, tight-lipped.

Bunny's eyes flashed. 'My father likes it on the table at twelve-thirty sharp. It's been late three days running.

'Where *is* your father?' Rebecca asked, suddenly sensing his absence.

Bunny seized her arm and drew her out of the kitchen, for she was always punctilious in keeping family matters from the servants' ears. 'Daddy had a letter this morning,' she confided when they were safely in the dining room. 'It put him in a terrible temper. He called out to Jim that he'd have to go to Birmingham right away.'

'Who was it from? Did he say?'

'I didn't dare ask; he was too vexed. But when he was reading it he shouted: "Damn, interfering woman!" '

'Ah . . . Mrs Skedgemore. Well, no use waiting dinner for him. Put his to keep hot.'

By three o'clock George had still not returned. 'What shall I do, Mama?' asked Bunny, who had run to the oven every quarter of an hour to examine her father's wilting dinner.

'Put it in the dogs' bucket. He's bound to have eaten by now.'

Ten minutes later Bunny was back, breathless with news. 'Aunt Charlotte's coming up the drive – on Aunt Louisa's bicycle! She almost crashed into the bank. You should see her, Mama; she looks a fright; red as a beetroot and her hair falling down!'

Charlotte? Pell-mell from the The Grange? And George gone hotfoot to Birmingham. 'Go and help her, then. And Bunny . . . ?'

'Yes?'

'When you have shown your aunt in here you can leave us. She and I will talk privately.'

Rebecca's hands, and the needlework they had been engaged upon, fell into her lap. She let her head fall to one side against the chair-back so that she could gaze through the garden window. How many moments of silence remained? Two? Three? A faint excitement stirred in her as she anticipated Charlotte, dishevelled in the doorway; for Charlotte had risked her neck and abandoned her dignity, not to see George, but to see her, the sister-in-law. Now why was that? It was to do with Mrs Skedgemore's letter and George's flight . . . A-ha! She caught her breath as understanding dawned: Charlotte was here to beg assistance in the management of George. She, Rebecca, was Charlotte's last hope. Her heart quickened – not unpleasantly – and thoughts of Charlotte over the years flashed through her memory like avenging angels.

Heavy feet were coming briskly through the hall; Rebecca assumed an air of calm detachment and took up her needlework.

'Rebecca!' Charlotte cried throatily, bursting, into the room. Then, advancing: 'My poor, dear Rebecca!'

'Why, Charlotte! Whatever has happened to you? Sit down and calm yourself.' Though her voice was mild, Rebecca indicated a chair with some firmness.

After a small hesitation, Charlotte forwent the kiss she had intended to plant on her sister-in-law's cheek, and sat down.

'Now, take a deep breath and tell me all about it.'

Charlotte's eyes darted from side to side. Her task was visibly hateful to her. She shuddered, and for a moment closed her eyes.

'Yes?' Rebecca prompted with palpably false sympathy.

Charlotte took hold of herself. She leaned forward and began: 'My dear, I would not distress you for the world. Please understand that it is only concern for your fragile state of health that brings me here with such urgency. But Rebecca, I must speak, to spare you even graver distress, perhaps *life-endangering* distress. Brace yourself, my dear.' Charlotte stretched out a hand, but Rebecca, intent upon her needlework, was able to overlook it.

'George . . .' – Charlotte paused and adjusted her voice to a dramatic hiss – 'George has been utterly reckless!'

Rebecca raised her head. 'Yes?' she murmured humouringly.

Bleakly, Charlotte took in that Rebecca was not yet roused. She steeled herself to greater effort. 'He has given notice to leave this farm! This house! He has allowed a foolish disagreement with Ada to cloud his judgment. Oh, I *know* she can be strong-willed – how I have *begged* George to allow me to handle her; but he's so stubborn, so headstrong! He just blew up; and over such a silly little thing – I'd have sorted it out in a trice if only I'd been given the chance. But no; he had to give notice then and there. Ada drove straight over to see me. I'm afraid she was quite worked up, too; in fact she was strongly inclined to take him at his word. Of course, my first thought was for *you* – an invalid, dependent for your very life on complete tranquillity! I saw at once that a move was out of the question. I made Ada promise to do nothing hasty. As soon as she had gone, I leapt on to Louisa's bicycle. "I must get to her before George," I thought. "She must not be alarmed unnecessarily. I must reassure poor, *delicate* Rebecca that I shall stand by her in opposition to this piece of folly!" ' There it was. She had thrown in her hand. Hardly daring to breathe, Charlotte fixed gimlet eyes upon her sister-in-law and waited for the response.

Rebecca took her time. She raised her work to the window and scrutinized it, then, with an air of satisfaction, ran a needle into the back of the canvas and put it down.

'But, Charlotte,' she began softly, 'surely you don't imagine that this comes as a surprise to me? I've been aware for some time that George wished to give this place up. Dear as your friend may be to you, she is hardly an ideal landlord; and George could never make an ideal tenant – he's far too independent. I'm surprised you haven't understood that yourself, having always been so close to him; though, of course, a sister can never know a man as thoroughly as a wife. But let me put your mind at rest. A move has been on the cards for some time, and now that I am so well recovered there is nothing to hold us back. No doubt this disagreement with Mrs Skedgemore has made George appear impetuous, but nothing could be further from the case. Of course, it *is* a pity that George decided so hastily on the Skedgemore arrangement in the first place. I think he regrets, now, that he didn't seek other, more considered advice – mine, for instance. . . . That aside, I quite relish a move; I've never felt particularly at home here, myself . . . There! I've reassured you. You feel quite easy now, I daresay.'

Charlotte's face was devoid of expression; her eyes fixed on Rebecca's as if they would never break away.

'Tea?' Rebecca suggested brightly. 'Be a dear and tell Bunny.'

Charlotte shook her head. 'I must go,' she mumbled, rising painfully.'

'George will be home soon. He can run you back. I expect the bicycle will go in the boot, otherwise Bunny will ride it back for you.'

But mention of George's return had galvanized Charlotte. 'No no,' she cried, on her way to the door.'

'But all that *pedalling* . . .'

She was gone.

Rebecca closed her eyes and waited for exultation to arrive. At last! she told herself; at last she had had the better of Charlotte – Charlotte who had schemed with George behind her back, who had contrived to deprive her of any say in her own destiny, who had put Sally beyond a doctor's reach. And she had handled Charlotte so cleverly . . . But exultation would not be conjured.

She rose from her chair and stood gazing into the garden. 'I cannot take pleasure from this; it is not my way,' she admitted, as self-knowledge crept up on her. 'I have never wished to make a battle of it. If only Charlotte had found it in her to accept me – as Caroline has at last – we could have rubbed along . . . perhaps not in our unyielding youth, but as the years went by, as life mellowed us . . .' She recalled the strain of the Lipscombe war years when George had been unable to confide his anxieties; she had been glad to think that Charlotte might comfort him. Yet Charlotte had never allowed that Rebecca had a part to play; she had striven to exclude her utterly. Be that as it may, she would not permit Charlotte, now, to put her in a false position. 'I shall be to her as I wish to be.' With an effort, she banished Charlotte from her mind. George would soon be home; and from George she had the right to expect fair dealings – and a newly-strengthened resolve to exact them.

He returned, looking white and apprehensive. After much nervous pacing of the sitting room, he evidently decided that matters could not, for the moment, be faced. 'Better go and see the cowman,' he muttered, making for the door.

'George! Sit down. Look, I know all about it. Charlotte's been here. She seemed to think I'd be surprised. I told her that, on the contrary, you'd made it perfectly clear to me that the situation here was unsatisfactory. I know we've never discussed it, George, but I assumed that sooner or later we'd be obliged to move. And now that I'm so much stronger, and as long as we do things sensibly – take our time to find somewhere suitable for us *both* – I'm sure I shall take it all in my stride.'

'Becky!' He sank to his knees at her side. 'I can't tell you what a relief it is to hear you say that! I wasn't sure you could stand it. But it just blew up. That woman'd provoke a saint. . .'

'Of course she would, darling.'

'You *are* a good stick, Becky. I'll find us the perfect place this time, just you trust old . . .'

'No, George. This time we'll find it together. Won't it be fun motoring out to look places over? Oh, I have missed our lovely days out.'

He frowned with the effort to take it in.

'You see, dear,' she explained, 'this time I shall have to be most particular about certain things, now that I'm rather an invalid. You know: the steepness of stairs, the arrangement of rooms . . . I shall consult Caroline before we make a final decision – she's always impressing upon me that I should get things organized so that there's no strain on my heart. It would be such a pity if you found the perfect farm, and the house turned out to be hopeless. Much better if we work together from the start.'

'I think I see what you're getting at . . .'

'Good.' She reached for his hand. 'I'm quite excited by the idea, aren't you?'

'Rather, old thing,' he said, feeling suddenly that he was.

'Willow Dasset Farm,' said Rebecca.

'Perfect 'cept for the house,' said George.

'Willow Dasset . . . It even sounds lovely. And only two miles from that nice market town.'

'First-class farm. Good garden, decent stable. Dilapidated house, though. No point thinking about it.'

'But beautifully proportioned. *Basically* it's all right. I mean, the stairs are shallow and the rooms are a good size.'

'No bathroom. Not been decorated this century.'

'Worth doing up, do you think?'

'Certainly. They're asking a very reasonable price. But you'd never stand the mess, Becky.'

'No. I wonder . . . George, how do you think it'd be if I stayed at The Crown while the work was done? Such a comfortable hotel – I'd enjoy it. Caroline could keep me company.'

'That's an idea, old thing! It's certainly an idea . . . I say, we could get it just as we want – you know, bathroom downstairs as well as up to save your strength. . . . We could plan it. It'd be like . . . um . . .'

'Like building Mallory House.'

'That's just what I was thinking. By Jove, Becky, I reckon you've hit on something.'

'We'll go into it.'

'Willow Dasset Farm. I must say, I like the sound of it. One thing though: it's the furthest from the grave of any place we've looked at. Won't you mind that?'

'I've told you before, George; I'm not drawn to her grave. Mind you, we ought to visit it soon; we haven't been since I was taken ill. I hope the sexton's keeping it tidy.'

'We'll go the Sunday after next. We'll take Pip.'

'Yes, that'd be nice. Perhaps we could call on Edith?'

'Of course we could. Give her a ring and tell her the news. We'll have to hire an architect chappie. By Jove, Becky; it feels quite like old times.'

7

'Here we are,' George announced without enthusiasm. To their left was the lych gate and churchyard, to their right the looming bulk of Knoller Knap.

'Is that it? Is that your hill?' asked Caroline, leaning over Rebecca's lap to peer up.

'Better get on with it, I suppose.' George wound up his window and opened the door. 'Grave inspection first. Then I'll go round to the sexton's cottage – give him a tip, or a piece of my mind.'

'And while your father calls on the sexton, you can show your aunt the church, Bunny,' Rebecca called to her daughter who was climbing out of the front passenger seat.

'Not coming?' asked Caroline.

Rebecca shook her head.

'Right-oh.' Caroline knew what it was: they had talked non-stop all the way down and now Rebecca was in need of silence and her own company. Rebecca was like that. Well, Caroline was content. The talk had been exhilarating, about Willow Dasset Farm, the alterations and additions, and the lovely weeks she and Rebecca were to spend queening it at The Crown. Then Rebecca had suddenly called to George that as soon as the work was done Charlotte and Louisa must be invited to Willow Dasset. 'Charlotte first, then Louisa. They'll enjoy it better separately. Tell them that, George.' And the back of George's neck had gone pink. (Of course, he and Charlotte had had an almighty row.) But Rebecca had been insistent. 'You're to tell them straight away, George. We don't want them to feel deserted.' Then she had settled back comfortably and smiled at Caroline. 'And you'll come as often as you can, I trust.'

'Come along, Miss Bunny,' Caroline now said to her niece, and they set off after the striding, disappearing George.

Rebecca closed her eyes until the fade of footfalls on gravel became silence. When she looked again the sun had come out, and the top of Knoller Knap was ablaze. 'The golden hill'! The phrase was Sally's, a familiar landmark in her stories. Had the child meant Knoller Knap? To Rebecca, Knoller Knap was dark and forbidding. But now, as she wound the window down and gazed upwards, it seemed possible, after all, that Knoller Knap was indeed the golden hill.

Ah . . . Sally – such a long, sad stretch before and after. But there *had been* a now and forever, even though she had wished the time away and longed for another place. There *had been* a collision, and Rebecca and Sally still reverberated up there – in the small garden, on the stony track, through the long grasses and with the wind at the rattly windows. And the thought pierced her like a shaft of sunlight that Sally had loved the hill; it was the world where she and the wind had danced.

Rebecca lay back against the hard leather seat, and watched the hill through half-shut eyes.

George came cheerfully through the lych gate to the car. When he saw her, his heart lurched. She was so still, so . . . not there. She was sleeping, he told himself sharply, and opened the car door to investigate.

She was not sleeping. Her lazy grin widened, and beneath the drooping, dark-fringed lids, her eyes were shining. 'Lord, Becky! You gave me a fright! What are you lying there grinning at, anyway?'

She was disinclined to move, and when her lips

parted it was reluctantly. At last it came: 'The hill,' she murmured indolently.

'Go on with you,' cried George. Knoller Knap had never been a laughing matter, least of all to Becky. And she was still grinning in that half-asleep way. Something had amused her. Something had caught her eye. He turned and crouched and squinted along her line of vision; but though he shaded his eyes and looked far and near, there was only the hill.

'I shan't come here again.'

He heard her with surprise; then, faintly alarmed, he straightened up and looked at her. 'Something up, old thing?'

'Not at all. I just want to remember it like this – the hill with the sun on it – Sally's place.'

'Oh, Becky . . .'

'Come here, George.' She pushed herself along the seat. 'Get in. Sit beside me. I've something to say.'

He climbed, somewhat dubiously, into the back of the car.

'Now' – she took his hand – 'about Charlotte. No, don't look cross – just listen. I meant what I said – you're to make it up with her, make it clear that she'll be welcome at Willow Dasset Farm. Life's too short for nastiness. And I'm not going to play tit for tat. You and she have been very close over the years – I'm sure she must be feeling her world's come to an end after quarrelling with you, and knowing that you're about to move away. You and I are lucky, George, we have so much to look forward to, we can afford to be generous. Now, do I have your promise?'

He nodded with a sheepish grin. ''Spose so. I'll admit it's been on my mind. Took the gilt off our plans, somehow – the bad feeling.' He shook his head. 'But I never thought to hear you take old Charlie's side.'

'I'm not taking anyone's side. I just want us all to make the best of it – live and let live – make room for one another. Seems to me it's our only hope.'

'Oh, Becky!' he cried chokily, and pressed her hand to his lips. 'You're an angel . . . It's all going to be just as you say. Before I'm done, that house at Willow Dasset'll be fit for a queen – you wait and see – trust old George!'

And her amused, heavy-lidded regard suggested that she would.

THE END

Brief Shining
Kathleen Rowntree

The sequel to *The Quiet War of Rebecca Sheldon*.

'CAPTURES THOSE PERFECT ENDLESS SUMMERS OF
CHILDHOOD . . . THE RUSTIC STYLE OF LAURIE LEE'S
NOSTALGIC PROSE IS MIXED WITH PUNGENT STABS
REMINISCENT OF KATHERINE MANSFIELD'
She

To Sally and Anne, Willow Dasset was a place of sun and poppy
fields and haymaking, and Grandpa Ludbury striding across the
farmyard to welcome them. Everything was perfect at Willow Dasset,
except their parents. Meg and Henry brought all their tensions and
resentments with them, and their pervading restlessness somehow
damaged the enchantment of summer at the farm.

As Sally, the elder, changed from a child into a young girl, she
realised that the tension came from her mother. Meg was a Ludbury,
with all the strangeness, the greeds and longings of that curious clan.
But now Meg's jealousy and resentment was centred on her own
daughter. Sally, reaching for a life of her own, realised that if she
wanted any kind of happiness, she had to fight her mother any way
she could. And the one thing she never forgot was her grandmother –
for Rebecca too had had to fight the Ludburys – and Rebecca had
won.

'THE NARRATIVE IS QUIETLY HAUNTING WITH MEMORABLE
CHARACTERS'
Publishers Weekly

0 552 99584 3

BLACK SWAN

A SELECTED LIST OF FINE NOVELS AVAILABLE FROM BLACK SWAN

THE PRICES SHOWN BELOW WERE CORRECT AT THE TIME OF GOING TO PRESS. HOWEVER TRANSWORLD PUBLISHERS RESERVE THE RIGHT TO SHOW NEW RETAIL PRICES ON COVERS WHICH MAY DIFFER FROM THOSE PREVIOUSLY ADVERTISED IN THE TEXT OR ELSEWHERE.

☐	99588 6	THE HOUSE OF THE SPIRITS	*Isabel Allende*	£6.99
☐	99313 1	OF LOVE AND SHADOWS	*Isabel Allende*	£6.99
☐	99564 9	JUST FOR THE SUMMER	*Judy Astley*	£6.99
☐	99537 1	GUPPIES FOR TEA	*Marika Cobbold*	£6.99
☐	99593 2	A RIVAL CREATION	*Marika Cobbold*	£6.99
☐	99488 X	SUGAR CAGE	*Connie May Fowler*	£5.99
☐	99656 4	THE TEN O'CLOCK HORSES	*Laurie Graham*	£5.99
☐	99610 6	THE SINGING HOUSE	*Janette Griffiths*	£5.99
☐	99449 9	DISAPPEARING ACTS	*Terry McMillan*	£6.99
☐	99503 7	WAITING TO EXHALE	*Terry McMillan*	£6.99
☐	99506 1	BETWEEN FRIENDS	*Kathleen Rowntree*	£6.99
☐	99584 3	BRIEF SHINING	*Kathleen Rowntree*	£5.99
☐	99561 4	TELL MRS POOLE I'M SORRY	*Kathleen Rowntree*	£6.99
☐	99606 8	OUTSIDE, LOOKING IN	*Kathleen Rowntree*	£5.99
☐	99608 4	LAURIE AND CLAIRE	*Kathleen Rowntree*	£6.99
☐	99529 0	OUT OF THE SHADOWS	*Titia Sutherland*	£5.99
☐	99460 X	THE FIFTH SUMMER	*Titia Sutherland*	£6.99
☐	99410 3	A VILLAGE AFFAIR	*Joanna Trollope*	£5.99
☐	99442 1	A PASSIONATE MAN	*Joanna Trollope*	£5.99
☐	99470 7	THE RECTOR'S WIFE	*Joanna Trollope*	£5.99
☐	99492 8	THE MEN AND THE GIRLS	*Joanna Trollope*	£6.99
☐	99082 5	JUMPING THE QUEUE	*Mary Wesley*	£6.99
☐	99548 7	HARNESSING PEACOCKS	*Mary Wesley*	£6.99
☐	99126 0	THE CAMOMILE LAWN	*Mary Wesley*	£6.99
☐	99495 2	A DUBIOUS LEGACY	*Mary Wesley*	£6.99
☐	99591 6	A MISLAID MAGIC	*Joyce Windsor*	£6.99

All Transworld titles are available by post from:

Book Service By Post, P.O. Box 29, Douglas, Isle of Man IM99 1BQ

Credit cards accepted. Please telephone 01624 675137, fax 01624 670923, Internet http://www.bookpost.co.uk or e-mail: bookshop@enterprise.net for details.

Free postage and packing in the UK. Overseas customers allow £1 per book (paperbacks) and £3 per book (hardbacks).